PENGUIN B

Orlan

Virginia Woolf is now recognized as a
great novelist and essayist and a key figure ... . as a ....
and a modernist. Born in 1882, she was the daughter of the editor and
critic Leslie Stephen, and suffered a traumatic adolescence after the
deaths of her mother, in 1895, and her step-sister Stella, in 1897, leaving
her subject to breakdowns for the rest of her life. Her father died in 1904
and two years later her favourite brother Thoby died suddenly of typhoid.
With her sister, the painter Vanessa Bell, she was drawn into the company of writers and artists such as Lytton Strachey and Roger Fry, later
known as the Bloomsbury Group. Among them she met Leonard Woolf,
whom she married in 1912, and together they founded the Hogarth Press
in 1917, which was to publish the work of T. S. Eliot, E. M. Forster and
Katherine Mansfield as well as the earliest translations of Freud. Woolf
lived an energetic life among friends and family, reviewing and writing,
and dividing her time between London and the Sussex Downs. In 1941,
fearing another attack of mental illness, she drowned herself.

Her first novel, *The Voyage Out*, appeared in 1915, and she then worked
through the transitional *Night and Day* (1919) to the highly experimental
and impressionistic *Jacob's Room* (1922). From then on her fiction became
a series of brilliant and extraordinarily varied experiments, each one
searching for a fresh way of presenting the relationship between individual lives and the forces of society and history. She was particularly
concerned with women's experience, not only in her novels but also in
her essays and her two books of feminist polemic, *A Room of One's Own*
(1929) and *Three Guineas* (1938). Her major novels include *Mrs Dalloway*
(1925), *To the Lighthouse* (1927), the historical fantasy *Orlando* (1928),
written for Vita Sackville-West, the extraordinarily poetic vision of *The
Waves* (1931), the family saga of *The Years* (1937), and *Between the Acts*
(1941). All these are published by Penguin, as are her *Diaries*, Volumes
I-V, selections from her essays and short stories, and *Flush* (1933), a
reconstruction of the life of Elizabeth Barrett Browning's spaniel.

Brenda Lyons is a doctoral candidate at Balliol College, Oxford, where
she is writing on 'Platonic Allusions in Virginia Woolf's Fiction'. She

holds an MA in English Literature from the University of Massachusetts, Amherst, and has been an editor, writer and educator since the publication of *Brahmins and Bullyboys: G. Frank Radway's Boston Album* (co-edited with Stephen Halpert, 1973).

Sandra M. Gilbert is Professor of English at the University of California and has published widely, including four volumes of poetry and a book on D. H. Lawrence. With Susan Gubar she has co-authored *The Madwoman in the Attic* and two volumes of *No Man's Land: The Place of the Woman Writer in the Twentieth Century* (Vol. 1: *The War of the Words* and Vol. 2: *Sex Change*) and co-edited *Shakespeare's Sisters* and the *Norton Anthology of Literature by Women: The Tradition in English*.

Julia Briggs is General Editor for the works of Virginia Woolf in Penguin.

ORLANDO
A Biography

VIRGINIA WOOLF

EDITED BY BRENDA LYONS WITH
AN INTRODUCTION AND
NOTES BY SANDRA M. GILBERT

PENGUIN BOOKS

PENGUIN BOOKS

Published by the Penguin Group
Penguin Books Ltd, 80 Strand, London WC2R 0RL, England
Penguin Putnam Inc., 375 Hudson Street, New York, New York 10014, USA
Penguin Books Australia Ltd, 250 Camberwell Road, Camberwell, Victoria 3124, Australia
Penguin Books Canada Ltd, 10 Alcorn Avenue, Toronto, Ontario, Canada M4V 3B2
Penguin Books India (P) Ltd, 11 Community Centre, Panchsheel Park, New Delhi – 110 017, India
Penguin Books (NZ) Ltd, Cnr Rosedale and Airborne Roads, Albany, Auckland, New Zealand
Penguin Books (South Africa) (Pty) Ltd, 24 Sturdee Avenue, Rosebank 2196, South Africa

Penguin Books Ltd, Registered Offices: 80 Strand, London WC2R 0RL, England

www.penguin.com

Orlando first published by The Hogarth Press 1928
This annotated edition published in Penguin Books 1993
Reprinted in Penguin Classics 2000

12

Introduction and notes copyright © Sandra M. Gilbert, 1993
Other editorial matter copyright © Brenda Lyons, 1993
All rights reserved

The moral right of the editors has been asserted

Typeset by DatIX International Limited, Bungay, Suffolk
Set in 10½/12½ pt Monophoto Garamond
Printed in England by Clays Ltd, St Ives plc

Opposite: facsimile of the dust jacket of the first edition.

ORLANDO

A BIOGRAPHY

VIRGINIA WOOLF

THE HOGARTH PRESS, 52 Tavistock Square, W.C.1

Contents

Bibliographical Note

The following is a list of abbreviated titles used in this edition.

Diary: *The Diary of Virginia Woolf*, 5 vols., ed. Anne Olivier Bell (Hogarth Press, 1977; Penguin Books, 1979).

Letters: *The Letters of Virginia Woolf*, 6 vols., ed. Nigel Nicolson and Joanne Trautmann (Hogarth Press, 1975–80).

Passionate Apprentice: *A Passionate Apprentice: The Early Journals, 1897–1909*, ed. Mitchell A. Leaska (Hogarth Press, 1990).

Essays: *The Essays of Virginia Woolf*, 6 vols., ed. Andrew McNeillie (Hogarth Press, 1986).

CE: *Collected Essays*, 4 vols., ed. Leonard Woolf (Chatto & Windus, 1966, 1967).

Moments of Being: *Moments of Being: Unpublished Autobiographical Writings of Virginia Woolf*, ed. Jeanne Schulkind (Hogarth Press, 1985).

Knole: *Knole and the Sackvilles*, Vita Sackville-West (Heinemann, 1922).

Letters of Vita: *The Letters of Vita Sackville-West to Virginia Woolf*, ed. Louise DeSalvo and Mitchell A. Leaska (Hutchinson, 1984).

Orlando: *Virginia Woolf's* Vita Nuova

In the autumn of 1927, Virginia Woolf was struggling to compose a critical book on 'Fiction, or some title to that effect'. *To the Lighthouse*, arguably her strongest novel, had been published a few months earlier to considerable acclaim, but she was bored and troubled by the work she was doing now. Suddenly she claimed to have had a surge of inspiration. As she told the story in a letter of 9 October 1927 to the aristocratic novelist-poet Vita Sackville-West, a close friend with whom she was more than half in love at this time:

> Yesterday morning I was in despair ... I couldn't screw a word from me; and at last dropped my head in my hands: dipped my pen in the ink, and wrote these words, as if automatically, on a clean sheet: Orlando: A Biography. No sooner had I done this than my body was flooded with rapture and my brain with ideas. I wrote rapidly till 12 ... But listen; suppose Orlando turns out to be Vita ...[1]

Thus began *Orlando*, a witty and parodic 'biography' that Woolf was later to describe as 'a writer's holiday', even while she conceded the compulsion she had felt to produce the book: 'How extraordinarily unwilled by me but potent in its own right ... Orlando was! as if it had shoved everything aside to come into existence.'[2]

In fact, although Woolf declared that she had embarked upon this *jeu d'esprit* in a kind of trance, she had been meditating a project of this sort for quite some time. In March 1927, when *To the Lighthouse* was at press, she commented in her diary that she was considering writing 'a Defoe narrative for fun'. She had, she noted, 'conceived a whole fantasy to be called "The Jessamy Brides"' about two women, 'poor, solitary at the top of a house' from which one could see 'anything (for this is all fantasy) the Tower Bridge, clouds, aeroplanes', adding that the work was

> to be written . . . at the top of my speed . . . Satire is to be the main note – satire & wildness . . . My own lyric vein is to be satirized. Everything mocked . . . For the truth is I feel the need of an escapade after these serious poetic experimental books whose form is always so closely considered. I want to kick up my heels & be off.[3]

As the months wore on, she had refined and transformed this idea, remarking even before she wrote to Vita that

> One of these days . . . I shall sketch here, like a grand historical picture, the outlines of all my friends . . . It might be a most amusing book . . . Vita should be Orlando, a young nobleman . . . & it should be truthful; but fantastic.[4]

A week or two later, she decided that the work would be 'a biography beginning in the year 1500 & continuing to the present day, called Orlando: Vita; only with a change about from one sex to another.'[5]

At this point in her career, Woolf was at the height of her impressive imaginative and intellectual powers. Born in 1882, to Leslie Stephen, an eminent Victorian man of letters, and his beautiful, lively second wife, Julia, she had been raised in, as she put it, 'a very communicative, literate, letter writing, visiting, articulate, late-nineteenth-century world'.[6] Even before her marriage in 1912 to the socialist intellectual Leonard Woolf, she had begun to move out of that world and into the centre of the radical and rebellious circle of artists and writers that was to become known as the 'Bloomsbury Group'. Among other activities, she had studied Greek (still at that time an unusual project for a young woman), taught at a working-women's college in South London, worked for the women's movement, and begun writing reviews for *The Times Literary Supplement*.

Now, at forty-five, Woolf was the author of five novels, which had become increasingly innovative in style, as well as a number of important critical essays and sketches. With her husband, Leonard, she owned and operated the Hogarth Press, a small but influential publishing house whose list included works by such key modernist figures as T. S. Eliot and Katherine Mansfield, along with the English translations of the complete works of Sigmund Freud. Never arrogant – she had indeed had a number of nervous breakdowns marked by severe depression and often possessed a distorted sense of her own 'failure' in life – she was nevertheless, in her best moments, serenely confident of her own abilities and continually determined to set herself new challenges. At the same time, having spent more than a decade developing what she called the 'tunnelling' method by which she conveyed the interior lives of her characters in such novels as *Mrs. Dalloway* and *To the Lighthouse*, she had every reason to want to take a 'writer's holiday'.

Metaphorically speaking, what better companion might she have on such a holiday than the eccentric and charismatic Vita Sackville-West? Where Woolf herself was the daughter of a 'literate, letter writing, visiting, articulate' *haut bourgeois* family, Vita (short for Victoria) was indubitably a scion of the aristocracy, a class with which Woolf had always been ambivalently fascinated. Where, despite her literary successes, Woolf continually worried about money, Vita was at least putatively the heiress to a vast fortune: although her claim to Knole, her ancestral estate, had involved a complex lawsuit, the place itself was ancient, luxurious and immense. While Woolf had married a socialist intellectual whom she herself once defined as a 'penniless Jew', Vita was married to a representative of the British 'establishment' – the debonair diplomat Harold Nicolson. Where Woolf was both childless and sexually timid, Vita was both the mother of two sons and a notorious 'Sapphist', who made no effort to conceal her attraction to, and affairs with, women. (Indeed, where Leonard Woolf was unswervingly monogamous, even uxorious, Harold Nicolson was as flamboyantly bisexual as his wife.)

In addition, though Woolf was (or felt she was) physically fragile and odd-looking, Vita was sturdily beautiful, with a dark sensuality that she had inherited (or so Woolf speculated) from a Spanish-dancer grandmother named 'Pepita de Oliva', who was said to be descended from gypsies. If Woolf was (at times) almost neurasthenically intellectual and unworldly, Vita was not only a woman of the world but also a woman of action and adventure, who had briefly run off to Paris with a female lover, Violet Trefusis, just five years after her marriage to Nicolson. Despite her famous wit and charm, Woolf was often anxious about her social self-presentation – her clothes, her demeanour, even on some occasions her manners – but Vita had the careless elegance and the offhand air of command bred by generations of power. And last, but certainly not least, where Woolf was a brilliant, driven and ambitious artist, Vita was considerably less talented; although she was a successful and prolific writer herself, she could not have been regarded as a serious literary competitor.

That Vita frankly and urgently confessed to being 'in love' with Woolf can only have multiplied her charms from the novelist's point of view. In a 1925 diary entry, the author-to-be of *Orlando* incisively summarized the traits that drew her to this compellingly seductive companion:

> I like her & being with her, & the splendour – she shines in the grocer's shop in Sevenoaks with a candle lit radiance, stalking on legs like beech trees, pink glowing, grape clustered, pearl hung. That is the secret of her glamour, I suppose. Anyhow she found me incredibly dowdy, no woman cared less for personal appearance – no one put on things in the way I did. Yet so beautiful, &c. What is the effect of all this on me? Very mixed. There is her maturity & full breastedness: her being so much in full sail on the high tides, where I am coasting down backwaters; her capacity I mean to take the floor in any company, to represent her country, to visit Chatsworth, to control silver, servants, chow dogs; her motherhood (but she is a little cold & offhand with her boys) her being in short (what I have never been) a real woman. Then there is some voluptuousness about her; the grapes are ripe; & not reflective. No. In brain & insight she is not as highly organised as I am. But then she is aware of this, & so lavishes on me the maternal protection which, for some reason, is what I have always most wished from everyone.[7]

From girlhood on, Woolf had enjoyed writing mock 'histories' of the lives of friends and relatives: in 1907 she produced a little work called 'Friendships Gallery', a playful life of Violet Dickinson, an older woman to whom she was much attached; and the following year she composed 'Reminiscences', a memoir of her sister Vanessa that was addressed to Vanessa's children. But now, as a mature writer, she had found so intriguing a subject that she was impelled to develop the kind of informal, personal sketch she had earlier dedicated to Violet and Vanessa into a full-length, professionally expert (albeit fantastic and parodic) tribute to a person who enthralled her, a tribute that Vita's son Nigel Nicolson was later to call 'the longest and most charming love letter in literature'.

Beyond the personal charisma that Woolf had described with such élan in her 1925 diary, what made Vita especially fascinating to this would-be 'biographer' was the combination of erotic intensity and sexual ambiguity that Woolf associated with Sapphism – that is, with lesbianism. 'These Sapphists *love* women; friendship is never untinged with amorosity,' she noted with interest.[8] Nor was her interest surprising, for the Bloomsbury Group, in which Woolf had moved almost from her adolescence, had long been 'radical in its rejection of sexual taboos', to quote her nephew and biographer Quentin Bell.[9]

Indeed, as the critic Alex Zwerdling has put it, the

> sexual permissiveness of the group really was extraordinary: homosexuality and lesbianism not only practised but openly discussed; adulterous liaisons becoming an accepted part of the family circle; *ménages à trois, à quatre, à cinq*; and all this happening shortly after the death of Queen Victoria, among people raised by the old rules.[10]

Woolf's sister Vanessa, for instance, married Clive Bell but had a long affair with the art historian Roger Fry and, after bearing Bell two sons, had a daughter by the painter Duncan Grant, with whom she settled into an amicable lifelong partnership.

Woolf's friend Lytton Strachey, to whom she was briefly engaged at one point, had numerous homosexual relationships, although he too settled into a long living-arrangement, in his case with Dora Carrington, a young woman who adored him, and her husband, Ralph Partridge, whom *he* adored.

Although the young Virginia Stephen tended to be an observer rather than a participant in these unconventional sexual configurations, her own feelings were never stifled by convention. As Quentin Bell observes, for example, she was clearly in love with Violet Dickinson, to whom she wrote 'passionate letters, enchanting, amusing, embarrassing ... from which one tries to conjure up a picture of the recipient'.[11] And, in fact, long before she had conceived the Sapphic tale of 'The Jessamy Brides' which was to metamorphose into *Orlando*, Woolf had depicted love between women with special fervour in her novels. Rachel Vinrace, the heroine of *The Voyage Out* (1915), develops a keen attachment to her friend and mentor Helen Ambrose, while Katharine Hilbery, the protagonist of *Night and Day* (1919), and the suffragist Mary Datchet are drawn together, and the painter Lily Briscoe, a major character in *To the Lighthouse*, is enthralled by Mrs Ramsay, the powerfully maternal figure who dominates the work.

Most strikingly, Clarissa Dalloway, the eponymous heroine of *Mrs. Dalloway* (1925), remembers the moment when her girlhood friend Sally Seton kissed her on the lips as the supreme erotic experience of her life and muses on her feelings for women in one of the most explicitly sexual passages Woolf ever wrote:

> ... she could not resist sometimes yielding to the charm of a woman, not a girl, of a woman confessing, as to her they often did, some scrape, some folly ... she did undoubtedly then feel what men felt. Only for a moment; but it was enough. It was a sudden revelation, a tinge like a blush which one tried to check and then, as it spread, one yielded to its expansion, and rushed to the farthest verge and there quivered and felt the world come closer, swollen with some astonishing significance, some pressure of rapture, which split its thin skin and gushed and poured with an extraordinary alleviation over the cracks and sores! Then, for

that moment, she had seen an illumination; a match burning in a crocus; an inner meaning almost expressed. But the close withdrew; the hard softened. It was over – the moment.[12]

'She did undoubtedly then feel what men felt.' Although this remark seems casual enough, what underlay it – and what would have given particular force to Woolf's attraction to Sapphism as well as to the fascination with transvestism and transsexualism so centrally dramatized in *Orlando* – was the rise in the early years of the century of the new enterprise of 'sexology', whose discourse complemented and supplemented the equally new (and equally sexualized) discourse of psychoanalysis that had now been taken up by so many of the writer's contemporaries. Where Victorian thinkers had preached that 'proper' masculinity and femininity were inborn, that sexuality was essentially immutable, the sexologists and their disciples began to call attention to both the fluidity and the artifice of gender.

Edward Carpenter, an open homosexual and the foremost British prophet of this way of thinking, argued in the 1890s for what he saw as the utopian existence of a 'third' or 'Intermediate Sex', whom he called 'Urnings' (from Urania, meaning heaven) because they were able to achieve a kind of androgynous transcendence of the narrow limits of heterosexuality. Specifically relating his definition of these privileged beings to the growing movement for women's rights in which Woolf was herself involved, he declared in 1896 that

in late years (and since the arrival of the New Woman amongst us) . . . there are some remarkable and (we think) indispensable types of character, in whom there is such a union or balance of the feminine and masculine qualities that these people become to a great extent the interpreters of men and women to each other.[13]

And that Carpenter's views would have been known to Woolf is more than likely, because he had met and influenced both E. M. Forster and G. Lowes Dickinson, two important figures who were closely associated with the Bloomsbury Group.

A theme similar to Carpenter's was later sounded by the playwright and Fabian socialist George Bernard Shaw, who also connected changing definitions of sexuality with the transformative impact of the suffrage movement. 'People are still full of the old idea that woman is a special creation,' Shaw commented in 1927 – just when Woolf was composing *Orlando* – but, he observed,

> I am bound to say that of late years she has been working extremely hard to eradicate that impression, and make one understand that *a woman is really only a man in petticoats, or if you like, that a man is a woman without petticoats* [emphasis mine].[14]

Thus, by 1933, Havelock Ellis, England's foremost theorist of 'sexology' and a friend of both Carpenter's and Shaw's, could succinctly summarize such new views of gender in his magisterial book *The Psychology of Sex*, with the comment that

> We may not know exactly what sex is, but we do know that it is mutable, with the possibility of one sex being changed into the other sex, that its frontiers are often uncertain, and that there are many stages between a complete male and a complete female.[15]

Recently, of course, theorists of gender and sexuality have sought to make careful distinctions between transvestism, transsexualism and (male or female) homosexuality. Male transvestites are not necessarily homosexuals. Clearly lesbians need not be transvestites. And homosexuals of either sex are only infrequently transsexuals – people who experience themselves as having been born into the 'wrong' sex. For Woolf's generation, however, such distinctions were less clear. Shortly after *Orlando* appeared, Radclyffe Hall's controversial *The Well of Loneliness* (1928), an ostensibly realistic portrait of the artist as a lesbian, characterized the 'invert' Stephen Gordon, its female protagonist, as a man trapped in a woman's body.

An avowed lesbian herself, Hall regularly cross-dressed, was called 'John' by her intimates, and moved in the Sapphic salons of Paris and London whose other habituées included such sexually rebellious women as her aristocratic lover Una Troubridge and the painter Romaine Brooks, as well as the writers Natalie Barney, Gertrude Stein and Vita Sackville-West. Yet, despite Hall's own apparently unproblematic repudiation of what the poet Adrienne Rich has lately called 'compulsory heterosexuality', the author of the significantly entitled *The Well of Loneliness* gave a tragic cast to Stephen Gordon's story, describing her as 'grotesque and splendid, like some primitive thing conceived in a turbulent age of transition'.[16] The bleakness of Hall's perspective was, in fact, very different from the light-heartedness with which Woolf presented Orlando's change of sex.

After her male protagonist has become a woman, Woolf observes insouciantly that 'in every other respect, [she] remained precisely as he had been' (p. 98), implying that sexually defined selves or roles are merely costumes and thus readily interchangeable. 'It was a change in Orlando herself that dictated her choice of woman's dress and of a woman's sex,' she explains later, in a clarification of this point, noting that 'Different though the sexes are, they intermix' (p. 132). Indeed, not only is Orlando him/herself a multiply sexed being who happily transcends gender because her 'form combine[s] in one the strength of a man and a woman's grace' (p. 98), but her lover and her husband also appear to have available rich wardrobes of multiform sexuality. After Orlando has become a woman, the Archduchess Harriet of Scand-op-Boom becomes Archduke Harry; he/she and Orlando act 'the parts of man and woman for ten minutes with great vigour and then [fall] into natural discourse' (p. 126). Similarly, after she has wed the comic but magical sea captain Marmaduke Bonthrop Shelmerdine, Orlando affectionately accuses her *simpatico* husband of being a woman, and he cheerfully accuses her of being a man, for 'it was to each . . . a revelation that a woman could be as tolerant and free-spoken as a man, and a man as strange and subtle as a woman' (p. 179).

Despite the pain explored in *The Well of Loneliness* and the pleasure represented in *Orlando*, the two works have in common an assumption about gender, fostered by the theories of such sexologists as Carpenter and Ellis, which radically contradicts Sigmund Freud's famous assertion that 'Anatomy is destiny'. Hall sees it as Stephen Gordon's doom that her sexual destiny has been, as it were, detached from her anatomy, while Woolf defines Orlando's ability to choose her own sexual destiny as a triumph over anatomy. But both at least implicitly protest against the notion that social or erotic gender roles are inevitably determined by biological sexuality. Thus, although Woolf thought *The Well of Loneliness* merely a 'meritorious dull book',[17] she offered to testify on its behalf when the work was seized and confiscated by government censors. Her defence of Hall's project must have been impelled as much by a sense of kinship with the rejection of 'compulsory heterosexuality' as it was by a commitment to freedom of speech.

Nor was Woolf alone among Bloomsbury intellectuals in her desire to disentangle anatomy from destiny. Quentin Bell notes that just before she was inspired by her romance with the Sapphic Vita Sackville-West to begin producing her own fantastic portrait of the artist as what we now call a transsexual, she had become fascinated by sex change at a social event where gender fluidity was virtually thematic:

> ... early in September [1927], Maynard and Lydia Keynes gave a party at Tilton. Jack ... Sheppard enacted the part of an Italian *prima donna*, words and music being supplied by a gramophone. Someone had brought a newspaper cutting with them; it reproduced the photograph of a pretty young woman who had become a man, and this for the rest of the evening became Virginia's main topic of conversation.[18]

When Woolf decided, therefore, that the 'writer's holiday' devoted to her friend Vita's life as 'Orlando, a young nobleman' should be simultaneously 'truthful' and 'fantastic', she was quite accurately articulating a particular vision of gender as well as of history. For if it was 'fantastic' to conceive of Vita living for 300 years, from the age of Elizabeth to the 'present day', it was, in Woolf's opinion, perfectly 'truthful' to imagine Vita changing her sex as easily and casually as she might change her clothes.

*

If Woolf's romantic fascination with Vita and with Vita's Sapphism was one of the major forces that compelled her to write *Orlando* with unprecedented speed and exhilaration, her longstanding interest in history and biography was another crucially influential factor. Her father, Leslie Stephen, had become the first editor of the prestigious *Dictionary of National Biography* in the year she was born, so she had been preoccupied with the personal but often 'official' genre of biography and its relationship to 'official' public historiography from early in her career. She was largely educated at home, moreover, and according to Quentin Bell, the studies her father prescribed for her in her adolescence had included most of the historical and biographical classics produced in the nineteenth century, among them Macaulay's *History of England*, Carlyle's *French Revolution*, Thomas Arnold's *History of Rome*, Gibbon's multi-volumed *Decline and Fall of the Roman Empire*, and Froude's *Life of Carlyle*. That most of these books centred on the lives and works of men, almost entirely omitting any discussion of the experiences and achievements of women, must have soon become irritating to a young proponent of women's rights who was eventually to produce two of our century's major feminist treatises – *A Room of One's Own* (1929) and *Three Guineas* (1938).

Perhaps, therefore, as a gesture of rebellion against both paternal and patriarchal authority, some of Virginia Stephen's first writings took shape as biographies and histories which drew upon the form in which her father and his associates worked, while not so subtly satirizing the Lives of Great Men that were the subjects of his dictionary, and which his friend Thomas Carlyle had, in *Heroes and Hero Worship*, proclaimed the substance of history itself. 'Friendships Gallery' and 'Reminiscences', her affectionate tributes to Violet Dickinson and Vanessa Bell, were in fact preceded by an attempted 'History of Women' (written in 1897 when she was just fifteen and unfortunately now lost) and later by a fanciful meditation on the past entitled 'The Journal of Mistress Joan Martyn' (1906), in which a woman historian named Rosamund Merridew discovers a set of documents purporting to record the life and times of one Joan Martyn, a fifteenth-century diarist who is also a sort of prototype of the mythical 'Judith Shakespeare' whose tragic and monitory tale Woolf was to invent in *A Room of One's Own*.

As Woolf matured, these early efforts to revise and reimagine a past that had always been depicted as primarily masculine branched out into three major biographical/historical projects that consistently concerned her both as a fiction-writer and as an essayist. First, she frequently attempted to rewrite official history so as to provide what the French feminist theorist Hélène Cixous has named 'the other history' – the history not of 'Great Men' but of women and of, in Woolf's own phrase, 'the obscure', the history that falls into the interstices between the chronicles of princes and kings so that, when told, it 'breaks the sequence' of recorded time. Second, she frequently sought to excavate and inspect *family* history – to investigate, that is, the chronicles of the person and the personal, the family romances, which stand behind both the Carlylean 'Lives of Great Men' and the Woolfian 'Lives of the Obscure'. Third, in such crucial texts as *A Room of One's Own* and *Three Guineas*, she produced meditations on education which simultaneously recounted her rejection of the 'old' history, her dream of a 'new' history, and her desire for a re-engendered education – literally (from the Latin *educere*) a 'leading into' – in the new.

Woolf was not, of course, alone in her disaffection with traditional history. As early as 1818, her favourite novelist, Jane Austen, had created in *Northanger Abbey* a naive young heroine named Catherine Morland who voiced a discontent that would have been congenial to the youthful Virginia Stephen. History, Catherine complained, 'tells me nothing that does not either vex or weary me. The quarrels of popes and kings, with wars or pestilences, in every page; the men all so good for nothing, and hardly any women at all – it is very tiresome.'[19] In seeking to remedy this problem, moreover, Woolf's own work significantly parallels (or in a few cases almost uncannily foreshadows) the research done by a range of real women historians in the early twentieth century, some of whose writings – for instance, Eileen Power's *Medieval People* (1924) – she would later read, but some of whose scholarship – for example, Mary Beard's *Woman as a Force in History* (1946) – she would not live to know.

When the Bloomsbury novelist first began to address the 'tiresomeness' of conventional male-dominated history, such feminist projects were virtually non-existent, even in her circle of radical intellectuals. Indeed, as late as 1921, the American historian Arthur Schlesinger had observed that

> If the silence of historians is taken to mean anything, it would appear that one half of our population have been negligible factors in our country's history. Before accepting the truth of this assumption, the facts of our history need to be raked over from a new point of view. It should not be forgotten . . . that all of our great historians have been men and were likely therefore to be influenced by a sex interpretation of history all the more potent because unconscious.[20]

Though she may never have encountered Schlesinger's statement, Woolf was to echo it shortly after completing *Orlando*: in *A Room of One's Own* she remarked acerbically that 'It was certainly an odd monster that one made up by reading the historians' [views of women] first, and the poets' afterwards – a worm winged like an eagle; the spirit of life and beauty in a kitchen chopping up suet.' To remedy the situation, she suggested that the students of Newnham and Girton 'should re-write history', for, she noted ironically, 'it often seems a little queer as it is, unreal, lop-sided'.[21]

Although she produced a number of essays on women's past and on female literary traditions that attempted just such re-writings, Woolf's most sustained attempts at historical revision paradoxically took the form of novels. In her view, as she explained in the 'novel-essay' *The Pargiters*, which was the germ of her late novel-history *The Years* (1937), 'it would be far easier to write history [than fiction but] that method of telling the truth seems to me so elementary, and so clumsy, that I prefer, where truth is important, to write fiction.'²² And this was a preference to which, from the start of her writing career, she had consistently clung.

Thus, as a history of the transformed and transforming self which criticizes standard histories and biographies at the same time that it proposes the possibility of an alternative life, *Orlando* is not an unprecedented work in Woolf's canon. In *The Voyage Out*, the arrogant St John Hirst finds it impossible to imagine that Rachel Vinrace has 'reached the age of twenty-four without reading Gibbon'. In *Jacob's Room* (1922), the form of biography encloses an absent subject – a mysterious young man 'over whom' we 'hang vibrating'. In *To the Lighthouse*, when 'Time Passes', major public events are related only parenthetically while an unidentified narrator describes the assaults of nature on the Ramsays' summer house, and then focuses on the restorative labours of two obscure cleaning women. Throughout these books (and others) Woolf persistently explored the mystifying relationship between the ineffable essence of human reality and the deceptive, usually patriarchal, substance of written records. By the time she came to compose her 'love letter' to Vita Sackville-West, therefore, she was ready not only for what she called 'an escapade' but also for the creation of what Leon Edel has seen as 'a fully-fledged theory of biography', formulated, now, not only in reaction to her father's ideas but perhaps also in response to the theories of such modernist contemporaries as Lytton Strachey, the flamboyant debunker of *Eminent Victorians*, and Harold Nicolson, the author of a treatise on biography that was to be published in 1928 by her own Hogarth Press.²³

In Edel's view, it was in fact Strachey himself who helped spark Woolf's desire to write a novel in the form of a parodic biography. Commenting on *Mrs. Dalloway*, Strachey proposed to Woolf that perhaps she should write a book with a 'wilder and more fantastic' structure than anything she had heretofore attempted, a 'framework that admits of anything, like *Tristram Shandy*'.²⁴ But the nature of the history that Woolf did 'take' as both structure and subject was far more subversive than anything Strachey had in mind. For while, in such volumes as *Eminent*

Victorians and *Queen Victoria*, Strachey did ridicule the pomposities of the late nineteenth century, he still preserved the contours of traditional history and biography. Setting himself against the patriotic proprieties of the Victorian establishment, he almost always acquiesced in the subtler pieties of the masculinist Cambridge to which he himself remained loyal. Woolf, however, produced a new kind of record – an exuberant account of a life which, though apparently lived on the edge of patriarchal history, nevertheless appropriates and transforms that history.

Just as Woolf's paradoxical decision that *Orlando* should be 'truthful but fantastic' accurately summarizes her vision of the gender transformation at the heart of the book, the phrase also offers an appropriate description of the narrative/historical enterprise she undertook as she embarked on this 'writer's holiday'. For the Lord/Lady Orlando is a nobleperson whom we first encounter as a young man in the sixteenth century, follow through the courts of Elizabeth I and Charles II to an ambassadorship in Turkey where *he* becomes a *she*, meet again living the life of a literary lady aristocrat in eighteenth- and nineteenth-century England, and finally see when she has become a prize-winning author in 'the present moment' of aeroplanes and motor-cars. Certainly, in the free-flying sweep and scope with which it wings over the gravities of history, this life goes beyond even the fantastic, Shandyan parameters Strachey prescribed. Yet at the same time, it is, as Woolf insisted, 'truthful' – truthful because it is true to Woolf's ongoing effort to reimagine history, and truthful because it is true to her developing vision of the secret psychological realities that shape even the most liberated woman's life.

Like Vita Sackville-West – and like Virginia Woolf herself – Orlando seems to have been born into a central and privileged position in society. At the same time, like both Woolf and Vita, he/she is always a kind of outsider, and even, from a conventional point of view, mad (*furioso*), like his/her literary ancestor, Ariosto's *Orlando Furioso*.[25] By rank a nobleman, he has 'a liking for low company, especially for that of lettered people', and even when he is more or less adopted by the great Queen Elizabeth, he has little enthusiasm for the doings of the court. During the timeless time of the Great Frost, when London seems to hang suspended on the ice of an eternal moment, he falls in love with the androgynous Sasha, a Russian Princess for whom he 'want[s] another landscape and another tongue', a place and a language outside the public English history that is forming all around him. When Sasha sails away in the flood of time that suddenly breaks up the ice, Orlando retreats to his country estate to become a writer, but even in the world of letters he is still an outsider. Gulled and galled by the literary impresario Nick Greene, he is haunted but mystified by the enigmatic face of Shakespeare and feels that no battle in which his ancestors fought was 'half so arduous as this which he now undertook to win immortality against the English language' (p. 57).

Again, as the English ambassador to Constantinople and, then, the ex-ambassadress living *al fresco* among a band of gypsies, Orlando never quite fits in. In the first case, *he* alarms the English by making a disreputable marriage to one 'Rosina Pepita', and in the second, *she* disturbs the gypsies by writing poems, admiring sunsets and longing for her English manor house. Finally, when she returns to England, the lady Orlando is always slightly out of step with the march of time around her. In the eighteenth century, she dresses as a man so that she can visit – and hear the tales told by – the communities of fallen women who walk the London pavements. In the nineteenth century, she marries a sea captain and produces 'lachrymose blot[s]' (p. 167) of poetry, but her husband is an eccentric explorer, not a Victorian patriarch, and her writing of sentimental verse is 'much against her natural temperament'. In the twentieth century, she finally wins a prize for her poem 'The Oak Tree' but wires her husband a sardonically encoded comment on the meaning of literary achievement: '"Rattigan Glumphoboo", which summed it up precisely' (p. 196). Always on the margins of history, she nevertheless glimpses Elizabeth, Shakespeare, Charles II, Nell Gwyn, Alexander Pope, the Carlyles and even, in the book's first draft, one 'Volumnia Fox' – a pseudonym for none other than Virginia Woolf.[26] But her glance passes over these luminaries with the luminous indifference of, say, a lighthouse beam. Within sight of shore, she is always offshore, at sea in the wilder waters of history.

Nevertheless, as Woolf depicts him/her, Orlando *is* history, if only because the light of her mind is the lamp that lights up time for Woolf's readers, and her stately mansion, with its allegorically resonant 365 bedrooms and 52 staircases, is the house whose endurance-through-change is the metaphor that Woolf gives us for human duration. Whether offshore or on the edge of time, Orlando's supposedly marginal perspective, a perspective both Stephen and Strachey might have excluded or ignored, becomes the central point of view from which we must view the world as we try to come to terms with the terms of history. In fact, as Woolf ranges over them – obliquely envisioning them, slyly appropriating them, subversively revising them – the terms of history become Orlando's terms, and finally even history itself becomes Orlando's story, the tale of a body now male, now female, which embodies that thread of alternative truth Woolf was to call, in *A Room of One's Own*, 'the common life which is the real life' as opposed to 'the little separate lives . . . we live as individuals'.[27]

Thus, the psychosexual development of this parentless creature (for Woolf never really introduces Orlando's parents into her 'biography') constitutes a novel narrative indeed, for it is generalized, parodied and ultimately transcended in the course of Orlando's fantastic intersections with history. Simultaneously redefining and questioning conventional periodization, the so-called Elizabethan period recapitulates Orlando's childhood and pre-adolescence, with a timeless pre-Oedipal frost and an Oedipal flood exaggerating and mocking the meaning of 'growing up'. Similarly, the seventeenth century, with its sex change, offers Orlando a new kind of adolescence, comically marking a moment of sexual transformation and self-realization, while the eighteenth century represents her ostensible (that is, what should be her) 'young ladyhood'. Again, the nineteenth century reproduces her bemused confrontation with the exigencies of patriarchally defined female maturity (wedlock, maternity); and the twentieth century, with its adumbration of an apocalyptic 'new world', reflects a mature 'moment of being', a liberating encounter with 'the Captain self, the Key self, which amalgamates and controls them all' (p. 214).

In this uncanny conflation of the personal and the political, both the processions of 'King following King' that make up official history and the permutations of 'the lives of the obscure' that constitute the 'other history' appear, to use a phrase of Wallace Stevens's 'more truly and more strange'. And specifically, the history Woolf herself had always defined as 'masculine' here becomes 'feminine', too – becomes, indeed, what the writer had heretofore implicitly defined as a contradiction in terms: a public history of the private woman – as Orlando, returning at last from Turkey to reclaim her English inheritance, becomes England's figurative land-lady: the Lady Or-land-o, Ur-land-o, Her-land-o.

That *Orlando* did begin as, and at base really is, a fantasy biography/family history of a particular woman Virginia Woolf loved is certainly also relevant here, not just because the novelist wanted to flatter and immortalize her friend, not just because that friend was the wife of the theorist of biography Harold Nicolson, but also because her commonly used nickname, Vita, means 'life', so that the *Vita Nuova* Woolf devised for her fancifully suggests the New Life that is the Life of the New Woman. Therefore, just as many of the illustrations scattered throughout the book are pictures of Vita herself or of her Sackville ancestors, many details of the plot reflect significant details of Vita's actual biography: her early impassioned affair with Violet Trefusis (who here becomes the Russian Sasha because Vita called her 'Lushka'); her Spanish grandmother (here, as in real life, 'Rosina Pepita'); her courtship by the foolish aristocrat Lord Lascelles (here the Duke/Duchess of Scand-op-Boom); her travels in the East (here the Turkish episode): her transvestism (here the eighteenth-century escapades); her winning of the Hawthornden Prize for 'The Land' (here the winning of the 'Burdett Coutts Prize' for 'The Oak Tree'); her legal fight for her ancestral property (here, as in real life, her Great Law Suit); her marriage to the supportive bisexual Harold Nicolson (here called Marmaduke Bonthrop Shelmerdine); and so forth.[28]

Equally important, Woolf's fantastic transformations of these details function to empower Vita. Thus this fictional *Vita Nuova* grants her not just the one 'life and a lover' she asks for as Orlando but many lives and many lovers. Thus, too, because Vita had grown up feeling like a boy – even, during the height of her affair with Violet Trefusis, posing as a wounded soldier named 'Julian' – and haunted by anxiety about her 'dual' sexuality, Woolf assures her that, yes, if she felt like a boy she was a boy. In fact, as if responding to the hope Vita expressed in her (then unpublished) autobiography that 'as centuries go on . . . the sexes [will] become more nearly merged on account of their increasing resemblances',[29] Woolf suggests in her simultaneous revision of history and sexuality that centuries have indeed gone on and the sexes have merged, or were never wholly separated – for 'Different though the sexes are, they intermix' (p. 132). Thus, finally, where Vita was ultimately barred from inheriting Knole, the Sackville estate, because of her sex, Woolf grants her perpetual possession of this house so that at last the dispossessed man/woman has not one but 365 rooms of her own – a figure whose symbolic cast, even if based on the extravagant reality of Knole, implies that he/she has inherited not just a place in time but time itself.[30]

As a 'theory of biography', then, *Orlando* is also both a comment on history and a meditation on time. To begin with, in her role as a sort of metabiographer – a writer who both deploys and criticizes the form in which she is working – Woolf wittily parodies the intrusive and often absurd speculations of the scholar who presumes to know the 'truth' about the 'life' and 'self' of his subject. Each of us, she argues, as she endows Orlando with a host of costumes and careers, has many 'lives' and many 'selves'. Nor can they ever, in their multiplicity, be properly understood by the voyeuristic researcher. In relegating some of the major turning points of Orlando's history (for instance, her sex change, some of her romances, the birth of her son, and even her completion of 'The Oak Tree') to offstage scenes, Woolf simultaneously mocks the feigned puritanism of biographers who shudder at scandals even while they recount them and emphasizes the singularity, opacity and privacy – indeed, the unknowability (at least to others) – of major personal 'events'.

Just as importantly, in resisting the usual definitions of a 'lifetime' (threescore and ten), Woolf points out that an individual's own perception of duration, as well as her or his sense of the varieties of her/his emotional and intellectual experience, may be far more dramatic than we ordinarily suppose. From adolescence to adulthood, one may undergo personal metamorphoses as radical as the public changes associated with the transformation of the fertile and unruly 'Elizabethan period' into the tidily rational 'eighteenth century' or the stickily sentimental 'Victorian period'. And one may feel, as 'time passes', that the gulf between one's adolescence and one's adulthood is so vast that it ought to be measured not in what we call 'years' but in what we term 'centuries'.

Conversely, by arbitrarily associating traditionally defined historical 'periods' with the life of a single individual, Woolf proposes that our definitions of historical moments – the 'Elizabethan', the 'Romantic', the 'Victorian', the 'modern' – may be equally arbitrary. If Orlando, as a kind of paradigmatic spirit of English letters, is still persistently him/herself, single yet multiple, various yet the same throughout these apparent metamorphoses of English society, perhaps historical 'changes' themselves are not as easily explicable or describable as we have been taught. Certainly the hilarious rhetoric that Woolf adopts (as her role of biographer/historian heralds each new 'age') deflates the pretensions of writers who imply that the complexities of the past can be interpreted through simplistic labels and categories.[31]

The funniest and best-known passage of such rhetoric is probably the one in which, while Orlando gazes at the 'serene and orderly' prospect of eighteenth-century London, remembering the 'tortuous Elizabethan highways', her parodic biographer suddenly describes a 'turbulent welter of cloud' gathering over the city at the stroke of midnight and proclaims that now 'All was darkness; all was doubt; all was confusion. The Eighteenth century was over; the Nineteenth century had begun' (p. 156). To be sure, Woolf is succinctly and metaphorically summarizing here the difference between the 'spirit' of one 'age' and the 'spirit' of another, but the abruptness and absurdity of the change she depicts puts the very idea of historical 'transition' in question. How and why the 'hypothetical orderliness' of the eighteenth century gave way to the supposed 'cloudiness' of the nineteenth are more difficult questions than most chroniclers are willing to concede.

Finally, Woolf shows, time itself – the material with which both biographers and historians must inevitably grapple – is far more mysterious than the average scholar would like to admit. Is time what we experience or is it what we are told we experience? Do we, in other words, live primarily by personal internal clocks or are we really governed by an abstract, culturally imposed chronology? These are questions Woolf had already addressed in a number of works. In *Mrs. Dalloway*, for instance, public, official time is represented by 'Big Ben . . . with his majesty laying down the law, so solemn, so just', while what we might call private, experiential time is symbolized by 'the other clock, the clock which always struck two minutes after Big Ben' and which 'came shuffling in with its lap full of odds and ends . . . all sorts of little things . . . flooding and lapping and dancing in on the wake of that solemn stroke'.[32] And as we have seen, in *To the Lighthouse* the culturally constructed time by which history is usually measured – the chronicler's time of births, deaths and wars – is so engulfed by a sort of undifferentiated 'natural' time that major events are related in parenthetical statements while the passage of ten years appears merely to occupy a single night.

As a meditation on comparable questions about temporality, however, *Orlando* is a good deal more radical than either of these precursor texts. Obviously, the elasticity of the medium through which the book's protagonist moves is metaphysically crucial: on the one hand, half of Orlando's life/time expands to include five centuries of English social and cultural history; on the other hand, five centuries of English history shrink, as it were, to half the span of this magical being's life/time. But in addition, Woolf intermittently comments not just on the arbitrariness of the 'ages' into which historical time has been organized by assorted historians, but also on the arbitrariness of temporal units themselves. At one point, for example, her narrator ridicules the calendar, which, as she dryly observes, has no meaning in and of itself unless a human significance is imported into it:

It was now November. After November, comes December. Then January, February, March, and April. After April comes May. June, July, August follow. Next is September. Then October, and so, behold, here we are back at November again, with a whole year accomplished.

This method of writing biography, though it has its merits, is a little bare, perhaps . . . (p. 184)

At another point, though, Woolf celebrates the centrality that the calendar – and the clock – can assume when their abstract signification coincides with the fullness of human experience. Achieving a sort of Joycean epiphany in the twentieth century, Orlando notices that

the immensely long tunnel in which she seemed to have been travelling for hundreds of years widened; the light poured in; her thoughts became mysteriously tightened . . . she could hear every whisper and crackle in the room so that the clock ticking on the mantelpiece beat like a hammer. And so for some seconds the light went on becoming brighter and brighter, and she saw everything more and more clearly and the clock ticked louder and louder until there was a terrific explosion right in her ear. Orlando leapt as if she had been violently struck on the head. Ten times she was struck. In fact it was ten o'clock in the morning. It was the eleventh of October. It was 1928. It was the present moment.

No one need wonder that Orlando started, pressed her hand to her heart, and turned pale. For what more terrifying revelation can there be than that it is the present moment? That we survive the shock at all is only possible because the past shelters us on one side and the future on another. (p. 206)

Hyperbolical though it is, this passage summarizes the radiant intensity of the temporal experience – the 'moment of being', to use Woolf's own phrase – that this writer continually sought to capture in her complex role as revisionary biographer/historian/novelist and that, in *Orlando*, she triumphantly bestowed upon Vita Sackville-West.

By the time Woolf finished *Orlando*, she had started to have doubts about this novel which had begun with such compelling exuberance as a 'writer's holiday'. 'It may fall between stools, be too long for a joke, & too frivolous for a serious book,' she worried on 22 March 1928, and a month later she dismissed the work as 'a freak'.[33] To her surprise, though, her first 'reviewer' – Leonard Woolf, to whom she regularly submitted all her manuscripts for comment as soon as she felt they had been properly completed – took the book 'more seriously than [she] had expected'. He 'Thinks it in some ways better than The Lighthouse', she noted in her diary on 31 May – 'about more interesting things, & with more attachment to life, & larger ... He says it is very original.'[34]

Nor was Leonard Woolf eccentric among the novel's early readers, for in his wife's own words, 'The reception [of *Orlando*] surpassed expectations',[35] in newspapers and magazines on both sides of the Atlantic. Writing for the *New York Herald Tribune*, the feminist novelist and essayist Rebecca West defined the work as 'a poetic masterpiece of the first rank',[36] an encomium which left Woolf feeling 'a little sheepish and silly', while other, equally enthusiastic critics praised Woolf's 'swift and sparkling prose', her 'delicious' fantasy, her 'exquisite' poetry, and her 'wit that plays like summer lightning'. 'Never, perhaps, has Mrs Woolf written with more verve: certainly she has never imagined more boldly,' pronounced *The Times Literary Supplement*. And though pre-publication orders for the book had been disheartening because, as Woolf explained to herself in her diary, 'No one wants biography'[37] – not even, evidently, mock biography – post-publication sales were the strongest Woolf had ever had. 'L. has just been in to consult about a 3rd edition of Orlando,' she noted in December 1928, adding that 'we have sold over 6,000 copies; & sales are still amazingly brisk – 150 today for instance; most days between 50 & 60; always to my surprise.' In fact, the success of Woolf's literary 'escapade' marked a turning point in her professional career. At last, she was able to decide, 'my room is secure. For the first time since I married . . . I have been spending money.'[38]

In the last few decades, however, a number of Woolf scholars and critics have tended to value *Orlando* less highly than its early readers did. Quentin Bell, for example, damns the work with faint praise as 'easy, amusing, and straightforward in its narrative'. Although he concedes that 'of all Virginia's novels [this is] the one that comes nearest to sexual, or rather to homosexual, feeling,' he characterizes its protagonist as 'near . . . to the glamorous creations of the novelette'.[39] Adopting a similar tone, Alex Zwerdling dismissively observes that in *Orlando* 'such serious Woolfian themes as androgyny, the passage of time, and artistic dedication are rather archly guyed', while Jane Marcus curtly remarks that 'more than "kind explanation" is needed to see in it a modern myth of historical development, what Rebecca West called the "high fountain" of genius', and most recently John Batchelor judges it 'not . . . a major work' but rather 'an experiment with a negative result'.[40] And indeed, despite the encomia of reviewers, Woolf herself had by November 1929 scornfully described the book as not just a 'freak' but, worse, 'mere child's play'.[41]

Yet Woolf's initial sense of *Orlando* as 'extraordinarily unwilled' but 'potent in its own right . . . as if it shoved everything aside to come into existence' should not be discounted. For besides being a happy 'escapade', a charming 'love letter', an exuberant analysis of gender roles and a witty meditation on history, this work occupies a particularly interesting and 'potent' position in Woolf's *oeuvre*: she began to contemplate *Orlando* shortly after she had completed *To the Lighthouse*, the elegiac examination of the traditional upper middle class Victorian family that was at least in part intended to exorcize the ghosts of her own parents, her own past; and after finishing *Orlando* she commented that 'I want to write a history, say of Newnham or the women's movement, in the same vein',[42] then turned almost immediately to her first major feminist treatise, *A Room of One's Own*. In a sense, it can be argued, *Orlando* functions as a crucial bridge between these two superficially very different texts.

Woolf herself understood quite well the psychic significance that *To the Lighthouse* had for her. As she initially conceived the novel, she noted that 'the centre is father's character, sitting in a boat, reciting We perished, each alone, while he crushes a dying mackerel',[43] and after she had completed it she observed that 'when it was written, I ceased to be obsessed by my mother. I no longer hear her voice; I do not see her.'[44] In a study of *Virginia Woolf and the Fictions of Psychoanalysis*, Elizabeth Abel has argued that 'Woolf's two versions of the genesis of her text depict different parental inspirations and distinct compositional processes that reproduce the psychoanalytic disputes over the narrative priority of each parent.'[45] Yet it may not be necessary to decide on the 'narrative priority' of either parent if one sees that the core project of the novel is both an exorcism of, and an elegy for, the sex roles of 'father' and 'mother' as they were prescribed during the years when Woolf was growing up. 'I suppose that I did for myself what psychoanalysts do for their patients. I expressed some very long felt and deeply felt emotion. And in expressing it I explained it and then laid it out to rest',[46] Woolf mused as she looked back on the composition of *To the Lighthouse*, and certainly in writing this book she had 'laid . . . to rest' the ghosts of traditionally defined parent figures who had haunted her work from *The Voyage Out* onwards.

Orlando is in fact the first Woolf novel in which a meditation on the configurations of the family as it is structured around the stereotypical heterosexual couple does not in some sense dominate the plot. Instead, this parodic but ultimately serious 'biography' takes as its starting point a character who may be said to have evolved as much from Lily Briscoe, the determinedly single woman artist of *To the Lighthouse*, as from Vita Sackville-West. What would Lily's life have been like, *Orlando* asks, if she had been set free to rove through history and discover that what Mrs Ramsay considered the 'universal law' of marriage (along with the sex roles on which that law was founded) was as much an artifice as the clothes she wore or as her own painting of the 'relation' of 'masses'? And what would Lily's life have become had all history been, for her, a surprisingly free space in which one could easily and insouciantly be woman *or* man? More, how would the engenderings of history appear to such a radically new kind of being? Would the two histories – the masculine chronicle solemnly produced by Big Ben and the feminine record more diffidently offered by the 'other clock' – retain their separateness, remain divided?

After she had explored these issues in *Orlando*, Woolf never again returned to the kinds of representations of the traditional family that had concerned her in her earlier books. *A Room of One's Own*, the work that immediately followed, was of course pioneering not only in its effort to excavate women's history but in its advocacy of a creative androgyny that recalls Edward Carpenter's celebration of a 'third' or 'intermediate sex', as well as in its imaginative resurrection of the lost woman poet 'Judith Shakespeare'. *The Waves* (1931), which Woolf was planning even as she wrote *Orlando* and began composing *A Room of One's Own*, focused on six speakers (three women and three men) whose family backgrounds are so blurred that one might almost think each had been parthenogenetically produced. And although in her last two novels, *The Years* and *Between the Acts*, Woolf did return to a scrutiny of family dynamics, she there approaches the history as well as the problems and pleasures of 'compulsory heterosexuality' even more sceptically and sardonically than she had before *Orlando* had 'shoved everything aside to come into existence'.

At the same time, however, all these works ask a question that was implicit in the revisionary history, the speculations on time past and time present, that so occupied the creator of a fantastic hero/heroine who lives through 500 years of cultural change. If history can be reimagined and sex roles reconstituted through such a reimagining, what might be the *future* towards which a newly conceived past and present would lead? This was a topic on which Woolf had also brooded throughout her career, beginning in the early 'Journal of Mistress Joan Martyn', whose fifteenth-century diarist confesses that each morning 'with my cheek leant upon the window pane I like to fancy that I am pressing as closely as can be upon the massy wall of time, which is for ever lifting & pulling & letting new spaces of life in upon us.'[47] Even at the end of her writing life, as Alex Zwerdling has reminded us, Woolf was still addressing this question. 'The outline for *Reading at Random*, the cultural history she left unfinished at the time of her death,' he notes, 'is reasonably familiar and straightforward from the Middle Ages through the nineteenth century. But then comes the injunction "Skip present day. A Chapter on the future".' Yet as he also observes, 'What eluded her was any understanding of how the present could conceivably lead to the future she imagined' – a future, I might add, in which the liberation symbolized by the lively shape-shiftings of Orlando and the reborn genius of 'Judith Shakespeare' would be not only literarily but literally possible.[48]

Perhaps, however, it was through the intensity of the highly metaphorical, lyrical, even incantatory language with which *Orlando* concludes that Woolf did begin to imagine at least the inception of a future that would be radically different from the past she had so yearningly revised. Certainly as her record of a changed and changing history mounts to an almost erotic climax on 'Thursday, the eleventh of October, Nineteen hundred and Twenty Eight', she offers us – not just comically but seriously –

a vision of transformative promise that amounts to a sort of annunciation, an impregnation of 'reality' by the forces of 'fantasy'. Imperiously invoking her husband while stationing herself beside the totemic natural object that has been her aesthetic subject for centuries ('"Marmaduke Bonthrop Shelmerdine!" she cried, standing by the oak tree'), Orlando bares 'her breast to the moon . . . so that her pearls glowed like the eggs of some vast moon-spider' (p. 227). And as she does so, she sets in motion a 'moment of being' that is also a moment of mysterious change.

Below her, Orlando sees what is figuratively speaking 'the great house' of the past, where all is 'lit as for the coming of a dead Queen'. Above her, the 'fine sea captain' Shelmerdine hovers, 'coming nearer and nearer' in an aeroplane. And then, in an allusion to the annunciatory gesture – the epiphany of dove or swan – through which the supernatural intervenes in human affairs, 'a single wild bird' springs up over Shelmerdine's head. Together, Woolf implies, the past of a dead queen and the present of October 1928, the culture of house and aeroplane and the nature of moon and 'moon-eggs', the sea of Shelmerdine the explorer and the earth of Orlando the land lady, all incarnated in the revisionary love of a 'womanly' man and a 'manly' woman, may conspire to conceive an 'unwilled' but 'potent' *vita nuova*.

Sandra M. Gilbert   1992

NOTES

1. Letter to Vita Sackville-West, 9 Oct. 1927, *Letters*, III, pp. 428–9.
2. *Diary*, III, 20 Dec. 1927, p. 168.
3. ibid., 14 March 1927, p. 131.
4. ibid., 20 Sept. 1927, p. 157.
5. ibid., 5 Oct. 1927, p. 161.
6. *Moments of Being*, p. 73.
7. *Diary*, III, 21 Dec. 1925, p. 52.
8. ibid.
9. Quentin Bell, *Bloomsbury* (Weidenfeld and Nicolson, 1973, p. 42).

10. Alex Zwerdling, *Virginia Woolf and the Real World* (University of California Press, 1986, p. 168).

11. Quentin Bell, *Virginia Woolf: A Biography*, I (Hogarth Press, 1972, p. 83).

12. Virginia Woolf, *Mrs. Dalloway* (1925; Penguin Books, 1992, pp. 34–5).

13. Edward Carpenter, *Love's Coming of Age* (1896; Mitchell Kennerley, 1911, pp. 120–21).

14. George Bernard Shaw, 'Woman-Man in Petticoats' in *Platform and Pulpit*, ed. Dan H. Laurence (Hill and Wang, 1961, p. 174).

15. Havelock Ellis, *The Psychology of Sex* (Ray Long and Richard R. Smith, 1933, p. 225).

16. Adrienne Rich, 'Compulsory Heterosexuality and the Lesbian Continuum' in *Blood, Bread and Poetry: Selected Prose 1979–1985* (W. W. Norton, 1986, pp. 23–75); Radclyffe Hall, *The Well of Loneliness* (1928; Avon, 1981, p. 52).

17. *Diary*, III, 31 Aug. 1928, p. 193.

18. Bell, *Virginia Woolf*, II, p. 132.

19. Jane Austen, *Northanger Abbey* (1818; Penguin Books, 1972, p. 123).

20. Arthur Schlesinger, 'The Role of Women in American History' in *New Viewpoints in American History* (Macmillan, 1921, p. 126).

21. Virginia Woolf, *A Room of One's Own* (1928; Penguin Books, 1945, pp. 45, 47).

22. Virginia Woolf, *The Pargiters*, ed. Mitchell A. Leaska (Hogarth Press, 1978, p. 9).

23. Leon Edel, *Literary Biography* (1959; Indiana University Press, 1973, p. 139).

24. ibid., p. 138.

25. On Ariosto's *Orlando Furioso* as a major precursor text for *Orlando*, see Beverley Ann Schlack, *Continuing Presences: Virginia Woolf's Use of Literary Allusion* (Pennsylvania State University Press, 1979, pp. 80–83). For a discussion of the comparable relevance of the Orlando/Rosalind plot in Shakespeare's *As You Like It*, see Joanne Trautmann, *The Jessamy Brides: The Friendship of Virginia Woolf and V. Sackville-West* (Pennsylvania State University Studies, No. 36, 1973, p. 41).

26. See 'Orlando: An Edition of the Manuscript', ed. Madeline Moore, in *Twentieth Century Literature* (No. 25, 1979, pp. 337–9).

27. Virginia Woolf, *A Room of One's Own* (1928; Penguin Books, 1945, p. 112).

28. For a more detailed discussion of parallels between Vita's life and Orlando's, see Schlack, op. cit., and Trautmann, op. cit.

29. Nigel Nicolson, *Portrait of a Marriage* (Weidenfeld and Nicolson, 1973, p. 107).

30. For Vita's own history of Knole and its extravagances, see Vita Sackville-West, *Knole and the Sackvilles* (Heinemann, 1922); see also the notes to this edition.

31. For an interesting (though somewhat different) analysis of *Orlando* as a 'deconstruction' of conventional biography and history, see Rachel Bowlby, *Virginia Woolf* (Basil Blackwell, 1988, pp. 128–45).

32. Virginia Woolf, *Mrs. Dalloway* (1925; Penguin Books, 1992, p. 140).

33. *Diary*, III, 22 March 1928, p. 177; 21 April 1928, p. 180.

34. ibid., 31 May 1928, p. 185.

35. ibid., 27 Oct. 1928, p. 200.

36. Rebecca West, *New York Herald Tribune*, 21 Oct. 1928, 11, pp. 1, 6.

37. *Diary*, III, 22 Sept. 1928, p. 198.

38. ibid., 18 Dec. 1928, p. 212.

39. Bell, *Virginia Woolf*, II, pp. 139–40, 118–19.

40. Zwerdling, op. cit., p. 56; Jane Marcus, 'Introduction: Virginia Woolf Aslant' in *Virginia Woolf: A Feminist Slant* (University of Nebraska Press, 1983, p. 2); John Batchelor, *Virginia Woolf: The Major Novels* (CUP, 1991, pp. 16, 18).

41. *Diary*, III, 5 Nov. 1929, p. 264.

42. ibid., 7 Nov. 1928, p. 203.

43. ibid., 14 May 1925, pp. 18–19.

44. *Moments of Being*, p. 90.

45. Elizabeth Abel, *Virginia Woolf and the Fictions of Psychoanalysis* (University of Chicago Press, 1989, p. 45).

46. *Moments of Being*, p. 90.

47. *Shorter Fiction*, p. 48.

48. Zwerdling, op. cit., p. 327.

Further Reading

PRIMARY

Vita Sackville-West

The Letters of Vita Sackville-West to Virginia Woolf, ed. Louise DeSalvo and Mitchell A. Leaska (Hutchinson, 1984).
Knole and the Sackvilles (Heinemann, 1922).

Virginia Woolf

The Diary of Virginia Woolf, 5 vols., ed. Anne Olivier Bell (Hogarth Press, 1977; Penguin Books, 1979).
The Essays of Virginia Woolf, 6 vols., ed. Andrew McNeillie (Hogarth Press, 1986).
The Letters of Virginia Woolf, 6 vols., ed. Nigel Nicolson and Joanne Trautmann (Hogarth Press, 1975–80).
Moments of Being: Unpublished Autobiographical Writings of Virginia Woolf, ed. Jeanne Schulkind (1975; 2nd edn, Hogarth Press, 1985).
A Writer's Diary, ed. Leonard Woolf (Hogarth Press, 1954).

SECONDARY

Susan Mary Alsop, *Lady Sackville: A Biography* (Weidenfeld and Nicolson, 1978).
Frank Baldanza, 'Orlando and the Sackvilles' in *PMLA* (*Proceedings of the Modern Language Association*) (No. 70, 1955, pp. 274–9).
Quentin Bell, *Virginia Woolf: A Biography*, 2 vols. (Hogarth Press, 1972).
Edward Bishop, *A Virginia Woolf Chronology* (Macmillan, 1989).
Louise DeSalvo, 'Lighting the Cave: The Relationship between Vita Sackville-West and Virginia Woolf' in *Signs: Journal of Women in Culture and Society* (Winter 1982, pp. 195–214).
——'A Note on the Orlando Tapestries at Knole House' in *Virginia Miscellany* (No. 13, 1979, pp. 3–4).

Leon Edel, *Literary Biography*, (1959; Indiana University Press, 1973, especially pp. 134–45).

Alice Fox, *Virginia Woolf and the English Renaissance* (OUP, 1990).

Victoria Glendinning, *Vita: The Life of Vita Sackville-West* (Weidenfeld and Nicolson, 1983).

David Bonnel Greene, 'Orlando and the Sackvilles: Addendum' in *PMLA* (No. 71, 1956, pp. 268–9).

Ellen Hawkes, 'Woolf's Magical Garden of Women' in *New Feminist Essays on Virginia Woolf*, ed. Jane Marcus (University of Nebraska Press, 1981, pp. 31–60).

Frederick Kellerman, 'A New Key to Virginia Woolf's *Orlando*' in *English Studies* (No. 59, 1978, pp. 138–50).

Sherron E. Knopp, '"If I Saw You Would You Kiss Me?" Sapphism and the Subversiveness of Virginia Woolf's *Orlando*' in *PMLA* (No. 103, 1988, pp. 24–34).

Betty Kushen, '"Dreams of Golden Domes": Manic Fusion in Virginia Woolf's *Orlando*' in *Literature and Psychology* (No. 29, 1979, pp. 53–66).

Jean O. Love, '*Orlando* and Its Genesis: Venturing and Experimenting in Art, Love and Sex' in *Virginia Woolf: Reevaluation and Continuity*, ed. Ralph Freedman (University of California Press, 1980, pp. 189–218).

Herbert Marder, *Feminism and Art: A Study of Virginia Woolf* (University of Chicago Press, 1968).

Madeline Moore, 'Orlando: An Edition of the Manuscript' in *Twentieth Century Literature* (No. 25, 1979, pp. 303–55).

Nigel Nicolson, *Portrait of a Marriage* (Weidenfeld and Nicolson, 1973).

Phyllis Rose, *Woman of Letters: A Life of Virginia Woolf* (OUP, 1978).

Sonya Rudikoff, 'How Many Lovers Had Virginia Woolf' in the *Hudson Review* (32, No. 4, 1979, pp. 540–66).

Beverly Ann Schlack, *Continuing Presences: Virginia Woolf's Use of Literary Allusion* (Pennsylvania State University Press, 1979).

Clifton Snider, '"A Single Self": A Jungian Interpretation of

Virginia Woolf's *Orlando*' in *Modern Fiction Studies* (No. 25, 1979, pp. 263–8).

Susan M. Squier, *Virginia Woolf and London: The Sexual Politics of the City* (University of North Carolina Press, 1985).

——'Tradition and Revision in Woolf's *Orlando*: Defoe and the Jessamy Brides' in *Women's Studies* (1984).

Lytton Strachey, *Elizabeth and Essex* (Harcourt Brace, 1928).

Pamela Transue, 'Orlando', Chapter V of *Virginia Woolf and the Politics of Style* (State University of New York Press, 1986, pp. 111–26).

Joanne Trautmann, *The Jessamy Brides: The Friendship of Virginia Woolf and Vita Sackville-West* (*Pennsylvania State University Studies*, No. 36, 1973).

Jean Moorcraft Wilson, *Virginia Woolf: Life and London, a Biography of Place* (Cecil Woolf, 1987).

Leonard Woolf, *An Autobiography*, 2 vols. (Hogarth Press, 1967–9; OUP, 1980).

Alex Zwerdling, *Virginia Woolf and the Real World* (University of California Press, 1986).

A Note on the Text

Woolf composed *Orlando* in a high state of exhilaration: 'I have written this book quicker than any: & it is all a joke; & yet gay & quick reading I think: a writers holiday.'[1] She began writing on 7 or 8 October 1927, and set down the last words shortly before 1 a.m. on the night of 17 March 1928.[2] She then revised it completely, while retaining most of the narrative structure of the first draft (some details of the passages she later cut can be found in the notes to this edition). A number of extracts from the original manuscript have subsequently been published: the first (a sequence from Chapter V that begins with an apologetic note from Miss Christina Rossetti) by Vita Sackville-West in an article for the *Listener* in 1955, based on a radio programme.[3] Transcripts of many passages that differ in the manuscript from the printed text are provided by Madeline Moore in her article on the subject.[4] The manuscript remains in perpetuity at Knole, the Sackville family estate at Sevenoaks, Kent, as part of a bequest to the National Trust from Vita's sons, Ben and Nigel Nicolson.

Woolf sent Vita a special leather-bound copy of *Orlando* on the morning of publication, 11 October 1928, the day on which the novel's last chapter takes place and Orlando arrives at the present time; she also gave Vita the manuscript. The first British edition of *Orlando* was published by the Woolfs at the Hogarth Press, having been printed in Edinburgh (by R. & R. Clark, Ltd), and the first American trade edition was published by Harcourt, Brace and Co. on 18 October, though both this and the Hogarth volume were preceded by a special limited edition, published on 2 October by Crosby Gaige of New York who printed 861 copies and a further 15 on green paper.[5] The American edition of *Orlando* differs in a large number of significant details from the British text. It was Woolf's practice to revise page-proofs for her British and American publishers independently, with the result that there are more than 150 variant readings. A list of these is given in an appendix to this volume. The page-proofs that Woolf corrected for Harcourt Brace are at Smith College. Some pages of the corrected typescript survive in private hands, several having been purchased by Frederick B. Adams, an American railways director.[6]

Orlando sold exceptionally well – more than 8,000 copies in Britain and more than 13,000 in the United States during its first six months. As Woolf's biographer John Mepham points out, it was 'the turning point in her career from the point of view of sales'. During her lifetime *Orlando*, along with *Flush* (1933, her spoof biography of Elizabeth Barrett Browning's cocker spaniel) and *The Years* (1937), sold best, but this pattern changed after the war when these titles were overtaken by the more serious modernism of *Mrs. Dalloway* (1925) and *To the Lighthouse* (1927).[7] Later editions of *Orlando* include the Uniform Edition (1933, strictly not a new edition, since it was a photo-offset reprint); the first Penguin edition of 1942, which identified Woolf as the daughter of Sir Leslie Stephen KCB and the wife of Leonard Woolf, cost nine pence and ran to 75,000 copies; there was also an edition in the Signet Classic series (New American Library) with an introduction by Elizabeth Bowen (1960). Harcourt Brace then published in paperback for Harvest Books an edition that, exceptionally, reproduced the original photographs; more than 38,000 of these were printed between October 1973 and December 1976.

This edition is based on the text of the first English (Hogarth) edition, with the following errors corrected (the first reading is from this Penguin edition, the second from the first English edition).

102.34	blank verse poem	]	blank version poem
131.26	seem to hint	]	seems to hint
218.6	strangers, but a little wary	]	strangers, but a little weary

NOTES

1. *Diary*, III, 18 March 1928, p. 177.
2. See Letter to Vita Sackville-West, 9 Oct. 1927, *Letters*, III, pp. 428–9; and *Diary*, III, 5 and 22 Oct. 1927, p. 161. The MS ends with the date 'March 17th 1928'; see also Letter to Vita Sackville-West, 20? March 1928, *Letters*, III, p. 474, and the diary entry, 'Orlando was finished yesterday as the clock struck one', *Diary*, III, 18 March 1928, p. 176 (confusingly repeated at the entry for 22 March, p. 177).
3. V. Sackville-West, 'Virginia Woolf and *Orlando*' (*Listener*, 27 January 1955, pp. 157–8).
4. Madeline Moore, '*Orlando*: An Edition of the Manuscript' in *Twentieth Century Literature* (No. 25, 1979, pp. 303–55).
5. Bibliographical details are taken from B. J. Kirkpatrick, *A Bibliography of Virginia Woolf* (3rd edn, OUP, 1980, pp. 34–8).
6. See note in *Letters*, V, p. 168.
7. John Mepham, *Virginia Woolf: A Literary Life* (Macmillan, 1991, pp. 130–31).

A Note on the Illustrations

Orlando is unique among Woolf's novels in presenting itself to readers as a biography, if parodically so:

> I am writing Orlando half in a mock style very clear & plain, so that people will understand every word. But the balance between truth & fantasy must be careful. It is based on Vita, Violet Trefusis, Lord Lascelles, Knole &c.[1]

In support of this claim the first edition features eight illustrations, plus a black and white portrait on the dust jacket which appears as the frontispiece to this edition. The photograph is of a painting or part of a painting of a gentleman in Elizabethan costume with a large shield before him (on previous occasions Vanessa Bell had designed and illustrated dust jackets for Woolf's novels). The first edition notes that this portrait (which looks like a modern pastiche) is reproduced by kind permission of the Worthing Art Gallery, but nothing more is known about it.

Woolf began assembling the photographs for *Orlando* in October 1927; three of these were of Vita Sackville-West, while three others were taken from portraits at Knole. Taking the pictures in order of their appearance, the first, which is also the frontispiece to the original volume ('Orlando as a Boy'), is the right-hand side of a double portrait at Knole. Painted by Cornelius Nuie, it shows two sons of Edward Sackville, fourth Earl of Dorset, as boys; the younger one, the Honourable Edward Sackville, is depicted here. Vita had also reproduced this picture in her book *Knole and the Sackvilles* (1922). The second ('The Russian Princess as a Child') is a photograph of Woolf's niece Angelica Bell (daughter of Vanessa Bell and Duncan Grant); it may be a collage, as the lower part of the photograph appears painted. The third ('The Archduchess Harriet') is Marcus Gheeraerts' portrait of Mary Curzon, fourth Countess of Dorset, then hanging in the parlour passage at Knole; while the fourth ('Orlando as Ambassador'), is from a pastel portrait of Lionel, first Duke of Dorset, by Rosalba Carriera, in the sitting room.[2] The fifth ('Orlando on her return to England') is a studio photograph of Vita, probably taken by Lenare. The sixth ('Orlando about the year 1840') seems to have been taken by Vanessa and Duncan on the afternoon of 14 November 1927.[3] The seventh ('Marmaduke Bonthrop Shelmerdine, Esquire') is the painting of a young man *c.* 1820 by an unidentified artist – he bears some resemblance to the young Harold Nicolson. Vita had bought it from a London dealer and it now hangs at Sissinghurst.[4] The eighth ('Orlando at the present time') is a photograph of Vita at Long Barn taken by Leonard Woolf, probably at the end of April 1928. Virginia wrote to Vita: 'It has now become essential to have a photograph of Orlando in country clothes in a wood. If you have films and a camera I thought Leonard might take you.'[5]

In this edition the photographs have been placed as closely as possible to their positions in the first edition.

NOTES

1. *Diary*, III, 22 Oct. 1927, p. 162.
2. The use of these three Knole portraits later led the new Lord Sackville to complain that they had been used without his permission – in fact Vita had obtained her father's permission before his death; see *Letters*, III, p. 558.
3. See letters to Vita, 6 and 11 Nov. 1927, *Letters*, III, pp. 434–5. Footnotes explain that three portraits of the Sackville family were used in *Orlando* (the frontispiece and the third and fourth pictures). A further footnote (p. 435) identifies the photograph of Vita in a hat, shawl and check skirt ('Orlando about the year 1840') as the work of Vanessa and Duncan. The earlier photograph of Vita in satin and pearls ('Orlando on her return to England') was probably taken by Lenare, since Virginia wrote to Vita, 'Nessa wants to photograph you at 2, that is if she thinks the Lenare too bad.' It looks as if, in addition to the fancy-dress '1840' picture, Vanessa and

Duncan took some photographs of Vita in the pink satin and pearls that were intended to suggest a Lely portrait because in Madeline Moore's book *The Short Season Between Two Silences* (Unwin Hyman, 1984) there is a photograph of a rather dishevelled Vita in pearls and satin, captioned, 'Vita ... posing as a lily [Lely?] in Vanessa Bell's studio, 1928'. In *Vita* (p. 182), Victoria Glendinning quotes an amusing account of one of these photographic sessions, though she later (p. 205) identifies the '1840' portrait as the one taken by Lenare, a view contradicted by the editors of the *Letters*.

4. See Letter to Vita, 17 April 1928, *Letters*, III, p. 484; and footnote.
5. Letter to Vita, 27 April 1928, *Letters*, III, p. 488. This photograph also appears in *Letters of Vita*. Two other versions, apparently taken on the same occasion, appear in *Vita* (here credited to Virginia, rather than Leonard) and in Nigel Nicolson's *Vita and Harold: The Letters of Vita Sackville-West and Harold Nicolson 1910–1962* (Weidenfeld and Nicolson, 1992).

Overleaf: facsimile of the frontispiece and title page of the first edition.

ORLANDO AS A BOY

ORLANDO

A BIOGRAPHY

VIRGINIA WOOLF

Published by Leonard and Virginia Woolf at the
Hogarth Press, 52 Tavistock Square, London, W.C.
1928

Preface

Many friends have helped me in writing this book. Some are dead and so illustrious that I scarcely dare name them, yet no one can read or write without being perpetually in the debt of Defoe, Sir Thomas Browne, Sterne, Sir Walter Scott, Lord Macaulay, Emily Brontë, De Quincey, and Walter Pater – to name the first that come to mind. Others are alive, and though perhaps as illustrious in their own way, are less formidable for that very reason. I am specially indebted to Mr. C. P. Sanger, without whose knowledge of the law of real property this book could never have been written. Mr. Sydney-Turner's wide and peculiar erudition has saved me, I hope, some lamentable blunders. I have had the advantage – how great I alone can estimate – of Mr. Arthur Waley's knowledge of Chinese. Madame Lopokova (Mrs. J. M. Keynes) has been at hand to correct my Russian. To the unrivalled sympathy and imagination of Mr. Roger Fry I owe whatever understanding of the art of painting I may possess. I have, I hope, profited in another department by the singularly penetrating, if severe, criticism of my nephew Mr. Julian Bell. Miss M. K. Snowdon's indefatigable researches in the archives of Harrogate and Cheltenham were none the less arduous for being vain. Other friends have helped me in ways too various to specify. I must content myself with naming Mr. Angus Davidson; Mrs. Cartwright; Miss Janet Case; Lord Berners (whose knowledge of Elizabethan music has proved invaluable); Mr. Francis Birrell; my brother, Dr. Adrian Stephen; Mr. F. L. Lucas; Mr. and Mrs. Desmond MacCarthy; that most inspiriting of critics, my brother-in-law, Mr. Clive Bell; Mr. G. H. Rylands; Lady Colefax; Miss Nellie Boxall; Mr. J. M. Keynes; Mr. Hugh Walpole; Miss Violet Dickinson; the Hon. Edward Sackville West; Mr. and Mrs. St. John Hutchinson; Mr. Duncan Grant; Mr. and Mrs. Stephen Tomlin; Mr. and Lady Ottoline

Morrell; my mother-in-law, Mrs. Sidney Woolf; Mr. Osbert Sitwell; Madame Jacques Raverat; Colonel Cory Bell; Miss Valerie Taylor; Mr. J. T. Sheppard; Mr. and Mrs. T. S. Eliot; Miss Ethel Sands; Miss Nan Hudson; my nephew Mr. Quentin Bell (an old and valued collaborator in fiction); Mr. Raymond Mortimer; Lady Gerald Wellesley; Mr. Lytton Strachey; the Viscountess Cecil; Miss Hope Mirrlees; Mr. E. M. Forster; the Hon. Harold Nicolson; and my sister, Vanessa Bell – but the list threatens to grow too long and is already far too distinguished. For while it rouses in me memories of the pleasantest kind it will inevitably wake expectations in the reader which the book itself can only disappoint. Therefore I will conclude by thanking the officials of the British Museum and Record Office for their wonted courtesy; my niece Miss Angelica Bell, for a service which none but she could have rendered; and my husband for the patience with which he has invariably helped my researches and for the profound historical knowledge to which these pages owe whatever degree of accuracy they may attain. Finally, I would thank, had I not lost his name and address, a gentleman in America, who has generously and gratuitously corrected the punctuation, the botany, the entomology, the geography, and the chronology of previous works of mine and will, I hope, not spare his services on the present occasion.

CONTENTS

Illustrations

Chapter I

He – for there could be no doubt of his sex, though the fashion of the time did something to disguise it – was in the act of slicing at the head of a Moor[1] which swung from the rafters. It was the colour of an old football, and more or less the shape of one, save for the sunken cheeks and a strand or two of coarse, dry hair, like the hair on a cocoanut. Orlando's father, or perhaps his grandfather, had struck it from the shoulders of a vast Pagan who had started up under the moon in the barbarian fields of Africa; and now it swung, gently, perpetually, in the breeze which never ceased blowing through the attic rooms of the gigantic house of the lord who had slain him.

Orlando's fathers had ridden in fields of asphodel,[2] and stony fields, and fields watered by strange rivers, and they had struck many heads of many colours off many shoulders, and brought them back to hang from the rafters. So too would Orlando, he vowed. But since he was sixteen only, and too young to ride with them in Africa or France, he would steal away from his mother and the peacocks in the garden and go to his attic room and there lunge and plunge and slice the air with his blade. Sometimes he cut the cord so that the skull bumped on the floor and he had to string it up again, fastening it with some chivalry almost out of reach so that his enemy grinned at him through shrunk, black lips triumphantly. The skull swung to and fro, for the house, at the top of which he lived, was so vast that there seemed trapped in it the wind itself, blowing this way, blowing that way, winter and summer. The green arras with the hunters on it moved perpetually. His fathers had been noble since they had been at all. They came out of the northern mists wearing coronets on their heads.[3] Were not the bars of darkness in the room, and the yellow pools which chequered the floor, made by the sun falling through the stained glass of a vast coat of arms in

the window? Orlando stood now in the midst of the yellow
body of an heraldic leopard.[4] When he put his hand on the
window-sill to push the window open, it was instantly coloured
red, blue, and yellow like a butterfly's wing. Thus, those who
like symbols, and have a turn for the deciphering of them, might
observe that though the shapely legs, the handsome body,[5] and
the well-set shoulders were all of them decorated with various
tints of heraldic light, Orlando's face, as he threw the window
open, was lit solely by the sun itself. A more candid, sullen face
it would be impossible to find. Happy the mother who bears,
happier still the biographer who records the life of such a one!
Never need she vex herself, nor he invoke the help of novelist or
poet. From deed to deed, from glory to glory, from office to
office he must go, his scribe following after, till they reach
whatever seat it may be that is the height of their desire. Orlando,
to look at, was cut out precisely for some such career. The red of
the cheeks was covered with peach down; the down on the lips
was only a little thicker than the down on the cheeks. The lips
themselves were short and slightly drawn back over teeth of an
exquisite and almond whiteness. Nothing disturbed the arrowy
nose in its short, tense flight; the hair was dark, the ears small,
and fitted closely to the head. But, alas, that these catalogues of
youthful beauty cannot end without mentioning forehead and
eyes. Alas, that people are seldom born devoid of all three; for
directly we glance at Orlando standing by the window, we must
admit that he had eyes like drenched violets, so large that the
water seemed to have brimmed in them and widened them; and
a brow like the swelling of a marble dome pressed between the
two blank medallions which were his temples. Directly we glance
at eyes and forehead, thus do we rhapsodise. Directly we glance
at eyes and forehead, we have to admit a thousand disagreeables
which it is the aim of every good biographer to ignore. Sights
disturbed him, like that of his mother, a very beautiful lady in
green walking out to feed the peacocks with Twitchett, her
maid, behind her; sights exalted him – the birds and the trees;
and made him in love with death – the evening sky, the homing

rooks; and so, mounting up the spiral stairway into his brain – which was a roomy one – all these sights, and the garden sounds too, the hammer beating, the wood chopping, began that riot and confusion of the passions and emotions which every good biographer detests. But to continue – Orlando slowly drew in his head, sat down at the table, and, with the half-conscious air of one doing what they do every day of their lives at this hour, took out a writing book labelled 'Aethelbert: A Tragedy in Five Acts',[6] and dipped an old stained goose quill in the ink.

Soon he had covered ten pages and more with poetry. He was fluent, evidently, but he was abstract. Vice, Crime, Misery were the personages of his drama; there were Kings and Queens of impossible territories; horrid plots confounded them; noble sentiments suffused them; there was never a word said as he himself would have said it, but all was turned with a fluency and sweetness which, considering his age – he was not yet seventeen – and that the sixteenth century had still some years of its course to run, were remarkable enough. At last, however, he came to a halt. He was describing, as all young poets are for ever describing, nature, and in order to match the shade of green precisely he looked (and here he showed more audacity than most) at the thing itself, which happened to be a laurel bush growing beneath the window. After that, of course, he could write no more. Green in nature is one thing, green in literature another. Nature and letters seem to have a natural antipathy; bring them together and they tear each other to pieces. The shade of green Orlando now saw spoilt his rhyme and split his metre. Moreover, nature has tricks of her own. Once look out of a window at bees among flowers, at a yawning dog, at the sun setting, once think 'how many more suns shall I see set', etc. etc. (the thought is too well known to be worth writing out) and one drops the pen, takes one's cloak, strides out of the room, and catches one's foot on a painted chest as one does so. For Orlando was a trifle clumsy.

He was careful to avoid meeting anyone. There was Stubbs, the gardener,[7] coming along the path. He hid behind a tree till he had passed. He let himself out at a little gate in the garden wall. He skirted all stables, kennels, breweries, carpenters' shops, wash-houses, places where they make tallow candles, kill oxen, forge horse-shoes, stitch jerkins – for the house was a town[8] ringing with men at work at their various crafts – and gained the ferny path leading uphill through the park unseen. There is perhaps a kinship among qualities; one draws another along with it; and the biographer should here call attention to the fact that this clumsiness is often mated with a love of solitude. Having stumbled over a chest, Orlando naturally loved solitary places, vast views, and to feel himself for ever and ever and ever alone.

So, after a long silence, 'I am alone', he breathed at last, opening his lips for the first time in this record. He had walked very quickly uphill through ferns and hawthorn bushes, startling deer and wild birds, to a place crowned by a single oak tree.[9] It was very high, so high indeed that nineteen English counties could be seen beneath; and on clear days thirty or perhaps forty, if the weather was very fine. Sometimes one could see the English Channel, wave reiterating upon wave. Rivers could be seen and pleasure boats gliding on them; and galleons setting out to sea; and armadas with puffs of smoke from which came the dull thud of cannon firing; and forts on the coast; and castles among the meadows; and here a watch tower; and there a fortress; and again some vast mansion like that of Orlando's father, massed like a town in the valley circled by walls. To the east there were the spires of London and the smoke of the city; and perhaps on the very sky line, when the wind was in the right quarter, the craggy top and serrated edges of Snowdon[10] herself showed mountainous among the clouds. For a moment Orlando stood counting, gazing, recognising. That was his father's house; that his uncle's. His aunt owned those three great turrets among the trees there. The heath was theirs and the forest; the pheasant and the deer, the fox, the badger, and the butterfly.

He sighed profoundly, and flung himself – there was a passion in his movements which deserves the word – on the earth at the foot of the oak tree. He loved, beneath all this summer transiency, to feel the earth's spine beneath him; for such he took the hard root of the oak tree to be; or, for image followed image, it was the back of a great horse that he was riding; or the deck of a tumbling ship – it was anything indeed, so long as it was hard, for he felt the need of something which he could attach his floating heart to; the heart that tugged at his side; the heart that seemed filled with spiced and amorous gales every evening about this time when he walked out. To the oak tree he tied it and as he lay there, gradually the flutter in and about him stilled itself; the little leaves hung, the deer stopped; the pale summer clouds stayed; his limbs grew heavy on the ground; and he lay so still that by degrees the deer stepped nearer and the rooks wheeled round him and the swallows dipped and circled and the dragon-flies shot past, as if all the fertility and amorous activity of a summer's evening were woven web-like about his body.

After an hour or so – the sun was rapidly sinking, the white clouds had turned red, the hills were violet, the woods purple, the valleys black – a trumpet sounded. Orlando leapt to his feet. The shrill sound came from the valley. It came from a dark spot down there; a spot compact and mapped out; a maze; a town, yet girt about with walls; it came from the heart of his own great house in the valley, which, dark before, even as he looked and the single trumpet duplicated and reduplicated itself with other shriller sounds, lost its darkness and became pierced with lights. Some were small hurrying lights, as if servants dashed along corridors to answer summonses; others were high and lustrous lights, as if they burnt in empty banqueting-halls made ready to receive guests who had not come; and others dipped and waved and sank and rose, as if held in the hands of troops of serving men, bending, kneeling, rising, receiving, guarding, and escort-ing with all dignity indoors a great Princess alighting from her chariot. Coaches turned and wheeled in the courtyard. Horses tossed their plumes. The Queen had come.

Orlando looked no more. He dashed downhill. He let himself in at a wicket gate. He tore up the winding staircase. He reached his room. He tossed his stockings to one side of the room, his jerkin to the other. He dipped his head. He scoured his hands. He pared his finger nails. With no more than six inches of looking-glass and a pair of old candles to help him, he had thrust on crimson breeches, lace collar, waistcoat of taffeta, and shoes with rosettes on them as big as double dahlias in less than ten minutes by the stable clock. He was ready. He was flushed. He was excited. But he was terribly late.

By short cuts known to him, he made his way now through the vast congeries of rooms and staircases to the banqueting-hall, five acres distant on the other side of the house. But half-way there, in the back quarters where the servants lived, he stopped. The door of Mrs. Stewkley's sitting-room stood open – she was gone, doubtless, with all her keys to wait upon her mistress. But there, sitting at the servants' dinner table with a tankard beside him and paper in front of him, sat a rather fat, rather shabby man, whose ruff was a thought dirty, and whose clothes were of hodden brown.[11] He held a pen in his hand, but he was not writing. He seemed in the act of rolling some thought up and down, to and fro in his mind till it gathered shape or momentum to his liking. His eyes, globed and clouded like some green stone of curious texture, were fixed. He did not see Orlando. For all his hurry, Orlando stopped dead. Was this a poet? Was he writing poetry? 'Tell me', he wanted to say, 'everything in the whole world' – for he had the wildest, most absurd, extravagant ideas about poets and poetry – but how speak to a man who does not see you? who sees ogres, satyrs, perhaps the depths of the sea instead? So Orlando stood gazing while the man turned his pen in his fingers, this way and that way; and gazed and mused; and then, very quickly, wrote half-a-dozen lines and looked up. Whereupon Orlando, overcome with shyness, darted off and reached the banqueting-hall only just in time to sink upon his knees and, hanging his head in confusion, to offer a bowl of rose water to the great Queen herself.[12]

Such was his shyness that he saw no more of her than her ringed hand in water; but it was enough. It was a memorable hand; a thin hand with long fingers always curling as if round orb or sceptre; a nervous, crabbed, sickly hand; a commanding hand, too; a hand that had only to raise itself for a head to fall; a hand, he guessed, attached to an old body that smelt like a cupboard in which furs are kept in camphor; which body was yet caparisoned in all sorts of brocades and gems; and held itself very upright though perhaps in pain from sciatica; and never flinched though strung together by a thousand fears; and the Queen's eyes were light yellow. All this he felt as the great rings flashed in the water and then something pressed his hair – which, perhaps, accounts for his seeing nothing more likely to be of use to a historian. And in truth, his mind was such a welter of opposites – of the night and the blazing candles, of the shabby poet and the great Queen, of silent fields and the clatter of serving men – that he could see nothing; or only a hand.

By the same showing, the Queen herself can have seen only a head. But if it is possible from a hand to deduce a body, informed with all the attributes of a great Queen, her crabbedness, courage, frailty, and terror, surely a head can be as fertile, looked down upon from a chair of state by a lady whose eyes were always, if the waxworks at the Abbey are to be trusted, wide open. The long, curled hair, the dark head bent so reverently, so innocently before her, implied a pair of the finest legs that a young nobleman has ever stood upright upon; and violet eyes; and a heart of gold; and loyalty and manly charm – all qualities which the old woman loved the more the more they failed her. For she was growing old and worn and bent before her time. The sound of cannon was always in her ears. She saw always the glistening poison drop and the long stiletto. As she sat at table she listened; she heard the guns in the Channel;[13] she dreaded – was that a curse, was that a whisper? Innocence, simplicity, were all the more dear to her for the dark background she set them against. And it was that same night, so tradition has it, when Orlando was sound asleep, that she made over formally, putting her hand and seal finally to the parchment, the gift of the great monastic house[14] that had been the Archbishop's and then the King's to Orlando's father.

Orlando slept all night in ignorance. He had been kissed by a queen without knowing it. And perhaps, for women's hearts are intricate, it was his ignorance and the start he gave when her lips touched him that kept the memory of her young cousin (for they had blood in common) green in her mind. At any rate, two years of this quiet country life had not passed, and Orlando had written no more perhaps than twenty tragedies and a dozen histories and a score of sonnets when a message came that he was to attend the Queen at Whitehall.

'Here', she said, watching him advance down the long gallery towards her, 'comes my innocent!' (There was a serenity about him always which had the look of innocence when, technically, the word was no longer applicable.)

'Come!' she said. She was sitting bolt upright beside the fire. And she held him a foot's pace from her and looked him up and down. Was she matching her speculations the other night with the truth now visible? Did she find her guesses justified? Eyes, mouth, nose, breast, hips, hands – she ran them over; her lips twitched visibly as she looked; but when she saw his legs she laughed out loud. He was the very image of a noble gentleman. But inwardly? She flashed her yellow hawk's eyes upon him as if she would pierce his soul. The young man withstood her gaze blushing only a damask rose as became him. Strength, grace, romance, folly, poetry, youth – she read him like a page. Instantly she plucked a ring from her finger (the joint was swollen rather) and as she fitted it to his, named him her Treasurer and Steward; next hung about him chains of office; and bidding him bend his knee, tied round it at the slenderest part the jewelled order of the Garter. Nothing after that was denied him. When she drove in state he rode at her carriage door. She sent him to Scotland on a sad embassy to the unhappy Queen. He was about to sail for the Polish wars when she recalled him. For how could she bear to think of that tender flesh torn and that curly head rolled in the dust? She kept him with her. At the height of her triumph when the guns were booming at the Tower[15] and the air was thick enough with gunpowder to make one sneeze and the huzzas of the people rang beneath the windows, she pulled him down among the cushions where her women had laid her (she was so worn and old) and made him bury his face in that astonishing composition – she had not changed her dress for a month – which smelt for all the world, he thought, recalling his boyish memory, like some old cabinet at home where his mother's furs were stored. He rose, half suffocated from the embrace. 'This', she breathed, 'is my victory!' – even as a rocket roared up and dyed her cheeks scarlet.

For the old woman loved him. And the Queen, who knew a man when she saw one, though not, it is said, in the usual way, plotted for him a splendid ambitious career. Lands were given him, houses assigned him. He was to be the son of her old age; the limb of her infirmity; the oak tree on which she leant her degradation. She croaked out these promises and strange domineering tendernesses (they were at Richmond[16] now) sitting bolt upright in her stiff brocades by the fire which, however high they piled it, never kept her warm.

Meanwhile, the long winter months drew on. Every tree in the Park was lined with frost. The river ran sluggishly. One day when the snow was on the ground and the dark panelled rooms were full of shadows and the stags were barking in the Park, she saw in the mirror, which she kept for fear of spies always by her, through the door, which she kept for fear of murderers always open, a boy – could it be Orlando? – kissing a girl – who in the Devil's name was the brazen hussy? Snatching at her golden-hilted sword she struck violently at the mirror. The glass crashed; people came running; she was lifted and set in her chair again; but she was stricken after that and groaned much, as her days wore to an end, of man's treachery.

It was Orlando's fault perhaps; yet, after all, are we to blame Orlando? The age was the Elizabethan; their morals were not ours; nor their poets; nor their climate; nor their vegetables even. Everything was different. The weather itself, the heat and cold of summer and winter, was, we may believe, of another temper altogether. The brilliant amorous day was divided as sheerly from the night as land from water. Sunsets were redder and more intense; dawns were whiter and more auroral. Of our crepuscular half-lights and lingering twilights they knew nothing. The rain fell vehemently, or not at all. The sun blazed or there was darkness. Translating this to the spiritual regions as their wont is, the poets sang beautifully how roses fade and petals fall. The moment is brief they sang; the moment is over; one long night is then to be slept by all. As for using the artifices of the greenhouse or conservatory to prolong or preserve these fresh pinks and roses, that was not their way. The withered intricacies and ambiguities of our more gradual and doubtful age were unknown to them. Violence was all. The flower bloomed and faded. The sun rose and sank. The lover loved and went. And what the poets said in rhyme, the young translated into practice. Girls were roses, and their seasons were short as the flowers'. Plucked they must be before nightfall; for the day was brief and the day was all. Thus, if Orlando followed the leading of the climate, of the poets, of the age itself, and plucked his flower in the window-seat even with the snow on the ground and the Queen vigilant in the corridor, we can scarcely bring ourselves to blame him. He was young; he was boyish; he did but as nature bade him do. As for the girl, we know no more than Queen Elizabeth herself did what her name was. It may have been Doris, Chloris, Delia, or Diana,[17] for he made rhymes to them all in turn; equally, she may have been a court lady, or some serving maid. For Orlando's taste was broad; he was no lover of garden flowers only; the wild and the weeds even had always a fascination for him.

Here, indeed, we lay bare rudely, as a biographer may, a curious trait in him, to be accounted for, perhaps, by the fact that a certain grandmother of his had worn a smock and carried milkpails. Some grains of the Kentish or Sussex earth were mixed with the thin, fine fluid which came to him from Normandy. He held that the mixture of brown earth and blue blood was a good one. Certain it is that he had always a liking for low company, especially for that of lettered people whose wits so often keep them under, as if there were the sympathy of blood between them. At this season of his life, when his head brimmed with rhymes and he never went to bed without striking off some conceit, the cheek of an innkeeper's daughter seemed fresher and the wit of a gamekeeper's niece seemed quicker than those of the ladies at Court. Hence, he began going frequently to Wapping Old Stairs[18] and the beer gardens at night, wrapped in a grey cloak to hide the star at his neck and the garter at his knee. There, with a mug before him, among the sanded alleys and bowling greens and all the simple architecture of such places, he listened to sailors' stories of hardship and horror and cruelty on the Spanish main; how some had lost their toes, others their noses – for the spoken story was never so rounded or so finely coloured as the written. Especially he loved to hear them volley forth their songs of the Azores, while the parrakeets, which they had brought from those parts, pecked at the rings in their ears, tapped with their hard acquisitive beaks at the rubies on their fingers, and swore as vilely as their masters. The women were scarcely less bold in their speech and less free in their manners than the birds. They perched on his knee, flung their arms round his neck and, guessing that something out of the common lay hid beneath his duffle cloak, were quite as eager to come at the truth of the matter as Orlando himself.

Nor was opportunity lacking. The river was astir early and late with barges, wherries, and craft of all description. Every day sailed to sea some fine ship bound for the Indies; now and again another blackened and ragged with hairy unknown men on board crept painfully to anchor. No one missed a boy or girl if they dallied a little on the water after sunset; or raised an eyebrow if gossip had seen them sleeping soundly among the treasure sacks safe in each other's arms. Such indeed was the adventure that befel Orlando, Sukey, and the Earl of Cumberland.[19] The day was hot; their loves had been active; they had fallen asleep among the rubies. Late that night the Earl, whose fortunes were much bound up in the Spanish ventures, came to check the booty alone with a lantern. He flashed the light on a barrel. He started back with an oath. Twined about the cask two spirits lay sleeping. Superstitious by nature, and his conscience laden with many a crime, the Earl took the couple – they were wrapped in a red cloak, and Sukey's bosom was almost as white as the eternal snows of Orlando's poetry – for a phantom sprung from the graves of drowned sailors to upbraid him. He crossed himself. He vowed repentance. The row of almshouses still standing in the Sheen Road is the visible fruit of that moment's panic. Twelve poor old women of the parish to-day drink tea and to-night bless his Lordship for a roof above their heads; so that illicit love in a treasure ship – but we omit the moral.

Soon, however, Orlando grew tired, not only of the discomfort of this way of life, and of the crabbed streets of the neighbourhood, but of the primitive manners of the people. For it has to be remembered that crime and poverty had none of the attraction for the Elizabethans that they have for us. They had none of our modern shame of book learning; none of our belief that to be born the son of a butcher is a blessing and to be unable to read a virtue; no fancy that what we call 'life' and 'reality' are somehow connected with ignorance and brutality; nor, indeed, any equivalent for these two words at all. It was not to seek 'life' that Orlando went among them; not in quest of 'reality' that he left them. But when he had heard a score of times how Jakes had lost his nose and Sukey her honour – and they told the stories admirably, it must be admitted – he began to be a little weary of the repetition, for a nose can only be cut off in one way and maidenhood lost in another – or so it seemed to him – whereas the arts and the sciences had a diversity about them which stirred his curiosity profoundly. So, always keeping them in happy memory, he left off frequenting the beer gardens and the skittle alleys, hung his grey cloak in his wardrobe, let his star shine at his neck and his garter twinkle at his knee, and appeared once more at the Court of King James. He was young, he was rich, he was handsome. No one could have been received with greater acclamation than he was.

It is certain indeed that many ladies were ready to show him their favours. The names of three at least were freely coupled with his in marriage – Clorinda, Favilla, Euphrosyne[20] – so he called them in his sonnets.

To take them in order; Clorinda was a sweet-mannered gentle lady enough – indeed Orlando was greatly taken with her for six months and a half; but she had white eyelashes and could not bear the sight of blood. A hare brought up roasted at her father's table turned her faint. She was much under the influence of the Priests too, and stinted her underlinen in order to give to the poor. She took it on her to reform Orlando of his sins, which sickened him, so that he drew back from the marriage, and did not much regret it when she died soon after of the small-pox.

Favilla, who comes next, was of a different sort altogether. She was the daughter of a poor Somersetshire gentleman; who, by sheer assiduity and the use of her eyes had worked her way up at court, where her address in horsemanship, her fine instep, and her grace in dancing won the admiration of all. Once, however, she was so ill-advised as to whip a spaniel that had torn one of her silk stockings (and it must be said in justice that Favilla had few stockings and those for the most part of drugget) within an inch of its life beneath Orlando's window. Orlando, who was a passionate lover of animals, now noticed that her teeth were crooked, and the two front turned inward, which, he said, is a sure sign of a perverse and cruel disposition in woman, and so broke the engagement that very night for ever.

The third, Euphrosyne, was by far the most serious of his flames. She was by birth one of the Irish Desmonds and had therefore a family tree of her own as old and deeply rooted as Orlando's itself. She was fair, florid, and a trifle phlegmatic. She spoke Italian well, had a perfect set of teeth in the upper jaw, though those on the lower were slightly discoloured. She was never without a whippet or spaniel at her knee; fed them with white bread from her own plate; sang sweetly to the virginals; and was never dressed before mid-day owing to the extreme care she took of her person. In short, she would have made a perfect wife for such a nobleman as Orlando, and matters had gone so far that the lawyers on both sides were busy with covenants, jointures, settlements, messuages, tenements, and whatever is needed before one great fortune can mate with another when, with the suddenness and severity that then marked the English climate, came the Great Frost.

The Great Frost[21] was, historians tell us, the most severe that has ever visited these islands. Birds froze in mid-air and fell like stones to the ground. At Norwich a young countrywoman started to cross the road in her usual robust health and was seen by the onlookers to turn visibly to powder and be blown in a puff of dust over the roofs as the icy blast struck her at the street corner. The mortality among sheep and cattle was enormous. Corpses froze and could not be drawn from the sheets. It was no uncommon sight to come upon a whole herd of swine frozen immovable upon the road. The fields were full of shepherds, ploughmen, teams of horses, and little bird-scaring boys all struck stark in the act of the moment, one with his hand to his nose, another with the bottle to his lips, a third with a stone raised to throw at the raven who sat, as if stuffed, upon the hedge within a yard of him. The severity of the frost was so extraordinary that a kind of petrifaction sometimes ensued; and it was commonly supposed that the great increase of rocks in some parts of Derbyshire was due to no eruption, for there was none, but to the solidification of unfortunate wayfarers who had been turned literally to stone where they stood. The Church could give little help in the matter, and though some landowners had these relics blessed, the most part preferred to use them either as landmarks, scratching-posts for sheep, or, when the form of the stone allowed, drinking troughs for cattle, which purposes they serve, admirably for the most part, to this day.

But while the country people suffered the extremity of want, and the trade of the country was at a standstill, London enjoyed a carnival of the utmost brilliancy. The Court was at Greenwich, and the new King seized the opportunity that his coronation gave him to curry favour with the citizens. He directed that the river, which was frozen to a depth of twenty feet and more for six or seven miles on either side, should be swept, decorated and given all the semblance of a park or pleasure ground, with arbours, mazes, alleys, drinking booths, etc., at his expense. For himself and the courtiers, he reserved a certain space immediately opposite the Palace gates; which, railed off from the public only by a silken rope, became at once the centre of the most brilliant society in England. Great statesmen, in their beards and ruffs, despatched affairs of state under the crimson awning of the Royal Pagoda. Soldiers planned the conquest of the Moor and the downfall of the Turk in striped arbours surmounted by plumes of ostrich feathers. Admirals strode up and down the narrow pathways, glass in hand, sweeping the horizon and telling stories of the north-west passage[22] and the Spanish Armada. Lovers dallied upon divans spread with sables. Frozen roses fell in showers when the Queen and her ladies walked abroad. Coloured balloons hovered motionless in the air. Here and there burnt vast bonfires of cedar and oak wood, lavishly salted, so that the flames were of green, orange, and purple fire. But however fiercely they burnt, the heat was not enough to melt the ice which, though of singular transparency, was yet of the hardness of steel. So clear indeed was it that there could be seen, congealed at a depth of several feet, here a porpoise, there a flounder. Shoals of eels lay motionless in a trance, but whether their state was one of death or merely of suspended animation which the warmth would revive puzzled the philosophers. Near London Bridge,[23] where the river had frozen to a depth of some twenty fathoms, a wrecked wherry boat was plainly visible, lying on the bed of the river where it had sunk last autumn, overladen with apples. The old bumboat woman, who was carrying her fruit to market on the Surrey side, sat there in her plaids and farthingales with her lap full of apples, for all the world as if she were about to serve a customer, though a certain blueness about the lips hinted the truth. 'Twas a sight King James specially liked to look upon, and he would bring a troupe of courtiers to gaze with him. In short, nothing could exceed the brilliancy and gaiety of the scene by day. But it was at night that the carnival was at its merriest. For the frost continued unbroken; the nights were of perfect stillness; the moon and stars blazed with the hard fixity of diamonds, and to the fine music of flute and trumpet the courtiers danced.

Orlando, it is true, was none of those who tread lightly the corantoe and lavolta;[24] he was clumsy and a little absent-minded. He much preferred the plain dances of his own country, which he had danced as a child to these fantastic foreign measures. He had indeed just brought his feet together about six in the evening of the seventh of January at the finish of some such quadrille or minuet when he beheld, coming from the pavilion of the Muscovite Embassy, a figure, which, whether boy's or woman's, for the loose tunic and trousers of the Russian fashion served to disguise the sex, filled him with the highest curiosity. The person, whatever the name or sex, was about middle height, very slenderly fashioned, and dressed entirely in oyster-coloured velvet, trimmed with some unfamiliar greenish-coloured fur. But these details were obscured by the extraordinary seductiveness which issued from the whole person. Images, metaphors of the most extreme and extravagant twined and twisted in his mind. He called her a melon, a pineapple, an olive tree, an emerald, and a fox in the snow all in the space of three seconds; he did not know whether he had heard her, tasted her, seen her, or all three together. (For though we must pause not a moment in the narrative we may here hastily note that all his images at this time were simple in the extreme to match his senses and were mostly taken from things he had liked the taste of as a boy. But if his senses were simple they were at the same time extremely strong. To pause therefore and seek the reasons of things is out of the question.) . . . A melon, an emerald, a fox in the snow – so he raved, so he stared. When the boy, for alas, a boy it must be – no woman could skate with such speed and vigour – swept almost on tiptoe past him, Orlando was ready to tear his hair with vexation that the person was of his own sex, and thus all embraces were out of the question. But the skater came closer.

Legs, hands, carriage, were a boy's, but no boy ever had a mouth like that; no boy had those breasts; no boy had eyes which looked as if they had been fished from the bottom of the sea. Finally, coming to a stop and sweeping a curtsey with the utmost grace to the King, who was shuffling past on the arm of some Lord-in-waiting, the unknown skater came to a standstill. She was not a handsbreadth off. She was a woman. Orlando stared; trembled; turned hot; turned cold; longed to hurl himself through the summer air; to crush acorns beneath his feet; to toss his arms with the beech trees and the oaks. As it was, he drew his lips up over his small white teeth; opened them perhaps half an inch as if to bite; shut them as if he had bitten. The Lady Euphrosyne hung upon his arm.

The stranger's name, he found, was the Princess Marousha Stanilovska Dagmar Natasha Iliana Romanovitch,[25] and she had come in the train of the Muscovite Ambassador, who was her uncle perhaps, or perhaps her father, to attend the coronation. Very little was known of the Muscovites. In their great beards and furred hats they sat almost silent; drinking some black liquid which they spat out now and then upon the ice. None spoke English, and French with which some at least were familiar was then little spoken at the English Court.

It was through this accident that Orlando and the Princess became acquainted. They were seated opposite each other at the great table spread under a huge awning for the entertainment of the notables. The Princess was placed between two young Lords, one Lord Francis Vere and the other the young Earl of Moray. It was laughable to see the predicament she soon had them in, for though both were fine lads in their way, the babe unborn had as much knowledge of the French tongue as they had. When at the beginning of dinner the Princess turned to the Earl and said, with a grace which ravished his heart, 'Je crois avoir fait la connaissance d'un gentilhomme qui vous était apparenté en Pologne l'été dernier', or 'La beauté des dames de la cour d'Angleterre me met dans le ravissement. On ne peut voir une dame plus gracieuse que votre reine, ni une coiffure plus belle que la sienne,'[26] both

Lord Francis and the Earl showed the highest embarrassment. The one helped her largely to horse-radish sauce, the other whistled to his dog and made him beg for a marrow bone. At this the Princess could no longer contain her laughter, and Orlando, catching her eyes across the boars' heads and stuffed peacocks, laughed too. He laughed, but the laugh on his lips froze in wonder. Whom had he loved, what had he loved, he asked himself in a tumult of emotion, until now? An old woman, he answered, all skin and bone. Red-cheeked trulls too many to mention. A puling nun. A hard-bitten cruel-mouthed adventuress. A nodding mass of lace and ceremony. Love had meant to him nothing but sawdust and cinders. The joys he had had of it tasted insipid in the extreme. He marvelled how he could have gone through with it without yawning. For as he looked the thickness of his blood melted; the ice turned to wine in his veins; he heard the waters flowing and the birds singing; spring broke over the hard wintry landscape; his manhood woke; he grasped a sword in his hand; he charged a more daring foe than Pole or Moor; he dived in deep water; he saw the flower of danger growing in a crevice; he stretched his hand – in fact he was rattling off one of his most impassioned sonnets when the Princess addressed him, 'Would you have the goodness to pass the salt?'

He blushed deeply.

'With all the pleasure in the world, Madame,' he replied, speaking French with a perfect accent. For, heaven be praised, he spoke the tongue as his own; his mother's maid had taught him. Yet perhaps it would have been better for him had he never learnt that tongue; never answered that voice; never followed the light of those eyes . . .

The Princess continued. Who were those bumpkins, she asked him, who sat beside her with the manners of stablemen? What was the nauseating mixture they had poured on her plate? Did the dogs eat at the same table with the men in England? Was that figure of fun at the end of the table with her hair rigged up like a Maypole (comme une grande perche mal fagotée) really the

Queen? And did the King always slobber like that? And which of those popinjays was George Villiers?[27] Though these questions rather discomposed Orlando at first, they were put with such archness and drollery that he could not help but laugh; and as he saw from the blank faces of the company that nobody understood a word, he answered her as freely as she asked him, speaking, as she did, in perfect French.

Thus began an intimacy between the two which soon became the scandal of the Court.

Soon it was observed Orlando paid the Muscovite far more attention than mere civility demanded. He was seldom far from her side, and their conversation, though unintelligible to the rest, was carried on with such animation, provoked such blushes and laughter, that the dullest could guess the subject. Moreover, the change in Orlando himself was extraordinary. Nobody had ever seen him so animated. In one night he had thrown off his boyish clumsiness; he was changed from a sulky stripling, who could not enter a ladies' room without sweeping half the ornaments from the table, to a nobleman, full of grace and manly courtesy. To see him hand the Muscovite (as she was called) to her sledge, or offer her his hand for the dance, or catch the spotted kerchief which she had let drop, or discharge any other of those manifold duties which the supreme lady exacts and the lover hastens to anticipate was a sight to kindle the dull eyes of age, and to make the quick pulse of youth beat faster. Yet over it all hung a cloud. The old men shrugged their shoulders. The young tittered between their fingers. All knew that Orlando was betrothed to another. The Lady Margaret O'Brien O'Dare O'Reilly Tyrconnel (for that was the proper name of Euphrosyne of the Sonnets) wore Orlando's splendid sapphire on the second finger of her left hand. It was she who had the supreme right to his attentions. Yet she might drop all the handkerchiefs in her wardrobe (of which she had many scores) upon the ice and Orlando never stooped to pick them up. She might wait twenty minutes for him to hand her to her sledge, and in the end have to be content with the services of her Blackamoor. When she skated, which she did rather clumsily, no one was at her elbow to encourage her, and, if she fell, which she did rather heavily, no one raised her to her feet and dusted the snow from her petticoats. Although she was naturally phlegmatic, slow to take offence, and more reluctant than most people to believe that a mere foreigner could oust her from Orlando's affections, still even the Lady Margaret herself was brought at last to suspect that something was brewing against her peace of mind.

Indeed, as the days passed, Orlando took less and less care to hide his feelings. Making some excuse or other, he would leave the company as soon as they had dined, or steal away from the skaters, who were forming sets for a quadrille. Next moment it would be seen that the Muscovite was missing too. But what most outraged the Court, and stung it in its tenderest part, which is its vanity, was that the couple was often seen to slip under the silken rope, which railed off the Royal enclosure from the public part of the river and to disappear among the crowd of common people. For suddenly the Princess would stamp her foot and cry, 'Take me away. I detest your English mob,' by which she meant the English Court itself. She could stand it no longer. It was full of prying old women, she said, who stared in one's face, and of bumptious young men who trod on one's toes. They smelt bad. Their dogs ran between her legs. It was like being in a cage. In Russia they had rivers ten miles broad on which one could gallop six horses abreast all day long without meeting a soul. Besides, she wanted to see the Tower, the Beefeaters, the Heads on Temple Bar, and the jewellers' shops in the city. Thus, it came about that Orlando took her to the city, showed her the Beefeaters and the rebels' heads, and bought her whatever took her fancy in the Royal Exchange.[28] But this was not enough. Each increasingly desired the other's company in privacy all day long where there were none to marvel or to stare. Instead of taking the road to London, therefore, they turned the other way about and were soon beyond the crowd among the frozen reaches of the Thames where, save for sea birds and some old country woman hacking at the ice in a vain attempt to draw a pailful of water or gathering what sticks or dead leaves she could find for firing, not a living soul ever came their way. The poor kept closely to their cottages, and the better sort, who could afford it, crowded for warmth and merriment to the city.

Hence, Orlando and Sasha, as he called her for short, and because it was the name of a white Russian fox[29] he had had as a boy – a creature soft as snow, but with teeth of steel, which bit him so savagely that his father had it killed – hence, they had the river to themselves. Hot with skating and with love they would throw themselves down in some solitary reach, where the yellow osiers fringed the bank, and wrapped in a great fur cloak Orlando would take her in his arms, and know, for the first time, he murmured, the delights of love. Then, when the ecstasy was over and they lay lulled in a swoon on the ice, he would tell her of his other loves, and how, compared with her, they had been of wood, of sackcloth, and of cinders. And laughing at his vehemence, she would turn once more in his arms and give him, for love's sake, one more embrace. And then they would marvel that the ice did not melt with their heat, and pity the poor old woman who had no such natural means of thawing it, but must hack at it with a chopper of cold steel. And then, wrapped in their sables, they would talk of everything under the sun; of sights and travels; of Moor and Pagan; of this man's beard and that woman's skin; of a rat that fed from her hand at table; of the arras that moved always in the hall at home;[30] of a face; of a feather. Nothing was too small for such converse, nothing was too great.

Then, suddenly Orlando would fall into one of his moods of melancholy; the sight of the old woman hobbling over the ice might be the cause of it, or nothing; and would fling himself face downwards on the ice and look into the frozen waters and think of death. For the philosopher is right[31] who says that nothing thicker than a knife's blade separates happiness from melancholy; and he goes on to opine that one is twin fellow to the other; and draws from this the conclusion that all extremes of feeling are allied to madness; and so bids us take refuge in the true Church (in his view the Anabaptist), which is the only harbour, port, anchorage, etc., he said, for those tossed on this sea.

'All ends in death,' Orlando would say, sitting upright, his face clouded with gloom. (For that was the way his mind worked now, in violent see-saws from life to death, stopping at nothing in between, so that the biographer must not stop either, but must fly as fast as he can and so keep pace with the unthinking passionate foolish actions and sudden extravagant words in which, it is impossible to deny, Orlando at this time of his life indulged.)

'All ends in death,' Orlando would say, sitting upright on the ice. But Sasha who after all had no English blood in her but was from Russia where the sunsets are longer, the dawns less sudden, and sentences often left unfinished from doubt as to how best to end them – Sasha stared at him, perhaps sneered at him, for he must have seemed a child to her, and said nothing. But at length the ice grew cold beneath them, which she disliked, so pulling him to his feet again, she talked so enchantingly, so wittily, so wisely (but unfortunately always in French, which notoriously loses its flavour in translation) that he forgot the frozen waters or night coming or the old woman or whatever it was, and would try to tell her – plunging and splashing among a thousand images which had gone as stale as the women who inspired them – what she was like. Snow, cream, marble, cherries, alabaster, golden wire? None of these. She was like a fox, or an olive tree; like the waves of the sea when you look down upon them from a height; like an emerald; like the sun on a green hill which is yet clouded – like nothing he had seen or known in England. Ransack the language as he might, words failed him. He wanted another landscape, and another tongue. English was too frank, too candid, too honeyed a speech for Sasha. For in all she said, however open she seemed and voluptuous, there was something hidden; in all she did, however daring, there was something concealed. So the green flame seems hidden in the emerald, or the sun prisoned in a hill. The clearness was only outward;

within was a wandering flame. It came; it went; she never shone
with the steady beam of an Englishwoman – here, however,
remembering the Lady Margaret and her petticoats, Orlando ran
wild in his transports and swept her over the ice, faster, faster,
vowing that he would chase the flame, dive for the gem, and so
on and so on, the words coming on the pants of his breath with
the passion of a poet whose poetry is half pressed out of him
by pain.

But Sasha was silent. When Orlando had done telling her that
she was a fox, an olive tree, or a green hill-top, and had given
her the whole history of his family; how their house was one of
the most ancient in Britain; how they had come from Rome with
the Caesars and had the right to walk down the Corso (which is
the chief street in Rome) under a tasselled palanquin,[32] which he
said is a privilege reserved only for those of imperial blood (for
there was an orgulous credulity about him which was pleasant
enough), he would pause and ask her, Where was her own
house? What was her father? Had she brothers? Why was she
here alone with her uncle? Then, somehow, though she answered
readily enough, an awkwardness would come between them. He
suspected at first that her rank was not as high as she would like;
or that she was ashamed of the savage ways of her people, for he
had heard that the women in Muscovy wear beards and the men
are covered with fur from the waist down; that both sexes are
smeared with tallow to keep the cold out, tear meat with their
fingers and live in huts where an English noble would scruple to
keep his cattle; so that he forbore to press her. But on reflection,
he concluded that her silence could not be for that reason; she
herself was entirely free from hair on the chin; she dressed in
velvet and pearls, and her manners were certainly not those of a
woman bred in a cattle-shed.

What, then, did she hide from him? The doubt underlying the
tremendous force of his feelings was like a quicksand beneath a
monument which shifts suddenly and makes the whole pile shake.
The agony would seize him suddenly. Then he would blaze out
in such wrath that she did not know how to quiet him. Perhaps

she did not want to quiet him; perhaps his rages pleased her and she provoked them purposely – such is the curious obliquity of the Muscovitish temperament.

To continue the story – skating farther than their wont that day they reached that part of the river where the ships had anchored and been frozen in midstream. Among them was the ship of the Muscovite Embassy flying its double-headed black eagle from the main mast, which was hung with many-coloured icicles several yards in length. Sasha had left some of her clothing on board, and supposing the ship to be empty they climbed on deck and went in search of it. Remembering certain passages in his own past, Orlando would not have marvelled had some good citizens sought this refuge before them; and so it turned out. They had not ventured far when a fine young man started up from some business of his own behind a coil of rope and saying, apparently, for he spoke Russian, that he was one of the crew and would help the Princess to find what she wanted, lit a lump of candle and disappeared with her into the lower parts of the ship.

Time went by, and Orlando, wrapped in his own dreams, thought only of the pleasures of life; of his jewel; of her rarity; of means for making her irrevocably and indissolubly his own. Obstacles there were and hardships to be overcome. She was determined to live in Russia, where there were frozen rivers and wild horses and men, she said, who gashed each other's throats open. It is true that a landscape of pine and snow, habits of lust and slaughter, did not entice him. Nor was he anxious to cease his pleasant country ways of sport and tree-planting; relinquish his office; ruin his career; shoot the reindeer instead of the rabbit; drink vodka instead of canary, and slip a knife up his sleeve – for what purpose, he knew not. Still, all this and more than all this he would do for her sake. As for his marriage with the Lady Margaret, fixed though it was for this day sennight,[33] the thing was so palpably absurd that he scarcely gave it a thought. Her kinsmen would abuse him for deserting a great lady; his friends would deride him for ruining the finest career in

THE RUSSIAN PRINCESS AS A CHILD

the world for a Cossack woman and a waste of snow – it weighed not a straw in the balance compared with Sasha herself. On the first dark night they would fly. They would take ship to Russia. So he pondered; so he plotted as he walked up and down the deck.

He was recalled, turning westward, by the sight of the sun, slung like an orange on the cross of St. Paul's.[34] It was blood-red and sinking rapidly. It must be almost evening. Sasha had been gone this hour and more. Seized instantly with those dark forebodings which shadowed even his most confident thoughts of her, he plunged the way he had seen them go into the hold of the ship; and, after stumbling among chests and barrels in the darkness, was made aware by a faint glimmer in a corner that they were seated there. For one second, he had a vision of them; saw Sasha seated on the sailor's knee; saw her bend towards him; saw them embrace before the light was blotted out in a red cloud by his rage. He blazed into such a howl of anguish that the whole ship echoed. Sasha threw herself between them, or the sailor would have been stifled before he could draw his cutlass. Then a deadly sickness came over Orlando, and they had to lay him on the floor and give him brandy to drink before he revived. And then, when he had recovered and was sat upon a heap of sacking on deck, Sasha hung over him, passing before his dizzied eyes softly, sinuously, like the fox that had bit him, now cajoling, now denouncing, so that he came to doubt what he had seen. Had not the candle guttered; had not the shadows moved? The box was heavy, she said; the man was helping her to move it. Orlando believed her one moment – for who can be sure that his rage has not painted what he most dreads to find? – the next was the more violent with anger at her deceit. Then Sasha herself turned white; stamped her foot on deck; said she would go that night, and called upon her Gods to destroy her, if she, a Romanovitch, had lain in the arms of a common seaman. Indeed, looking at them together (which he could hardly bring himself to do) Orlando was outraged by the foulness of his imagination that could have painted so frail a creature in the paws of that hairy sea brute. The man was huge; stood six feet four in his stockings; wore common wire rings in his ears; and looked like a dray horse upon which some wren or robin has perched in its flight. So he yielded; believed her; and asked her pardon. Yet, when they were going down the ship's side, lovingly again, Sasha paused with her hand on the ladder, and called back to this tawny wide-cheeked monster a volley of Russian greetings, jests, or endearments, not a word of which Orlando could understand. But there was something in her tone (it might be the fault of the Russian consonants) that reminded Orlando of a scene some nights since, when he had come upon her in secret gnawing a candle-end in a corner, which she had picked from the floor. True, it was pink; it was gilt; and it was from the King's table; but it was tallow, and she gnawed it. Was there not, he thought, handing her on to the ice, something rank in her, something coarse flavoured, something peasant born? And he fancied her at forty grown unwieldy though she was now slim as a reed, and lethargic though she was now blithe as a lark. But again as they skated towards London such suspicions melted in his breast, and he felt as if he had been hooked by a great fish through the nose and rushed through the waters unwillingly, yet with his own consent.

It was an evening of astonishing beauty. As the sun sank, all the domes, spires, turrets, and pinnacles of London rose in inky blackness against the furious red sunset clouds. Here was the fretted cross at Charing; there the dome of St. Paul's; there the massy square of the Tower buildings; there like a grove of trees stripped of all leaves save a knob at the end were the heads on the pikes at Temple Bar. Now the Abbey windows were lit up and burnt like a heavenly, many-coloured shield (in Orlando's fancy); now all the west seemed a golden window with troops of angels (in Orlando's fancy again) passing up and down the heavenly stairs perpetually. All the time they seemed to be skating on fathomless depths of air, so blue the ice had become; and so glassy smooth was it that they sped quicker and quicker to the city with the white gulls circling about them, and cutting in the air with their wings the very same sweeps that they cut on the ice with their skates.

Sasha, as if to reassure him, was tenderer than usual and even more delightful. Seldom would she talk about her past life, but now she told him how, in winter in Russia, she would listen to the wolves howling across the steppes, and thrice, to show him, she barked like a wolf. Upon which he told her of the stags in the snow at home, and how they would stray into the great hall for warmth and be fed by an old man with porridge from a bucket.[35] And then she praised him; for his love of beasts; for his gallantry; for his legs. Ravished with her praises and shamed to think how he had maligned her by fancying her on the knees of a common sailor and grown fat and lethargic at forty, he told her that he could find no words to praise her; yet instantly bethought him how she was like the spring and green grass and rushing waters, and seizing her more tightly than ever, he swung her with him half across the river so that the gulls and the cormorants swung too. And halting at length, out of breath, she said, panting slightly, that he was like a million-candled Christmas tree (such as they have in Russia) hung with yellow globes; incandescent; enough to light a whole street by; (so one might translate it) for what with his glowing cheeks, his dark curls, his black and crimson cloak, he looked as if he were burning with his own radiance, from a lamp lit within.

All the colour, save the red of Orlando's cheeks, soon faded. Night came on. As the orange light of sunset vanished it was succeeded by an astonishing white glare from the torches, bonfires, flaming cressets, and other devices by which the river was lit up and the strangest transformation took place. Various churches and noblemen's palaces, whose fronts were of white stone showed in streaks and patches as if floating on the air. Of St. Paul's, in particular, nothing was left but a gilt cross. The Abbey appeared like the grey skeleton of a leaf. Everything suffered emaciation and transformation. As they approached the carnival, they heard a deep note like that struck on a tuning-fork which boomed louder and louder until it became an uproar.

Every now and then a great shout followed a rocket into the air. Gradually they could discern little figures breaking off from the vast crowd and spinning hither and thither like gnats on the surface of a river. Above and around this brilliant circle like a bowl of darkness pressed the deep black of a winter's night. And then into this darkness there began to rise with pauses, which kept the expectation alert and the mouth open, flowering rockets; crescents; serpents; a crown. At one moment the woods and distant hills showed green as on a summer's day; the next all was winter and blackness again.

By this time Orlando and the Princess were close to the Royal enclosure and found their way barred by a great crowd of the common people, who were pressing as near to the silken rope as they dared. Loth to end their privacy and encounter the sharp eyes that were on the watch for them, the couple lingered there, shouldered by apprentices; tailors; fishwives; horse dealers; cony catchers;[36] starving scholars; maid-servants in their whimples; orange girls; ostlers; sober citizens; bawdy tapsters; and a crowd of little ragamuffins such as always haunt the outskirts of a crowd, screaming and scrambling among people's feet – all the riff-raff of the London streets indeed was there, jesting and jostling, here casting dice, telling fortunes, shoving, tickling, pinching; here uproarious, there glum; some of them with mouths gaping a yard wide; others as little reverent as daws on a house-top; all as variously rigged out as their purse or stations allowed; here in fur and broadcloth; there in tatters with their feet kept from the ice only by a dishclout bound about them. The main press of people, it appeared, stood opposite a booth or stage something like our Punch and Judy show[37] upon which some kind of theatrical performance was going forward. A black man was waving his arms and vociferating. There was a woman in white laid upon a bed. Rough though the staging was, the actors running up and down a pair of steps and sometimes tripping, and the crowd stamping their feet and whistling, or when they were bored, tossing a piece of orange peel on to the ice which a dog would scramble for, still the astonishing, sinuous melody of the words stirred Orlando like music. Spoken with extreme speed and a daring agility of tongue which reminded him of the sailors singing in the beer gardens at Wapping, the words even without meaning were as wine to him. But now and again a single phrase would come to him over the ice which was as if torn from the depths of his heart. The frenzy of the Moor seemed to him his own frenzy, and when the Moor suffocated the woman in her bed it was Sasha he killed with his own hands.

At last the play was ended. All had grown dark. The tears streamed down his face. Looking up into the sky there was nothing but blackness there too. Ruin and death, he thought, cover all. The life of man ends in the grave. Worms devour us.

> Methinks it should be now a huge eclipse
> Of sun and moon, and that the affrighted globe
> Should yawn—[38]

Even as he said this a star of some pallor rose in his memory. The night was dark; it was pitch dark; but it was such a night as this that they had waited for; it was on such a night as this that they had planned to fly. He remembered everything. The time had come. With a burst of passion he snatched Sasha to him, and hissed in her ear 'Jour de ma vie!'[39] It was their signal. At midnight they would meet at an inn near Blackfriars. Horses waited there. Everything was in readiness for their flight. So they parted, she to her tent, he to his. It still wanted an hour of the time.

Long before midnight Orlando was in waiting. The night was of so inky a blackness that a man was on you before he could be seen, which was all to the good, but it was also of the most solemn stillness so that a horse's hoof, or a child's cry, could be heard at a distance of half a mile. Many a time did Orlando, pacing the little courtyard, hold his heart at the sound of some nag's steady footfall on the cobbles, or at the rustle of a woman's dress. But the traveller was only some merchant, making home belated; or some woman of the quarter whose errand was nothing so innocent. They passed, and the street was quieter than before. Then those lights which burnt downstairs in the small, huddled quarters where the poor of the city lived moved up to the sleeping-rooms, and then, one by one, were extinguished. The street lanterns in these purlieus were few at most; and the negligence of the night watchman often suffered them to expire long before dawn. The darkness then became even deeper than before. Orlando looked to the wicks of his lantern, saw to the saddle girths; primed his pistols; examined his holsters; and did all these things a dozen times at least till he could find nothing more needing his attention. Though it still lacked some twenty minutes to midnight, he could not bring himself to go indoors to the inn parlour, where the hostess was still serving sack and the cheaper sort of canary wine to a few seafaring men, who would sit there trolling their ditties, and telling their stories of Drake, Hawkins, and Grenville,⁴⁰ till they toppled off the benches and rolled asleep on the sanded floor. The darkness was more compassionate to his swollen and violent heart. He listened to every footfall; speculated on every sound. Each drunken shout and each wail from some poor wretch laid in the straw or in other distress cut his heart to the quick, as if it boded ill omen to his venture. Yet, he had no fear for Sasha. Her courage made nothing of the adventure. She would come alone, in her cloak and trousers, booted like a man. Light as her footfall was, it would hardly be heard, even in this silence.

So he waited in the darkness. Suddenly he was struck in the face by a blow, soft, yet heavy, on the side of his cheek. So strung with expectation was he, that he started and put his hand to his sword. The blow was repeated a dozen times on forehead and cheek. The dry frost had lasted so long that it took him a minute to realise that these were raindrops falling; the blows were the blows of the rain. At first, they fell slowly, deliberately, one by one. But soon the six drops became sixty; then six hundred; then ran themselves together in a steady spout of water. It was as if the hard and consolidated sky poured itself forth in one profuse fountain. In the space of five minutes Orlando was soaked to the skin.

Hastily putting the horses under cover, he sought shelter

beneath the lintel of the door whence he could still observe the courtyard. The air was thicker now than ever, and such a steaming and droning rose from the downpour that no footfall of man or beast could be heard above it. The roads, pitted as they were with great holes, would be under water and perhaps impassable. But of what effect this would have upon their flight he scarcely thought. All his senses were bent upon gazing along the cobbled pathway – gleaming in the light of the lantern – for Sasha's coming. Sometimes, in the darkness, he seemed to see her wrapped about with rain strokes. But the phantom vanished. Suddenly, with an awful and ominous voice, a voice full of horror and alarm which raised every hair of anguish in Orlando's soul, St. Paul's struck the first stroke of midnight. Four times more it struck remorselessly. With the superstition of a lover, Orlando had made out that it was on the sixth stroke that she would come. But the sixth stroke echoed away, and the seventh came and the eighth, and to his apprehensive mind they seemed notes first heralding and then proclaiming death and disaster. When the twelfth struck he knew that his doom was sealed. It was useless for the rational part of him to reason; she might be late; she might be prevented; she might have missed her way. The passionate and feeling heart of Orlando knew the truth. Other clocks struck, jangling one after another. The whole world seemed to ring with the news of her deceit and his derision. The old suspicions subterraneously at work in him rushed forth from concealment openly. He was bitten by a swarm of snakes, each more poisonous than the last. He stood in the doorway in the tremendous rain without moving. As the minutes passed, he sagged a little at the knees. The downpour rushed on. In the thick of it, great guns seemed to boom. Huge noises as of the tearing and rending of oak trees could be heard. There were also wild cries and terrible inhuman groanings. But Orlando stood there immovable till Paul's clock struck two, and then, crying aloud with an awful irony, and all his teeth showing, 'Jour de ma vie!' he dashed the lantern to the ground, mounted his horse and galloped he knew not where.

Some blind instinct, for he was past reasoning, must have driven him to take the river bank in the direction of the sea. For when the dawn broke, which it did with unusual suddenness, the sky turning a pale yellow and the rain almost ceasing, he found himself on the banks of the Thames off Wapping. Now a sight of the most extraordinary nature met his eyes. Where, for three months and more, there had been solid ice of such thickness that it seemed permanent as stone, and a whole gay city had been stood on its pavement, was now a race of turbulent yellow waters. The river had gained its freedom in the night. It was as if a sulphur spring (to which view many philosophers inclined) had risen from the volcanic regions beneath and burst the ice asunder with such vehemence that it swept the huge and massy fragments furiously apart. The mere look of the water was enough to turn one giddy. All was riot and confusion. The river was strewn with icebergs. Some of these were as broad as a bowling green and as high as a house; others no bigger than a man's hat, but most fantastically twisted. Now would come down a whole convoy of ice blocks sinking everything that stood in their way. Now, eddying and swirling like a tortured serpent, the river would seem to be hurtling itself between the fragments and tossing them from bank to bank, so that they could be heard smashing against the piers and pillars. But what was the most awful and inspiring of terror was the sight of the human creatures who had been trapped in the night and now paced their twisting and precarious islands in the utmost agony of spirit. Whether they jumped into the flood or stayed on the ice their doom was certain. Sometimes quite a cluster of these poor creatures would come down together, some on their knees, others suckling their babies. One old man seemed to be reading aloud from a holy book. At other times, and his fate perhaps was the most dreadful, a solitary wretch would stride his narrow tenement alone. As they swept out to sea, some could be heard crying vainly for help, making wild promises to amend their ways, confessing their sins and vowing altars and wealth if God would hear their prayers. Others were so dazed with terror that they sat immovable and silent looking steadfastly before them. One crew of young watermen or post-boys, to judge by their liveries, roared and shouted the lewdest tavern songs, as if in bravado, and were dashed against a tree and sunk with blasphemies on their lips. An old nobleman – for such his furred gown and golden chain proclaimed him – went down not far from where Orlando stood, calling vengeance upon the Irish rebels,[41] who, he cried with his last breath, had plotted this devilry. Many perished clasping some silver pot or other treasure to their breasts; and at least a score of poor wretches were drowned by their own cupidity, hurling themselves from the bank into the flood rather than let a gold goblet escape them, or see before their eyes the disappearance of some furred gown. For furniture, valuables, possessions of all sorts were carried away on the icebergs. Among other strange sights was to be seen a cat suckling its young; a table laid sumptuously for a supper of twenty; a couple in bed; together with an extraordinary number of cooking utensils.

Dazed and astounded, Orlando could do nothing for some time but watch the appalling race of waters as it hurled itself past him. At last, seeming to recollect himself, he clapped spurs to his horse and galloped hard along the river bank in the direction of the sea. Rounding a bend of the river, he came opposite that reach where, not two days ago, the ships of the Ambassadors had seemed immovably frozen. Hastily, he made count of them all; the French; the Spanish; the Austrian; the Turk. All still floated, though the French had broken loose from her moorings, and the Turkish vessel had taken a great rent in her side and was fast filling with water. But the Russian ship was nowhere to be seen. For one moment Orlando thought it must have foundered; but, raising himself in his stirrups and shading his eyes, which had the sight of a hawk's, he could just make out the shape of a ship on the horizon. The black eagles were flying from the mast head. The ship of the Muscovite Embassy was standing out to sea.[42]

Flinging himself from his horse, he made, in his rage, as if he would breast the flood. Standing knee-deep in water he hurled at the faithless woman all the insults that have ever been the lot of her sex. Faithless, mutable, fickle, he called her; devil, adulteress, deceiver; and the swirling waters took his words, and tossed at his feet a broken pot and a little straw.

Chapter II

The biographer is now faced with a difficulty which it is better perhaps to confess than to gloss over. Up to this point in telling the story of Orlando's life, documents, both private and historical, have made it possible to fulfil the first duty of a biographer, which is to plod, without looking to right or left, in the indelible footprints of truth;[1] unenticed by flowers; regardless of shade; on and on methodically till we fall plump into the grave and write *finis* on the tombstone above our heads. But now we come to an episode which lies right across our path, so that there is no ignoring it. Yet it is dark, mysterious, and undocumented; so that there is no explaining it. Volumes might be written in interpretation of it; whole religious systems founded upon the signification of it. Our simple duty is to state the facts as far as they are known, and so let the reader make of them what he may.

In the summer of that disastrous winter which saw the frost, the flood, the deaths of many thousands, and the complete downfall of Orlando's hopes – for he was exiled from Court; in deep disgrace with the most powerful nobles of his time; the Irish house of Desmond was justly enraged; the King had already trouble enough with the Irish not to relish this further addition – in that summer Orlando retired to his great house in the country and there lived in complete solitude. One June morning – it was Saturday the 18th – he failed to rise at his usual hour, and when his groom went to call him he was found fast asleep. Nor could he be awakened. He lay as if in a trance, without perceptible breathing; and though dogs were set to bark under his window; cymbals, drums, bones beaten perpetually in his room; a gorse bush put under his pillow; and mustard plasters applied to his feet, still he did not wake, take food, or show any sign of life for seven whole days. On the seventh day he woke at

47

his usual time (a quarter before eight, precisely) and turned the whole posse of caterwauling wives and village soothsayers out of his room; which was natural enough; but what was strange was that he showed no consciousness of any such trance, but dressed himself and sent for his horse as if he had woken from a single night's slumber. Yet some change, it was suspected, must have taken place in the chambers of his brain, for though he was perfectly rational and seemed graver and more sedate in his ways than before, he appeared to have an imperfect recollection of his past life. He would listen when people spoke of the great frost or the skating or the carnival, but he never gave any sign, except by passing his hand across his brow as if to wipe away some cloud, of having witnessed them himself. When the events of the past six months were discussed, he seemed not so much distressed as puzzled, as if he were troubled by confused memories of some time long gone or were trying to recall stories told him by another. It was observed that if Russia was mentioned or Princesses or ships, he would fall into a gloom of an uneasy kind and get up and look out of the window or call one of the dogs to him, or take a knife and carve a piece of cedar wood. But the doctors were hardly wiser then than they are now, and after prescribing rest and exercise, starvation and nourishment, society and solitude, that he should lie in bed all day and ride forty miles between lunch and dinner, together with the usual sedatives and irritants, diversified, as the fancy took them, with possets of newt's slobber on rising, and draughts of peacock's gall on going to bed, they left him to himself, and gave it as their opinion that he had been asleep for a week.

But if sleep it was, of what nature, we can scarcely refrain from asking, are such sleeps as these? Are they remedial measures – trances in which the most galling memories, events that seem likely to cripple life for ever, are brushed with a dark wing which rubs their harshness off and gilds them, even the ugliest and basest, with a lustre, an incandescence? Has the finger of death to be laid on the tumult of life from time to time lest it rend us asunder? Are we so made that we have to take death in small doses daily or we could not go on with the business of living? And then what strange powers are these that penetrate our most secret ways and change our most treasured possessions without our willing it? Had Orlando, worn out by the extremity of his suffering, died for a week, and then come to life again? And if so, of what nature is death and of what nature life?[2] Having waited well over half an hour for an answer to these questions, and none coming, let us get on with the story.

Now Orlando gave himself up to a life of extreme solitude. His disgrace at Court and the violence of his grief were partly the reason of it, but as he made no effort to defend himself and seldom invited anyone to visit him (though he had many friends who would willingly have done so) it appeared as if to be alone in the great house of his fathers suited his temper. Solitude was his choice. How he spent his time, nobody quite knew. The servants, of whom he kept a full retinue, though much of their business was to dust empty rooms and to smooth the coverlets of beds that were never slept in, watched, in the dark of the evening, as they sat over their cakes and ale, a light passing along the galleries, through the banqueting-halls, up the staircases, into the bedrooms, and knew that their master was perambulating the house alone. None dared follow him, for the house was haunted by a great variety of ghosts, and the extent of it made it easy to lose one's way and either fall down some hidden staircase or open a door which, should the wind blow it to, would shut upon one for ever – accidents of no uncommon occurrence, as the frequent discovery of the skeletons of men and animals in attitudes of great agony made evident. Then the light would be lost altogether, and Mrs. Grimsditch,[3] the housekeeper, would say to Mr. Dupper, the chaplain, how she hoped his Lordship had not met with some bad accident. Mr. Dupper would opine that his Lordship was on his knees, no doubt, among the tombs of his ancestors in the Chapel, which was in the Billiard Table Court, half a mile away on the south side. For he had sins on his conscience, Mr. Dupper was afraid; upon which Mrs. Grimsditch would retort, rather sharply, that so had

most of us; and Mrs. Stewkley and Mrs. Field and old Nurse
Carpenter would all raise their voices in his Lordship's praise;
and the grooms and the stewards would swear that it was a
thousand pities to see so fine a nobleman moping about the
house when he might be hunting the fox or chasing the deer;
and even the little laundry maids and scullery maids, the Judys
and the Faiths, who were handing round the tankards and cakes,
would pipe up their testimony to his Lordship's gallantry; for
never was there a kinder gentleman, or one more free with those
little pieces of silver which serve to buy a knot of ribbon or put
a posy in one's hair; until even the Blackamoor whom they
called Grace Robinson by way of making a Christian woman of
her, understood what they were at, and agreed that his Lordship
was a handsome, pleasant, darling gentleman in the only way she
could, that is to say by showing all her teeth at once in a broad
grin. In short, all his serving men and women held him in high
respect, and cursed the foreign Princess (but they called her by a
coarser name than that) who had brought him to this pass.

But though it was probably cowardice, or love of hot ale, that
led Mr. Dupper to imagine his Lordship safe among the tombs
so that he need not go in search of him, it may well have been
that Mr. Dupper was right. Orlando now took a strange delight
in thoughts of death and decay, and, after pacing the long galleries and ballrooms with a taper in his hand, looking at picture
after picture as if he sought the likeness of somebody whom he
could not find, would mount into the family pew and sit for
hours watching the banners stir and the moonlight waver with a
bat or death's head moth to keep him company. Even this was
not enough for him, but he must descend into the crypt where
his ancestors lay,[4] coffin piled upon coffin, for ten generations
together. The place was so seldom visited that the rats had made
free with the lead work, and now a thigh bone would catch at
his cloak as he passed, or he would crack the skull of some old
Sir Malise as it rolled beneath his foot. It was a ghastly sepulchre;
dug deep beneath the foundations of the house as if the first
Lord of the family, who had come from France with the Con-

queror, had wished to testify how all pomp is built upon corruption; how the skeleton lies beneath the flesh; how we that dance and sing above must lie below; how the crimson velvet turns to dust; how the ring (here Orlando, stooping his lantern, would pick up a gold circle lacking a stone, that had rolled into a corner) loses its ruby and the eye which was so lustrous shines no more. 'Nothing remains of all these Princes', Orlando would say, indulging in some pardonable exaggeration of their rank, 'except one digit,' and he would take a skeleton hand in his and bend the joints this way and that. 'Whose hand was it?' he went on to ask. 'The right or the left? The hand of man or woman, of age or youth? Had it urged the war-horse, or plied the needle? Had it plucked the rose, or grasped cold steel? Had it—' but here either his invention failed him or, what is more likely, provided him with so many instances of what a hand can do that he shrank, as his wont was, from the cardinal labour of composition, which is excision, and he put it with the other bones, thinking how there was a writer called Thomas Browne,[5] a Doctor of Norwich, whose writing upon such subjects took his fancy amazingly.

So, taking his lantern and seeing that the bones were in order, for though romantic, he was singularly methodical and detested nothing so much as a ball of string on the floor, let alone the skull of an ancestor, he returned to that curious, moody pacing down the galleries, looking for something among the pictures, which was interrupted at length by a veritable spasm of sobbing, at the sight of a Dutch snow scene by an unknown artist. Then it seemed to him that life was not worth living any more. Forgetting the bones of his ancestors and how life is founded on a grave, he stood there shaken with sobs, all for the desire of a woman in Russian trousers, with slanting eyes, a pouting mouth, and pearls about her neck. She had gone. She had left him. He was never to see her again. And so he sobbed. And so he found his way back to his own rooms; and Mrs. Grimsditch, seeing the light in the window, put the tankard from her lips and said Praise be to God, his Lordship was safe in his room again; for she had been thinking all this while that he was foully murdered.

Orlando now drew his chair up to the table; opened the works of Sir Thomas Browne and proceeded to investigate the delicate articulation of one of the doctor's longest and most marvellously contorted cogitations.

For though these are not matters on which a biographer can profitably enlarge it is plain enough to those who have done a reader's part in making up from bare hints dropped here and there the whole boundary and circumference of a living person; can hear in what we only whisper a living voice; can see, often when we say nothing about it, exactly what he looked like; know without a word to guide them precisely what he thought – and it is for readers such as these that we write – it is plain then to such a reader that Orlando was strangely compounded of many humours – of melancholy, of indolence, of passion, of love of solitude, to say nothing of all those contortions and subtleties of temper which were indicated on the first page, when he slashed at a dead nigger's head; cut it down; hung it chivalrously out of his reach again and then betook himself to the window-seat with a book. The taste for books was an early one. As a child he was sometimes found at midnight by a page still reading. They took his taper away, and he bred glow-worms to serve his purpose. They took the glow-worms away, and he almost burnt the house down with a tinder. To put it in a nutshell, leaving the novelist to smooth out the crumpled silk and all its implications, he was a nobleman afflicted with a love of literature. Many people of his time, still more of his rank, escaped the infection and were thus free to run or ride or make love at their own sweet will. But some were early infected by a germ said to be bred of the pollen of the asphodel[6] and to be blown out of Greece and Italy, which was of so deadly a nature that it would shake the hand as it was raised to strike, cloud the eye as it sought its prey, and make the tongue stammer as it declared its love. It was the fatal nature of this disease to substitute a phantom for reality, so that Orlando, to whom fortune had given every gift – plate, linen, houses, men-servants, carpets, beds in profusion – had only to open a book for the whole vast accumulation to turn to mist. The nine acres of stone which were his house vanished; one hundred and fifty indoor servants disappeared; his eighty riding horses became invisible; it would take too long to count the carpets, sofas, trappings, china, plate, cruets, chafing dishes and other movables often of beaten gold,[7] which evaporated like so much sea mist under the miasma. So it was, and Orlando would sit by himself, reading, a naked man.

The disease gained rapidly upon him now in his solitude. He would read often six hours into the night; and when they came to him for orders about the slaughtering of cattle or the harvesting of wheat, he would push away his folio and look as if he did not understand what was said to him. This was bad enough and wrung the hearts of Hall, the falconer, of Giles, the groom, of Mrs. Grimsditch, the housekeeper, of Mr. Dupper, the chaplain. A fine gentleman like that, they said, had no need of books. Let him leave books, they said, to the palsied or the dying. But worse was to come. For once the disease of reading has laid hold upon the system it weakens it so that it falls an easy prey to that other scourge which dwells in the inkpot and festers in the quill. The wretch takes to writing. And while this is bad enough in a poor man, whose only property is a chair and a table set beneath a leaky roof – for he has not much to lose, after all – the plight of a rich man, who has houses and cattle, maid-servants, asses and linen, and yet writes books, is pitiable in the extreme. The flavour of it all goes out of him; he is riddled by hot irons; gnawed by vermin. He would give every penny he has (such is the malignity of the germ) to write one little book and become famous; yet all the gold in Peru will not buy him the treasure of a well-turned line. So he falls into consumption and sickness, blows his brains out, turns his face to the wall. It matters not in what attitude they find him. He has passed through the gates of Death and known the flames of Hell.

Happily, Orlando was of a strong constitution and the disease (for reasons presently to be given) never broke him down as it has broken many of his peers. But he was deeply smitten with it, as the sequel shows. For when he had read for an hour or so in

Sir Thomas Browne, and the bark of the stag and the call of the
night watchman showed that it was the dead of night and all safe
asleep, he crossed the room, took a silver key from his pocket
and unlocked the doors of a great inlaid cabinet which stood in
the corner. Within were some fifty drawers of cedar wood[8] and
upon each was a paper neatly written in Orlando's hand. He
paused, as if hesitating which to open. One was inscribed 'The
Death of Ajax', another 'The Birth of Pyramus', another 'Iphi-
genia in Aulis', another 'The Death of Hippolytus', another
'Meleager', another 'The Return of Odysseus' – in fact there
was scarcely a single drawer that lacked the name of some mytho-
logical personage at a crisis of his career. In each drawer lay a
document of considerable size all written over in Orlando's hand.
The truth was that Orlando had been afflicted thus for many
years. Never had any boy begged apples as Orlando begged
paper; nor sweetmeats as he begged ink. Stealing away from talk
and games, he had hidden himself behind curtains, in priest's
holes, or in the cupboard behind his mother's bedroom which
had a great hole in the floor and smelt horribly of starling's
dung, with an inkhorn in one hand, a pen in another, and on his
knee a roll of paper. Thus had been written, before he was
turned twenty-five, some forty-seven plays, histories, romances,
poems; some in prose, some in verse; some in French, some in
Italian; all romantic, and all long. One he had had printed by
John Ball of the Feathers and Coronet opposite St. Paul's Cross,
Cheapside; but though the sight of it gave him extreme delight, he had never dared show it even to his mother, since to
write, much more to publish, was, he knew, for a nobleman an
inexpiable disgrace.

Now, however, that it was the dead of night and he was
alone, he chose from this repository one thick document called
'Xenophila a Tragedy' or some such title, and one thin one,
called simply 'The Oak Tree' (this was the only monosyllabic
title among the lot), and then he approached the inkhorn,
fingered the quill, and made other such passes as those addicted
to this vice begin their rites with. But he paused.

As this pause was of extreme significance in his history, more so, indeed, than many acts which bring men to their knees and make rivers run with blood, it behoves us to ask why he paused; and to reply, after due reflection, that it was for some such reason as this. Nature, who has played so many queer tricks upon us, making us so unequally of clay and diamonds, of rainbow and granite,[9] and stuffed them into a case, often of the most incongruous, for the poet has a butcher's face and the butcher a poet's; nature, who delights in muddle and mystery, so that even now (the first of November 1927) we know not why we go upstairs, or why we come down again, our most daily movements are like the passage of a ship on an unknown sea, and the sailors at the mast-head ask, pointing their glasses to the horizon; Is there land or is there none? to which, if we are prophets, we make answer 'Yes'; if we are truthful we say 'No'; nature, who has so much to answer for besides the perhaps unwieldy length of this sentence, has further complicated her task and added to our confusion by providing not only a perfect rag-bag of odds and ends within us – a piece of a policeman's trousers lying cheek by jowl with Queen Alexandra's wedding veil – but has contrived that the whole assortment shall be lightly stitched together by a single thread. Memory is the seamstress, and a capricious one at that. Memory runs her needle in and out, up and down, hither and thither. We know not what comes next, or what follows after. Thus, the most ordinary movement in the world, such as sitting down at a table and pulling the inkstand towards one, may agitate a thousand odd, disconnected fragments, now bright, now dim, hanging and bobbing and dipping and flaunting, like the underlinen of a family of fourteen on a line in a gale of wind. Instead of being a single, downright, bluff piece of work of which no man need feel ashamed, our commonest deeds are set about with a fluttering and flickering of wings, a rising and falling of lights. Thus it was that Orlando, dipping his pen in the ink, saw the mocking face of the lost Princess and asked himself a million questions instantly which were as arrows dipped in gall. Where was she; and why had she left him? Was the Ambassador her uncle or her lover? Had they plotted? Was she forced? Was she married? Was she dead? – all of which so drove their venom into him that, as if to vent his agony somewhere, he plunged his quill so deep into the inkhorn that the ink spirted over the table, which act, explain it how one may (and no explanation perhaps is possible – Memory is inexplicable), at once substituted for the face of the Princess a face of a very different sort. But whose was it, he asked himself? And he had to wait, perhaps half a minute, looking at the new picture which lay on top of the old, as one lantern slide is half seen through the next, before he could say to himself, 'This is the face of that rather fat, shabby man who sat in Twitchett's room[10] ever so many years ago when old Queen Bess came here to dine; and I saw him,' Orlando continued, catching at another of those little coloured rags, 'sitting at the table, as I peeped in on my way downstairs, and he had the most amazing eyes,' said Orlando, 'that ever were, but who the devil was he?' Orlando asked, for here Memory added to the forehead and eyes, first, a coarse, grease-stained ruffle, then a brown doublet, and finally a pair of thick boots such as citizens wear in Cheapside. 'Not a Nobleman; not one of us,' said Orlando (which he would not have said aloud, for he was the most courteous of gentlemen; but it shows what an effect noble birth has upon the mind and incidentally how difficult it is for a nobleman to be a writer[11]), 'a poet, I dare say.' By all the laws, Memory, having disturbed him sufficiently, should now have blotted the whole thing out completely, or have fetched up something so idiotic and out of keeping – like a dog chasing a cat or an old woman blowing her nose into a red cotton handkerchief – that, in despair of keeping pace with her vagaries, Orlando should have struck his pen in earnest against his paper. (For we can, if we have the resolution, turn the hussy, Memory, and all her ragtag and bobtail out of the house.) But Orlando paused. Memory still held before him the image of a shabby man with big, bright eyes. Still he looked, still he paused. It is these pauses that are our undoing. It is then that sedition enters the fortress and our troops rise in insurrection. Once before he had paused, and love with its horrid rout, its shawms, its cymbals, and its heads with gory locks torn from the shoulders had burst in.[12] From love he had suffered the tortures of the damned. Now, again, he paused, and into the breach thus made, leapt Ambition, the harridan, and Poetry, the witch, and Desire of Fame, the strumpet; all joined hands and made of his heart their dancing ground. Standing upright in the solitude of his room, he vowed that he would be the first poet of his race and bring immortal lustre upon his name. He said (reciting the names and exploits of his ancestors) that Sir Boris had fought and killed the Paynim; Sir Gawain, the Turk; Sir Miles, the Pole; Sir Andrew, the Frank; Sir Richard, the Austrian; Sir Jordan, the Frenchman; and Sir Herbert, the Spaniard.[13] But of all that killing and campaigning, that drinking and love-making, that spending and hunting and riding and eating, what remained? A skull; a finger. Whereas, he said, turning to the page of Sir Thomas Browne, which lay open upon the table – and again he paused. Like an incantation rising from all parts of the room, from the night wind and the moonlight, rolled the divine melody of those words which, lest they should outstare this page, we will leave where they lie entombed, not dead, embalmed rather, so fresh is their colour, so sound their breathing – and Orlando, comparing that achievement with those of his ancestors, cried out that they and their deeds were dust and ashes, but this man and his words were immortal.

He soon perceived, however, that the battles which Sir Miles and the rest had waged against armed knights to win a kingdom, were not half so arduous as this which he now undertook to win immortality against the English language. Anyone moderately familiar with the rigours of composition will not need to be told the story in detail; how he wrote and it seemed good; read and it seemed vile; corrected and tore up; cut out; put in; was in ecstasy; in despair; had his good nights and bad mornings; snatched at ideas and lost them; saw his book plain before him and it vanished; acted his people's parts as he ate; mouthed them as he walked; now cried; now laughed; vacillated between this style and that; now preferred the heroic and pompous; next the plain and simple; now the vales of Tempe;[14] then the fields of Kent or Cornwall; and could not decide whether he was the divinest genius or the greatest fool in the world.

It was to settle this last question that he decided, after many months of such feverish labour, to break the solitude of years and communicate with the outer world. He had a friend in London, one Giles Isham of Norfolk,[15] who, though of gentle birth, was acquainted with writers and could doubtless put him in touch with some member of that blessed, indeed sacred, fraternity. For, to Orlando in the state he was now in, there was a glory about a man who had written a book and had it printed, which outshone all the glories of blood and state.[16] To his imagination it seemed as if even the bodies of those instinct with such divine thoughts must be transfigured. They must have aureoles for hair, incense for breath, and roses must grow between their lips – which was certainly not true either of himself or Mr. Dupper. He could think of no greater happiness than to be allowed to sit behind a curtain and hear them talk. Even the imagination of that bold and various discourse made the memory of what he and his courtier friends used to talk about – a dog, a horse, a woman, a game of cards – seem brutish in the extreme. He bethought him with pride that he had always been called a scholar, and sneered at for his love of solitude and books. He had never been apt at pretty phrases. He would stand stock still, blush, and stride like a grenadier in a ladies' drawing-room. He had twice fallen, in sheer abstraction, from his horse. He had broken Lady Winchilsea's fan[17] once while making a rhyme. Eagerly recalling these and other instances of his unfitness for the life of society, an ineffable hope, that all the turbulence of his youth, his clumsiness, his blushes, his long walks, and his love of the country proved that he himself belonged to the sacred race rather than to the noble – was by birth a writer, rather than an aristocrat – possessed him. For the first time since the night of the great flood he was happy.

He now commissioned Mr. Isham of Norfolk to deliver to

Mr. Nicholas Greene of Clifford's Inn[18] a document which set forth Orlando's admiration for his works (for Nick Greene was a very famous writer at that time) and his desire to make his acquaintance; which he scarcely dared ask; for he had nothing to offer in return; but if Mr. Nicholas Greene would condescend to visit him, a coach and four would be at the corner of Fetter Lane at whatever hour Mr. Greene chose to appoint, and bring him safely to Orlando's house. One may fill up the phrases which then followed; and figure Orlando's delight when, in no long time, Mr. Greene signified his acceptance of the Noble Lord's invitation; took his place in the coach and was set down in the hall to the south of the main building punctually at seven o'clock on Monday, April the twenty-first.

Many Kings, Queens, and Ambassadors had been received there; Judges had stood there in their ermine. The loveliest ladies of the land had come there; and the sternest warriors. Banners hung there which had been at Flodden and at Agincourt.[19] There were displayed the painted coats of arms with their lions and their leopards and their coronets. There were the long tables where the gold and silver plate was stood; and there the vast fireplaces of wrought Italian marble where nightly a whole oak tree, with its million leaves and its nests of rook and wren, was burnt to ashes. Nicholas Greene, the poet stood there now, plainly dressed in his slouched hat and black doublet, carrying in one hand a small bag.

That Orlando as he hastened to greet him was slightly disappointed was inevitable. The poet was not above middle height; was of a mean figure; was lean and stooped somewhat, and, stumbling over the mastiff on entering, the dog bit him. Moreover, Orlando for all his knowledge of mankind was puzzled where to place him. There was something about him which belonged neither to servant, squire, or noble. The head with its rounded forehead and beaked nose was fine, but the chin receded. The eyes were brilliant, but the lips hung loose and slobbered. It was the expression of the face as a whole, however, that was disquieting. There was none of that stately composure which makes the faces of the nobility so pleasing to look at; nor had it anything of the dignified servility of a well-trained domestic's face; it was a face seamed, puckered, and drawn together. Poet though he was, it seemed as if he were more used to scold than to flatter; to quarrel than to coo; to scramble than to ride; to struggle than to rest; to hate than to love. This, too, was shown by the quickness of his movements; and by something fiery and suspicious in his glance. Orlando was somewhat taken aback. But they went to dinner.

Here, Orlando, who usually took such things for granted, was, for the first time, unaccountably ashamed of the number of his servants and of the splendour of his table. Stranger still, he bethought him with pride – for the thought was generally distasteful – of that great grandmother Moll who had milked the cows. He was about somehow to allude to this humble woman and her milk-pails, when the poet forestalled him by saying that it was odd, seeing how common the name of Greene was, that the family had come over with the Conqueror and was of the highest nobility in France. Unfortunately, they had come down in the world and done little more than leave their name to the royal borough of Greenwich. Further talk of the same sort, about lost castles, coats of arms, cousins who were baronets in the north, intermarriage with noble families in the west, how some Greens spelt the name with an e at the end, and others without, lasted till the venison was on the table. Then Orlando contrived to say something of Grandmother Moll and her cows, and had eased his heart a little of its burden by the time the wild fowl were before them. But it was not until the Malmsey[20] was passing freely that Orlando dared mention what he could not help thinking a more important matter than the Greens or the cows; that is to say the sacred subject of poetry. At the first mention of the word, the poet's eyes flashed fire; he dropped the fine gentleman airs he had worn; thumped his glass on the table, and launched into one of the longest, most intricate, most passionate, and bitterest stories that Orlando had ever heard, save from the lips of a jilted woman, about a play of his; another poet; and a critic.

Of the nature of poetry itself, Orlando only gathered that it was harder to sell than prose, and though the lines were shorter took longer in the writing. So the talk went on with ramifications interminable, until Orlando ventured to hint that he had himself been so rash as to write – but here the poet leapt from his chair. A mouse had squeaked in the wainscot, he said. The truth was, he explained, that his nerves were in a state where a mouse's squeak upset them for a fortnight. Doubtless the house was full of vermin, but Orlando had not heard them. The poet then gave Orlando the full story of his health for the past ten years or so. It had been so bad that one could only marvel that he still lived. He had had the palsy, the gout, the ague, the dropsy, and the three sorts of fever in succession; added to which he had an enlarged heart, a great spleen, and a diseased liver. But, above all, he had, he told Orlando, sensations in his spine which defied description. There was one knob about the third from the top which burnt like fire; another about the second from the bottom which was cold as ice. Sometimes he woke with a brain like lead; at others it was as if a thousand wax tapers were alight and people were throwing fireworks inside him. He could feel a rose leaf through his mattress, he said; and knew his way almost about London by the feel of the cobbles. Altogether he was a piece of machinery so finely made and so curiously put together (here he raised his hand as if unconsciously, and indeed it was of the finest shape imaginable) that it confounded him to think that he had only sold five hundred copies of his poem, but that of course was largely due to the conspiracy against him. All he could say, he concluded, banging his fist upon the table, was that the art of poetry was dead in England.

How that could be with Shakespeare, Marlowe, Ben Jonson, Browne, Donne,[21] all now writing or just having written, Orlando, reeling off the names of his favourite heroes, could not think.

Greene laughed sardonically. Shakespeare, he admitted, had written some scenes that were well enough; but he had taken them chiefly from Marlowe. Marlowe was a likely boy, but what

61

could you say of a lad who died before he was thirty? As for Browne, he was for writing poetry in prose, and people soon got tired of such conceits as that. Donne was a mountebank who wrapped up his lack of meaning in hard words. The gulls were taken in; but the style would be out of fashion twelve months hence. As for Ben Jonson – Ben Jonson was a friend of his and he never spoke ill of his friends.

No, he concluded, the great age of literature is past; the great age of literature was the Greek; the Elizabethan age was inferior in every respect to the Greek. In such ages men cherished a divine ambition which he might call *La Gloire*[22] (he pronounced it Glawr, so that Orlando did not at first catch his meaning). Now all young writers were in the pay of the booksellers and poured out any trash that would sell. Shakespeare was the chief offender in this way and Shakespeare was already paying the penalty. Their own age, he said, was marked by precious conceits and wild experiments – neither of which the Greeks would have tolerated for a moment. Much though it hurt him to say it – for he loved literature as he loved his life – he could see no good in the present and had no hope of the future. Here he poured himself out another glass of wine.

Orlando was shocked by these doctrines; yet could not help observing that the critic himself seemed by no means downcast. On the contrary, the more he denounced his own time, the more complacent he became. He could remember, he said, a night at the Cock Tavern in Fleet Street[23] when Kit Marlowe was there and some others. Kit was in high feather, rather drunk, which he easily became, and in a mood to say silly things. He could see him now, brandishing his glass at the company and hiccoughing out, 'Stap my vitals, Bill' (this was to Shakespeare), 'there's a great wave coming and you're on the top of it,' by which he meant, Greene explained, that they were trembling on the verge of a great age in English literature, and that Shakespeare was to be a poet of some importance. Happily for himself, he was killed two nights later in a drunken brawl, and so did not live to see how this prediction turned out. 'Poor foolish fellow,' said Greene, 'to go and say a thing like that. A great age, forsooth – the Elizabethan a great age!'

'So, my dear Lord,' he continued, settling himself comfortably in his chair and rubbing the wine-glass between his fingers, 'we must make the best of it, cherish the past and honour those writers – there are still a few left of 'em – who take antiquity for their model and write, not for pay but for Glawr.' (Orlando could have wished him a better accent.) 'Glawr', said Greene, 'is the spur of noble minds. Had I a pension of three hundred pounds a year paid quarterly, I would live for Glawr alone. I would lie in bed every morning reading Cicero.[24] I would imitate his style so that you couldn't tell the difference between us. That's what I call fine writing,' said Greene; 'that's what I call Glawr. But it's necessary to have a pension to do it.'

By this time Orlando had abandoned all hope of discussing his own work with the poet; but this mattered the less as the talk now got upon the lives and characters of Shakespeare, Ben Jonson, and the rest, all of whom Greene had known intimately and about whom he had a thousand anecdotes of the most amusing kind to tell. Orlando had never laughed so much in his life. These, then, were his gods! Half were drunken and all were amorous. Most of them quarrelled with their wives; not one of them was above a lie or an intrigue of the most paltry kind. Their poetry was scribbled down on the backs of washing bills held to the heads of printer's devils at the street door. Thus Hamlet went to press; thus Lear; thus Othello. No wonder, as Greene said, that these plays show the faults they do. The rest of the time was spent in carousings and junketings in taverns and in beer gardens, when things were said that passed belief for wit, and things were done that made the utmost frolic of the courtiers seem pale in comparison. All this Greene told with a spirit that roused Orlando to the highest pitch of delight. He had a power of mimicry that brought the dead to life, and could say the finest things of books provided they were written three hundred years ago.[25]

So time passed, and Orlando felt for his guest a strange mixture of liking and contempt, of admiration and pity, as well as something too indefinite to be called by any one name, but had something of fear in it and something of fascination. He talked incessantly about himself, yet was such good company that one could listen to the story of his ague for ever. Then he was so witty; then he was so irreverent; then he made so free with the names of God and Woman; then he was so full of queer crafts and had such strange lore in his head; could make salad in three hundred different ways; knew all that could be known of the mixing of wines; played half-a-dozen musical instruments, and was the first person, and perhaps the last, to toast cheese in the great Italian fireplace. That he did not know a geranium from a carnation, an oak from a birch tree, a mastiff from a greyhound, a teg from a ewe,[26] wheat from barley, plough land from fallow; was ignorant of the rotation of the crops; thought oranges grew under ground and turnips on trees; preferred any townscape to any landscape – all this and much more amazed Orlando, who had never met anybody of his kind before. Even the maids, who despised him, tittered at his jokes, and the men-servants, who loathed him, hung about to hear his stories. Indeed, the house had never been so lively as now that he was there – all of which gave Orlando a great deal to think about, and caused him to compare this way of life with the old. He recalled the sort of talk he had been used to about the King of Spain's apoplexy or the mating of a bitch; he bethought him how the day passed between the stables and the dressing closet; he remembered how the Lords snored over their wine and hated anybody who woke them up. He bethought him how active and valiant they were in body; how slothful and timid in mind. Worried by these thoughts, and unable to strike a proper balance, he came to the conclusion that he had admitted to his house a plaguey spirit of unrest that would never suffer him to sleep sound again.

At the same moment, Nick Greene came to precisely the opposite conclusion. Lying in bed of a morning on the softest pillows between the smoothest sheets and looking out of his oriel window upon turf which for three centuries had known neither dandelion nor dock weed, he thought that unless he could somehow make his escape, he should be smothered alive. Getting up and hearing the pigeons coo, dressing and hearing the fountains fall, he thought that unless he could hear the drays roar upon the cobbles of Fleet Street, he would never write another line. If this goes on much longer, he thought, hearing the footman mend the fire and spread the table with silver dishes next door, I shall fall asleep and (here he gave a prodigious yawn) sleeping die.

So he sought Orlando in his room, and explained that he had not been able to sleep a wink all night because of the silence. (Indeed, the house was surrounded by a park fifteen miles in circumference and a wall ten feet high.) Silence, he said, was of all things the most oppressive to his nerves. He would end his visit, by Orlando's leave, that very morning. Orlando felt some relief at this, yet also a great reluctance to let him go. The house, he thought, would seem very dull without him. On parting (for he had never yet liked to mention the subject), he had the temerity to press his play upon the Death of Hercules upon the poet and ask his opinion of it. The poet took it; muttered something about Glawr and Cicero, which Orlando cut short by promising to pay the pension quarterly; whereupon Greene, with many protestations of affection, jumped into the coach and was gone.

The great hall had never seemed so large, so splendid, or so empty as the chariot rolled away. Orlando knew that he would never have the heart to make toasted cheese in the Italian fireplace again. He would never have the wit to crack jokes about Italian pictures; never have the skill to mix punch as it should be mixed; a thousand good quips and cranks would be lost to him. Yet what a relief to be out of the sound of that querulous voice, what a luxury to be alone once more, so he could not help reflecting, as he unloosed the mastiff which had been tied up these six weeks because it never saw the poet without biting him.

Nick Greene was set down at the corner of Fetter Lane that same afternoon, and found things going on much as he had left them. Mrs. Greene, that is to say, was giving birth to a baby in one room; Tom Fletcher was drinking gin in another. Books were tumbled all about the floor; dinner – such as it was – was set on a dressing-table where the children had been making mud pies. But this, Greene felt, was the atmosphere for writing; here he could write, and write he did. The subject was made for him. A noble Lord at home. A visit to a Nobleman in the country – his new poem was to have some such title as that. Seizing the pen with which his little boy was tickling the cat's ears, and dipping it in the egg-cup which served for inkpot, Greene dashed off a very spirited satire there and then. It was so done to a turn that no one could doubt that the young Lord who was roasted was Orlando; his most private sayings and doings, his enthusiasms and follies, down to the very colour of his hair and the foreign way he had of rolling his r's, were there to the life. And if there had been any doubt about it, Greene clinched the matter by introducing, with scarcely any disguise, passages from that aristocratic tragedy, the Death of Hercules, which he found as he expected, wordy and bombastic in the extreme.

The pamphlet, which ran at once into several editions, and paid the expenses of Mrs. Greene's tenth lying-in, was soon sent by friends who take care of such matters to Orlando himself. When he had read it, which he did with deadly composure from start to finish, he rang for the footman; delivered the document to him at the end of a pair of tongs; bade him drop it in the filthiest heart of the foulest midden on the estate. Then, when the man was turning to go he stopped him, 'Take the swiftest horse in the stable,' he said, 'ride for dear life to Harwich. There embark upon a ship which you will find bound for Norway. Buy for me from the King's own kennels the finest elk-hounds [27] of the Royal strain, male and female. Bring them back without delay. For', he murmured, scarcely above his breath as he turned to his books, 'I have done with men.'

The footman, who was perfectly trained in his duties, bowed and disappeared. He fulfilled his task so efficiently that he was back that day three weeks, leading in his hand a leash of the finest elk-hounds, one of whom, a female, gave birth that very night under the dinner-table to a litter of eight fine puppies. Orlando had them brought to his bed-chamber.

'For', he said, 'I have done with men.'

Nevertheless, he paid the pension quarterly.

Thus, at the age of thirty, or thereabouts, this young Nobleman had not only had every experience that life has to offer, but had seen the worthlessness of them all. Love and ambition, women and poets were all equally vain. Literature was a farce. The night after reading Greene's Visit to a Nobleman in the Country, he burnt in a great conflagration fifty-seven poetical works, only retaining 'The Oak Tree', which was his boyish dream and very short. Two things alone remained to him in which he now put any trust: dogs and nature; an elk-hound and a rose bush. The world, in all its variety, life in all its complexity, had shrunk to that. Dogs and a bush were the whole of it. So feeling quit of a vast mountain of illusion, and very naked in consequence, he called his hounds to him and strode through the Park.

So long had he been secluded, writing and reading, that he had half forgotten the amenities of nature, which in June can be great. When he reached that high mound whence on fine days half of England with a slice of Wales and Scotland thrown in can be seen, he flung himself under his favourite oak tree and felt that if he need never speak to another man or woman so long as he lived; if his dogs did not develop the faculty of speech; if he never met a poet or a Princess again, he might make out what years remained to him in tolerable content.

Here he came then, day after day, week after week, month after month, year after year. He saw the beech trees turn golden and the young ferns unfurl; he saw the moon sickle and then circular; he saw – but probably the reader can imagine the passage which should follow and how every tree and plant in the neighbourhood is described first green, then golden; how moons rise and suns set; how spring follows winter and autumn summer; how night succeeds day and day night; how there is first a storm and then fine weather; how things remain much as they are for two or three hundred years or so, except for a little dust and a few cobwebs which one old woman can sweep up in half an hour; a conclusion which, one cannot help feeling, might have been reached more quickly by the simple statement that 'Time passed'[28] (here the exact amount could be indicated in brackets) and nothing whatever happened.

But Time, unfortunately, though it makes animals and vegetables bloom and fade with amazing punctuality, has no such simple effect upon the mind of man. The mind of man, moreover, works with equal strangeness upon the body of time. An hour, once it lodges in the queer element of the human spirit, may be stretched to fifty or a hundred times its clock length; on the other hand, an hour may be accurately represented on the timepiece of the mind by one second. This extraordinary discrepancy between time on the clock and time in the mind is less known than it should be and deserves fuller investigation. But the biographer, whose interests are, as we have said, highly restricted, must confine himself to one simple statement: when a man has reached the age of thirty, as Orlando now had, time when he is thinking becomes inordinately long; time when he is doing becomes inordinately short. Thus Orlando gave his orders and did the business of his vast estates in a flash; but directly he was alone on the mound under the oak tree, the seconds began to round and fill until it seemed as if they would never fall. They filled themselves, moreover, with the strangest variety of objects. For not only did he find himself confronted by problems which have puzzled the wisest of men, such as What is love? What friendship? What truth? but directly he came to think about them, his whole past, which seemed to him of extreme length and variety, rushed into the falling second, swelled it a dozen times its natural size, coloured it a thousand tints, and filled it with all the odds and ends in the universe.

In such thinking (or by whatever name it should be called) he spent months and years of his life. It would be no exaggeration to say that he would go out after breakfast a man of thirty and come home to dinner a man of fifty-five at least. Some weeks added a century to his age, others no more than three seconds at most. Altogether, the task of estimating the length of human life (of the animals' we presume not to speak) is beyond our capacity, for directly we say that it is ages long, we are reminded that it is briefer than the fall of a rose leaf to the ground. Of the two forces which alternately, and what is more confusing still, at the same moment, dominate our unfortunate numbskulls – brevity and diuturnity – Orlando was sometimes under the influence of the elephant-footed deity, then of the gnat-winged fly. Life seemed to him of prodigious length. Yet even so, it went like a flash. But even when it stretched longest and the moments swelled biggest and he seemed to wander alone in deserts of vast eternity,[29] there was no time for the smoothing out and decipher-ing of those thickly scored parchments which thirty years among men and women had rolled tight in his heart and brain. Long before he had done thinking about Love (the oak tree had put forth its leaves and shaken them to the ground a dozen times in the process) Ambition would jostle it off the field, to be replaced by Friendship or Literature. And as the first question had not been settled – What is Love? – back it would come at the least provocation or none, and hustle Books or Metaphors or What one lives for into the margin, there to wait till they saw their chance to rush into the field again. What made the process still longer was that it was profusely illustrated, not only with pic-tures, as that of old Queen Elizabeth, laid on her tapestry couch in rose-coloured brocade with an ivory snuff-box in her hand and a gold-hilted sword by her side, but with scents – she was strongly perfumed – and with sounds; the stags were barking in Richmond Park that winter's day. And so, the thought of love would be all ambered over with snow and winter; with log fires burning; with Russian women, gold swords, and the bark of stags; with old King James' slobbering and fireworks and sacks of treasure in the holds of Elizabethan sailing ships. Every single thing, once he tried to dislodge it from its place in his mind, he found thus cumbered with other matter like the lump of glass which, after a year at the bottom of the sea, is grown about with bones and dragon-flies, and coins and the tresses of drowned women.

'Another metaphor by Jupiter!' he would exclaim as he said this (which will show the disorderly and circuitous way in which his mind worked and explain why the oak tree flowered and faded so often before he came to any conclusion about Love). 'And what's the point of it?' he would ask himself. 'Why not say simply in so many words—' and then he would try to think for half an hour – or was it two years and a half? – how to say simply in many words what love is. 'A figure like that is manifestly untruthful,' he argued, 'for no dragon-fly, unless under very exceptional circumstances, could live at the bottom of the sea. And if literature is not the Bride and Bedfellow of Truth, what is she? Confound it all,' he cried, 'why say Bedfellow when one's already said Bride? Why not simply say what one means and leave it?'

So then he tried saying the grass is green and the sky is blue and so to propitiate the austere spirit of poetry whom still, though at a great distance, he could not help reverencing. 'The sky is blue,' he said, 'the grass is green.' Looking up, he saw that, on the contrary, the sky is like the veils which a thousand Madonnas have let fall from their hair; and the grass fleets[30] and darkens like a flight of girls fleeing the embraces of hairy satyrs from enchanted woods. 'Upon my word,' he said (for he had fallen into the bad habit of speaking aloud), 'I don't see that one's more true than another. Both are utterly false.' And he despaired of being able to solve the problem of what poetry is and what truth is and fell into a deep dejection.

And here we may profit by a pause in his soliloquy to reflect how odd it was to see Orlando stretched there on his elbow on a June day and to reflect that this fine fellow with all his faculties about him and a healthy body, witness cheeks and limbs – a man who never thought twice about heading a charge or fighting a duel – should be so subject to the lethargy of thought, and rendered so susceptible by it, that when it came to a question of poetry, or his own competence in it, he was as shy as a little girl behind her mother's cottage door. In our belief, Greene's ridicule of his tragedy hurt him as much as the Princess' ridicule of his love. But to return—

Orlando went on thinking. He kept looking at the grass and at the sky and trying to bethink him what a true poet, who has his verses published in London, would say about them. Memory meanwhile (whose habits have already been described) kept steady before his eyes the face of Nicholas Greene, as if that sardonic loose-lipped man, treacherous as he had proved himself, were the Muse in person, and it was to him that Orlando must do homage. So Orlando, that summer morning, offered him a variety of phrases, some plain, others figured, and Nick Greene kept shaking his head and sneering and muttering something about Glawr and Cicero and the death of poetry in our time. At length, starting to his feet (it was now winter and very cold) Orlando swore one of the most remarkable oaths of his lifetime, for it bound him to a servitude than which none is stricter. 'I'll be blasted', he said, 'if I ever write another word, or try to write another word, to please Nick Greene or the Muse. Bad, good, or indifferent, I'll write, from this day forward, to please myself'; and here he made as if he were tearing a whole budget[31] of papers across and tossing them in the face of that sneering loose-lipped man. Upon which, as a cur ducks if you stoop to shy a stone at him, Memory ducked her effigy of Nick Greene out of sight; and substituted for it – nothing whatever.

But Orlando, all the same, went on thinking. He had indeed much to think of. For when he tore the parchment across, he tore, in one rending, the scrolloping,[32] emblazoned scroll which he had made out in his own favour in the solitude of his room appointing himself, as the King appoints Ambassadors, the first poet of his race, the first writer of his age, conferring eternal immortality upon his soul and granting his body a grave among laurels and the intangible banners of a people's reverence perpetually. Eloquent as this all was, he now tore it up and threw it in the dust-bin. 'Fame', he said, 'is like' (and since there was no Nick Greene to stop him, he went on to revel in images of which we will choose only one or two of the quietest) 'a braided coat which hampers the limbs; a jacket of silver which curbs the heart; a painted shield which covers a scarecrow,' etc. etc. The pith of his phrases was that while fame impedes and constricts, obscurity wraps about a man like a mist; obscurity is dark, ample, and free; obscurity lets the mind take its way unimpeded. Over the obscure man is poured the merciful suffusion of darkness. None knows where he goes or comes. He may seek the truth and speak it; he alone is free; he alone is truthful; he alone is at peace. And so he sank into a quiet mood, under the oak tree, the hardness of whose roots, exposed above the ground, seemed to him rather comfortable than otherwise.

Sunk for a long time in profound thoughts as to the value of obscurity, and the delight of having no name, but being like a wave which returns to the deep body of the sea; thinking how obscurity rids the mind of the irk of envy and spite; how it sets running in the veins the free waters of generosity and magnanimity; and allows giving and taking without thanks offered or praise given; which must have been the way of all great poets, he supposed (though his knowledge of Greek was not enough to bear him out), for, he thought, Shakespeare must have written like that, and the church builders built like that, anonymously, needing no thanking or naming, but only their work in the daytime and a little ale perhaps at night – 'What an admirable life this is,' he thought, stretching his limbs out under the oak tree. 'And why not enjoy it this very moment?' The thought struck him like a bullet. Ambition dropped like a plummet. Rid of the heart-burn of rejected love, and of vanity rebuked, and all the other stings and pricks which the nettle-bed of life had burnt upon him when ambitious of fame, but could no longer inflict upon one careless of glory, he opened his eyes, which had been wide open all the time, but had seen only thoughts, and saw, lying in the hollow beneath him, his house.

There it lay in the early sunshine of spring.[33] It looked a town rather than a house, but a town built, not hither and thither, as this man wished or that, but circumspectly, by a single architect with one idea in his head. Courts and buildings, grey, red, plum colour, lay orderly and symmetrical; the courts were some of them oblong and some square; in this was a fountain; in that a statue; the buildings were some of them low, some pointed; here was a chapel, there a belfry; spaces of the greenest grass lay in between and clumps of cedar trees and beds of bright flowers; all were clasped – yet so well set out was it that it seemed that every part had room to spread itself fittingly – by the roll of a massive wall; while smoke from innumerable chimneys curled perpetually into the air. This vast, yet ordered building, which could house a thousand men and perhaps two thousand horses, was built, Orlando thought, by workmen whose names are unknown. Here have lived, for more centuries than I can count, the obscure generations of my own obscure family. Not one of these Richards, Johns, Annes, Elizabeths has left a token of himself behind him, yet all, working together with their spades and their needles, their love-making and their child-bearing, have left this.

Never had the house looked more noble and humane.

Why, then, had he wished to raise himself above them? For it seemed vain and arrogant in the extreme to try to better that anonymous work of creation; the labours of those vanished hands. Better was it to go unknown and leave behind you an arch, a potting shed, a wall where peaches ripen, than to burn like a meteor and leave no dust. For after all, he said, kindling as he looked at the great house on the greensward below, the unknown lords and ladies who lived there never forgot to set aside something for those who come after; for the roof that will leak; for the tree that will fall. There was always a warm corner for the old shepherd in the kitchen; always food for the hungry; always their goblets were polished, though they lay sick; and their windows were lit though they lay dying. Lords though they were, they were content to go down into obscurity with the molecatcher and the stone-mason. Obscure noblemen, forgotten builders – thus he apostrophised them with a warmth that entirely gainsaid such critics as called him cold, indifferent, slothful (the truth being that a quality often lies just on the other side of the wall from where we seek it) – thus he apostrophised his house and race in terms of the most moving eloquence; but when it came to the peroration – and what is eloquence that lacks a peroration? – he fumbled. He would have liked to have ended with a flourish to the effect that he would follow in their footsteps and add another stone to their building. Since, however, the building already covered nine acres, to add even a single stone seemed superfluous. Could one mention furniture in a peroration? Could one speak of chairs and tables and mats to lie beside people's beds? For whatever the peroration wanted, that was what the house stood in need of. Leaving his speech unfinished for the moment, he strode down hill again resolved henceforward to devote himself to the furnishing of the mansion. The news – that she was to attend him instantly – brought tears to the eyes of good old Mrs. Grimsditch, now grown somewhat old. Together they perambulated the house.

The towel horse in the King's bedroom ('and that was King Jamie, my Lord,'[34] she said, hinting that it was many a day since a King had slept under their roof; but the odious Parliament days were over and there was now a Crown in England again) lacked a leg; there were no stands to the ewers in the little closet leading into the waiting room of the Duchess's page; Mr. Greene had made a stain on the carpet with his nasty pipe smoking, which she and Judy, for all their scrubbing, had never been able to wash out. Indeed, when Orlando came to reckon up the matter of furnishing with rosewood chairs and cedar-wood cabinets, with silver basins, china bowls, and Persian carpets, every one of the three hundred and sixty-five bedrooms[35] which the house contained, he saw that it would be no light one; and if some thousands of pounds of his estate remained over, these would do little more than hang a few galleries with tapestry, set the dining hall with fine, carved chairs and provide mirrors of solid silver and chairs of the same metal (for which he had an inordinate passion) for the furnishing of the royal bed-chambers.

He now set to work in earnest, as we can prove beyond a doubt if we look at his ledgers. Let us glance at an inventory of what he bought at this time, with the expenses totted up in the margin – but these we omit.

'To fifty pairs of Spanish blankets, ditto curtains of crimson and
white taffeta; the valence to them of white satin embroidered
with crimson and white silk . . .

'To seventy yellow satin chairs and sixty stools, suitable with
their buckram covers to them all . . .

'To sixty-seven walnut tree tables . . .

'To seventeen dozen boxes containing each dozen five dozen of
Venice glasses . . .

'To one hundred and two mats, each thirty yards long . . .

'To ninety-seven cushions of crimson damask laid with silver
parchment lace and footstools of cloth of tissue and chairs
suitable . . .

'To fifty branches for a dozen lights apiece . . .'

Already – it is an effect lists have upon us – we are beginning
to yawn. But if we stop, it is only that the catalogue is tedious,
not that it is finished. There are ninety-nine pages more of it and
the total sum disbursed ran into many thousands – that is to say
millions of our money. And if his day was spent like this, at
night again, Lord Orlando might be found reckoning out what
it would cost to level a million molehills, if the men were paid
tenpence an hour; and again, how many hundredweight of nails
at 5½d. a gill were needed to repair the fence round the park,
which was fifteen miles in circumference. And so on and so on.

The tale, we say, is tedious, for one cupboard is much like
another, and one molehill not much different from a million.
Some pleasant journeys it cost him; and some fine adventures.
As, for instance, when he set a whole city of blind women near
Bruges to stitch hangings for a silver canopied bed; and the
story of his adventure with a Moor in Venice of whom he
bought (but only at the sword's point) his lacquered cabinet,
might, in other hands, prove worth the telling. Nor did the
work lack variety; for here would come, drawn by teams from
Sussex, great trees, to be sawn across and laid along the gallery
for flooring;[36] and then a chest from Persia, stuffed with wool
and sawdust, from which, at last, he would take a single plate, or
one topaz ring.

At length, however, there was no room in the galleries for another table; no room on the tables for another cabinet; no room in the cabinet for another rose-bowl; no room in the bowl for another handful of pot-pourri; there was no room for anything anywhere; in short the house was furnished. In the garden snowdrops, crocuses, hyacinths, magnolias, roses, lilies, asters, the dahlia in all its varieties, pear trees and apple trees and cherry trees and mulberry trees, with an enormous quantity of rare and flowering shrubs, of trees evergreen and perennial, grew so thick on each other's roots that there was no plot of earth without its bloom, and no stretch of sward without its shade. In addition, he had imported wild fowl with gay plumage; and two Malay bears, the surliness of whose manners concealed, he was certain, trusty hearts.

All now was ready; and when it was evening and the innumerable silver sconces were lit and the light airs which for ever moved about the galleries stirred the blue and green arras, so that it looked as if the huntsmen were riding and Daphne flying; when the silver shone and lacquer glowed and wood kindled; when the carved chairs held their arms out and dolphins swam upon the walls with mermaids on their backs;[37] when all this and much more than all this was complete and to his liking, Orlando walked through the house with his elk-hounds following and felt content. He had matter now, he thought, to fill out his peroration. Perhaps it would be well to begin the speech all over again. Yet, as he paraded the galleries he felt that still something was lacking. Chairs and tables, however richly gilt and carved, sofas, resting on lions' paws with swans' necks curving under them, beds even of the softest swansdown are not by themselves enough. People sitting in them, people lying in them improve them amazingly. Accordingly Orlando now began a series of very splendid entertainments to the nobility and gentry of the neighbourhood. The three hundred and sixty-five bedrooms were full for a month at a time. Guests jostled each other on the fifty-two staircases. Three hundred servants bustled about the pantries. Banquets took place almost nightly. Thus, in a very few years, Orlando had worn the nap off his velvet, and spent the half of his fortune; but he had earned the good opinion of his neighbours, held a score of offices in the county, and was annually presented with perhaps a dozen volumes dedicated to his Lordship in rather fulsome terms by grateful poets. For though he was careful not to consort with writers at that time and kept himself always aloof from ladies of foreign blood, still, he was excessively generous both to women and to poets, and both adored him.

But when the feasting was at its height and his guests were at their revels, he was apt to take himself off to his private room alone. There when the door was shut, and he was certain of privacy, he would have out an old writing book, stitched together with silk stolen from his mother's workbox, and labelled in a round schoolboy hand,[38] 'The Oak Tree, A Poem'. In this he would write till midnight chimed and long after. But as he scratched out as many lines as he wrote in, the sum of them was often, at the end of the year, rather less than at the beginning, and it looked as if in the process of writing the poem would be completely unwritten. For it is for the historian of letters to remark that he had changed his style amazingly. His floridity was chastened; his abundance curbed; the age of prose was congealing those warm fountains. The very landscape outside was less stuck about with garlands and the briars themselves were less thorned and intricate. Perhaps the senses were a little duller and honey and cream less seductive to the palate. Also that the streets were better drained and the houses better lit had its effect upon the style, it cannot be doubted.

One day he was adding a line or two with enormous labour to 'The Oak Tree, A Poem', when a shadow crossed the tail of his eye. It was no shadow, he soon saw, but the figure of a very tall lady in riding hood and mantle crossing the quadrangle on which his room looked out. As this was the most private of the courts, and the lady was a stranger to him, Orlando marvelled how she had got there. Three days later the same apparition appeared again; and on Wednesday noon appeared once more.

This time, Orlando was determined to follow her, nor apparently was she afraid to be found, for she slackened her steps as he came up and looked him full in the face. Any other woman thus caught in a Lord's private grounds would have been afraid; any other woman with that face, headdress, and aspect would have thrown her mantilla across her shoulders to hide it. For this lady resembled nothing so much as a hare; a hare startled, but obdurate; a hare whose timidity is overcome by an immense and foolish audacity; a hare that sits upright and glowers at its pursuer with great, bulging eyes; with ears erect but quivering, with nose pointed, but twitching. This hare, moreover, was six feet high and wore a headdress into the bargain of some antiquated kind which made her look still taller. Thus confronted, she stared at Orlando with a stare in which timidity and audacity were most strangely combined.

First, she asked him, with a proper, but somewhat clumsy curtsey, to forgive her her intrusion. Then, rising to her full height again, which must have been something over six feet two, she went on to say – but with such a cackle of nervous laughter, so much tee-heeing and haw-hawing that Orlando thought she must have escaped from a lunatic asylum – that she was the Archduchess Harriet[39] Griselda of Finster-Aarhorn and Scand-op-Boom in the Roumanian territory. She desired above all things to make his acquaintance, she said. She had taken lodging over a baker's shop at the Park Gates. She had seen his picture and it was the image of a sister of hers who was – here she guffawed – long since dead. She was visiting the English court. The Queen was her Cousin. The King was a very good fellow but seldom went to bed sober. Here she tee-heed and haw-hawed again. In short, there was nothing for it but to ask her in and give her a glass of wine.

Indoors, her manners regained the hauteur natural to a Roumanian Archduchess; and had she not shown a knowledge of wines rare in a lady, and made some observations upon firearms and the customs of sportsmen in her country, which were sensible enough, the talk would have lacked spontaneity. Jumping to her

THE ARCHDUCHESS HARRIET

feet at last, she announced that she would call the following day, swept another prodigious curtsey and departed. The following day, Orlando rode out. The next, he turned his back; on the third he drew his curtain. On the fourth it rained, and as he could not keep a lady in the wet, nor was altogether averse to company, he invited her in and asked her opinion whether a suit of armour, which belonged to an ancestor of his, was the work of Jacobi or of Topp.[40] He inclined to Topp. She held another opinion − it matters very little which. But it is of some importance to the course of our story that, in illustrating her argument, which had to do with the working of the tie pieces, the Archduchess Harriet took the golden shin case and fitted it to Orlando's leg.

That he had a pair of the shapeliest legs that any Nobleman has ever stood upright upon has already been said.

Perhaps something in the way she fastened the ankle buckle; or her stooping posture; or Orlando's long seclusion; or the natural sympathy which is between the sexes; or the Burgundy; or the fire − any of these causes may have been to blame; for certainly blame there is on one side or another, when a Nobleman of Orlando's breeding, entertaining a lady in his house, and she his elder by many years, with a face a yard long and staring eyes, dressed somewhat ridiculously too, in a mantle and riding cloak though the season was warm − blame there is when such a Nobleman is so suddenly and violently overcome by passion of some sort that he has to leave the room.

But what sort of passion, it may well be asked, could this be? And the answer is double faced as Love herself. For Love − but leaving Love out of the argument for a moment, the actual event was this:

When the Archduchess Harriet Griselda stooped to fasten the buckle, Orlando heard, suddenly and unaccountably, far off the beating of Love's wings. The distant stir of that soft plumage roused in him a thousand memories of rushing waters, of loveliness in the snow and faithlessness in the flood; and the sound came nearer; and he blushed and trembled; and he was moved as he had thought never to be moved again; and he was ready to raise his hands and let the bird of beauty alight upon his shoulders, when – horror! – a creaking sound like that the crows make tumbling over the trees began to reverberate; the air seemed dark with coarse black wings; voices croaked; bits of straw, twigs, and feathers dropped; and there pitched down upon his shoulders the heaviest and foulest of the birds; which is the vulture. Thus he rushed from the room and sent the footman to see the Archduchess Harriet to her carriage.

For Love, to which we may now return, has two faces; one white, the other black; two bodies; one smooth, the other hairy. It has two hands, two feet, two tails, two, indeed, of every member and each one is the exact opposite of the other. Yet, so strictly are they joined together that you cannot separate them. In this case, Orlando's love began her flight towards him with her white face turned, and her smooth and lovely body outwards. Nearer and nearer she came wafting before her airs of pure delight. All of a sudden (at the sight of the Archduchess presumably) she wheeled about, turned the other way round; showed herself black, hairy, brutish; and it was Lust the vulture, not Love, the Bird of Paradise, that flopped, foully and disgustingly, upon his shoulders. Hence he ran; hence he fetched the footman.

But the harpy is not so easily banished as all that. Not only did the Archduchess continue to lodge at the Baker's, but Orlando was haunted every day and night by phantoms of the foulest kind. Vainly, it seemed, had he furnished his house with silver and hung the walls with arras, when at any moment a dung-bedraggled fowl could settle upon his writing-table. There she was, flopping about among the chairs; he saw her waddling ungracefully across the galleries. Now, she perched, top heavy upon a fire screen. When he chased her out, back she came and pecked at the glass till she broke it.

Thus realising that his home was uninhabitable, and that steps must be taken to end the matter instantly, he did what any other young man would have done in his place, and asked King Charles to send him as Ambassador Extraordinary to

Constantinople. The King was walking in Whitehall. Nell Gwyn was on his arm.[41] She was pelting him with hazel nuts. 'Twas a thousand pities, that amorous lady sighed, that such a pair of legs should leave the country.

Howbeit, the Fates were hard; she could do no more than toss one kiss over her shoulder before Orlando sailed.

Chapter III

It is, indeed, highly unfortunate, and much to be regretted that at this stage of Orlando's career, when he played a most important part in the public life of his country, we have least information to go upon. We know that he discharged his duties to admiration – witness his Bath and his Dukedom.[1] We know that he had a finger in some of the most delicate negotiations between King Charles and the Turks – to that, treaties in the vault of the Record Office bear testimony. But the revolution which broke out during his period of office, and the fire[2] which followed, have so damaged or destroyed all those papers from which any trustworthy record could be drawn, that what we can give is lamentably incomplete. Often the paper was scorched a deep brown in the middle of the most important sentence. Just when we thought to elucidate a secret that has puzzled historians for a hundred years, there was a hole in the manuscript big enough to put your finger through. We have done our best to piece out a meagre summary from the charred fragments that remain; but often it has been necessary to speculate, to surmise, and even to use the imagination.

Orlando's day was passed, it would seem, somewhat in this fashion. About seven, he would rise, wrap himself in a long Turkish cloak, light a cheroot,[3] and lean his elbows on the parapet. Thus he would stand, gazing at the city beneath him, apparently entranced. At this hour the mist would lie so thick that the domes of Santa Sofia[4] and the rest would seem to be afloat; gradually the mist would uncover them; the bubbles would be seen to be firmly fixed; there would be the river; there the Galata Bridge; there the green-turbaned pilgrims without eyes or noses, begging alms; there the pariah dogs picking up offal; there the shawled women; there the innumerable donkeys; there men on horses carrying long poles. Soon, the whole town would be astir with the cracking of whips, the beating of gongs, cryings to prayer, lashing of mules, and rattle of brass-bound wheels, while sour odours, made from bread fermenting and incense, and spice, rose even to the heights of Pera itself and seemed the very breath of the strident multi-coloured and barbaric population.

Nothing, he reflected, gazing at the view which was now sparkling in the sun, could well be less like the counties of Surrey and Kent or the towns of London and Tunbridge Wells. To the right and left rose in bald and stony prominence the inhospitable Asian mountains, to which the arid castle of a robber chief or two might hang; but parsonage there was none, nor manor house, nor cottage, nor oak, elm, violet, ivy, or wild eglantine. There were no hedges for ferns to grow on, and no fields for sheep to graze. The houses were white as egg-shells and as bald. That he, who was English root and fibre, should yet exult to the depths of his heart in this wild panorama, and gaze and gaze at those passes and far heights planning journeys there alone on foot[5] where only the goat and shepherd had gone before; should feel a passion of affection for the bright, unseasonable flowers, love the unkempt, pariah dogs beyond even his elk-hounds at home, and snuff the acrid, sharp smell of the streets eagerly into his nostrils, surprised him. He wondered if, in the season of the Crusades, one of his ancestors had taken up with a Circassian[6] peasant woman; thought it possible; fancied a certain darkness in his complexion; and, going indoors again, withdrew to his bath.

An hour later, properly scented, curled, and anointed, he would receive visits from secretaries and other high officials carrying, one after another, red boxes which yielded only to his own golden key. Within were papers of the highest importance, of which only fragments, here a flourish, there a seal firmly attached to a piece of burnt silk, now remain. Of their contents then, we cannot speak, but can only testify that Orlando was kept busy, what with his wax and seals, his various coloured ribbons which had to be diversely attached, his engrossing of titles and making of flourishes round capital letters, till luncheon came – a splendid meal of perhaps thirty courses.

After luncheon, lackeys announced that his coach and six was at the door, and he went, preceded by purple Janissaries[7] running on foot and waving great ostrich-feather fans above their heads, to call upon the other ambassadors and dignitaries of state. The ceremony was always the same. On reaching the courtyard, the Janissaries struck with their fans upon the main portal, which immediately flew open revealing a large chamber, splendidly furnished. Here were seated two figures, generally of the opposite sexes. Profound bows and curtseys were exchanged. In the first room, it was permissible only to mention the weather. Having said that it was fine or wet, hot or cold, the Ambassador then passed on to the next chamber, where again, two figures rose to greet him. Here it was only permissible to compare Constantinople as a place of residence with London; and the Ambassador naturally said that he preferred Constantinople, and his hosts naturally said, though they had not seen it, that they preferred London. In the next chamber, King Charles's and the Sultan's healths had to be discussed at some length. In the next were discussed the Ambassador's health and that of his host's wife, but more briefly. In the next the Ambassador complimented his host upon his furniture, and the host complimented the Ambassador upon his dress. In the next, sweetmeats were offered, the host deploring their badness, the Ambassador extolling their goodness. The ceremony ended at length with the smoking of a hookah[8] and the drinking of a glass of coffee; but though the motions of smoking and drinking were gone through punctiliously there was neither tobacco in the pipe nor coffee in the glass, as, had either smoke or drink been real, the human frame would have sunk beneath the surfeit. For, no sooner had the Ambassador despatched one such visit, than another had to be undertaken. The same ceremonies were gone through in precisely the same order six or seven times over at the houses of the other great officials, so that it was often late at night before the Ambassador reached home. Though Orlando performed these tasks to admiration and never denied that they are, perhaps, the most important part of a diplomatist's duties, he was undoubtedly

ORLANDO AS AMBASSADOR

fatigued by them, and often depressed to such a pitch of gloom that he preferred to take his dinner alone with his dogs. To them, indeed, he might be heard talking in his own tongue. And sometimes, it is said, he would pass out of his own gates late at night so disguised that the sentries did not know him. Then he would mingle with the crowd on the Galata Bridge; or stroll through the bazaars; or throw aside his shoes and join the worshippers in the Mosques. Once, when it was given out that he was ill of a fever, shepherds, bringing their goats to market, reported that they had met an English Lord on the mountain top and heard him praying to his God. This was thought to be Orlando himself, and his prayer was, no doubt, a poem said aloud, for it was known that he still carried about with him, in the bosom of his cloak, a much scored manuscript; and servants, listening at the door, heard the Ambassador chanting something in an odd, sing-song voice when he was alone.

It is with fragments such as these that we must do our best to make up a picture of Orlando's life and character at this time. There exist, even to this day, rumours, legends, anecdotes of a floating and unauthenticated kind about Orlando's life in Constantinople – (we have quoted but a few of them) which go to prove that he possessed, now that he was in the prime of life, the power to stir the fancy and rivet the eye which will keep a memory green long after all that more durable qualities can do to preserve it is forgotten. The power is a mysterious one compounded of beauty, birth, and some rarer gift, which we may call glamour and have done with it. 'A million candles', as Sasha had said, burnt in him without his being at the trouble of lighting a single one. He moved like a stag, without any need to think about his legs. He spoke in his ordinary voice and echo beat a silver gong. Hence rumours gathered round him. He became the adored of many women and some men. It was not necessary that they should speak to him or even that they should see him; they conjured up before them especially when the scenery was romantic, or the sun was setting, the figure of a noble gentleman in silk stockings. Upon the poor and uneducated, he had the same power as upon the rich. Shepherds, gipsies, donkey drivers, still sing songs about the English Lord 'who dropped his emeralds in the well', which undoubtedly refer to Orlando, who once, it seems, tore his jewels from him in a moment of rage or intoxication and flung them in a fountain; whence they were fished by a page boy. But this romantic power, it is well known, is often associated with a nature of extreme reserve. Orlando seems to have made no friends. As far as is known, he formed no attachments. A certain great lady came all the way from England in order to be near him, and pestered him with her attentions, but he continued to discharge his duties so indefatigably that he had not been Ambassador at the Horn more than two years and a half before King Charles signified his intention of raising him to the highest rank in the peerage. The envious said that this was Nell Gwyn's tribute to the memory of a leg. But, as she had seen him once only, and was then busily engaged in pelting her royal master with nutshells, it is likely that it was his merits that won him his Dukedom, not his calves.

Here we must pause, for we have reached a moment of great significance in his career. For the conferring of the Dukedom was the occasion of a very famous, and indeed, much disputed incident, which we must now describe, picking our way among burnt papers and little bits of tape as best we may. It was at the end of the great fast of Ramadan[9] that the Order of the Bath and the patent of nobility arrived in a frigate commanded by Sir Adrian Scrope; and Orlando made this the occasion for an entertainment more splendid than any that has been known before or since in Constantinople. The night was fine; the crowd immense, and the windows of the Embassy brilliantly illuminated. Again, details are lacking, for the fire had its way with all such records, and has left only tantalising fragments which leave the most important points obscure. From the diary of John Fenner Brigge,[10] however, an English naval officer, who was among the guests, we gather that people of all nationalities 'were packed like herrings in a barrel' in the courtyard. The crowd pressed so unpleasantly close that Brigge soon climbed into a Judas tree, the better to observe the proceedings. The rumour had got about among the natives (and here is additional proof of Orlando's mysterious power over the imagination) that some kind of miracle was to be performed. 'Thus,' writes Brigge (but his manuscript is full of burns and holes, some sentences being quite illegible), 'when the rockets began to soar into the air, there was considerable uneasiness among us lest the native population should be seized . . . fraught with unpleasant consequences to all . . . English ladies in the company, I own that my hand went to my cutlass. Happily,' he continues in his somewhat long-winded style, 'these fears seemed, for the moment, groundless and, observing the demeanour of the natives . . . I came to the conclusion that this demonstration of our skill in the art of pyrotechny was valuable, if only because it impressed upon them . . . the superiority of the British . . . Indeed, the sight was one of indescribable magnificence. I found myself alternately praising the Lord that he had permitted . . . and wishing that my poor, dear mother . . . By the Ambassador's orders, the long windows, which are so imposing a feature of Eastern architecture, for though ignorant in many ways . . . were thrown wide; and within, we could see a tableau vivant or theatrical display in which English ladies and gentlemen . . . represented a masque the work of one . . . The words were inaudible, but the sight of so many of our countrymen and women, dressed with the highest elegance and distinction . . . moved me to emotions of which I am certainly not ashamed, though unable . . . I was intent upon observing the astonishing conduct of Lady — which was of a nature to fasten the eyes of all upon her, and to bring discredit upon her sex and country, when' – unfortunately a branch of the Judas tree broke, Lieutenant Brigge fell to the ground, and the rest of the entry records only his gratitude to Providence (who plays a very large part in the diary) and the exact nature of his injuries.

Happily, Miss Penelope Hartopp, daughter of the General of that name, saw the scene from inside and carries on the tale in a letter, much defaced too, which ultimately reached a female friend at Tunbridge Wells. Miss Penelope was no less lavish in her enthusiasm than the gallant officer. 'Ravishing,' she exclaims ten times on one page, 'wondrous ... utterly beyond description ... gold plate ... candelabras ... negroes in plush breeches ... pyramids of ice ... fountains of negus ... jellies made to represent His Majesty's ships ... swans made to represent water lilies ... birds in golden cages ... gentlemen in slashed crimson velvet ... Ladies' headdresses *at least* six foot high ... musical boxes ... Mr. Peregrine said I looked *quite* lovely which I only repeat to you, my dearest, because I know ... Oh! how I longed for you all! ... surpassing anything we have seen at the Pantiles ... oceans to drink ... some gentlemen overcome ... Lady Betty ravishing ... Poor Lady Bonham made the unfortunate mistake of sitting down without a chair beneath her ... Gentlemen all very gallant ... wished a thousand times for you and dearest Betsy ... But the sight of all others, the cynosure of all eyes ... as all admitted, for none could be so vile as to deny it, was the Ambassador himself. Such a leg! Such a countenance!! Such princely manners!!! To see him come into the room! To see him go out again! And something *interesting* in the expression, which makes one feel, one scarcely knows why, that he has *suffered*! They say a lady was the cause of it. The heartless monster!!! How can one of our *reputed tender sex* have had the effrontery!!! He is unmarried, and half the ladies in the place are wild for love of him ... A thousand, thousand kisses to Tom, Gerry, Peter, and dearest Mew' [presumably her cat].

From the Gazette of the time, we gather that 'as the clock struck twelve, the Ambassador appeared on the centre Balcony which was hung with priceless rugs. Six Turks of the Imperial Body Guard, each over six foot in height, held torches to his right and left. Rockets rose into the air at his appearance, and a great shout went up from the people, which the Ambassador acknowledged, bowing deeply, and speaking a few words of thanks in the Turkish language, which it was one of his accomplishments to speak with fluency. Next, Sir Adrian Scrope, in the full dress of a British Admiral, advanced; the Ambassador knelt on one knee; the Admiral placed the Collar of the Most

Noble Order of the Bath round his neck, then pinned the Star to his breast; after which another gentleman of the diplomatic corps advancing in a stately manner placed on his shoulders the ducal robes, and handed him on a crimson cushion, the ducal coronet.'

At length, with a gesture of extraordinary majesty and grace, first bowing profoundly, then raising himself proudly erect, Orlando took the golden circlet of strawberry leaves and placed it, with a gesture which none that saw it ever forgot, upon his brows. It was at this point that the first disturbance began. Either the people had expected a miracle – some say a shower of gold was prophesied to fall from the skies – which did not happen, or this was the signal chosen for the attack to begin; nobody seems to know; but as the coronet settled on Orlando's brows a great uproar rose. Bells began ringing; the harsh cries of the prophets were heard above the shouts of the people; many Turks fell flat to the ground and touched the earth with their foreheads. A door burst open. The natives pressed into the banqueting-rooms. Women shrieked. A certain lady, who was said to be dying for love of Orlando, seized a candelabra and dashed it to the ground. What might not have happened, had it not been for the presence of Sir Adrian Scrope and a squad of British blue-jackets,[11] nobody can say. But the Admiral ordered the bugles to be sounded; a hundred blue-jackets stood instantly at attention; the disorder was quelled, and quiet, at least for the time being, fell upon the scene.

So far, we are on the firm, if rather narrow, ground of ascertained truth. But nobody has ever known exactly what took place later that night. The testimony of the sentries and others seems, however, to prove that the Embassy was empty of company, and shut up for the night in the usual way by two A.M. The Ambassador was seen to go to his room, still wearing the insignia of his rank, and shut the door. Some say he locked it, which was against his custom. Others maintain that they heard music of a rustic kind, such as shepherds play, later that night in the courtyard under the Ambassador's window. A washer-woman, who was kept awake by a toothache, said that she saw a man's figure, wrapped in a cloak or dressing gown, come out upon the balcony. Then, she said, a woman, much muffled, but apparently of the peasant class, was drawn up by means of a rope which the man let down to her on to the balcony. There, the washer-woman said, they embraced passionately 'like lovers', and went into the room together, drawing the curtains so that no more could be seen.

Next morning, the Duke, as we must now call him, was found by his secretaries sunk in profound slumber amid bed clothes that were much tumbled. The room was in some disorder, his coronet having rolled on the floor, and his cloak and garter being flung all of a heap on a chair. The table was littered with papers. No suspicion was felt at first, as the fatigues of the night had been great. But when afternoon came and he still slept, a doctor was summoned. He applied remedies which had been used on the previous occasion, plasters, nettles, emetics, etc., but without success. Orlando slept on. His secretaries then thought it their duty to examine the papers on the table. Many were scribbled over with poetry, in which frequent mention was made of an oak tree. There were also various state papers and others of a private nature concerning the management of his estates in England. But at length they came upon a document of far greater significance. It was nothing less, indeed, than a deed of marriage, drawn up, signed, and witnessed between his Lordship, Orlando, Knight of the Garter, etc., etc., etc., and Rosina Pepita,[12] a dancer, father unknown, but reputed a gipsy, mother also unknown but reputed a seller of old iron in the market-place over against the Galata Bridge. The secretaries looked at each other in dismay. And still Orlando slept. Morning and evening they watched him, but, save that his breathing was regular and his cheeks still flushed their habitual deep rose, he gave no sign of life. Whatever science or ingenuity could do to waken him they did. But still he slept.

On the seventh day of his trance (Thursday, May the 10th) the first shot was fired of that terrible and bloody insurrection of which Lieutenant Brigge had detected the first symptoms. The

Turks rose against the Sultan, set fire to the town, and put every foreigner they could find, either to the sword or to the basti-nado.[13] A few English managed to escape; but, as might have been expected, the gentlemen of the British Embassy preferred to die in defence of their red boxes,[14] or, in extreme cases, to swallow bunches of keys rather than let them fall into the hands of the Infidel. The rioters broke into Orlando's room, but seeing him stretched to all appearance dead they left him untouched, and only robbed him of his coronet and the robes of the Garter.

And now again obscurity descends, and would indeed that it were deeper! Would, we almost have it in our hearts to exclaim, that it were so deep that we could see nothing whatever through its opacity! Would that we might here take the pen and write Finis to our work! Would that we might spare the reader what is to come and say to him in so many words, Orlando died and was buried. But here, alas, Truth, Candour, and Honesty, the austere Gods who keep watch and ward by the inkpot of the biographer, cry No! Putting their silver trumpets to their lips they demand in one blast, Truth! And again they cry Truth! and sounding yet a third time in concert they peal forth, The Truth and nothing but the Truth!

At which – Heaven be praised! for it affords us a breathing space – the doors gently open, as if a breath of the gentlest and holiest zephyr had wafted them apart, and three figures enter.[15] First, comes our Lady of Purity; whose brows are bound with fillets of the whitest lamb's wool; whose hair is as an avalanche of the driven snow; and in whose hand reposes the white quill of a virgin goose. Following her, but with a statelier step, comes our Lady of Chastity; on whose brow is set like a turret of burning but unwasting fire a diadem of icicles; her eyes are pure stars, and her fingers, if they touch you, freeze you to the bone. Close behind her, sheltering indeed in the shadow of her more stately sisters, comes our Lady of Modesty, frailest and fairest of the three; whose face is only shown as the young moon shows when it is thin and sickle shaped and half hidden among clouds. Each advances towards the centre of the room where Orlando still lies sleeping; and with gestures at once appealing and commanding, *Our Lady of Purity* speaks first:

'I am the guardian of the sleeping fawn; the snow is dear to me; and the moon rising; and the silver sea. With my robes I cover the speckled hen's eggs and the brindled sea shell; I cover vice and poverty. On all things frail or dark or doubtful, my veil descends. Wherefore, speak not, reveal not. Spare, O spare!'

Here the trumpets peal forth.

'Purity Avaunt! Begone Purity!'

Then *Our Lady Chastity* speaks:

'I am she whose touch freezes and whose glance turns to stone. I have stayed the star in its dancing, and the wave as it falls. The highest Alps are my dwelling place; and when I walk, the lightnings flash in my hair; where my eyes fall, they kill. Rather than let Orlando wake, I will freeze him to the bone. Spare, O spare!'

Here the trumpets peal forth.

'Chastity Avaunt! Begone Chastity!'

Then *Our Lady of Modesty* speaks, so low that one can hardly hear:

'I am she that men call Modesty. Virgin I am and ever shall be. Not for me the fruitful fields and the fertile vineyard. Increase is odious to me; and when the apples burgeon or the flocks breed, I run, I run; I let my mantle fall. My hair covers my eyes. I do not see. Spare, O spare!'

Again the trumpets peal forth:

'Modesty Avaunt! Begone Modesty!'

With gestures of grief and lamentation the three sisters now join hands and dance slowly, tossing their veils and singing as they go:

'Truth come not out from your horrid den. Hide deeper, fearful Truth. For you flaunt in the brutal gaze of the sun things that were better unknown and undone; you unveil the shameful; the dark you make clear, Hide! Hide! Hide!'

Here they make as if to cover Orlando with their draperies. The trumpets, meanwhile, still blare forth,

'The Truth and nothing but the Truth.'

At this the Sisters try to cast their veils over the mouths of the trumpets so as to muffle them, but in vain, for now all the trumpets blare forth together,

'Horrid Sisters, go!'

The sisters become distracted and wail in unison, still circling and flinging their veils up and down.

'It has not always been so! But men want us no longer; the women detest us. We go; we go. I (*Purity says this*) to the hen roost. I (*Chastity says this*) to the still unravished heights of Surrey. I (*Modesty says this*) to any cosy nook where there are ivy and curtains in plenty.'

'For there, not here (all speak together joining hands and making gestures of farewell and despair towards the bed where Orlando lies sleeping) dwell still in nest and boudoir, office and lawcourt those who love us; those who honour us, virgins and city men; lawyers and doctors; those who prohibit; those who deny; those who reverence without knowing why; those who praise without understanding; the still very numerous (Heaven be praised) tribe of the respectable; who prefer to see not; desire to know not; love the darkness; those still worship us, and with reason; for we have given them Wealth, Prosperity, Comfort, Ease. To them we go, you we leave. Come, Sisters, come! This is no place for us here.'

They retire in haste, waving their draperies over their heads, as if to shut out something that they dare not look upon and close the door behind them.

We are, therefore, now left entirely alone in the room with the sleeping Orlando and the trumpeters. The trumpeters, ranging themselves side by side in order, blow one terrific blast –

'THE TRUTH!'

at which Orlando woke.

He stretched himself. He rose. He stood upright in complete nakedness before us, and while the trumpets pealed Truth! Truth! Truth! we have no choice left but confess – he was a woman.

*

The sound of the trumpets died away and Orlando stood stark naked. No human being, since the world began, has ever looked more ravishing. His form combined in one the strength of a man and a woman's grace. As he stood there, the silver trumpets prolonged their note, as if reluctant to leave the lovely sight which their blast had called forth; and Chastity, Purity, and Modesty, inspired, no doubt, by Curiosity, peeped in at the door and threw a garment like a towel at the naked form which, unfortunately, fell short by several inches. Orlando looked himself up and down in a long looking-glass, without showing any signs of discomposure, and went, presumably, to his bath.

We may take advantage of this pause in the narrative to make certain statements. Orlando had become a woman – there is no denying it. But in every other respect, Orlando remained precisely as he had been. The change of sex, though it altered their future, did nothing whatever to alter their identity. Their faces remained, as their portraits prove, practically the same. His memory – but in future we must, for convention's sake, say 'her' for 'his', and 'she' for 'he' – her memory then, went back through all the events of her past life without encountering any obstacle. Some slight haziness there may have been, as if a few dark drops had fallen into the clear pool of memory; certain things had become a little dimmed; but that was all. The change seemed to have been accomplished painlessly and completely and in such a way that Orlando herself showed no surprise at it. Many people, taking this into account, and holding that such a change of sex is against nature, have been at great pains to prove (1) that Orlando had always been a woman, (2) that Orlando is at this moment a man. Let biologists and psychologists determine. It is enough for us to state the simple fact; Orlando was a man till the age of thirty; when he became a woman and has remained so ever since.

But let other pens treat of sex and sexuality;[16] we quit such odious subjects as soon as we can. Orlando had now washed, and dressed herself in those Turkish coats and trousers which can be worn indifferently by either sex; and was forced to consider her position. That it was precarious and embarrassing in the extreme must be the first thought of every reader who has followed her story with sympathy. Young, noble, beautiful, she had woken to find herself in a position than which we can conceive none more delicate for a young lady of rank. We should not have blamed her had she rung the bell, screamed, or fainted. But Orlando showed no such signs of perturbation. All her actions were deliberate in the extreme, and might indeed have been thought to show tokens of premeditation. First, she carefully examined the papers on the table; took such as seemed to be written in poetry, and secreted them in her bosom; next she called her Seleuchi hound,[17] which had never left her bed all these days, though half famished with hunger, fed and combed him; then stuck a pair of pistols in her belt; finally wound about her person several strings of emeralds and pearls of the finest orient which had formed part of her Ambassadorial wardrobe. This done, she leant out of the window, gave one low whistle, and descended the shattered and blood-stained staircase, now strewn with the litter of waste-paper baskets, treaties, despatches, seals, sealing wax, etc., and so entered the courtyard. There, in the shadow of a giant fig tree, waited an old gipsy on a donkey. He led another by the bridle. Orlando swung her leg over it; and thus, attended by a lean dog, riding a donkey, in company of a gipsy, the Ambassador of Great Britain at the Court of the Sultan left Constantinople.

They rode for several days and nights and met with a variety of adventures, some at the hands of men, some at the hands of nature, in all of which Orlando acquitted herself with courage. Within a week they reached the high ground outside Broussa,[18] which was then the chief camping ground of the gipsy tribe to which Orlando had allied herself. Often she had looked at those mountains from her balcony at the Embassy; often had longed to be there; and to find oneself where one has longed to be always, to a reflective mind, gives food for thought. For some time, however, she was too well pleased with the change to spoil it by thinking. The pleasure of having no documents to seal or sign, no flourishes to make, no calls to pay, was enough. The gipsies followed the grass; when it was grazed down, on they moved again. She washed in streams if she washed at all; no boxes, red, blue, or green, were presented to her; there was not a key, let alone a golden key, in the whole camp; as for 'visiting', the word was unknown. She milked the goats; she collected brushwood; she stole a hen's egg now and then, but always put a coin or a pearl in place of it; she herded cattle; she stripped vines; she trod the grape; she filled the goat-skin and drank from it; and when she remembered how, at about this time of day, she should have been making the motions of drinking and smoking over an empty coffee-cup and a pipe which lacked tobacco, she laughed aloud, cut herself another hunch of bread, and begged for a puff from old Rustum's pipe, filled though it was with cow dung.

The gipsies, with whom it is obvious that she must have been in secret communication before the revolution, seem to have looked upon her as one of themselves (which is always the highest compliment a people can pay), and her dark hair and dark complexion bore out the belief that she was, by birth, one of them and had been snatched by an English Duke from a nut tree when she was a baby and taken to that barbarous land where people live in houses because they are too feeble and diseased to stand the open air. Thus, though in many ways inferior to them, they were willing to help her to become more like them; taught her their arts of cheese-making and basket-weaving, their science of stealing and bird-snaring, and were even prepared to consider letting her marry among them.

But Orlando had contracted in England some of the customs or diseases (whatever you choose to consider them) which cannot, it seems, be expelled. One evening, when they were all sitting round the camp fire and the sunset was blazing over the Thessalian hills,[19] Orlando exclaimed:

'How good to eat!' (The gipsies have no word for 'beautiful'. This is the nearest.)

All the young men and women burst out laughing uproariously. The sky good to eat, indeed! The elders, however, who had seen more of foreigners than they had, became suspicious. They noticed that Orlando often sat for whole hours doing nothing whatever, except look here and then there; they would come upon her on some hill-top staring straight in front of her, no matter whether the goats were grazing or straying. They began to suspect that she had other beliefs than their own, and the older men and women thought it probable that she had fallen into the clutches of the vilest and cruellest among all the Gods, which is Nature. Nor were they far wrong. The English disease, a love of Nature, was inborn in her, and here, where Nature was so much larger and more powerful than in England, she fell into its hands as she had never done before. The malady is too well known, and has been, alas, too often described to need describing afresh, save very briefly. There were mountains; there were valleys; there were streams. She climbed the mountains; roamed the valleys; sat on the banks of the streams. She likened the hills to ramparts, to the breasts of doves, and the flanks of kine. She compared the flowers to enamel and the turf to Turkey rugs worn thin. Trees were withered hags, and sheep were grey boulders. Everything, in fact, was something else. She found the tarn on the mountain-top and almost threw herself in to seek the wisdom she thought lay hid there; and when, from the mountain-top, she beheld far off, across the Sea of Marmara, the plains of Greece, and made out (her eyes were admirable) the Acropolis with a white streak or two which must, she thought, be the Parthenon,[20] her soul expanded with her eyeballs, and she prayed that she might share the majesty of the hills, know the serenity of the plains, etc. etc., as all such believers do. Then, looking down, the red hyacinth, the purple iris wrought her to cry out in ecstasy at the goodness, the beauty of nature; raising her eyes again, she beheld the eagle soaring, and imagined its raptures and made them her own. Returning home, she saluted each star, each peak, and each watch-fire as if they signalled to her alone; and at last, when she flung herself upon her mat in the gipsies' tent, she could not help bursting out again, How good to eat! How good to eat! (For it is a curious fact that though human beings have such imperfect means of communication, that they can only say 'good to eat' when they mean 'beautiful' and the other way about, they will yet endure ridicule and misunderstanding rather than keep any experience to themselves.) All the young gipsies laughed. But Rustum el Sadi, the old man who had brought Orlando out of Constantinople on his donkey, sat silent. He had a nose like a scimitar; his cheeks were furrowed as if from the age-long descent of iron hail; he was brown and keen-eyed, and as he sat tugging at his hookah he observed Orlando narrowly. He had the deepest suspicion that her God was Nature. One day he found her in tears. Interpreting this to mean that her God had punished her, he told her that he was not surprised. He showed her the fingers of his left hand, withered by the frost; he showed her his right foot, crushed where a rock had fallen. This, he said, was what her God did to men. When she said, 'But so beautiful', using the English word, he shook his head; and when she repeated it he was angry. He saw that she did not believe what he believed, and that was enough, wise and ancient as he was, to enrage him.

This difference of opinion disturbed Orlando, who had been perfectly happy until now. She began to think, was Nature beautiful or cruel; and then she asked herself what this beauty was; whether it was in things themselves, or only in herself; so she went on to the nature of reality, which led her to truth, which in its turn led to Love, Friendship, Poetry (as in the days on the high mound at home); which meditations, since she could impart no word of them, made her long, as she had never longed before, for pen and ink.

'Oh! if only I could write!' she cried (for she had the odd conceit of those who write that words written are shared). She had no ink; and but little paper. But she made ink from berries and wine; and finding a few margins and blank spaces in the manuscript of 'The Oak Tree', managed, by writing a kind of shorthand, to describe the scenery in a long, blank verse poem, and to carry on a dialogue with herself about this Beauty and Truth concisely enough. This kept her extremely happy for hours on end. But the gipsies became suspicious. First, they noticed that she was less adept than before at milking and cheese-making; next, she often hesitated before replying; and once a gipsy boy who had been asleep, woke in a terror feeling her eyes upon him. Sometimes this constraint would be felt by the whole tribe, numbering some dozens of grown men and women. It sprang from the sense they had (and their senses are very sharp and much in advance of their vocabulary) that whatever they were doing crumbled like ashes in their hands. An old woman making a basket, a boy skinning a sheep, would be singing or crooning contentedly at their work, when Orlando would come into the camp, fling herself down by the fire and gaze into the flames. She need not even look at them, and yet they felt, here is someone who doubts; (we make a rough-and-ready translation from the gipsy language) here is someone who does not do the thing for the sake of doing; nor looks for looking's sake; here is someone who believes neither in sheep-skin nor basket; but sees (here they looked apprehensively about the tent) something else. Then a vague but most unpleasant feeling would begin to work in the boy and in the old woman. They broke their withys;[21] they cut their fingers. A great rage filled them. They wished Orlando would leave the tent and never come near them again. Yet she was of a cheerful and willing disposition, they owned; and one of her pearls was enough to buy the finest herd of goats in Broussa.

Slowly, she began to feel that there was some difference between her and the gipsies which made her hesitate sometimes to marry and settle down among them for ever. At first she tried to account for it by saying that she came of an ancient and civilised race, whereas these gipsies were an ignorant people, not much better than savages. One night when they were questioning her about England she could not help with some pride describing the house where she was born, how it had 365 bedrooms and had been in the possession of her family for four or five hundred years. Her ancestors were earls, or even dukes, she added. At this she noticed again that the gipsies were uneasy; but not angry as before when she had praised the beauty of nature. Now they were courteous, but concerned as people of fine breeding are when a stranger has been made to reveal his low birth or poverty. Rustum followed her out of the tent alone and said that she need not mind if her father were a Duke, and possessed all the bedrooms and furniture that she described. They would none of them think the worse of her for that. Then she was seized with a shame that she had never felt before. It was clear that Rustum and the other gipsies thought a descent of four or five hundred years only the meanest possible. Their own families went back at least two or three thousand years. To the gipsy whose ancestors had built the Pyramids centuries before Christ was born, the genealogy of Howards and Plantagenets [22] was no better and no worse than that of the Smiths and the Joneses: both were negligible. Moreover, where the shepherd boy had a lineage of such antiquity, there was nothing specially memorable or desirable in ancient birth; vagabonds and beggars all shared it. And then, though he was too courteous to speak openly, it was clear that the gipsy thought that there was no more vulgar ambition than to possess bedrooms by the hundred (they were on top of a hill as they spoke; it was night; the mountains rose around them) when the whole earth is ours. Looked at from the gipsy point of view, a Duke, Orlando understood, was nothing but a profiteer or robber who snatched land and money from people who rated these things of little worth, and could think of nothing better to do than to build three hundred and sixty-five bedrooms when one was enough, and none was even better than one. She could not deny that her ancestors had accumulated field after field; house after house; honour after honour; yet had none of them been saints or heroes, or great benefactors of the human race. Nor could she counter the argument (Rustum was too much of a gentleman to press it, but she understood) that any man who did now what her ancestors had done three or four hundred years ago would be denounced – and by her own family most loudly – for a vulgar upstart, an adventurer, a *nouveau riche*.

She sought to answer such arguments by the familiar if oblique method of finding the gipsy life itself rude and barbarous; and so, in a short time, much bad blood was bred between them. Indeed, such differences of opinion are enough to cause bloodshed and revolution. Towns have been sacked for less, and a million martyrs have suffered at the stake rather than yield an inch upon any of the points here debated. No passion is stronger in the breast of man than the desire to make others believe as he believes. Nothing so cuts at the root of his happiness and fills him with rage as the sense that another rates low what he prizes high. Whigs and Tories, Liberal party and Labour party – for what do they battle except their own prestige? It is not love of truth but desire to prevail that sets quarter against quarter and makes parish desire the downfall of parish. Each seeks peace of mind and subserviency rather than the triumph of truth and the exaltation of virtue – but these moralities belong, and should be left to the historian, since they are as dull as ditch water.

'Four hundred and seventy-six bedrooms mean nothing to them,' sighed Orlando.

'She prefers a sunset to a flock of goats,' said the gipsies.

What was to be done, Orlando could not think. To leave the gipsies and become once more an Ambassador seemed to her intolerable. But it was equally impossible to remain for ever where there was neither ink nor writing paper, neither reverence for the Talbots nor respect for a multiplicity of bedrooms. So she was thinking, one fine morning on the slopes of Mount Athos,[23] when minding her goats. And then Nature, in whom she trusted, either played her a trick or worked a miracle – again, opinions differ too much for it to be possible to say which. Orlando was gazing rather disconsolately at the steep hill-side in front of her. It was now midsummer, and if we must compare the landscape to anything, it would have been to a dry bone; to a sheep's skeleton; to a gigantic skull picked white by a thousand vultures. The heat was intense, and the little fig tree under which Orlando lay only served to print patterns of fig-leaves upon her light burnous.[24]

Suddenly a shadow, though there was nothing to cast a

shadow, appeared on the bald mountain-side opposite. It deepened quickly and soon a green hollow showed where there had been barren rock before. As she looked, the hollow deepened and widened, and a great park-like space opened in the flank of the hill. Within, she could see an undulating and grassy lawn; she could see oak trees dotted here and there; she could see the thrushes hopping among the branches. She could see the deer stepping delicately from shade to shade, and could even hear the hum of insects and the gentle sighs and shivers of a summer's day in England. After she had gazed entranced for some time, snow began falling; soon the whole landscape was covered and marked with violet shades instead of yellow sunlight. Now she saw heavy carts coming along the roads, laden with tree trunks,[25] which they were taking, she knew, to be sawn for firewood; and then there appeared the roofs and belfries and towers and courtyards of her own home. The snow was falling steadily, and she could now hear the slither and flop which it made as it slid down the roof and fell to the ground. The smoke went up from a thousand chimneys. All was so clear and minute that she could see a daw pecking for worms in the snow. Then, gradually, the violet shadows deepened and closed over the carts and the lawns and the great house itself. All was swallowed up. Now there was nothing left of the grassy hollow, and instead of the green lawns was only the blazing hill-side which a thousand vultures seemed to have picked bare. At this, she burst into a passion of tears, and striding back to the gipsies' camp, told them that she must sail for England the very next day.

It was happy for her that she did so. Already the young men had plotted her death. Honour, they said, demanded it, for she did not think as they did. Yet they would have been sorry to cut her throat; and welcomed the news of her departure. An English merchant ship, as luck would have it, was already under sail in the harbour about to return to England; and Orlando, by breaking off another pearl from her necklace, not only paid her passage but had some bank-notes left over in her wallet. These she

would have liked to present to the gipsies. But they d
wealth she knew; and she had to content herself with emb
which on her part were sincere.

Chapter IV

With some of the guineas left from the sale of the tenth pearl of her string, Orlando had bought herself a complete outfit of such clothes as women then wore, and it was in the dress of a young Englishwoman of rank that she now sat on the deck of the *Enamoured Lady*. It is a strange fact, but a true one, that up to this moment she had scarcely given her sex a thought. Perhaps the Turkish trousers which she had hitherto worn had done something to distract her thoughts; and the gipsy women, except in one or two important particulars, differ very little from the gipsy men. At any rate, it was not until she felt the coil of skirts about her legs and the Captain offered, with the greatest politeness, to have an awning spread for her on deck, that she realised with a start the penalties and the privileges of her position. But that start was not of the kind that might have been expected.

It was not caused, that is to say, simply and solely by the thought of her chastity and how she could preserve it. In normal circumstances a lovely young woman alone would have thought of nothing else; the whole edifice of female government is based on that foundation stone; chastity is their jewel, their centre-piece, which they run mad to protect, and die when ravished of. But if one has been a man for thirty years or so, and an Ambassador into the bargain, if one has held a Queen in one's arms and one or two other ladies, if report be true, of less exalted rank, if one has married a Rosina Pepita, and so on, one does not perhaps give such a very great start about that. Orlando's start was of a very complicated kind, and not to be summed up in a trice. Nobody, indeed, ever accused her of being one of those quick wits who run to the end of things in a minute. It took her the entire length of the voyage to moralise out the meaning of her start, and so, at her own pace, we will follow her.

'Lord,' she thought, when she had recovered from her start,

stretching herself out at length under her awning, 'this is a pleasant, lazy way of life, to be sure. But', she thought, giving her legs a kick, 'these skirts are plaguey things to have about one's heels. Yet the stuff (flowered paduasoy¹) is the loveliest in the world. Never have I seen my own skin (here she laid her hand on her knee) look to such advantage as now. Could I, however, leap overboard and swim in clothes like these? No! Therefore, I should have to trust to the protection of a blue-jacket. Do I object to that? Now do I?' she wondered, here encountering the first knot in the smooth skein of her argument.

Dinner came before she had untied it, and then it was the Captain himself – Captain Nicholas Benedict Bartolus, a sea-captain of distinguished aspect, who did it for her as he helped her to a slice of corned beef.

'A little of the fat, Ma'am?' he asked. 'Let me cut you just the tiniest little slice the size of your finger nail.' At those words a delicious tremor ran through her frame. Birds sang; the torrents rushed. It recalled the feeling of indescribable pleasure with which she had first seen Sasha, hundreds of years ago. Then she had pursued, now she fled. Which is the greater ecstasy? The man's or the woman's? And are they not perhaps the same? No, she thought, this is the most delicious (thanking the Captain but refusing), to refuse, and see him frown. Well, she would, if he wished it, have the very thinnest, smallest shiver² in the world. This was the most delicious of all, to yield and see him smile. 'For nothing', she thought, regaining her couch on deck, and continuing the argument, 'is more heavenly than to resist and to yield; to yield and to resist. Surely it throws the spirit into such a rapture as nothing else can. So that I'm not sure', she continued, 'that I won't throw myself overboard, for the mere pleasure of being rescued by a blue-jacket after all.'

(It must be remembered that she was like a child entering into possession of a pleasaunce³ or toy cupboard; her arguments would not commend themselves to mature women, who have had the run of it all their lives.)

'But what used we young fellows in the cockpit of the *Marie*

Rose to say about a woman who threw herself overboard for the pleasure of being rescued by a blue-jacket?' she said. 'We had a word for them. Ah! I have it . . .' (But we must omit that word; it was disrespectful in the extreme and passing strange on a lady's lips.) 'Lord! Lord!' she cried again at the conclusion of her thoughts, 'must I then begin to respect the opinion of the other sex, however monstrous I think it? If I wear skirts, if I can't swim, if I have to be rescued by a blue-jacket, by God!' she cried, 'I must!' Upon which a gloom fell over her. Candid by nature, and averse to all kinds of equivocation, to tell lies bored her. It seemed to her a roundabout way of going to work. Yet, she reflected, the flowered paduasoy – the pleasure of being rescued by a blue-jacket – if these were only to be obtained by roundabout ways, roundabout one must go, she supposed. She remembered how, as a young man, she had insisted that women must be obedient, chaste, scented, and exquisitely apparelled. 'Now I shall have to pay in my own person for those desires,' she reflected; 'for women are not (judging by my own short experience of the sex) obedient, chaste, scented, and exquisitely apparelled by nature. They can only attain these graces, without which they may enjoy none of the delights of life, by the most tedious discipline. There's the hairdressing,' she thought, 'that alone will take an hour of my morning; there's looking in the looking-glass, another hour; there's staying and lacing; there's washing and powdering; there's changing from silk to lace and from lace to paduasoy; there's being chaste year in year out . . .' Here she tossed her foot impatiently, and showed an inch or two of calf. A sailor on the mast, who happened to look down at the moment, started so violently that he missed his footing and only saved himself by the skin of his teeth. 'If the sight of my ankles means death to an honest fellow who, no doubt, has a wife and family to support, I must, in all humanity, keep them covered,' Orlando thought. Yet her legs were among her chiefest beauties. And she fell to thinking what an odd pass we have come to when all a woman's beauty has to be kept covered lest a sailor may fall from a mast-head. 'A pox on them!' she said, realising

ORLANDO ON HER RETURN TO ENGLAND

for the first time what, in other circumstances, she would have been taught as a child, that is to say, the sacred responsibilities of womanhood.

'And that's the last oath I shall ever be able to swear,' she thought; 'once I set foot on English soil. And I shall never be able to crack a man over the head, or tell him he lies in his teeth, or draw my sword and run him through the body, or sit among my peers, or wear a coronet, or walk in procession, or sentence a man to death, or lead an army, or prance down Whitehall on a charger, or wear seventy-two different medals on my breast. All I can do, once I set foot on English soil, is to pour out tea and ask my lords how they like it. D'you take sugar. D'you take cream?' And mincing out the words, she was horrified to perceive how low an opinion she was forming of the other sex, the manly, to which it had once been her pride to belong. 'To fall from a mast-head', she thought, 'because you see a woman's ankles; to dress up like a Guy Fawkes⁴ and parade the streets, so that women may praise you; to deny a woman teaching lest she may laugh at you; to be the slave of the frailest chit in petticoats, and yet to go about as if you were the Lords of creation – Heavens!' she thought, 'what fools they make of us – what fools we are!' And here it would seem from some ambiguity in her terms that she was censuring both sexes equally, as if she belonged to neither; and indeed, for the time being, she seemed to vacillate; she was man; she was woman; she knew the secrets, shared the weaknesses of each. It was a most bewildering and whirligig state of mind to be in. The comforts of ignorance seemed utterly denied her. She was a feather blown on the gale. Thus it is no great wonder, as she pitted one sex against the other, and found each alternately full of the most deplorable infirmities, and was not sure to which she belonged – it was no great wonder that she was about to cry out that she would return to Turkey and become a gipsy again when the anchor fell with a great splash into the sea; the sails came tumbling on deck, and she perceived (so sunk had she been in thought that she had seen nothing for several days) that the ship was anchored off the coast of Italy. The Captain at once sent to ask the honour of her company ashore with him in the long-boat.

When she returned the next morning, she stretched herself on her couch under the awning and arranged her draperies with the greatest decorum about her ankles.

'Ignorant and poor as we are compared with the other sex,' she thought, continuing the sentence which she had left unfinished the other day, 'armoured with every weapon as they are, while they debar us even from a knowledge of the alphabet' (and from these opening words it is plain that something had happened during the night to give her a push towards the female sex, for she was speaking more as a woman speaks than as a man, yet with a sort of content after all), 'still – they fall from the mast-head.' Here she gave a great yawn and fell asleep. When she woke, the ship was sailing before a fair breeze so near the shore that towns on the cliffs' edge seemed only kept from slipping into the water by the interposition of some great rock or the twisted roots of some ancient olive tree. The scent of oranges wafted from a million trees, heavy with the fruit, reached her on deck. A score of blue dolphins, twisting their tails, leapt high now and again into the air. Stretching her arms out (arms, she had learnt already, have no such fatal effects as legs), she thanked Heaven that she was not prancing down Whitehall on a war-horse, nor even sentencing a man to death. 'Better is it', she thought, 'to be clothed with poverty and ignorance, which are the dark garments of the female sex; better to leave the rule and discipline of the world to others; better be quit of martial ambition, the love of power, and all the other manly desires if so one can more fully enjoy the most exalted raptures known to the human spirit, which are', she said aloud, as her habit was when deeply moved, 'contemplation, solitude, love.'

'Praise God that I'm a woman!' she cried, and was about to run into the extreme folly – than which none is more distressing in woman or man either – of being proud of her sex, when she paused over the singular word, which, for all we can do to put it in its place, has crept in at the end of the last sentence: Love. 'Love,' said Orlando. Instantly – such is its impetuosity – love took a human shape – such is its pride. For where other thoughts are content to remain abstract, nothing will satisfy this one but to put on flesh and blood, mantilla and petticoats, hose and jerkin. And as all Orlando's loves had been women, now, through the culpable laggardry of the human frame to adapt itself to convention, though she herself was a woman, it was still a woman she loved; and if the consciousness of being of the same sex had any effect at all, it was to quicken and deepen those feelings which she had had as a man. For now a thousand hints and mysteries became plain to her that were then dark. Now, the obscurity, which divides the sexes and lets linger innumerable impurities in its gloom, was removed, and if there is anything in what the poet says about truth and beauty, this affection gained in beauty what it lost in falsity. At last, she cried, she knew Sasha as she was, and in the ardour of this discovery, and in the pursuit of all those treasures which were now revealed, she was so rapt and enchanted that it was as if a cannon ball had exploded at her ear when a man's voice said, 'Permit me, Madam,' a man's hand raised her to her feet; and the fingers of a man with a three-masted sailing ship tattooed on the middle finger pointed to the horizon.

'The cliffs of England, Ma'am,' said the Captain, and he raised the hand which had pointed at the sky to the salute. Orlando now gave a second start, even more violent than the first.

'Christ Jesus!' she cried.

Happily, the sight of her native land after long absence excused both start and exclamation, or she would have been hard put to it to explain to Captain Bartolus the raging and conflicting emotions which now boiled within her. How tell him that she, who now trembled on his arm, had been a Duke and an Ambassador? How explain to him that she, who had been lapped like a lily in folds of paduasoy, had hacked heads off, and lain with loose women among treasure sacks in the holds of pirate ships on summer nights when the tulips were abloom and the bees buzzing off Wapping Old Stairs? Not even to herself could she explain the giant start she gave, as the resolute right hand of the sea-captain indicated the cliffs of the British Islands.

'To refuse and to yield,' she murmured, 'how delightful; to pursue and to conquer, how august; to perceive and to reason, how sublime.' Not one of these words so coupled together seemed to her wrong; nevertheless, as the chalky cliffs loomed nearer, she felt culpable; dishonoured; unchaste, which, for one who had never given the matter a thought, was strange. Closer and closer they drew, till the samphire gatherers,[5] hanging half-way down the cliff, were plain to the naked eye. And watching them, she felt, scampering up and down within her, like some derisive ghost who in another instant will pick up her skirts and flaunt out of sight, Sasha the lost, Sasha the memory, whose reality she had proved just now so surprisingly – Sasha, she felt, mopping and mowing and making all sorts of disrespectful gestures towards the cliffs and the samphire gatherers; and when the sailors began chanting, 'So good-bye and adieu to you, Ladies of Spain', the words echoed in Orlando's sad heart, and she felt that however much landing there meant comfort, meant opulence, meant consequence and state (for she would doubtless pick up some noble Prince and reign, his consort, over half Yorkshire),[6] still, if it meant conventionality, meant slavery, meant deceit, meant denying her love, fettering her limbs, pursing her lips, and restraining her tongue, then she would turn about with the ship and set sail once more for the gipsies.

Among the hurry of these thoughts, however, there now rose, like a dome of smooth, white marble, something which, whether fact or fancy, was so impressive to her fevered imagination that she settled upon it as one has seen a swarm of vibrant dragon-flies alight, with apparent satisfaction, upon the glass bell which shelters some tender vegetable. The form of it, by the hazard of fancy, recalled that earliest, most persistent memory – the man with the big forehead in Twitchett's sitting-room, the man who sat writing, or rather looking, but certainly not at her, for he never seemed to see her poised there in all her finery, lovely boy though she must have been, she could not deny it – and whenever she thought of him, the thought spread round it, like the risen moon on turbulent waters, a sheet of silver calm. Now her hand went to her bosom (the other was still in the Captain's keeping), where the pages of her poem were hidden safe. It might have been a talisman that she kept there. The distraction of sex, which hers was, and what it meant, subsided; she thought now only of the glory of poetry, and the great lines of Marlowe, Shakespeare, Ben Jonson, Milton began booming and reverberating, as if a golden clapper beat against a golden bell in the cathedral tower which was her mind. The truth was that the image of the marble dome which her eyes had first discovered so faintly that it suggested a poet's forehead[7] and thus started a flock of irrelevant ideas, was no figment, but a reality; and as the ship advanced down the Thames before a favouring gale, the image with all its associations gave place to the truth, and revealed itself as nothing more and nothing less than the dome of a vast cathedral rising among a fretwork of white spires.

'St. Paul's,' said Captain Bartolus, who stood by her side. 'The Tower of London,' he continued. 'Greenwich Hospital, erected in memory of Queen Mary by her husband, his late majesty, William the Third. Westminster Abbey. The Houses of Parliament.' As he spoke, each of these famous buildings rose to view. It was a fine September morning. A myriad of little water-craft plied from bank to bank. Rarely has a gayer, or more interesting, spectacle presented itself to the gaze of a returned traveller. Orlando hung over the prow, absorbed in wonder. Her eyes had been used too long to savages and nature not to be entranced by these urban glories. That, then, was the dome of St. Paul's which Mr. Wren had built during her absence. Near by, a shock of golden hair burst from a pillar – Captain Bartolus was at her side to inform her that that was the Monument; there had been a plague and a fire during her absence, he said. Do what she would to restrain them, the tears came to her eyes, until, remembering that it is becoming in a woman to weep, she let them flow. Here, she thought, had been the great carnival. Here, where the waves slapped briskly, had stood the Royal Pavilion. Here she had first met Sasha. About here (she looked down into the sparkling waters) one had been used to see the frozen bumboat woman with her apples on her lap. All that splendour and corruption was gone. Gone, too, was the dark night, the monstrous downpour, the violent surges of the flood. Here, where yellow icebergs had raced circling with a crew of terror-stricken wretches on top, a covey of swans floated, orgulous, undulant, superb.[8] London itself had completely changed since she had last seen it. Then, she remembered, it had been a huddle of little black, beetle-browed houses. The heads of rebels had grinned on pikes at Temple Bar. The cobbled pavements had reeked of garbage and ordure. Now, as the ship sailed past Wapping, she caught glimpses of broad and orderly thoroughfares. Stately coaches drawn by teams of well-fed horses stood at the doors of houses whose bow windows, whose plate glass, whose polished knockers, testified to the wealth and modest dignity of the dwellers within. Ladies in flowered silk (she put the Captain's glass to her eye) walked on raised footpaths. Citizens in broidered coats took snuff at street corners under lamp-posts. She caught sight of a variety of painted signs swinging in the breeze and could form a rapid notion from what was painted on them of the tobacco, of the stuff, of the silk, of the gold, of the silver ware, of the gloves, of the perfumes, and of a thousand other articles which were sold within. Nor could she do more as the ship sailed to its anchorage by London Bridge than glance at coffee-house windows where, on balconies, since the weather was fine, a great number of decent citizens sat at ease, with china dishes in front of them, clay pipes by their sides, while one among them read from a news sheet, and was frequently interrupted by the laughter or the comments of the others. Were these taverns, were these wits, were these poets? she asked of Captain Bartolus, who obligingly informed her that even now – if she turned her head a little to the left and looked along the line of his first finger – so – they were passing the Cocoa Tree, where – yes, there he was – one might see Mr. Addison taking his coffee; the other two gentlemen – 'there, Ma'am, a little to the right of the lamp-post, one of 'em humped, t'other much the same as you or me' – were Mr. Dryden and Mr. Pope.* 'Sad dogs,' said the Captain, by which he meant that they were Papists,[9] 'but men of parts, none the less,' he added, hurrying aft to superintend the arrangements for landing.

'Addison, Dryden, Pope,' Orlando repeated as if the words were an incantation. For one moment she saw the high mountains above Broussa, the next, she had set her foot upon her native shore.

But now Orlando was to learn how little the most tempestuous flutter of excitement avails against the iron countenance of the law; how harder than the stones of London Bridge it is, and than the lips of a cannon more severe. No sooner had she returned to her home in Blackfriars than she was made aware by a succession of Bow Street runners and other grave emissaries from the Law Courts that she was a party to three major suits[10] which had been preferred against her during her absence, as well as innumerable minor litigations, some arising out of, others depending on them. The chief charges against her were (1) that she was dead, and therefore could not hold any property whatsoever; (2) that she was a woman, which amounts to much the same thing; (3) that she was an English Duke who had married one Rosina Pepita, a dancer; and had had by her three sons, which sons now declaring that their father was deceased, claimed that all his property descended to them. Such grave charges as these would, of course, take time and money to dispose of. All her estates were put in Chancery[11] and her titles pronounced in abeyance while the suits were under litigation. Thus it was in a highly ambiguous condition, uncertain whether she was alive or dead, man or woman, Duke or nonentity, that she posted down to her country seat,

---

* The Captain must have been mistaken, as a reference to any textbook of literature will show; but the mistake was a kindly one, and so we let it stand.

where, pending the legal judgment, she had the Law's permission to reside in a state of incognito or incognita, as the case might turn out to be.

It was a fine evening in December when she arrived and the snow was falling and the violet shadows were slanting much as she had seen them from the hill-top at Broussa. The great house lay more like a town than a house, brown and blue, rose and purple in the snow, with all its chimneys smoking busily as if inspired with a life of their own. She could not restrain a cry as she saw it there tranquil and massive, couched upon the meadows. As the yellow coach entered the park and came bowling along the drive between the trees, the red deer raised their heads as if expectantly, and it was observed that instead of showing the timidity natural to their kind, they followed the coach and stood about the courtyard when it drew up. Some tossed their antlers, others pawed the ground as the step was let down and Orlando alighted. One, it is said, actually knelt in the snow before her. She had not time to reach her hand towards the knocker before both wings of the great door were flung open, and there, with lights and torches held above their heads, were Mrs. Grimsditch, Mr. Dupper, and a whole retinue of servants come to greet her. But the orderly procession was interrupted first by the impetuosity of Canute,[12] the elk-hound, who threw himself with such ardour upon his mistress that he almost knocked her to the ground; next, by the agitation of Mrs. Grimsditch, who, making as if to curtsey, was overcome with emotion and could do no more than gasp Milord! Milady! Milady! Milord! until Orlando comforted her with a hearty kiss upon both her cheeks. After that, Mr. Dupper began to read from a parchment, but the dogs barking, the huntsmen winding their horns, and the stags, who had come into the courtyard in the confusion, baying the moon, not much progress was made, and the company dispersed within after crowding about their Mistress, and testifying in every way to their great joy at her return.

No one showed an instant's suspicion that Orlando was not the Orlando they had known. If any doubt there was in the human mind the action of the deer and the dogs would have been enough to dispel it, for the dumb creatures, as is well known, are far better judges both of identity and character than we are. Moreover, said Mrs. Grimsditch, over her dish of china tea, to Mr. Dupper that night, if her Lord was a Lady now, she had never seen a lovelier one, nor was there a penny piece to choose between them; one was as well-favoured as the other; they were as like as two peaches on one branch; which, said Mrs. Grimsditch, becoming confidential, she had always had her suspicions (here she nodded her head very mysteriously), which it was no surprise to her (here she nodded her head very knowingly), and for her part, a very great comfort; for what with the towels wanting mending and the curtains in the chaplain's parlour being moth-eaten round the fringes, it was time they had a Mistress among them.

'And some little masters and mistresses to come after her,' Mr. Dupper added, being privileged by virtue of his holy office to speak his mind on such delicate matters as these.

So, while the old servants gossiped in the servants' hall, Orlando took a silver candle in her hand and roamed once more through the halls, the galleries, the courts, the bedrooms; saw loom down at her again the dark visage of this Lord Keeper, that Lord Chamberlain, among her ancestors; sat now in this chair of state, now reclined on that canopy of delight; observed the arras, how it swayed; watched the huntsmen riding and Daphne flying; bathed her hand, as she had loved to do as a child, in the yellow pool of light which the moonlight made falling through the heraldic Leopard in the window; slid along the polished planks of the gallery, the other side of which was rough timber; touched this silk, that satin; fancied the carved dolphins swam; brushed her hair with King James' silver brush; buried her face in the pot-pourri,[13] which was made as the Conqueror had taught them many hundred years ago and from the same roses; looked at the garden and imagined the sleeping crocuses, the dormant dahlias; saw the frail nymphs gleaming white in the snow and the great yew hedges, thick as a house, black behind them; saw the orangeries and the giant medlars; − all this she saw, and each sight and sound, rudely as we write it down, filled her heart with such a lust and balm of joy, that at length, tired out, she entered the Chapel and sank into the old red arm-chair in which her ancestors used to hear service. There she lit a cheroot ('twas a habit she had brought back from the East) and opened the Prayer Book.

It was a little book bound in velvet, stitched with gold, which had been held by Mary Queen of Scots on the scaffold, and the eye of faith could detect a brownish stain, said to be made of a drop of the Royal blood.[14] But what pious thoughts it roused in Orlando, what evil passions it soothed asleep, who dare say, seeing that of all communions this with the deity is the most inscrutable? Novelist, poet, historian all falter with their hand on that door; nor does the believer himself enlighten us, for is he more ready to die than other people, or more eager to share his goods? Does he not keep as many maids and carriage horses as the rest? and yet with it all, holds a faith he says which should make goods a vanity and death desirable. In the Queen's prayer book, along with the blood-stain, was also a lock of hair and a crumb of pastry; Orlando now added to these keepsakes a flake of tobacco, and so, reading and smoking, was moved by the humane jumble of them all − the hair, the pastry, the blood-stain, the tobacco − to such a mood of contemplation as gave her a reverent air suitable in the circumstances, though she had, it is said, no traffic with the usual God. Nothing, however, can be more arrogant, though nothing is commoner than to assume that of Gods there is only one, and of religions none but the speaker's. Orlando, it seemed, had a faith of her own. With all the religious ardour in the world, she now reflected upon her sins and the imperfections that had crept into her spiritual state. The letter S, she reflected, is the serpent in the poet's Eden. Do what she would there were still too many of these sinful reptiles in the first stanzas of 'The Oak Tree'. But 'S' was nothing, in her opinion, compared with the termination 'ing'. The present participle is the Devil himself, she thought (now that we are in the place for believing in Devils). To evade such temptations is the first duty of the poet, she concluded, for as the ear is the antechamber to the soul, poetry can adulterate and destroy more surely than lust or gunpowder. The poet's, then, is the highest office of all, she continued. His words reach where others fall short. A silly song of Shakespeare's has done more for the poor and the wicked than all the preachers and philanthropists in the world. No time, no devotion, can be too great, therefore, which makes the vehicle of our message less distorting. We must shape our words till they are the thinnest integument for our thoughts. Thoughts are divine, etc. Thus it is obvious that she was back in the confines of her own religion which time had only strengthened in her absence, and was rapidly acquiring the intolerance of belief.

'I am growing up,' she thought, taking her taper at last. 'I am losing some illusions,' she said, shutting Queen Mary's book, 'perhaps to acquire others,' and she descended among the tombs where the bones of her ancestors lay.

But even the bones of her ancestors, Sir Miles, Sir Gervase, and the rest, had lost something of their sanctity since Rustum el Sadi had waved his hand that night in the Asian mountains. Somehow the fact that only three or four hundred years ago these skeletons had been men with their way to make in the world like any modern upstart, and that they had made it by acquiring houses and offices, garters and ribbands, as any other upstart does, while poets, perhaps, and men of great mind and breeding had preferred the quietude of the country, for which choice they paid the penalty by extreme poverty, and now hawked broadsheets in the Strand, or herded sheep in the fields, filled her with remorse. She thought of the Egyptian pyramids and what bones lie beneath them as she stood in the crypt; and the vast, empty hills which lie above the Sea of Marmara seemed, for the moment, a finer dwelling-place than this many-roomed mansion in which no bed lacked its quilt and no silver dish its silver cover.

'I am growing up,' she thought, taking her taper. 'I am losing my illusions, perhaps to acquire new ones,' and she paced down the long gallery to her bedroom. It was a disagreeable process, and a troublesome. But it was interesting, amazingly, she thought, stretching her legs out to her log fire (for no sailor was present), and she reviewed, as if it were an avenue of great edifices, the progress of her own self along her own past.

How she had loved sound when she was a boy, and thought the volley of tumultuous syllables from the lips the finest of all poetry. Then – it was the effect of Sasha and her disillusionment perhaps – into this high frenzy was let fall some black drop, which turned her rhapsody to sluggishness. Slowly there had opened within her something intricate and many-chambered, which one must take a torch to explore, in prose not verse; and she remembered how passionately she had studied that doctor at Norwich, Browne,[15] whose book was at her hand there. She had formed here in solitude after her affair with Greene, or tried to form, for Heaven knows these growths are agelong in coming, a spirit capable of resistance. 'I will write', she had said, 'what I enjoy writing'; and so had scratched out twenty-six volumes. Yet still, for all her travels and adventures and profound thinkings and turnings this way and that, she was only in process of fabrication. What the future might bring, Heaven only knew. Change was incessant, and change perhaps would never cease. High battlements of thought,[16] habits that had seemed durable as stone, went down like shadows at the touch of another mind and left a naked sky and fresh stars twinkling in it. Here she went to the window, and in spite of the cold could not help unlatching it. She leant out into the damp night air. She heard a fox bark in the woods, and the clutter of a pheasant trailing through the branches. She heard the snow slither and flop from the roof to the ground. 'By my life,' she exclaimed, 'this is a thousand times better than Turkey. Rustum,' she cried, as if she were arguing with the gipsy (and in this new power of bearing an argument in mind and continuing it with someone who was not there to contradict she showed again the development of her soul), 'you were wrong. This is better than Turkey. Hair, pastry, tobacco –

of what odds and ends are we compounded,' she said (thinking of Queen Mary's prayer book). 'What a phantasmagoria the mind is and meeting-place of dissemblables![17] At one moment we deplore our birth and state and aspire to an ascetic exaltation; the next we are overcome by the smell of some old garden path and weep to hear the thrushes sing.' And so bewildered as usual by the multitude of things which call for explanation and imprint their message without leaving any hint as to their meaning, she threw her cheroot out of the window and went to bed.

Next morning, in pursuance of these thoughts, she had out her pen and paper, and started afresh upon 'The Oak Tree', for to have ink and paper in plenty when one has made do with berries and margins is a delight not to be conceived. Thus she was now striking out a phrase in the depths of despair, now in the heights of ecstasy writing one in, when a shadow darkened the page. She hastily hid her manuscript.

As her window gave on to the most central of the courts, as she had given orders that she would see no one, as she knew no one and was herself legally unknown, she was first surprised at the shadow, then indignant at it, then (when she looked up and saw what caused it) overcome with merriment. For it was a familiar shadow, a grotesque shadow, the shadow of no less a personage than the Archduchess Harriet Griselda of Finster-Aarhorn and Scand-op-Boom in the Roumanian territory. She was loping across the court in her old black riding-habit and mantle as before. Not a hair of her head was changed. This then was the woman who had chased her from England! This was the eyrie of that obscene vulture[18] – this the fatal fowl herself! At the thought that she had fled all the way to Turkey to avoid her seductions (now become excessively flat), Orlando laughed aloud. There was something inexpressibly comic in the sight. She resembled, as Orlando had thought before, nothing so much as a monstrous hare. She had the staring eyes, the lank cheeks, the high headdress of that animal. She stopped now, much as a hare sits erect in the corn when thinking itself unobserved, and stared at Orlando, who stared back at her from the window.

After they had stared like this for a certain time, there was nothing for it but to ask her in, and soon the two ladies were exchanging compliments while the Archduchess struck the snow from her mantle.

'A plague on women,' said Orlando to herself, going to the cupboard to fetch a glass of wine, 'they never leave one a moment's peace. A more ferreting, inquisiting, busybodying set of people don't exist. It was to escape this Maypole that I left England, and now' – here she turned to present the Archduchess with the salver, and behold – in her place stood a tall gentleman in black. A heap of clothes lay in the fender. She was alone with a man.

Recalled thus suddenly to a consciousness of her sex, which she had completely forgotten, and of his, which was now remote enough to be equally upsetting, Orlando felt seized with faintness.

'La!' she cried, putting her hand to her side, 'how you frighten me!'

'Gentle creature,' cried the Archduchess, falling on one knee and at the same time pressing a cordial to Orlando's lips, 'forgive me for the deceit I have practised on you!'

Orlando sipped the wine and the Archduke knelt and kissed her hand.

In short, they acted the parts of man and woman for ten minutes with great vigour and then fell into natural discourse. The Archduchess (but she must in future be known as the Archduke) told his story – that he was a man and always had been one; that he had seen a portrait of Orlando and fallen hopelessly in love with him; that to compass his ends, he had dressed as a woman and lodged at the Baker's shop; that he was desolated when he fled to Turkey; that he had heard of her change and hastened to offer his services (here he teed and heed intolerably). For to him, said the Archduke Harry, she was and would ever be the Pink, the Pearl, the Perfection of her sex. The three p's would have been more persuasive if they had not been interspersed with tee-hees and haw-haws of the strangest kind.

'If this is love,' said Orlando to herself, looking at the Archduke on the other side of the fender, and now from the woman's point of view, 'there is something highly ridiculous about it.'

Falling on his knees, the Archduke Harry made the most passionate declaration of his suit. He told her that he had something like twenty million ducats in a strong box at his castle. He had more acres than any nobleman in England. The shooting was excellent: he could promise her a mixed bag of ptarmigan and grouse such as no English moor, or Scotch either, could rival. True, the pheasants had suffered from the gape[19] in his absence, and the does had slipped their young, but that could be put right, and would be with her help when they lived in Roumania together.

As he spoke, enormous tears formed in his rather prominent eyes and ran down the sandy tracts of his long and lanky cheeks.

That men cry as frequently and as unreasonably as women, Orlando knew from her own experience as a man; but she was beginning to be aware that women should be shocked when men display emotion in their presence, and so, shocked she was.

The Archduke apologised. He commanded himself sufficiently to say that he would leave her now, but would return on the following day for his answer.

That was a Tuesday. He came on Wednesday; he came on Thursday; he came on Friday; and he came on Saturday. It is true that each visit began, continued, or concluded with a declaration of love, but in between there was much room for silence. They sat on either side of the fireplace and sometimes the Archduke knocked over the fire-irons and Orlando picked them up again.[20] Then the Archduke would bethink him how he had shot an elk in Sweden, and Orlando would ask, was it a very big elk, and the Archduke would say that it was not as big as the reindeer which he had shot in Norway; and Orlando would ask, had he ever shot a tiger, and the Archduke would say he had shot an albatross, and Orlando would say (half hiding her yawn) was an albatross as big as an elephant, and the Archduke would say – something very sensible, no doubt, but Orlando heard it not, for she was looking at her writing-table, out of the window, at the door. Upon which the Archduke would say, 'I adore you', at the very same moment that Orlando said 'Look, it's beginning to rain', at which they were both much embarrassed, and blushed scarlet, and could neither of them think what to say next. Indeed, Orlando was at her wit's end what to talk about and had she not bethought her of a game called Fly Loo,[21] at which great sums of money can be lost with very little expense of spirit, she would have had to marry him, she supposed; for how else to get rid of him she knew not. By this device, however, and it was a simple one, needing only three lumps of sugar and a sufficiency of flies, the embarrassment of conversation was overcome and the necessity of marriage avoided. For now, the Archduke would bet her five hundred pounds to a tester that a fly would settle on this lump and not on that. Thus, they would have occupation for a whole morning watching the flies (who were naturally sluggish at this season and often spent an hour or so circling round the ceiling) until at length some fine blue-bottle made his choice and the match was won. Many hundreds of pounds changed hands between them at this game, which the Archduke, who was a born gambler, swore was every bit as good as horse racing, and vowed he could play at for ever. But Orlando soon began to weary.

'What's the good of being a fine young woman in the prime of life', she asked, 'if I have to pass all my mornings watching blue-bottles with an Archduke?'

She began to detest the sight of sugar; flies made her dizzy. Some way out of the difficulty there must be, she supposed, but she was still awkward in the arts of her sex, and as she could no longer knock a man over the head or run him through the body with a rapier, she could think of no better method than this. She caught a blue-bottle, gently pressed the life out of it (it was half dead already, or her kindness for the dumb creatures would not have permitted it) and secured it by a drop of gum arabic to a lump of sugar. While the Archduke was gazing at the ceiling, she deftly substituted this lump for the one she had laid her money on, and crying 'Loo Loo!' declared that she had won her bet. Her reckoning was that the Archduke, with all his knowledge of sport and horse-racing, would detect the fraud and, as to cheat at Loo is the most heinous of crimes, and men have been banished from the society of mankind to that of apes in the tropics for ever because of it, she calculated that he would be manly enough to refuse to have anything further to do with her. But she misjudged the simplicity of the amiable nobleman. He was no nice judge of flies. A dead fly looked to him much the same as a living one. She played the trick twenty times on him and he paid her over £17,250 (which is about £40,885 : 6 : 8 of our own money) before Orlando cheated so grossly that even he could be deceived no longer. When he realised the truth at last, a painful scene ensued. The Archduke rose to his full height. He coloured scarlet. Tears rolled down his cheeks one by one. That she had won a fortune from him was nothing – she was welcome to it; that she had deceived him was something – it hurt him to think her capable of it; but that she had cheated at Loo was everything. To love a woman who cheated at play was, he said, impossible. Here he broke down completely. Happily, he said, recovering slightly, there were no witnesses. She was, after all, only a woman, he said. In short, he was preparing in the chivalry of his heart to forgive her and had bent to ask her pardon for the violence of his language, when she cut the matter short, as he stooped his proud head, by dropping a small toad between his skin and his shirt.

In justice to her, it must be said that she would infinitely have preferred a rapier. Toads are clammy things to conceal about one's person a whole morning. But if rapiers are forbidden, one must have recourse to toads. Moreover toads and laughter between them sometimes do what cold steel cannot. She laughed. The Archduke blushed. She laughed. The Archduke cursed. She laughed. The Archduke slammed the door.

'Heaven be praised!' cried Orlando still laughing. She heard the sound of chariot wheels driven at a furious pace down the courtyard. She heard them rattle along the road. Fainter and fainter the sound became. Now it faded away altogether.

'I am alone,' said Orlando, aloud since there was no one to hear.

That silence is more profound after noise still wants the confirmation of science. But that loneliness is more apparent directly after one has been made love to, many women would take their oath. As the sound of the Archduke's chariot wheels died away, Orlando felt drawing further from her and further from her an Archduke (she did not mind that), a fortune (she did not mind that), a title (she did not mind that), the safety and circumstance of married life (she did not mind that), but life she heard going from her, and a lover. 'Life and a lover,' she murmured; and going to her writing-table she dipped her pen in the ink and wrote:

'Life and a lover' – a line which did not scan and made no sense with what went before – something about the proper way of dipping sheep to avoid the scab.[22] Reading it over she blushed and repeated,

'Life and a lover.' Then laying her pen aside she went into her bedroom, stood in front of her mirror, and arranged her pearls about her neck. Then since pearls do not show to advantage against a morning gown of sprigged cotton, she changed to a dove-grey taffeta; thence to one of peach bloom; thence to a wine-coloured brocade. Perhaps a dash of powder was needed, and if her hair were disposed – so – about her brow, it might become her. Then she slipped her feet into pointed slippers, and drew an emerald ring upon her finger. 'Now,' she said when all was ready and lit the silver sconces on either side of the mirror. What woman would not have kindled to see what Orlando saw then burning in the snow – for all about the looking-glass were snowy lawns, and she was like a fire, a burning bush, and the candle flames about her head were silver leaves; or again, the glass was green water, and she a mermaid, slung with pearls, a siren in a cave, singing so that oarsmen leant from their boats and fell down, down to embrace her; so dark, so bright, so hard, so soft,[23] was she, so astonishingly seductive that it was a thousand pities that there was no one there to put it in plain English, and say outright, 'Damn it, Madam, you are loveliness incarnate,' which was the truth. Even Orlando (who had no conceit of her person) knew it, for she smiled the involuntary smile which women smile when their own beauty, which seems not their own, forms like a drop falling or a fountain rising [24] and confronts them all of a sudden in the glass – this smile she smiled and then she listened for a moment and heard only the leaves blowing and the sparrows twittering, and then she sighed, 'Life, a lover,' and then she turned on her heel with extraordinary rapidity; whipped her pearls from her neck, stripped the satins from her back, stood erect in the neat black silk knickerbockers of an ordinary nobleman, and rang the bell. When the servant came, she told him to order a coach and six to be in readiness instantly. She was summoned by urgent affairs to London. Within an hour of the Archduke's departure, off she drove. [25]

And as she drove, we may seize the opportunity, since the landscape was of a simple English kind which needs no description, to draw the reader's attention more particularly than we could at the moment to one or two remarks which have slipped in here and there in the course of the narrative. For example, it may have been observed that Orlando hid her manuscripts when interrupted. Next, that she looked long and intently in the glass; and now, as she drove to London, one might notice her starting and suppressing a cry when the horses galloped faster than she liked. Her modesty as to her writing, her vanity as to her person, her fears for her safety all seem to hint that what was said a short time ago about there being no change in Orlando the man and Orlando the woman, was ceasing to be altogether true. She was becoming a little more modest, as women are, of her brains, and a little more vain, as women are, of her person. Certain susceptibilities were asserting themselves, and others were diminishing. The change of clothes had, some philosophers will say, much to do with it. Vain trifles as they seem, clothes have, they say, more important offices than merely to keep us warm. They change our view of the world and the world's view of us. For example, when Captain Bartolus saw Orlando's skirt, he had an awning stretched for her immediately, pressed her to take another slice of beef, and invited her to go ashore with him in the long-boat. These compliments would certainly not have been paid her had her skirts, instead of flowing, been cut tight to her legs in the fashion of breeches. And when we are paid compliments, it behoves us to make some return. Orlando curtseyed; she complied; she flattered the good man's humours as she would not have done had his neat breeches been a woman's skirts, and his braided coat a woman's satin bodice. Thus, there is much to support the view that it is clothes that wear us and not we them; we may make them take the mould of arm or breast, but they mould our hearts, our brains, our tongues to their liking. So, having now worn skirts for a considerable time, a certain change was visible in Orlando, which is to be found if the reader will look at page 111, even in her face.[26] If we compare the picture of Orlando as a man with that of Orlando as a woman we shall see that though both are undoubtedly one and the same person, there are certain changes. The man has his hand free to seize his sword, the woman must use hers to keep the satins from slipping from her shoulders. The man looks the world full in the face, as if it were made for his uses and fashioned to his liking. The woman takes a sidelong glance at it, full of subtlety, even of suspicion. Had they both worn the same clothes, it is possible that their outlook might have been the same.

That is the view of some philosophers and wise ones, but on the whole, we incline to another. The difference between the sexes is, happily, one of great profundity. Clothes are but a symbol of something hid deep beneath. It was a change in Orlando herself that dictated her choice of a woman's dress and of a woman's sex. And perhaps in this she was only expressing rather more openly than usual – openness indeed was the soul of her nature – something that happens to most people without being thus plainly expressed. For here again, we come to a dilemma. Different though the sexes are, they intermix. In every human being a vacillation from one sex to the other takes place,

and often it is only the clothes that keep the male or female
likeness, while underneath the sex is the very opposite of what it
is above. Of the complications and confusions which thus result
everyone has had experience; but here we leave the general
question and note only the odd effect it had in the particular case
of Orlando herself.

For it was this mixture in her of man and woman, one being
uppermost and then the other, that often gave her conduct an
unexpected turn. The curious of her own sex would argue, for
example, if Orlando was a woman,[27] how did she never take
more than ten minutes to dress? And were not her clothes
chosen rather at random, and sometimes worn rather shabby?
And then they would say, still, she has none of the formality of a
man, or a man's love of power. She is excessively tender-hearted.
She could not endure to see a donkey beaten or a kitten drowned.
Yet again, they noted, she detested household matters, was up at
dawn and out among the fields in summer before the sun had
risen. No farmer knew more about the crops than she did. She
could drink with the best and liked games of hazard. She rode
well and drove six horses at a gallop over London Bridge. Yet
again, though bold and active as a man, it was remarked that the
sight of another in danger brought on the most womanly palpita-
tions. She would burst into tears on slight provocation. She was
unversed in geography, found mathematics intolerable, and held
some caprices which are more common among women than
men, as for instance that to travel south is to travel downhill.
Whether, then, Orlando was most man or woman, it is difficult
to say and cannot now be decided. For her coach was now
rattling on the cobbles. She had reached her home in the city.
The steps were being let down; the iron gates were being opened.
She was entering her father's house at Blackfriars, which, though
fashion was fast deserting that end of the town, was still a
pleasant, roomy mansion, with gardens running down to the
river, and a pleasant grove of nut trees to walk in.

Here she took up her lodging and began instantly to look about

her for what she had come in search of – that is to say, life and a
lover. About the first there might be some doubt; the second she
found without the least difficulty two days after her arrival. It
was a Tuesday that she came to town. On Thursday she went for
a walk in the Mall, as was then the habit of persons of quality.
She had not made more than a turn or two of the avenue before
she was observed by a little knot of vulgar people who go there
to spy upon their betters. As she came past them, a common
woman carrying a child at her breast stepped forward, peered
familiarly into Orlando's face, and cried out, 'Lawk upon us, if it
ain't the Lady Orlando!' Her companions came crowding round,
and Orlando found herself in a moment the centre of a mob of
staring citizens and tradesmen's wives, all eager to gaze upon the
heroine of the celebrated lawsuit.[28] Such was the interest that the
case excited in the minds of the common people. She might,
indeed, have found herself gravely discommoded by the pressure
of the crowd – she had forgotten that ladies are not supposed to
walk in public places alone – had not a tall gentleman at once
stepped forward and offered her the protection of his arm. It
was the Archduke. She was overcome with distress and yet with
some amusement at the sight. Not only had this magnanimous
nobleman forgiven her, but in order to show that he took her
levity with the toad in good part, he had procured a jewel made
in the shape of that reptile which he pressed upon her with a
repetition of his suit as he handed her to her coach.

What with the crowd, what with the Duke, what with the
jewel, she drove home in the vilest temper imaginable. Was it
impossible then to go for a walk without being half-suffocated,
presented with a toad set in emeralds, and asked in marriage by
an Archduke? She took a kinder view of the case next day when
she found on her breakfast table half a dozen billets[29] from some
of the greatest ladies in the land – Lady Suffolk, Lady Salisbury,
Lady Chesterfield, Lady Tavistock, and others who reminded
her in the politest manner of old alliances between their families
and her own, and desired the honour of her acquaintance. Next
day, which was a Saturday, many of these great ladies waited on

her in person. On Tuesday, about noon, their footmen brought cards of invitation to various routs,[30] dinners, and assemblies in the near future; so that Orlando was launched without delay, and with some splash and foam at that, upon the waters of London society.

To give a truthful account of London society at that or indeed at any other time, is beyond the powers of the biographer or the historian. Only those who have little need of the truth, and no respect for it – the poets and the novelists – can be trusted to do it, for this is one of the cases where the truth does not exist. Nothing exists. The whole thing is a miasma – a mirage. To make our meaning plain – Orlando would come home from one of these routs at three or four in the morning with cheeks like a Christmas tree and eyes like stars. She would untie a lace, pace the room a score of times, untie another lace, stop, and pace the room again. Often the sun would be blazing over Southwark chimneys before she could persuade herself to get into bed, and there she would lie, pitching and tossing, laughing and sighing for an hour or longer before she slept at last. And what was all this stir about? Society. And what had society said or done to throw a reasonable lady into such an excitement? In plain language, nothing. Rack her memory as she would, next day Orlando could never remember a single word to magnify into the name something. Lord O. had been gallant. Lord A. polite. The Marquis of C. charming. Mr. M. amusing. But when she tried to recollect in what their gallantry, politeness, charm, or wit had consisted, she was bound to suppose her memory at fault, for she could not name a thing. It was the same always. Nothing remained over the next day, yet the excitement of the moment was intense. Thus we are forced to conclude that society is one of those brews such as skilled housekeepers serve hot about Christmas time, whose flavour depends upon the proper mixing and stirring of a dozen different ingredients. Take one out, and it is in itself insipid. Take away Lord O., Lord A., Lord C., or Mr. M. and separately each is nothing. Stir them all together and they combine to give off the most intoxicating of flavours, the most seductive of scents. Yet this intoxication, this seductiveness, entirely evade our analysis. At one and the same time, therefore, society is everything and society is nothing. Society is the most powerful concoction in the world and society has no existence whatsoever. Such monsters the poets and the novelists alone can deal with; with such something-nothings their works are stuffed out to prodigious size; and to them with the best will in the world we are content to leave it.

Following the example of our predecessors, therefore, we will only say that society in the reign of Queen Anne[31] was of unparalleled brilliance. To have the entry there was the aim of every well-bred person. The graces were supreme. Fathers instructed their sons, mothers their daughters. No education was complete for either sex which did not include the science of deportment, the art of bowing and curtseying, the management of the sword and the fan, the care of the teeth, the conduct of the leg, the flexibility of the knee, the proper methods of entering and leaving the room, with a thousand etceteras, such as will immediately suggest themselves to anybody who has himself been in society. Since Orlando had won the praise of Queen Elizabeth for the way she handed a bowl of rose water as a boy, it must be supposed that she was sufficiently expert to pass muster. Yet it is true that there was an absent-mindedess about her which sometimes made her clumsy; she was apt to think of poetry when she should have been thinking of taffeta; her walk was a little too much of a stride for a woman, perhaps, and her gestures, being abrupt, might endanger a cup of tea on occasion.

Whether this slight disability was enough to counterbalance the splendour of her bearing, or whether she inherited a drop too much of that black humour which ran in the veins of all her race, certain it is that she had not been in the world more than a score of times before she might have been heard to ask herself, had there been anybody but her spaniel Pippin[32] to hear her, 'What the devil is the matter with me?' The occasion was Tuesday, the 16th of June 1712; she had just returned from a great ball at Arlington House; the dawn was in the sky, and she was pulling off her stockings. 'I don't care if I never meet another soul as long as I live,' cried Orlando, bursting into tears. Lovers she had in plenty, but life, which is, after all, of some importance in its way, escaped her. 'Is this', she asked – but there was none to answer, 'is this', she finished her sentence all the same, 'what people call life?' The spaniel raised her forepaw in token of sympathy. The spaniel licked Orlando with her tongue. Orlando stroked the spaniel with her hand. Orlando kissed the spaniel with her lips. In short, there was the truest sympathy between them that can be between a dog and its mistress, and yet it cannot be denied that the dumbness of animals is a great impediment to the refinements of intercourse. They wag their tails; they bow the front part of the body and elevate the hind; they roll, they jump, they paw, they whine, they bark, they slobber, they have all sorts of ceremonies and artifices of their own, but the whole thing is of no avail, since speak they cannot. Such was her quarrel, she thought, setting the dog gently on to the floor, with the great people at Arlington House. They, too, wag their tails, bow, roll, jump, paw, and slobber, but talk they cannot. 'All these months that I've been out in the world', said Orlando, pitching one stocking across the room, 'I've heard nothing but what Pippin might have said. I'm cold. I'm happy. I'm hungry. I've caught a mouse. I've buried a bone. Please kiss my nose.' And it was not enough.

How, in so short a time, she had passed from intoxication to disgust we will only seek to explain by supposing that this mysterious composition which we call society, is nothing absolutely good or bad in itself, but has a spirit in it, volatile but potent, which either makes you drunk when you think it, as Orlando thought it, delightful, or gives you a headache when you think it, as Orlando thought it, repulsive. That the faculty of speech has much to do with it either way, we take leave to doubt. Often a dumb hour is the most ravishing of all; brilliant wit can be tedious beyond description. But to the poets we leave it, and so on with our story.

Orlando threw the second stocking after the first and went to bed dismally enough, determined that she would forswear society for ever. But again as it turned out, she was too hasty in coming to her conclusions. For the very next morning she woke to find, among the usual cards of invitation upon her table, one from a certain great Lady, the Countess of R. Having determined overnight that she would never go into society again, we can only explain Orlando's behaviour – she sent a messenger hot-foot to R— House to say that she would attend her Ladyship with all the pleasure in the world – by the fact that she was still suffering from the effect of three honeyed words dropped into her ear on the deck of the *Enamoured Lady* by Captain Nicholas Benedict Bartolus as they sailed down the Thames. Addison, Dryden, Pope, he had said, pointing to the Cocoa Tree, and Addison, Dryden, Pope had chimed in her head like an incantation ever since. Who can credit such folly? but so it was. All her experience with Nick Greene had taught her nothing. Such names still exercised over her the most powerful fascination. Something, perhaps, we must believe in, and as Orlando, we have said, had no belief in the usual divinities she bestowed her credulity upon great men – yet with a distinction. Admirals, soldiers, statesmen, moved her not at all. But the very thought of a great writer stirred her to such a pitch of belief that she almost believed him to be invisible.[33] Her instinct was a sound one. One can only believe entirely, perhaps, in what one cannot see. The little glimpse she had of these great men from the deck of the ship was of the nature of a vision. That the cup was china, or the gazette paper, she doubted. When Lord O. said one day that he had dined with Dryden the night before, she flatly disbelieved him. Now, the Lady R.'s reception room had the reputation of being the antechamber to the presence room of genius; it was the place where men and women met to swing censers and chant hymns to the bust of genius in a niche in the wall. Sometimes the God himself vouchsafed his presence for a moment. Intellect alone admitted the suppliant, and nothing (so the report ran) was said inside that was not witty.

It was thus with great trepidation that Orlando entered the

room. She found a company already assembled in a semicircle round the fire. Lady R., an oldish lady, of dark complexion, with a black lace mantilla on her head, was seated in a great arm-chair in the centre. Thus being somewhat deaf, she could control the conversation on both sides of her. On both sides of her sat men and women of the highest distinction. Every man, it was said, had been a Prime Minister and every woman, it was whispered, had been the mistress of a king. Certain it is that all were brilliant, and all were famous. Orlando took her seat with a deep reverence in silence ... After three hours, she curtseyed profoundly and left.

But what, the reader may ask with some exasperation, happened in between? In three hours, such a company must have said the wittiest, the profoundest, the most interesting things in the world. So it would seem indeed. But the fact appears to be that they said nothing. It is a curious characteristic which they share with all the most brilliant societies that the world has seen. Old Madame du Deffand[34] and her friends talked for fifty years without stopping. And of it all, what remains? Perhaps three witty sayings. So that we are at liberty to suppose either that nothing was said, or that nothing witty was said, or that the fraction of three witty sayings lasted eighteen thousand two hundred and fifty nights, which does not leave a liberal allowance of wit for any one of them.

The truth would seem to be – if we dare use such a word in such a connection – that all these groups of people lie under an enchantment. The hostess is our modern Sibyl.[35] She is a witch who lays her guests under a spell. In this house they think themselves happy; in that witty; in a third profound. It is all an illusion (which is nothing against it, for illusions are the most valuable and necessary of all things, and she who can create one is among the world's greatest benefactors), but as it is notorious that illusions are shattered by conflict with reality, so no real happiness, no real wit, no real profundity are tolerated where the illusion prevails. This serves to explain why Madame du Deffand said no more than three witty things in the course of fifty years.

Had she said more, her circle would have been destroyed. The witticism, as it left her lips, bowled over the current conversation as a cannon ball lays low the violets and the daisies. When she made her famous 'mot de Saint Denis' the very grass was singed. Disillusionment and desolation followed. Not a word was uttered. 'Spare us another such, for Heaven's sake, Madame!' her friends cried with one accord. And she obeyed. For almost seventeen years she said nothing memorable and all went well. The beautiful counterpane of illusion lay unbroken on her circle as it lay unbroken on the circle of Lady R. The guests thought that they were happy, thought that they were witty, thought that they were profound, and, as they thought this, other people thought it still more strongly; and so it got about that nothing was more delightful than one of Lady R.'s assemblies; everyone envied those who were admitted; those who were admitted envied themselves because other people envied them; and so there seemed no end to it – except that which we have now to relate.

For about the third time Orlando went there a certain incident occurred. She was still under the illusion that she was listening to the most brilliant epigrams in the world, though, as a matter of fact, old General C. was only saying, at some length, how the gout had left his left leg and gone to his right, while Mr. L. interrupted when any proper name was mentioned, 'R.? Oh! I know Billy R. as well as I know myself. S.? My dearest friend. T.? Stayed with him a fortnight in Yorkshire' – which, such is the force of illusion, sounded like the wittiest repartee, the most searching comment upon human life, and kept the company in a roar; when the door opened and a little gentleman entered whose name Orlando did not catch. Soon a curiously disagreeable sensation came over her. To judge from their faces, the rest began to feel it as well. One gentleman said there was a draught. The Marchioness of C. feared a cat must be under the sofa. It was as if their eyes were being slowly opened after a pleasant dream and nothing met them but a cheap wash-stand and a dirty counterpane. It was as if the fumes of some delicious wine were slowly leaving them. Still the General talked and still Mr. L. remembered. But it became more and more apparent how red the General's neck was, how bald Mr. L.'s head was. As for what they said – nothing more tedious and trivial could be imagined. Everybody fidgeted and those who had fans yawned behind them. At last Lady R. rapped with hers upon the arm of her great chair. Both gentlemen stopped talking.

Then the little gentleman said,

He said next,

He said finally,*

Here, it cannot be denied, was true wit, true wisdom, true profundity. The company was thrown into complete dismay. One such saying was bad enough; but three, one after another, on the same evening! No society could survive it.

'Mr. Pope,' said old Lady R. in a voice trembling with sarcastic fury, 'you are pleased to be witty.' Mr. Pope flushed red. Nobody spoke a word. They sat in dead silence some twenty minutes. Then, one by one, they rose and slunk from the room. That they would ever come back after such an experience was doubtful. Link-boys[36] could be heard calling their coaches all down South Audley Street. Doors were slammed and carriages drove off. Orlando found herself near Mr. Pope on the staircase. His lean and misshapen frame was shaken by a variety of emotions. Darts of malice, rage, triumph, wit, and terror (he was shaking like a leaf) shot from his eyes. He looked like some squat reptile set with a burning topaz in its forehead. At the same time, the strangest tempest of emotion seized now upon the luckless Orlando. A disillusionment so complete as that inflicted not an hour ago leaves the mind rocking from side to side. Everything appears ten times more bare and stark than before. It is a moment fraught with the highest danger for the human spirit. Women turn nuns and men priests in such moments. In such moments, rich men sign away their wealth; and happy men cut their throats

---

* These sayings are too well known to require repetition, and besides, they are all to be found in his published works.

with carving knives. Orlando would have done all willingly, but there was a rasher thing still for her to do, and this she did. She invited Mr. Pope to come home with her.

For if it is rash to walk into a lion's den unarmed, rash to navigate the Atlantic in a rowing boat, rash to stand on one foot on the top of St. Paul's, it is still more rash to go home alone with a poet. A poet is Atlantic and lion in one. While one drowns us the other gnaws us. If we survive the teeth, we succumb to the waves. A man who can destroy illusions is both beast and flood. Illusions are to the soul what atmosphere is to the earth. Roll up that tender air and the plant dies, the colour fades. The earth we walk on is a parched cinder. It is marl we tread and fiery cobbles scorch our feet. By the truth we are undone. Life is a dream. 'Tis waking that kills us. He who robs us of our dreams robs us of our life – (and so on for six pages if you will, but the style is tedious and may well be dropped).

On this showing, however, Orlando should have been a heap of cinders by the time the chariot drew up at her house in Blackfriars. That she was still flesh and blood, though certainly exhausted, is entirely due to a fact to which we drew attention earlier in the narrative. The less we see the more we believe. Now the streets that lie between Mayfair and Blackfriars were at that time very imperfectly lit. True, the lighting was a great improvement upon that of the Elizabethan age. Then the benighted traveller had to trust to the stars or the red flame of some night watchman to save him from the gravel pits at Park Lane or the oak woods where swine rootled in the Tottenham Court Road. But even so it wanted much of our modern efficiency. Lamp-posts lit with oil-lamps occurred every two hundred yards or so, but between lay a considerable stretch of pitch darkness. Thus for ten minutes Orlando and Mr. Pope would be in blackness; and then for about half a minute again in the light. A very strange state of mind was thus bred in Orlando. As the light faded, she began to feel steal over her the most delicious balm. 'This is indeed a very great honour for a young woman, to be driving with Mr. Pope,' she began to think, looking at the outline of his nose. 'I am the most blessed of my sex. Half an inch from me – indeed, I feel the knot of his knee ribbons pressing against my thigh – is the greatest wit in Her Majesty's dominions. Future ages will think of us with curiosity and envy me with fury.' Here came the lamp-post again. 'What a foolish wretch I am!' she thought. 'There is no such thing as fame and glory. Ages to come will never cast a thought on me or on Mr. Pope either. What's an "age", indeed? What are "we"?' and their progress through Berkeley Square seemed the groping of two blind ants, momentarily thrown together without interest or concern in common, across a blackened desert. She shivered. But here again was darkness. Her illusion revived. 'How noble his brow is,' she thought (mistaking a hump on a cushion for Mr. Pope's forehead in the darkness). 'What a weight of genius lives in it! What wit, wisdom, and truth – what a wealth of all those jewels, indeed, for which people are ready to barter their lives! Yours is the only light that burns for ever. But for you the human pilgrimage would be performed in utter darkness'; (here the coach gave a great lurch as it fell into a rut in Park Lane) 'without genius we should be upset and undone. Most august, most lucid of beams' – thus she was apostrophising the hump on the cushion when they drove beneath one of the street lamps in Berkeley Square and she realised her mistake. Mr. Pope had a forehead no bigger than another man's. 'Wretched man,' she thought, 'how you have deceived me! I took that hump for your forehead. When one sees you plain, how ignoble, how despicable you are! Deformed and weakly, there is nothing to venerate in you, much to pity, most to despise.'

Again they were in darkness and her anger became modified directly she could see nothing but the poet's knees.

'But it is I that am a wretch,' she reflected, once they were in complete obscurity again, 'for base as you may be, am I not still baser? It is you who nourish and protect me, you who scare the wild beast, frighten the savage, make me clothes of the silk-worm's wool, and carpets of the sheep's. If I want to worship, have you not provided me with an image of yourself and set it in the sky? Are not evidences of your care everywhere? How humble, how grateful, how docile, should I not be, therefore? Let it be all my joy to serve, honour, and obey you.'

Here they reached the big lamp-post at the corner of what is now Piccadilly Circus. The light blazed in her eyes, and she saw, besides some degraded creatures of her own sex,[37] two wretched pigmies on a stark desert land. Both were naked, solitary, and defenceless. The one was powerless to help the other. Each had enough to do to look after itself. Looking Mr. Pope full in the face, 'It is equally vain', she thought, 'for you to think you can protect me, or for me to think I can worship you. The light of truth beats upon us without shadow, and the light of truth is damnably unbecoming to us both.'

All this time, of course, they went on talking agreeably, as people of birth and education use, about the Queen's temper and the Prime Minister's gout, while the coach went from light to darkness down the Haymarket, along the Strand, up Fleet Street, and reached, at length, her house in Blackfriars. For some time the dark spaces between the lamps had been becoming brighter and the lamps themselves less bright – that is to say, the sun was rising, and it was in the equable but confused light of a summer's morning in which everything is seen but nothing is seen distinctly that they alighted, Mr. Pope handing Orlando from her carriage and Orlando curtseying Mr. Pope to precede her into her mansion with the most scrupulous attention to the rites of the Graces.

From the foregoing passage, however, it must not be supposed that genius (but the disease is now stamped out in the British Isles, the late Lord Tennyson, it is said, being the last person to suffer from it) is constantly alight, for then we should see everything plain and perhaps should be scorched to death in the process. Rather it resembles the lighthouse in its working, which sends one ray and then no more for a time; save that genius is much more capricious in its manifestations and may flash six or seven beams in quick succession (as Mr. Pope did that night) and then lapse into darkness for a year or for ever. To steer by

its beams is therefore impossible, and when the dark spell is on
them men of genius are, it is said, much like other people.

It was happy for Orlando, though at first disappointing, that
this should be so, for she now began to live much in the company
of men of genius. Nor were they so different from the rest of us
as one might have supposed. Addison, Pope, Swift, proved, she
found, to be fond of tea. They liked arbours. They collected
little bits of coloured glass. They adored grottos. Rank was not
distasteful to them. Praise was delightful. They wore plum-
coloured suits one day and grey another. Mr. Swift had a fine
malacca cane. Mr. Addison scented his handkerchiefs. Mr. Pope
suffered with his head. A piece of gossip did not come amiss.
Nor were they without their jealousies. (We are jotting down a
few reflections that came to Orlando higgledy-piggledy.) At first,
she was annoyed with herself for noticing such trifles, and kept a
book in which to write down their memorable sayings, but the
page remained empty. All the same, her spirits revived, and she
took to tearing up her cards of invitation to great parties; kept
her evenings free; began to look forward to Mr. Pope's visit, to
Mr. Addison's, to Mr. Swift's – and so on and so on. If the
reader will here refer to the *Rape of the Lock*, to the *Spectator*, to
Gulliver's Travels, he will understand precisely what these mysterious words may mean. Indeed, biographers and critics might save
themselves all their labours if readers would only take this advice.
For when we read:

> Whether the Nymph shall break Diana's Law,
> Or some frail China Jar receive a Flaw,
> Or stain her Honour, or her new Brocade,
> Forget her Pray'rs or miss a Masquerade,
> Or lose her Heart, or Necklace, at a Ball.[38]

– we know as if we heard him how Mr. Pope's tongue flickered
like a lizard's, how his eyes flashed, how his hand trembled, how
he loved, how he lied, how he suffered. In short, every secret of
a writer's soul, every experience of his life, every quality of his
mind is written large in his works, yet we require critics to

explain the one and biographers to expound the other. That time hangs heavy on people's hands is the only explanation of the monstrous growth.

So, now that we have read a page or two of the *Rape of the Lock*, we know exactly why Orlando was so much amused and so much frightened and so very bright-cheeked and bright-eyed that afternoon.

Mrs. Nelly then knocked at the door to say that Mr. Addison waited on her Ladyship. At this, Mr. Pope got up with a wry smile, made his congee,[39] and limped off. In came Mr. Addison. Let us, as he takes his seat, read the following passage from the *Spectator*:[40]

'I consider woman as a beautiful, romantic animal, that may be adorned with furs and feathers, pearls and diamonds, ores and silks. The lynx shall cast its skin at her feet to make her a tippet, the peacock, parrot and swan shall pay contributions to her muff; the sea shall be searched for shells, and the rocks for gems, and every part of nature furnish out its share towards the embellishment of a creature that is the most consummate work of it. All this, I shall indulge them in, but as for the petticoat I have been speaking of, I neither can, nor will allow it.'

We hold that gentleman, cocked hat and all, in the hollow of our hands. Look once more into the crystal. Is he not clear to the very wrinkle in his stocking? Does not every ripple and curve of his wit lie exposed before us, and his benignity and his timidity and his urbanity and the fact that he would marry a Countess and die very respectably in the end? All is clear. And when Mr. Addison has said his say, there is a terrific rap at the door, and Mr. Swift, who had these arbitrary ways with him, walks in unannounced. One moment, where is *Gulliver's Travels*?[41] Here it is! Let us read a passage from the voyage to the Houyhnhnms:

'I enjoyed perfect Health of Body and Tranquillity of Mind; I did not find the Treachery or Inconstancy of a Friend, nor the Injuries of a secret or open Enemy. I had no occasion of bribing, flattering or pimping, to procure the Favour of any great Man or of his Minion. I wanted no Fence against Fraud or Oppression; Here was neither Physician to destroy my Body, nor Lawyer to ruin my Fortune; No Informer to watch my Words, and Actions, or forge Accusations against me for Hire: Here were no Gibers, Censurers, Backbiters, Pickpockets, Highwaymen, House-breakers, Attorneys, Bawds, Buffoons, Gamesters, Politicians, Wits, splenetick tedious Talkers . . .'

But stop, stop your iron pelt of words, lest you flay us all alive, and yourself too! Nothing can be plainer than that violent man. He is so coarse and yet so clean; so brutal, yet so kind; scorns the whole world, yet talks baby language to a girl, and will die, can we doubt it? in a madhouse.

So Orlando poured out tea for them all; and sometimes, when the weather was fine, she carried them down to the country with her, and feasted them royally in the Round Parlour,[42] which she had hung with their pictures all in a circle, so that Mr. Pope could not say that Mr. Addison came before him, or the other way about. They were very witty, too (but their wit is all in their books), and taught her the most important part of style, which is the natural run of the voice in speaking – a quality which none that has not heard it can imitate, not Greene even, with all his skill; for it is born of the air, and breaks like a wave on the furniture, and rolls and fades away, and is never to be recaptured, least of all by those who prick up their ears, half a century later, and try. They taught her this, merely by the cadence of their voices in speech; so that her style changed somewhat, and she wrote some very pleasant, witty verses and characters in prose. And so she lavished her wine on them and put bank-notes, which they took very kindly, beneath their plates at dinner,[43] and accepted their dedications, and thought herself highly honoured by the exchange.

Thus time ran on, and Orlando could often be heard saying to herself with an emphasis which might, perhaps, make the hearer a little suspicious, 'Upon my soul, what a life this is!' (For she was still in search of that commodity.) But circumstances soon forced her to consider the matter more narrowly.

One day she was pouring out tea for Mr. Pope while, as anyone can tell from the verses quoted above, he sat very bright-eyed, observant, and all crumpled up in a chair by her side.

'Lord,' she thought, as she raised the sugar tongs, 'how women in ages to come will envy me! And yet—' she paused; for Mr. Pope needed her attention. And yet – let us finish her thought for her – when anybody says 'How future ages will envy me', it is safe to say that they are extremely uneasy at the present moment. Was this life quite so exciting, quite so flattering, quite so glorious as it sounds when the memoir writer has done his work upon it? For one thing, Orlando had a positive hatred of tea; for another, the intellect, divine as it is, and all-worshipful, has a habit of lodging in the most seedy of carcases, and often, alas, acts the cannibal among the other faculties so that often, where the Mind is biggest, the Heart, the Senses, Magnanimity, Charity, Tolerance, Kindliness, and the rest of them scarcely have room to breathe. Then the high opinion poets have of themselves; then the low one they have of others; then the enmities, injuries, envies, and repartees in which they are constantly engaged; then the volubility with which they impart them; then the rapacity with which they demand sympathy for them; all this, one may whisper, lest the wits may overhear us, makes pouring out tea a more precarious and, indeed, arduous occupation than is generally allowed. Added to which (we whisper again lest the women may overhear us), there is a little secret which men share among them; Lord Chesterfield[44] whispered it to his son with strict injunctions to secrecy, 'Women are but children of a larger growth . . . A man of sense only trifles with them, plays with them, humours and flatters them', which, since children always hear what they are not meant to, and sometimes, even, grow up, may have somehow leaked out, so that the whole ceremony of pouring out tea is a curious one. A woman knows very well that, though a wit sends her his poems, praises her judgment, solicits her criticism, and drinks her tea, this by no means signifies that he respects her opinions, admires her understanding, or will refuse, though the rapier is denied him, to run

her through the body with his pen. All this, we say, whisper it as
low as we can, may have leaked out by now; so that even with
the cream jug suspended and the sugar tongs distended the
ladies may fidget a little, look out of the window a little, yawn a
little, and so let the sugar fall with a great plop – as Orlando did
now – into Mr. Pope's tea. Never was any mortal so ready to
suspect an insult or so quick to avenge one as Mr. Pope. He
turned to Orlando and presented her instantly with the rough
draught of a certain famous line in the 'Characters of Women'.[45]
Much polish was afterwards bestowed on it, but even in the
original it was striking enough. Orlando received it with a curtsey. Mr. Pope left her with a bow. Orlando, to cool her cheeks,
for really she felt as if the little man had struck her, strolled in
the nut grove at the bottom of the garden. Soon the cool breezes
did their work. To her amazement she found that she was hugely
relieved to find herself alone. She watched the merry boatloads
rowing up the river. No doubt the sight put her in mind of one
or two incidents in her past life. She sat herself down in profound
meditation beneath a fine willow tree. There she sat till the stars
were in the sky. Then she rose, turned, and went into the house,
where she sought her bedroom and locked the door. Now she
opened a cupboard in which hung still many of the clothes she
had worn as a young man of fashion, and from among them
she chose a black velvet suit richly trimmed with Venetian lace. It
was a little out of fashion, indeed, but it fitted her to perfection
and dressed in it she looked the very figure of a noble Lord. She
took a turn or two before the mirror to make sure that her
petticoats had not lost her the freedom of her legs, and then let
herself secretly out of doors.

It was a fine night early in April. A myriad stars mingling
with the light of a sickle moon, which again was enforced by the
street lamps, made a light infinitely becoming to the human
countenance and to the architecture of Mr. Wren. Everything
appeared in its tenderest form, yet, just as it seemed on the point
of dissolution, some drop of silver sharpened it to animation.
Thus it was that talk should be, thought Orlando (indulging in

foolish reverie); that society should be, that friendship should be, that love should be. For, Heaven knows why, just as we have lost faith in human intercourse some random collocation of barns and trees or a haystack and a waggon presents us with so perfect a symbol of what is unattainable that we begin the search again.

She entered Leicester Square as she made these observations. The buildings had an airy yet formal symmetry not theirs by day. The canopy of the sky seemed most dexterously washed in to fill up the outline of roof and chimney. A young woman who sat dejectedly with one arm drooping by her side, the other reposing in her lap, on a seat beneath a plane tree in the middle of the square seemed the very figure of grace, simplicity, and desolation. Orlando swept her hat off to her in the manner of a gallant paying his addresses to a lady of fashion in a public place. The young woman raised her head. It was of the most exquisite shapeliness. The young woman raised her eyes. Orlando saw them to be of a lustre such as is sometimes seen on teapots but rarely in a human face. Through this silver glaze the young woman looked up at him (for a man he was to her) appealing, hoping, trembling, fearing. She rose; she accepted his arm. For – need we stress the point? – she was of the tribe which nightly burnishes their wares, and sets them in order on the common counter to wait the highest bidder. She led Orlando to the room in Gerrard Street which was her lodging. To feel her hanging lightly yet like a suppliant on her arm, roused in Orlando all the feelings which become a man. She looked, she felt, she talked like one. Yet, having been so lately a woman herself, she suspected that the girl's timidity and her hesitating answers and the very fumbling with the key in the latch and the fold of her cloak and the droop of her wrist were all put on to gratify her masculinity. Upstairs they went, and the pains which the poor creature had been at to decorate her room and hide the fact that she had no other deceived Orlando not a moment. The deception roused her scorn; the truth roused her pity. One thing showing through the other bred the oddest assortment of feeling, so that she did not know whether to laugh or to cry. Meanwhile Nell, as the girl called herself, unbuttoned her gloves; carefully concealed the left-hand thumb, which wanted mending; then drew behind a screen, where, perhaps, she rouged her cheeks, arranged her clothes, fixed a new kerchief round her neck – all the time prattling as women do, to amuse her lover, though Orlando could have sworn, from the tone of her voice, that her thoughts were elsewhere. When all was ready, out she came, prepared – but here Orlando could stand it no longer. In the strangest torment of anger, merriment, and pity she flung off all disguise and admitted herself a woman.

At this, Nell burst into such a roar of laughter as might have been heard across the way.

'Well, my dear,' she said, when she had somewhat recovered, 'I'm by no means sorry to hear it. For the plain Dunstable of the matter [46] is' (and it was remarkable how soon, on discovering that they were of the same sex, her manner changed and she dropped her plaintive, appealing ways), 'the plain Dunstable of the matter is, that I'm not in the mood for the society of the other sex to-night. Indeed, I'm in the devil of a fix.' Whereupon, drawing up the fire and stirring a bowl of punch, she told Orlando the whole story of her life. Since it is Orlando's life that engages us at present, we need not relate the adventures of the other lady, but it is certain that Orlando had never known the hours speed faster or more merrily, though Mistress Nell had not a particle of wit about her, and when the name of Mr. Pope came up in talk asked innocently if he were connected with the perruque maker of that name in Jermyn Street. Yet, to Orlando, such is the charm of ease and the seduction of beauty, this poor girl's talk, larded though it was with the commonest expressions of the street corners, tasted like wine after the fine phrases she had been used to, and she was forced to the conclusion that there was something in the sneer of Mr. Pope, in the condescension of Mr. Addison, and in the secret of Lord Chesterfield which took away her relish for the society of wits, deeply though she must continue to respect their works.

These poor creatures, she ascertained, for Nell brought Prue, and Prue Kitty, and Kitty Rose, had a society of their own of which they now elected her a member. Each would tell the story of the adventures which had landed her in her present way of life. Several were the natural daughters of earls and one was a good deal nearer than she should have been to the King's person. None was too wretched or too poor but to have some ring or handkerchief in her pocket which stood her in lieu of pedigree. So they would draw round the punch-bowl which Orlando made it her business to furnish generously, and many were the fine tales they told and many the amusing observations they made, for it cannot be denied that when women get together – but hist – they are always careful to see that the doors are shut and that not a word of it gets into print. All they desire is – but hist again – is that not a man's step on the stair? All they desire, we were about to say when the gentleman took the very words out of our mouths. Women have no desires, says this gentleman, coming into Nell's parlour; only affectations. Without desires (she has served him and he is gone) their conversation cannot be of the slightest interest to anyone. 'It is well known,' says Mr. S. W., 'that when they lack the stimulus of the other sex, women can find nothing to say to each other. When they are alone, they do not talk, they scratch.' And since they cannot talk together and scratching cannot continue without interruption and it is well known (Mr. T. R. has proved it) 'that women are incapable of any feeling of affection for their own sex and hold each other in the greatest aversion', what can we suppose that women do when they seek out each other's society? [47]

As that is not a question that can engage the attention of a sensible man, let us, who enjoy the immunity of all biographers and historians from any sex whatever, pass it over, and merely state that Orlando professed great enjoyment in the society of her own sex, and leave it to the gentlemen to prove, as they are very fond of doing, that this is impossible.

But to give an exact and particular account of Orlando's life at this time becomes more and more out of the question. As we peer and grope in the ill-lit, ill-paved, ill-ventilated courtyards that lay about Gerrard Street and Drury Lane at that time, we seem now to catch sight of her and then again to lose it. The task is made still more difficult by the fact that she found it convenient at this time to change frequently from one set of clothes to another. Thus she often occurs in contemporary memoirs as 'Lord' So-and-so, who was in fact her cousin; her bounty is ascribed to him, and it is he who is said to have written the poems that were really hers. She had, it seems, no difficulty in sustaining the different parts, for her sex changed far more frequently than those who have worn only one set of clothing can conceive; nor can there be any doubt that she reaped a twofold harvest by this device; the pleasures of life were increased and its experiences multiplied. For the probity of breeches she exchanged the seductiveness of petticoats and enjoyed the love of both sexes equally.

So then one may sketch her spending her morning in a China robe of ambiguous gender among her books; then receiving a client or two (for she had many scores of suppliants) in the same garment; then she would take a turn in the garden and clip the nut trees[48] – for which knee-breeches were convenient; then she would change into a flowered taffeta which best suited a drive to Richmond and a proposal of marriage from some great nobleman; and so back again to town, where she would don a snuff-coloured gown like a lawyer's and visit the courts to hear how her cases were doing – for her fortune was wasting hourly and the suits seemed no nearer consummation than they had been a hundred years ago; and so, finally, when night came, she would more often than not become a nobleman complete from head to toe and walk the streets in search of adventure.

Returning from some of these junketings – of which there were many stories told at the time, as, that she fought a duel, served on one of the King's ships as a captain, was seen to dance naked on a balcony, and fled with a certain lady to the Low Countries where the lady's husband followed them[49] – but of the truth or otherwise of these stories, we express no opinion –

returning from whatever her occupation may have been, she made a point sometimes of passing beneath the windows of a coffee house, where she could see the wits without being seen, and thus could fancy from their gestures what wise, witty, or spiteful things they were saying without hearing a word of them; which was perhaps an advantage; and once she stood half an hour watching three shadows on the blind drinking tea together in a house in Bolt Court.

Never was any play so absorbing. She wanted to cry out, Bravo! Bravo! For, to be sure, what a fine drama it was – what a page torn from the thickest volume of human life! There was the little shadow with the pouting lips, fidgeting this way and that on his chair, uneasy, petulant, officious; there was the bent female shadow, crooking a finger in the cup to feel how deep the tea was, for she was blind; and there was the Roman-looking rolling shadow in the big arm-chair – he who twisted his fingers so oddly and jerked his head from side to side and swallowed down the tea in such vast gulps. Dr. Johnson, Mr. Boswell, and Mrs. Williams – those were the shadows' names.[50] So absorbed was she in the sight, that she forgot to think how other ages would have envied her, though it seems probable that on this occasion they would. She was content to gaze and gaze. At length Mr. Boswell rose. He saluted the old woman with tart asperity. But with what humility did he not abase himself before the great Roman shadow, who now rose to its full height and rocking somewhat as he stood there rolled out the most magnificent phrases that ever left human lips; so Orlando thought them, though she never heard a word that any of the three shadows said as they sat there drinking tea.

At length she came home one night after one of these saunterings and mounted to her bedroom. She took off her laced coat and stood there in shirt and breeches looking out of the window. There was something stirring in the air which forbade her to go to bed. A white haze lay over the town, for it was a frosty night in midwinter and a magnificent vista lay all round her. She could see St. Paul's, the Tower, Westminster Abbey, with all the spires and domes of the city churches, the smooth bulk of its banks, the opulent and ample curves of its halls and meeting-places. On the north rose the smooth, shorn heights of Hampstead, and in the west the streets and squares of Mayfair shone out in one clear radiance. Upon this serene and orderly prospect the stars looked down, glittering, positive, hard, from a cloudless sky. In the extreme clearness of the atmosphere the line of every roof, the cowl of every chimney was perceptible; even the cobbles in the streets showed distinct one from another, and Orlando could not help comparing this orderly scene with the irregular and huddled purlieus which had been the city of London in the reign of Queen Elizabeth. Then, she remembered, the city, if such one could call it, lay crowded, a mere huddle and conglomeration of houses, under her windows at Blackfriars. The stars reflected themselves in deep pits of stagnant water which lay in the middle of the streets. A black shadow at the corner where the wine shop used to stand was, as likely as not, the corpse of a murdered man. She could remember the cries of many a one wounded in such night brawlings, when she was a little boy, held to the diamond-paned window in her nurse's arms. Troops of ruffians, men and women, unspeakably interlaced, lurched down the streets, trolling out wild songs with jewels flashing in their ears, and knives gleaming in their fists. On such a night as this the impermeable tangle of the forests on Highgate and Hampstead would be outlined, writhing in contorted intricacy against the sky. Here and there, on one of the hills which rose above London, was a stark gallows tree, with a corpse nailed to rot or parch on its cross; for danger and insecurity, lust and violence, poetry and filth swarmed over the tortuous Elizabethan highways and buzzed and stank – Orlando could remember even now the smell of them on a hot night – in the little rooms and narrow pathways of the city. Now – she leant out of her window – all was light, order, and serenity.[51] There was the faint rattle of a coach on the cobbles. She heard the far-away cry of the night watchman – 'Just twelve o'clock on a frosty morning'. No sooner had the words left his lips than the first stroke of midnight sounded. Orlando then for the first time noticed a small cloud gathered behind the dome of St. Paul's. As the strokes sounded, the cloud increased, and she saw it darken and spread with extraordinary speed. At the same time a light breeze rose and by the time the sixth stroke of midnight had struck the whole of the eastern sky was covered with an irregular moving darkness, though the sky to the west and north stayed clear as ever. Then the cloud spread north. Height upon height above the city was engulfed by it. Only Mayfair, with all its lights shining, burnt more brilliantly than ever by contrast. With the eighth stroke, some hurrying tatters of cloud sprawled over Piccadilly. They seemed to mass themselves and to advance with extraordinary rapidity towards the west end. As the ninth, tenth, and eleventh strokes struck, a huge blackness sprawled over the whole of London. With the twelfth stroke of midnight, the darkness was complete. A turbulent welter of cloud covered the city. All was darkness; all was doubt; all was confusion. The Eighteenth century was over; the Nineteenth century had begun.

Chapter V

The great cloud which hung, not only over London, but over the whole of the British Isles on the first day of the nineteenth century stayed, or rather, did not stay, for it was buffeted about constantly by blustering gales, long enough to have extraordinary consequences upon those who lived beneath its shadow. A change seemed to have come over the climate of England. Rain fell frequently, but only in fitful gusts, which were no sooner over than they began again. The sun shone, of course, but it was so girt about with clouds and the air was so saturated with water, that its beams were discoloured and purples, oranges, and reds of a dull sort took the place of the more positive landscapes of the eighteenth century. Under this bruised and sullen canopy the green of the cabbages was less intense, and the white of the snow was muddied. But what was worse, damp now began to make its way into every house – damp, which is the most insidious of all enemies, for while the sun can be shut out by blinds, and the frost roasted by a hot fire, damp steals in while we sleep; damp is silent, imperceptible, ubiquitous. Damp swells the wood, furs the kettle, rusts the iron, rots the stone. So gradual is the process, that it is not until we pick up some chest of drawers, or coal scuttle, and the whole thing drops to pieces in our hands, that we suspect even that the disease is at work.

Thus, stealthily and imperceptibly, none marking the exact day or hour of the change, the constitution of England was altered[1] and nobody knew it. Everywhere the effects were felt. The hardy country gentleman, who had sat down gladly to a meal of ale and beef in a room designed, perhaps by the brothers Adam,[2] with classic dignity, now felt chilly. Rugs appeared; beards were grown; trousers were fastened tight under the instep. The chill which he felt in his legs the country gentleman soon transferred to his house; furniture was muffled; walls and tables were covered; nothing was left bare. Then a change of diet became essential. The muffin was invented and the crumpet.[3] Coffee supplanted the after-dinner port, and, as coffee led to a drawing-room in which to drink it, and a drawing-room to glass cases, and glass cases to artificial flowers, and artificial flowers to mantelpieces, and mantelpieces to pianofortes, and pianofortes to drawing-room ballads, and drawing-room ballads (skipping a stage or two) to innumerable little dogs, mats, and china ornaments, the home – which had become extremely important – was completely altered.

Outside the house – it was another effect of the damp – ivy grew in unparalleled profusion. Houses that had been of bare stone were smothered in greenery. No garden, however formal its original design, lacked a shrubbery, a wilderness, a maze. What light penetrated to the bedrooms where children were born was naturally of an obfusc green,[4] and what light penetrated to the drawing-rooms where grown men and women lived came through curtains of brown and purple plush. But the change did not stop at outward things. The damp struck within. Men felt the chill in their hearts; the damp in their minds. In a desperate effort to snuggle their feelings into some sort of warmth one subterfuge was tried after another. Love, birth, and death were all swaddled in a variety of fine phrases. The sexes drew further and further apart. No open conversation was tolerated. Evasions and concealments were sedulously practised on both sides. And just as the ivy and the evergreen rioted in the damp earth outside, so did the same fertility show itself within. The life of the average woman was a succession of childbirths. She married at nineteen and had fifteen or eighteen children by the time she was thirty; for twins abounded. Thus the British Empire came into existence;[5] and thus – for there is no stopping damp; it gets into the inkpot as it gets into the woodwork – sentences swelled, adjectives multiplied, lyrics became epics, and little trifles that had been essays a column long were now encyclopaedias in ten or twenty volumes. But Eusebius Chubb shall be our witness to the effect this all had upon the mind of a sensitive man who could do nothing to stop it. There is a passage towards the end of his memoirs where he describes how, after writing thirty-five folio pages one morning 'all about nothing' he screwed the lid on his inkpot and went for a turn in his garden. Soon he found himself involved in the shrubbery. Innumerable leaves creaked and glistened above his head. He seemed to himself 'to crush the mould of a million more under his feet'. Thick smoke exuded from a damp bonfire at the end of the garden. He reflected that no fire on earth could ever hope to consume that vast vegetable encumbrance. Wherever he looked, vegetation was rampant. Cucumbers 'came scrolloping⁶ across the grass to his feet'. Giant cauliflowers towered deck above deck till they rivalled, to his disordered imagination, the elm trees themselves. Hens laid incessantly eggs of no special tint. Then, remembering with a sigh his own fecundity and his poor wife Jane, now in the throes of her fifteenth confinement indoors, how, he asked himself, could he blame the fowls? He looked upwards into the sky. Did not heaven itself, or that great frontispiece of heaven, which is the sky, indicate the assent, indeed, the instigation of the heavenly hierarchy? For there, winter or summer, year in year out, the clouds turned and tumbled, like whales, he pondered, or elephants rather; but no, there was no escaping the simile which was pressed upon him from a thousand airy acres; the whole sky itself as it spread wide above the British Isles was nothing but a vast feather bed; and the undistinguished fecundity of the garden, the bedroom and the henroost was copied there. He went indoors, wrote the passage quoted above, laid his head in a gas oven, and when they found him later he was past revival.

While this went on in every part of England, it was all very well for Orlando to mew herself in her house at Blackfriars and pretend that the climate was the same; that one could still say what one liked and wear knee-breeches or skirts as the fancy took one. Even she, at length, was forced to acknowledge that times were changed. One afternoon in the early part of the century she was driving through St. James's Park in her old panelled coach when one of those sunbeams, which occasionally, though not often, managed to come to earth, struggled through, marbling the clouds with strange prismatic colours as it passed. Such a sight was sufficiently strange after the clear and uniform skies of the eighteenth century to cause her to pull the window down and look at it. The puce and flamingo clouds made her think with a pleasurable anguish, which proves that she was insensibly afflicted with the damp already, of dolphins dying in Ionian seas. But what was her surprise when, as it struck the earth, the sunbeam seemed to call forth, or to light up, a pyramid, hecatomb, or trophy[7] (for it had something of a banquet-table air) – a conglomeration at any rate of the most heterogeneous and ill-assorted objects, piled higgledy-piggledy in a vast mound where the statue of Queen Victoria now stands! Draped about a vast cross of fretted and floriated gold were widow's weeds and bridal veils; hooked on to other excrescences were crystal palaces, bassinettes, military helmets, memorial wreaths, trousers, whiskers, wedding cakes, cannon, Christmas trees, telescopes, extinct monsters, globes, maps, elephants, and mathematical instruments – the whole supported like a gigantic coat of arms on the right side by a female figure clothed in flowing white; on the left, by a portly gentleman wearing a frock-coat and sponge-bag trousers. The incongruity of the objects, the association of the fully clothed and the partly draped, the garishness of the different colours and their plaid-like juxtapositions afflicted Orlando with the most profound dismay. She had never, in all her life, seen anything at once so indecent, so hideous, and so monumental. It might, and indeed it must be, the effect of the sun on the water-logged air; it would vanish with the first breeze that blew; but for all that, it looked, as she drove past, as if it were destined to endure for ever. Nothing, she felt, sinking back into the corner of her coach, no wind, rain, sun, or thunder, could ever demolish that garish erection. Only the noses would mottle and the trumpets would rust; but there they would remain, pointing east, west, south, and north, eternally. She looked back as her coach swept up Constitution Hill. Yes, there it was, still beaming placidly in a light which – she pulled her watch out of her fob – was, of course, the light of twelve o'clock mid-day. None other could be so prosaic, so matter-of-fact, so impervious to any hint of dawn or sunset, so seemingly calculated to last for ever. She was determined not to look again. Already she felt the tides of her blood run sluggishly. But what was more peculiar, a blush, vivid and singular, overspread her cheeks as she passed Buckingham Palace and her eyes seemed forced by a superior power down upon her knees. Suddenly she saw with a start that she was wearing black breeches. She never ceased blushing till she had reached her country house, which, considering the time it takes four horses to trot thirty miles, will be taken, we hope, as a signal proof of her chastity.

Once there, she followed what had now become the most imperious need of her nature and wrapped herself as well as she could in a damask quilt which she snatched from her bed. She explained to the Widow Bartholomew (who had succeeded good old Grimsditch as housekeeper) that she felt chilly.

'So do we all, m'lady,' said the Widow, heaving a profound sigh. 'The walls is sweating,' she said, with a curious, lugubrious complacency, and sure enough, she had only to lay her hand on the oak panels for the finger prints to be marked there. The ivy had grown so profusely that many windows were now sealed up. The kitchen was so dark that they could scarcely tell a kettle from a cullender. A poor black cat had been mistaken for coals and shovelled on the fire. Most of the maids were already wearing three or four red-flannel petticoats, though the month was August.

'But is it true, m'lady,' the good woman asked, hugging herself, while the golden crucifix heaved on her bosom, 'that the Queen, bless her, is wearing a what d'you call it, a —' the good woman hesitated and blushed.

'A crinoline,'[8] Orlando helped her out with it (for the word had reached Blackfriars). Mrs. Bartholomew nodded. The tears were already running down her cheeks, but as she wept she smiled. For it was pleasant to weep. Were they not all of them weak women? wearing crinolines the better to conceal the fact;

the great fact; the only fact; but, nevertheless, the deplorable fact; which every modest woman did her best to deny until denial was impossible; the fact that she was about to bear a child? to bear fifteen or twenty children indeed, so that most of a modest woman's life was spent, after all, in denying what, on one day at least of every year, was made obvious.

'The muffins is keepin' 'ot', said Mrs. Bartholomew, mopping up her tears, 'in the liberry.'

And wrapped in a damask bed quilt, to a dish of muffins Orlando now sat down.

'The muffins is keepin' 'ot in the liberry' – Orlando minced out the horrid cockney phrase in Mrs. Bartholomew's refined cockney accents as she drank – but no, she detested the mild fluid – her tea. It was in this very room, she remembered, that Queen Elizabeth had stood astride the fireplace with a flagon of beer in her hand, which she suddenly dashed on the table when Lord Burghley tactlessly used the imperative instead of the subjunctive. 'Little man, little man' – Orlando could hear her say – 'is "must" a word to be addressed to princes?'[9] And down came the flagon on the table: there was the mark of it still.

But when Orlando leapt to her feet, as the mere thought of that great Queen commanded, the bed quilt tripped her up, and she fell back in her arm-chair with a curse. To-morrow she would have to buy twenty yards or more of black bombazine,[10] she supposed, to make a skirt. And then (here she blushed), she would have to buy a crinoline, and then (here she blushed) a bassinette, and then another crinoline, and so on . . . The blushes came and went with the most exquisite iteration of modesty and shame imaginable. One might see the spirit of the age blowing, now hot, now cold, upon her cheeks. And if the spirit of the age blew a little unequally, the crinoline being blushed for before the husband, her ambiguous position must excuse her (even her sex was still in dispute) and the irregular life she had lived before.

At length the colour on her cheeks resumed its stability and it seemed as if the spirit of the age – if such indeed it were – lay dormant for a time. Then Orlando felt in the bosom of her shirt as if for some locket or relic of lost affection, and drew out no such thing, but a roll of paper, sea-stained, blood-stained, travel-stained – the manuscript of her poem, 'The Oak Tree'. She had carried this about with her for so many years now, and in such hazardous circumstances, that many of the pages were stained, some were torn, while the straits she had been in for writing paper when with the gipsies, had forced her to overscore the margins and cross the lines till the manuscript looked like a piece of darning most conscientiously carried out. She turned back to the first page and read the date, 1586, written in her own boyish hand. She had been working at it for close on three hundred years now.[11] It was time to make an end. Meanwhile she began turning and dipping and reading and skipping and thinking as she read, how very little she had changed all these years. She had been a gloomy boy, in love with death, as boys are; and then she had been amorous and florid; and then she had been sprightly and satirical; and sometimes she had tried prose and sometimes she had tried drama. Yet through all these changes she had remained, she reflected, fundamentally the same. She had the same brooding meditative temper, the same love of animals and nature, the same passion for the country and the seasons.

'After all,' she thought, getting up and going to the window, 'nothing has changed. The house, the garden are precisely as they were. Not a chair has been moved, not a trinket sold. There are the same walks, the same lawns, the same trees, and the same pool, which, I dare say, has the same carp in it. True, Queen Victoria is on the throne and not Queen Elizabeth, but what difference . . .'

No sooner had the thought taken shape, than, as if to rebuke it, the door was flung wide and in marchèd Basket, the butler, followed by Bartholomew, the housekeeper, to clear away tea. Orlando, who had just dipped her pen in the ink, and was about to indite some reflection upon the eternity of all things, was much annoyed to be impeded by a blot, which spread and mean-dered round her pen. It was some infirmity of the quill, she supposed; it was split or dirty. She dipped it again. The blot increased. She tried to go on with what she was saying; no words came. Next she began to decorate the blot with wings and whiskers, till it became a round-headed monster, something between a bat and a wombat. But as for writing poetry with Basket and Bartholomew in the room, it was impossible. No sooner had she said 'Impossible' than, to her astonishment and alarm, the pen began to curve and caracole with the smoothest possible fluency. Her page was written in the neatest sloping Italian hand with the most insipid verse she had ever read in her life:[12]

> I am myself but a vile link
> Amid life's weary chain,
> But I have spoken hallow'd words,
> Oh, do not say in vain!

> Will the young maiden, when her tears,
> Alone in moonlight shine,
> Tears for the absent and the loved,
> Murmur—

she wrote without a stop as Bartholomew and Basket grunted and groaned about the room, mending the fire, picking up the muffins.
  Again she dipped her pen and off it went –

> She was so changed, the soft carnation cloud
> Once mantling o'er her cheek like that which eve
> Hangs o'er the sky, glowing with roseate hue,
> Had faded into paleness, broken by
> Bright burning blushes, torches of the tomb,

but here, by an abrupt movement she spilt the ink over the page and blotted it from human sight she hoped for ever. She was all of a quiver, all of a stew. Nothing more repulsive could be imagined than to feel the ink flowing thus in cascades of involuntary inspiration. What had happened to her? Was it the damp, was it Bartholomew, was it Basket, what was it? she demanded. But the room was empty. No one answered her, unless the dripping of the rain in the ivy could be taken for an answer.

Meanwhile, she became conscious, as she stood at the window, of an extraordinary tingling and vibration all over her, as if she were made of a thousand wires upon which some breeze or errant fingers were playing scales. Now her toes tingled; now her marrow. She had the queerest sensations about the thigh bones. Her hairs seemed to erect themselves. Her arms sang and twanged as the telegraph wires would be singing and twanging in twenty years or so. But all this agitation seemed at length to concentrate in her hands; and then in one hand, and then in one finger of that hand, and then finally to contract itself so that it made a ring of quivering sensibility about the second finger of the left hand. And when she raised it to see what caused this agitation, she saw nothing – nothing but the vast solitary emerald which Queen Elizabeth had given her. And was that not enough? she asked. It was of the finest water. It was worth ten thousand pounds at least. The vibration seemed, in the oddest way (but remember we are dealing with some of the darkest manifestations of the human soul) to say No, that is not enough; and, further, to assume a note of interrogation, as though it were asking, what did it mean, this hiatus, this strange oversight? till poor Orlando felt positively ashamed of the second finger of her left hand without in the least knowing why. At this moment, Bartholomew came in to ask which dress she should lay out for dinner, and Orlando, whose senses were much quickened, instantly glanced at Bartholomew's left hand, and instantly perceived what she had never noticed before – a thick ring of rather jaundiced yellow circling the third finger where her own was bare.

'Let me look at your ring, Bartholomew,' she said, stretching her hand to take it.

At this, Bartholomew made as if she had been struck in the breast by a rogue. She started back a pace or two, clenched her hand and flung it away from her with a gesture that was noble in the extreme. 'No,' she said, with resolute dignity, her Ladyship might look if she pleased, but as for taking off her wedding ring, not the Archbishop nor the Pope nor Queen Victoria on her throne could force her to do that. Her Thomas had put it on her finger twenty-five years, six months, three weeks ago; she had slept in it; worked in it; washed in it; prayed in it; and proposed to be buried in it. In fact, Orlando understood her to say, but her voice was much broken with emotion, that it was by the gleam on her wedding ring that she would be assigned her station among the angels and its lustre would be tarnished for ever if she let it out of her keeping for a second.

'Heaven help us,' said Orlando, standing at the window and watching the pigeons at their pranks, 'what a world we live in! What a world to be sure!' Its complexities amazed her. It now seemed to her that the whole world was ringed with gold. She went in to dinner. Wedding rings abounded. She went to church. Wedding rings were everywhere. She drove out. Gold, or pinchbeck,[13] thin, thick, plain, smooth, they glowed dully on every hand. Rings filled the jewellers' shops, not the flashing pastes and diamonds of Orlando's recollection, but simple bands without a stone in them. At the same time, she began to notice a new habit among the town people. In the old days, one would meet a boy trifling with a girl under a hawthorn hedge frequently enough. Orlando had flicked many a couple with the tip of her whip and laughed and passed on. Now, all that was changed. Couples trudged and plodded in the middle of the road indissolubly linked together.[14] The woman's right hand was invariably passed through the man's left and her fingers were firmly gripped by his. Often it was not till the horses' noses were on them that they budged, and then, though they moved it was all in one piece, heavily, to the side of the road. Orlando could only suppose that some new discovery had been made about the race; that they were somehow stuck together, couple after couple, but who had made it, and when, she could not guess. It did not seem to be Nature. She looked at the doves and the rabbits and the elk-hounds and she could not see that Nature had changed her ways or mended them, since the time of Elizabeth at least. There was no indissoluble alliance among the brutes that she could see. Could it be Queen Victoria then, or Lord Melbourne?[15] Was it from them that the great discovery of marriage proceeded? Yet the Queen, she pondered, was said to be fond of dogs, and Lord Melbourne, she had heard, was said to be fond of women. It was strange – it was distasteful; indeed, there was something in this indissolubility of bodies which was repugnant to her sense of decency and sanitation. Her ruminations, however, were accompanied by such a tingling and twangling of the afflicted finger that she could scarcely keep her ideas in order. They were languishing and ogling like a housemaid's fancies. They made her blush. There was nothing for it but to buy one of those ugly bands and wear it like the rest. This she did, slipping it, overcome with shame, upon her finger in the shadow of a curtain; but without avail. The tingling persisted more violently, more indignantly than ever. She did not sleep a wink that night. Next morning when she took up the pen to write, either she could think of nothing, and the pen make one large lachrymose blot after another, or it ambled off, more alarmingly still, into mellifluous fluencies[16] about early death and corruption, which were worse than no thinking at all. For it would seem – her case proved it – that we write, not with the fingers, but with the whole person. The nerve which controls the pen winds itself about every fibre of our being, threads the heart, pierces the liver. Though the seat of her trouble seemed to be the left hand, she could feel herself poisoned through and through, and was forced at length to consider the most desperate of remedies, which was to yield completely and submissively to the spirit of the age, and take a husband.

That this was much against her natural temperament has been sufficiently made plain. When the sound of the Archduke's chariot wheels died away, the cry that rose to her lips was 'Life! A Lover!' not 'Life! A Husband!' and it was in pursuit of this aim that she had gone to town and run about the world as has been shown in the previous chapter. Such is the indomitable nature of the spirit of the age, however, that it batters down anyone who tries to make stand against it far more effectually than those who bend its own way. Orlando had inclined herself naturally to the Elizabethan spirit, to the Restoration spirit, to the spirit of the eighteenth century, and had in consequence scarcely been aware of the change from one age to the other. But the spirit of the nineteenth century was antipathetic to her in the extreme, and thus it took her and broke her, and she was aware of her defeat at its hands as she had never been before. For it is probable that the human spirit has its place in time assigned to it; some are born of this age, some of that; and now that Orlando was grown a woman, a year or two past thirty indeed, the lines of her character were fixed, and to bend them the wrong way was intolerable.

So she stood mournfully at the drawing-room window (Bartholomew had so christened the library) dragged down by the weight of the crinoline which she had submissively adopted. It was heavier and more drab than any dress she had yet worn. None had ever so impeded her movements. No longer could she stride through the garden with her dogs, or run lightly to the high mound and fling herself beneath the oak tree. Her skirts collected damp leaves and straw. The plumed hat tossed on the breeze. The thin shoes were quickly soaked and mud-caked. Her muscles had lost their pliancy. She became nervous lest there should be robbers behind the wainscot and afraid, for the first time in her life, of ghosts in the corridors. All these things inclined her, step by step, to submit to the new discovery, whether Queen Victoria's or another's, that each man and each woman has another allotted to it for life, whom it supports, by whom it is supported, till death them do part. It would be a comfort, she felt, to lean; to sit down; yes, to lie down; never, never, never to get up again. Thus did the spirit work upon her, for all her past pride, and as she came sloping down the scale of emotion to this lowly and unaccustomed lodging-place, those twanglings and tinglings which had been so captious and so interrogative modulated into the sweetest melodies, till it seemed as if angels were plucking harp-strings with white fingers and her whole being was pervaded by a seraphic harmony.

But whom could she lean upon? She asked that question of

the wild autumn winds. For it was now October, and wet as usual. Not the Archduke; he had married a very great lady and had hunted hares in Roumania these many years now; nor Mr. M.; he was become a Catholic; nor the Marquis of C.; he made sacks in Botany Bay;[17] nor the Lord O.; he had long been food for fishes. One way or another, all her old cronies were gone now, and the Nells and the Kits of Drury Lane, much though she favoured them, scarcely did to lean upon.

'Whom', she asked, casting her eyes upon the revolving clouds, clasping her hands as she knelt on the window-sill, and looking the very image of appealing womanhood as she did so, 'can I lean upon?' Her words formed themselves, her hands clasped themselves, involuntarily, just as her pen had written of its own accord. It was not Orlando who spoke, but the spirit of the age. But whichever it was, nobody answered it. The rooks were tumbling pell-mell among the violet clouds of autumn. The rain had stopped at last and there was an iridescence in the sky which tempted her to put on her plumed hat and her little stringed shoes and stroll out before dinner.

'Everyone is mated except myself,' she mused, as she trailed disconsolately across the courtyard. There were the rooks; Canute and Pippin[18] even – transitory as their alliances were, still each this evening seemed to have a partner. 'Whereas, I, who am mistress of it all,' Orlando thought, glancing as she passed at the innumerable emblazoned windows of the hall, 'am single, am mateless, am alone.'

Such thoughts had never entered her head before. Now they bore her down unescapably. Instead of thrusting the gate open, she tapped with a gloved hand for the porter to unfasten it for her. One must lean on someone, she thought, if it is only on a porter; and half wished to stay behind and help him to grill his chop on a bucket of fiery coals, but was too timid to ask it. So she strayed out into the park alone, faltering at first and apprehensive lest there might be poachers or gamekeepers or even errand-boys to marvel that a great lady should walk alone.

At every step she glanced nervously lest some male form

should be hiding behind a furze bush or some savage cow be lowering its horns to toss her. But there were only the rooks flaunting in the sky. A steel-blue plume from one of them fell among the heather. She loved wild birds' feathers. She had used to collect them as a boy. She picked it up and stuck it in her hat. The air blew upon her spirit somewhat and revived it. As the rooks went whirling and wheeling above her head and feather after feather fell gleaming through the purplish air, she followed them, her long cloak floating behind her, over the moor, up the hill. She had not walked so far for years. Six feathers[19] had she picked from the grass and drawn between her finger tips and pressed to her lips to feel their smooth, glinting plumage, when she saw, gleaming on the hill-side, a silver pool, mysterious as the lake into which Sir Bedivere flung the sword of Arthur.[20] A single feather quivered in the air and fell into the middle of it. Then, some strange ecstasy came over her. Some wild notion she had of following the birds to the rim of the world and flinging herself on the spongy turf and there drinking forgetfulness, while the rooks' hoarse laughter sounded over her. She quickened her pace; she ran; she tripped; the tough heather roots flung her to the ground. Her ankle was broken. She could not rise. But there she lay content. The scent of the bog myrtle and the meadow-sweet was in her nostrils. The rooks' hoarse laughter was in her ears. 'I have found my mate,' she murmured. 'It is the moor. I am nature's bride,' she whispered, giving herself in rapture to the cold embraces of the grass as she lay folded in her cloak in the hollow by the pool. 'Here will I lie. (A feather fell upon her brow.) I have found a greener laurel than the bay. My forehead will be cool always. There are wild birds' feathers – the owl's, the nightjar's. I shall dream wild dreams. My hands shall wear no wedding ring,' she continued, slipping it from her finger. 'The roots shall twine about them. Ah!' she sighed, pressing her head luxuriously on its spongy pillow, 'I have sought happiness through many ages and not found it; fame and missed it; love and not known it; life – and behold, death is better. I have known many men and many women,' she continued; 'none

ORLANDO ABOUT THE YEAR 1840

have I understood. It is better that I should lie at peace here with only the sky above me – as the gipsy told me years ago. That was in Turkey.' And she looked straight up into the marvellous golden foam into which the clouds had churned themselves, and saw next moment a track in it, and camels passing in single file through the rocky desert among clouds of red dust; and then, when the camels had passed, there were only mountains, very high and full of clefts and with pinnacles of rock, and she fancied she heard goat bells ringing in their passes, and in their folds were fields of irises and gentian. So the sky changed and her eyes slowly lowered themselves down and down till they came to the rain-darkened earth and saw the great hump of the South Downs, flowing in one wave along the coast; and where the land parted, there was the sea, the sea with ships passing; and she fancied she heard a gun far out at sea, and thought at first, 'That's the Armada', and then thought 'No, it's Nelson',[21] and then remembered how those wars were over and the ships were busy merchant ships; and the sails on the winding river were those of pleasure boats. She saw, too, cattle sprinkled on the dark fields, sheep and cows, and she saw the lights coming here and there in farm-house windows, and lanterns moving among the cattle as the shepherd went his rounds and the cowman; and then the lights went out and the stars rose and tangled themselves about the sky. Indeed, she was falling asleep with the wet feathers on her face and her ear pressed to the ground when she heard, deep within, some hammer on an anvil, or was it a heart beating? Tick-tock, tick-tock, so it hammered, so it beat, the anvil, or the heart in the middle of the earth; until, as she listened, she thought it changed to the trot of a horse's hoofs; one, two, three, four, she counted; then she heard a stumble; then, as it came nearer and nearer, she could hear the crack of a twig and the suck of the wet bog in its hoofs. The horse was almost on her. She sat upright. Towering dark against the yellow-slashed sky of dawn, with the plovers rising and falling about him, she saw a man on horseback.[22] He started. The horse stopped.

'Madam,' the man cried, leaping to the ground, 'you're hurt!'
'I'm dead, sir!' she replied.

A few minutes later, they became engaged.

The morning after, as they sat at breakfast, he told her his name. It was Marmaduke Bonthrop Shelmerdine, Esquire.[23]

'I knew it!' she said, for there was something romantic and chivalrous, passionate, melancholy, yet determined about him which went with the wild, dark-plumed name – a name which had, in her mind, the steel-blue gleam of rooks' wings, the hoarse laughter of their caws, the snake-like twisting descent of their feathers in a silver pool, and a thousand other things which will be described presently.

'Mine is Orlando,' she said. He had guessed it. For if you see a ship in full sail coming with the sun on it proudly sweeping across the Mediterranean from the South Seas, one says at once, 'Orlando', he explained.

In fact, though their acquaintance had been so short, they had guessed, as always happens between lovers, everything of any importance about each other in two seconds at the utmost, and it now remained only to fill in such unimportant details as what they were called; where they lived; and whether they were beggars or people of substance. He had a castle in the Hebrides, but it was ruined, he told her. Gannets feasted in the banqueting-hall. He had been a soldier and a sailor, and had explored the East. He was on his way now to join his brig[24] at Falmouth, but the wind had fallen and it was only when the gale blew from the South-west that he could put out to sea. Orlando looked hastily from the breakfast-room window at the gilt leopard on the weather vane. Mercifully its tail pointed due east and was steady as a rock. 'Oh! Shel, don't leave me!' she cried. 'I'm passionately in love with you,' she said. No sooner had the words left her mouth than an awful suspicion rushed into both their minds simultaneously,

'You're a woman, Shel!' she cried.

'You're a man, Orlando!' he cried.

Never was there such a scene of protestation and demonstration as then took place since the world began. When it was over and they were seated again she asked him, what was this talk of a South-west gale? Where was he bound for?

'For the Horn,' he said briefly, and blushed. (For a man had to blush as a woman had, only at rather different things.) It was only by dint of great pressure on her side and the use of much intuition that she gathered that his life was spent in the most desperate and splendid of adventures – which is to voyage round Cape Horn in the teeth of a gale. Masts had been snapped off; sails torn to ribbons (she had to drag the admission from him). Sometimes the ship had sunk, and he had been left the only survivor on a raft with a biscuit.

'It's about all a fellow can do nowadays,' he said sheepishly, and helped himself to great spoonfuls of strawberry jam. The vision which she had thereupon of this boy (for he was little more) sucking peppermints, for which he had a passion, while the masts snapped and the stars reeled and he roared brief orders to cut this adrift, to heave that overboard, brought the tears to her eyes, tears, she noted, of a finer flavour than any she had cried before. 'I am a woman,' she thought, 'a real woman, at last.' She thanked Bonthrop from the bottom of her heart for having given her this rare and unexpected delight. Had she not been lame in the left foot, she would have sat upon his knee.

'Shel, my darling,' she began again, 'tell me . . .' and so they talked two hours or more, perhaps about Cape Horn, perhaps not, and really it would profit little to write down what they said, for they knew each other so well that they could say anything, which is tantamount to saying nothing, or saying such stupid, prosy things as how to cook an omelette, or where to buy the best boots in London, things which have no lustre taken from their setting, yet are positively of amazing beauty within it. For it has come about, by the wise economy of nature, that our modern spirit can almost dispense with language; the commonest expressions do, since no expressions do; hence the most ordinary conversation is often the most poetic, and the most poetic is precisely that which cannot be written down. For which reasons we leave a great blank here, which must be taken to indicate that the space is filled to repletion.

After some days more of this kind of talk,

'Orlando, my dearest,' Shel was beginning, when there was a scuffling outside, and Basket the butler entered with the information that there was a couple of Peelers[25] downstairs with a warrant from the Queen.

'Show 'em up,' said Shelmerdine briefly, as if on his own quarter-deck, taking up, by instinct, a stand with his hands behind him in front of the fireplace. Two officers in bottle-green uniforms with truncheons at their hips then entered the room and stood at attention. Formalities being over, they gave into Orlando's own hands, as their commission was, a legal document of some very impressive sort, judging by the blobs of sealing wax, the ribbons, the oaths, and the signatures, which were all of the highest importance.

Orlando ran her eyes through it and then, using the first finger of her right hand as pointer, read out the following facts as being most germane to the matter.

'The lawsuits are settled,' she read out . . . 'some in my favour, as for example . . . others not. Turkish marriage annulled (I was ambassador in Constantinople, Shel,' she explained). 'Children pronounced illegitimate (they said I had three sons by Pepita, a Spanish dancer). So they don't inherit, which is all to the good . . . Sex? Ah! what about sex? My sex', she read out with some solemnity, 'is pronounced indisputably, and beyond the shadow of a doubt (what was I telling you a moment ago, Shel?), female. The estates which are now desequestrated in perpetuity descend and are tailed and entailed upon the heirs male of my body, or in default of marriage' – but here she grew impatient with this legal verbiage, and said, 'but there won't be any default of marriage, nor of heirs either, so the rest can be taken as read.' Whereupon she appended her own signature beneath Lord Palmerston's[26] and entered from that moment into the undisturbed possession of her titles, her house, and her estate – which was now so much shrunk, for the cost of the lawsuits had been prodigious, that, though she was infinitely noble again, she was also excessively poor.

When the result of the lawsuit was made known (and rumour flew much quicker than the telegraph which has supplanted it), the whole town was filled with rejoicings.[27]

[Horses were put into carriages for the sole purpose of being taken out. Empty barouches and landaus were trundled up and down the High Street incessantly. Addresses were read from the Bull. Replies were made from the Stag. The town was illuminated. Gold caskets were securely sealed in glass cases. Coins were well and duly laid under stones. Hospitals were founded. Rat and Sparrow clubs were inaugurated. Turkish women by the dozen were burnt in effigy in the market-place, together with scores of peasant boys with the label 'I am a base Pretender', lolling from their mouths. The Queen's cream-coloured ponies were soon seen trotting up the avenue with a command to Orlando to dine and sleep at the Castle, that very same night. Her table, as on a previous occasion, was snowed under with invitations from the Countess of R., Lady Q., Lady Palmerston, the Marchioness of P., Mrs. W. E. Gladstone,[28] and others, beseeching the pleasure of her company, reminding her of ancient alliances between their family and her own, etc.] – all of which is properly enclosed in square brackets, as above, for the good reason that a parenthesis it was without any importance in Orlando's life.[29] She skipped it, to get on with the text. For when the bonfires were blazing in the market-place, she was in the dark woods with Shelmerdine alone. So fine was the weather that the trees stretched their branches motionless above them, and if a leaf fell, it fell, spotted red and gold, so slowly that one could watch it for half an hour fluttering and falling till it came to rest at last, on Orlando's foot.

'Tell me, Mar,' she would say (and here it must be explained, that when she called him by the first syllable of his first name, she was in a dreamy, amorous, acquiescent mood, domestic, languid a little, as if spiced logs were burning, and it was evening, yet not time to dress, and a thought wet perhaps outside, enough to make the leaves glisten, but a nightingale might be singing even so among the azaleas, two or three dogs barking at distant farms, a cock crowing – all of which the reader should imagine in her voice) – 'Tell me, Mar,' she would say, 'about Cape Horn.' Then Shelmerdine would make a little model on the ground of the Cape with twigs and dead leaves and an empty snail shell or two.

'Here's the north,' he would say. 'There's the south. The wind's coming from hereabouts. Now the brig is sailing due west; we've just lowered the top-boom mizzen; and so you see – here, where this bit of grass is, she enters the current which you'll find marked – where's my map and compasses, Bo'sun? – Ah! thanks, that'll do, where the snail shell is. The current catches her on the starboard side, so we must rig the jib-boom or we shall be carried to the larboard,[30] which is where that beech leaf is – for you must understand my dear –' and so he would go on, and she would listen to every word; interpreting them rightly, so as to see, that is to say, without his having to tell her, the phosphorescence on the waves; the icicles clanking in the shrouds; how he went to the top of the mast in a gale; there reflected on the destiny of man; came down again; had a whisky and soda; went on shore; was trapped by a black woman; repented; reasoned it out; read Pascal;[31] determined to write philosophy; bought a monkey; debated the true end of life; decided in favour of Cape Horn, and so on. All this and a thousand other things she understood him to say, and so when she replied, Yes, negresses are seductive, aren't they? he having told her that the supply of biscuits now gave out, he was surprised and delighted to find how well she had taken his meaning.

'Are you positive you aren't a man?' he would ask anxiously, and she would echo,

'Can it be possible you're not a woman?' and then they must put it to the proof without more ado. For each was so surprised at the quickness of the other's sympathy, and it was to each such a revelation that a woman could be as tolerant and free-spoken as a man, and a man as strange and subtle as a woman, that they had to put the matter to the proof at once.

And so they would go on talking or rather, understanding, which has become the main art of speech in an age when words are growing daily so scanty in comparison with ideas that 'the biscuits ran out' has to stand for kissing a negress in the dark when one has just read Bishop Berkeley's[32] philosophy for the tenth time. (And from this it follows that only the most profound masters of style can tell the truth, and when one meets a simple one-syllabled writer, one may conclude, without any doubt at all, that the poor man is lying.)

So they would talk; and then, when her feet were fairly covered with spotted autumn leaves, Orlando would rise and stroll away into the heart of the woods in solitude, leaving Bonthrop sitting there among the snail shells, making models of Cape Horn. 'Bonthrop,' she would say, 'I'm off,' and when she called him by his second name, 'Bonthrop', it should signify to the reader that she was in a solitary mood, felt them both as specks on a desert, was desirous only of meeting death by herself, for people die daily, die at dinner-tables, or like this, out of doors in the autumn woods; and with the bonfires blazing and Lady Palmerston or Lady Derby[33] asking her out every night to dinner, the desire for death would overcome her, and so saying 'Bonthrop', she said in effect, 'I'm dead', and pushed her way as a spirit might through the spectre-pale beech trees, and so oared herself deep into solitude as if the little flicker of noise and movement were over and she were free now to take her way – all of which the reader should hear in her voice when she said 'Bonthrop'; and should also add, the better to illumine the word, that for him too the same word signified, mystically, separation and isolation and the disembodied pacing the deck of his brig in unfathomable seas.

After some hours of death, suddenly a jay shrieked 'Shelmerdine', and stooping, she picked one of those autumn crocuses which to some people signify that very word, and put it with the jay's feather that came tumbling blue through the beech woods, in her breast. Then she called 'Shelmerdine' and the word went shooting this way and that way through the woods and struck him where he sat, making models out of snail shells in the grass. He saw her, and heard her coming to him with the crocus and the jay's feather in her breast, and cried 'Orlando', which meant (and it must be remembered that when bright colours like blue and yellow mix themselves in our eyes, some of it rubs off on our thoughts) first the bowing and swaying of bracken as if something were breaking through; which proved to be a ship in full sail, heaving and tossing a little dreamily, rather as if she had a whole year of summer days to make her voyage in; and so the ship bears down, heaving this way, heaving that way, nobly, indolently, and rides over the crest of this wave and sinks into the hollow of that one, and so, suddenly stands over you (who are in a little cockle shell of a boat, looking up at her) with all her sails quivering,[34] and then, behold, they drop all of a heap on deck – as Orlando dropped now into the grass beside him.

Eight or nine days had been spent thus, but on the tenth, which was the 26th of October, Orlando was lying in the bracken, while Shelmerdine recited Shelley (whose entire works he had by heart), when a leaf which had started to fall slowly enough from a tree-top whipped briskly across Orlando's foot. A second leaf followed and then a third. Orlando shivered and turned pale. It was the wind. Shelmerdine – but it would be more proper now to call him Bonthrop – leapt to his feet.

'The wind!' he cried.

Together they ran through the woods, the wind plastering them with leaves as they ran, to the great court and through it and the little courts, frightened servants leaving their brooms and their saucepans to follow after till they reached the Chapel,[35] and there a scattering of lights was lit as fast as could be, one knocking over this bench, another snuffing out that taper. Bells were rung. People were summoned. At length there was Mr. Dupper catching at the ends of his white tie and asking where was the prayer book. And they thrust Queen Mary's prayer book in his hands and he searched hastily fluttering the pages, and said, 'Marmaduke Bonthrop Shelmerdine, and Lady Orlando, kneel down'; and they knelt down, and now they were bright and now they were dark as the light and shadow came flying helter-skelter through the painted windows; and among the banging of innumerable doors and a sound like brass pots beating, the organ sounded, its growl coming loud and faint alternately, and Mr. Dupper, who was grown a very old man, tried now to raise his voice above the uproar and could not be heard and then all was quiet for a moment, and one word – it might be 'the jaws of death' – rang out clear, while all the estate servants kept pressing in with rakes and whips still in their hands to listen, and some sang aloud and others prayed, and now a bird was dashed against the pane, and now there was a clap of thunder, so that no one heard the word Obey spoken or saw, except as a golden flash, the ring pass from hand to hand. All was movement and confusion. And up they rose with the organ booming and the lightning playing and the rain pouring, and the Lady Orlando, with her ring on her finger, went out into the court in her thin dress and held the swinging stirrup, for the horse was bitted and bridled and the foam was still on his flank, for her husband to mount, which he did with one bound, and the horse leapt forward and Orlando, standing there, cried out Marmaduke Bonthrop Shelmerdine! and he answered her Orlando! and the words went dashing and circling like wild hawks together among the belfries and higher and higher, further and further, faster and faster they circled, till they crashed and fell in a shower of fragments to the ground; and she went in.

Chapter VI

Orlando went indoors. It was completely still. It was very silent. There was the inkpot: there was the pen; there was the manuscript of her poem, broken off in the middle of a tribute to eternity. She had been about to say, when Basket and Bartholomew interrupted with the tea things, nothing changes. And then, in the space of three seconds and a half, everything had changed – she had broken her ankle, fallen in love, married Shelmerdine.

There was the wedding ring on her finger to prove it. It was true that she had put it there herself before she met Shelmerdine, but that had proved worse than useless. She now turned the ring round and round, with superstitious reverence, taking care lest it should slip past the joint of her finger.

'The wedding ring has to be put on the third finger of the left hand', she said, like a child cautiously repeating its lesson, 'for it to be of any use at all.'

She spoke thus, aloud and rather more pompously than was her wont, as if she wished someone whose good opinion she desired to overhear her. Indeed, she had in mind, now that she was at last able to collect her thoughts, the effect that her behaviour would have had upon the spirit of the age. She was extremely anxious to be informed whether the steps she had taken in the matter of getting engaged to Shelmerdine and marrying him met with its approval. She was certainly feeling more herself. Her finger had not tingled once, or nothing to count, since that night on the moor. Yet, she could not deny that she had her doubts. She was married, true; but if one's husband was always sailing round Cape Horn, was it marriage? If one liked him, was it marriage? If one liked other people, was it marriage? And finally, if one still wished, more than anything in the whole world, to write poetry, was it marriage? She had her doubts.

But she would put it to the test. She looked at the ring. She looked at the inkpot. Did she dare? No, she did not. But she must. No, she could not. What should she do then? Faint, if possible. But she had never felt better in her life.

'Hang it all!' she cried, with a touch of her old spirit, 'Here goes!'

And she plunged her pen neck deep in the ink. To her enormous surprise, there was no explosion. She drew the nib out. It was wet, but not dripping. She wrote. The words were a little long in coming, but come they did. Ah! but did they make sense? she wondered, a panic coming over her lest the pen might have been at some of its involuntary pranks again. She read,

> And then I came to a field where the springing grass
> Was dulled by the hanging cups of fritillaries,
> Sullen and foreign-looking, the snaky flower,
> Scarfed in dull purple, like Egyptian girls – [1]

As she wrote she felt some power (remember we are dealing with the most obscure manifestations of the human spirit) reading over her shoulder, and when she had written 'Egyptian girls', the power told her to stop. Grass, the power seemed to say, going back with a ruler such as governesses use to the beginning, is all right; the hanging cups of fritillaries – admirable; the snaky flower – a thought, strong from a lady's pen, perhaps, but Wordsworth, no doubt, sanctions it; but – girls? Are girls necessary? You have a husband at the Cape, you say? Ah, well, that'll do.

And so the spirit passed on.

Orlando now performed in spirit (for all this took place in spirit) a deep obeisance to the spirit of her age, such as – to compare great things with small – a traveller, conscious that he has a bundle of cigars in the corner of his suit case, makes to the customs officer who has obligingly made a scribble of white chalk on the lid. For she was extremely doubtful whether, if the spirit had examined the contents of her mind carefully, it would not have found something highly contraband for which she would have had to pay the full fine. She had only escaped by the skin of her teeth. She had just managed, by some dexterous deference to the spirit of the age, by putting on a ring and finding a man on a moor, by loving nature and being no satirist, cynic, or psychologist – any one of which goods would have been discovered at once – to pass its examination successfully. And she heaved a deep sigh of relief, as, indeed, well she might, for the transaction between a writer and the spirit of the age is one of infinite delicacy, and upon a nice arrangement between the two the whole fortune of his works depends. Orlando had so ordered it that she was in an extremely happy position; she need neither fight her age, nor submit to it; she was of it, yet remained herself. Now, therefore, she could write, and write she did. She wrote. She wrote. She wrote.

It was now November. After November, comes December. Then January, February, March, and April. After April comes May. June, July, August follow. Next is September. Then October, and so, behold, here we are back at November again, with a whole year accomplished.

This method of writing biography, though it has its merits, is a little bare, perhaps, and the reader, if we go on with it, may complain that he could recite the calendar for himself and so save his pocket whatever sum the Hogarth Press² may think proper to charge for this book. But what can the biographer do when his subject has put him in the predicament into which Orlando has now put us? Life, it has been agreed by everyone whose opinion is worth consulting, is the only fit subject for novelist or biographer; life, the same authorities have decided, has nothing whatever to do with sitting still in a chair and thinking. Thought and life are as the poles asunder. Therefore – since sitting in a chair and thinking is precisely what Orlando is doing now – there is nothing for it but to recite the calendar, tell one's beads, blow one's nose, stir the fire, look out of the window, until she has done. Orlando sat so still that you could have heard a pin drop. Would, indeed, that a pin had dropped!

MARMADUKE BONTHROP SHELMERDINE, ESQUIRE

That would have been life of a kind. Or if a butterfly had fluttered through the window and settled on her chair, one could write about that. Or suppose she had got up and killed a wasp. Then, at once, we could out with our pens and write. For there would be bloodshed, if only the blood of a wasp. Where there is blood there is life. And if killing a wasp is the merest trifle compared with killing a man, still it is a fitter subject for novelist or biographer than this mere wool-gathering; this thinking; this sitting in a chair day in, day out, with a cigarette and a sheet of paper and a pen and an inkpot. If only subjects, we might complain (for our patience is wearing thin), had more consideration for their biographers! What is more irritating than to see one's subject, on whom one has lavished so much time and trouble, slipping out of one's grasp altogether and indulging – witness her sighs and gasps, her flushing, her palings, her eyes now bright as lamps, now haggard as dawns – what is more humiliating than to see all this dumb show of emotion and excitement gone through before our eyes when we know that what causes it – thought and imagination – are of no importance whatsoever?

But Orlando was a woman – Lord Palmerston had just proved it. And when we are writing the life of a woman, we may, it is agreed, waive our demand for action, and substitute love instead. Love, the poet[3] has said, is woman's whole existence. And if we look for a moment at Orlando writing at her table, we must admit that never was there a woman more fitted for that calling. Surely, since she is a woman, and a beautiful woman, and a woman in the prime of life, she will soon give over this pretence of writing and thinking and begin at least to think of a gamekeeper[4] (and as long as she thinks of a man, nobody objects to a woman thinking). And then she will write him a little note (and as long as she writes little notes nobody objects to a woman writing either) and make an assignation for Sunday dusk and Sunday dusk will come; and the gamekeeper will whistle under the window – all of which is, of course, the very stuff of life and the only possible subject for fiction. Surely Orlando must have done one of these things? Alas – a thousand times, alas, Orlando did none of them. Must it then be admitted that Orlando was one of those monsters of iniquity who do not love? She was kind to dogs, faithful to friends, generosity itself to a dozen starving poets, had a passion for poetry. But love – as the male novelists define it – and who, after all, speak with greater authority? – has nothing whatever to do with kindness, fidelity, generosity, or poetry. Love is slipping off one's petticoat and— But we all know what love is. Did Orlando do that? Truth compels us to say no, she did not. If then, the subject of one's biography will neither love nor kill, but will only think and imagine, we may conclude that he or she is no better than a corpse and so leave her.

The only resource now left us is to look out of the window. There were sparrows; there were starlings; there were a number of doves, and one or two rooks, all occupied after their fashion. One finds a worm, another a snail. One flutters to a branch, another takes a little run on the turf. Then a servant crosses the courtyard, wearing a green baize apron. Presumably he is engaged on some intrigue with one of the maids in the pantry, but as no visible proof is offered us, in the courtyard, we can but hope for the best and leave it. Clouds pass, thin or thick, with some disturbance of the colour of the grass beneath. The sundial registers the hour in its usual cryptic way. One's mind begins tossing up a question or two, idly, vainly, about this same life. Life, it sings, or croons rather, like a kettle on a hob, Life, life, what art thou? Light or darkness, the baize apron of the under footman or the shadow of the starling on the grass?

Let us go, then,[5] exploring, this summer morning, when all are adoring the plum blossom and the bee. And humming and hawing, let us ask of the starling (who is a more sociable bird than the lark) what he may think on the brink of the dust-bin, whence he picks among the sticks combings of scullion's hair. What's life, we ask, leaning on the farmyard gate; Life, Life, Life! cries the bird, as if he had heard, and knew precisely, what we meant by this bothering prying habit of ours of asking questions indoors and out and peeping and picking at daisies as the way is of writers when they don't know what to say next. Then they come here, says the bird, and ask me what life is; Life, Life, Life!

We trudge on then by the moor path, to the high brow of the wine-blue purple-dark hill, and fling ourselves down there, and dream there and see there a grasshopper, carting back to his home in the hollow, a straw. And he says (if sawings like his can be given a name so sacred and tender) Life's labour, or so we interpret the whirr of his dust-choked gullet. And the ant agrees and the bees, but if we lie here long enough to ask the moths, when they come at evening, stealing among the paler heather bells, they will breathe in our ears such wild nonsense as one hears from telegraph wires in snow storms; tee-hee, haw-haw. Laughter, Laughter! the moths say.

Having asked then of man and of bird and the insects, for fish, men tell us, who have lived in green caves, solitary for years to hear them speak, never, never say, and so perhaps know what life is – having asked them all and grown no wiser, but only older and colder (for did we not pray once in a way to wrap up in a book something so hard, so rare, one could swear it was life's meaning?) back we must go and say straight out to the reader who waits a-tiptoe to hear what life is – alas, we don't know.

At this moment, but only just in time to save the book from extinction, Orlando pushed away her chair, stretched her arms, dropped her pen, came to the window, and exclaimed, 'Done!'

She was almost felled to the ground by the extraordinary sight which now met her eyes. There was the garden and some birds. The world was going on as usual. All the time she was writing the world had continued.

'And if I were dead, it would be just the same!' she exclaimed.

Such was the intensity of her feelings that she could even imagine that she had suffered dissolution, and perhaps some faintness actually attacked her. For a moment she stood looking at the fair, indifferent spectacle with staring eyes. At length she was revived in a singular way. The manuscript which reposed above her heart began shuffling and beating as if it were a living thing, and, what was still odder, and showed how fine a sympathy was between them, Orlando, by inclining her head, could make out what it was that it was saying. It wanted to be read. It must be read. It would die in her bosom if it were not read. For the first time in her life she turned with violence against nature. Elk-hounds and rose bushes were about her in profusion. But elk-hounds and rose bushes can none of them read. It is a lamentable oversight on the part of Providence which had never struck her before. Human beings alone are thus gifted. Human beings had become necessary. She rang the bell. She ordered the carriage to take her to London at once.

'There's just time to catch the eleven forty-five, M'Lady,' said Basket. Orlando had not yet realised the invention of the steam engine, but such was her absorption in the sufferings of a being, who, though not herself, yet entirely depended on her, that she saw a railway train for the first time, took her seat in a railway carriage, and had the rug arranged about her knees without giving a thought to 'that stupendous invention, which had (the historians say) completely changed the face of Europe in the past twenty years' (as, indeed, happens much more frequently than historians suppose). She noticed only that it was extremely smutty; rattled horribly; and the windows stuck. Lost in thought, she was whirled up to London in something less than an hour and stood on the platform at Charing Cross, not knowing where to go.

The old house at Blackfriars, where she had spent so many pleasant days in the eighteenth century, was now sold, part to the Salvation Army, part to an umbrella factory. She had bought another in Mayfair[6] which was sanitary, convenient, and in the heart of the fashionable world, but was it in Mayfair that her poem would be relieved of its desire? Pray God, she thought, remembering the brightness of their ladyships' eyes and the symmetry of their lordships' legs, they haven't taken to reading there. For that would be a thousand pities. Then there was Lady R.'s. The same sort of talk would be going on there still, she had no doubt. The gout might have shifted from the General's left leg to his right, perhaps. Mr. L. might have stayed ten days with R. instead of T. Then Mr. Pope would come in. Oh! but Mr. Pope was dead. Who were the wits now, she wondered – but that was not a question one could put to a porter, and so she moved on. Her ears were now distracted by the jingling of innumerable bells on the heads of innumerable horses. Fleets of the strangest little boxes on wheels were drawn up by the pavement. She walked out into the Strand. There the uproar was even worse. Vehicles of all sizes, drawn by blood horses and by dray horses, conveying one solitary dowager or crowded to the top by whiskered men in silk hats, were inextricably mixed. Carriages, carts, and omnibuses seemed to her eyes, so long used to the look of a plain sheet of foolscap, alarmingly at loggerheads; and to her ears, attuned to a pen scratching, the uproar of the street sounded violently and hideously cacophonous. Every inch of the pavement was crowded. Streams of people, threading in and out between their own bodies and the lurching and lumbering traffic with incredible agility, poured incessantly east and west. Along the edge of the pavement stood men, holding out trays of toys, and bawled. At corners, women sat beside great baskets of spring flowers and bawled. Boys running in and out of the horses' noses, holding printed sheets to their bodies, bawled too, Disaster! Disaster! At first Orlando supposed that she had arrived at some moment of national crisis; but whether it was happy or tragic, she could not tell. She looked anxiously at people's faces. But that confused her still more. Here would come by a man sunk in despair, muttering to himself as if he knew some terrible sorrow. Past him would nudge a fat, jolly-faced fellow, shouldering his way along as if it were a festival for all the world. Indeed, she came to the conclusion that there was neither rhyme nor reason in any of it. Each man and each woman was bent on his own affairs. And where was she to go?

She walked on without thinking, up one street and down

another, by vast windows piled with handbags, and mirrors, and dressing gowns, and flowers, and fishing rods, and luncheon baskets; while stuff of every hue and pattern, thickness or thinness, was looped and festooned and ballooned across and across. Sometimes she passed down avenues of sedate mansions, soberly numbered 'one', 'two', 'three', and so on right up to two or three hundred, each the copy of the other, with two pillars and six steps and a pair of curtains neatly drawn and family luncheons laid on tables, and a parrot looking out of one window and a man servant out of another, until her mind was dizzied with the monotony. Then she came to great open squares with black, shiny, tightly buttoned statues of fat men in the middle, and war-horses prancing, and columns rising and fountains falling and pigeons fluttering. So she walked and walked along pavements between houses until she felt very hungry, and something fluttering above her heart rebuked her with having forgotten all about it. It was her manuscript, 'The Oak Tree'.

She was confounded at her own neglect. She stopped dead where she stood. No coach was in sight. The street, which was wide and handsome, was singularly empty. Only one elderly gentleman was approaching. There was something vaguely familiar to her in his walk. As he came nearer, she felt certain that she had met him at some time or other. But where? Could it be that this gentleman, so neat, so portly, so prosperous, with a cane in his hand and a flower in his button-hole, with a pink, plump face, and combed white moustaches, could it be, Yes, by jove, it was! – her old, her very old friend, Nick Greene!

At the same time he looked at her; remembered her; recognised her. 'The Lady Orlando!' he cried, sweeping his silk hat almost in the dust.

'Sir Nicholas!'[7] she exclaimed. For she was made aware intuitively by something in his bearing that the scurrilous penny-a-liner, who had lampooned her and many another in the time of Queen Elizabeth, was now risen in the world and become certainly a Knight and doubtless a dozen other fine things into the bargain.

With another bow, he acknowledged that her conclusion was correct; he was a Knight; he was a Litt.D.; he was a Professor. He was the author of a score of volumes. He was, in short, the most influential critic of the Victorian age.

A violent tumult of emotion besieged her at meeting the man who had caused her, years ago, so much pain. Could this be the plaguey, restless fellow who had burnt holes in her carpets, and toasted cheese in the Italian fireplace and told such merry stories of Marlowe and the rest that they had seen the sun rise nine nights out of ten? He was now sprucely dressed in a grey morning suit, had a pink flower in his button-hole, and grey suede gloves to match. But even as she marvelled, he made another profound bow, and asked her whether she would honour him by lunching with him? The bow was a thought overdone perhaps, but the imitation of fine breeding was creditable. She followed him, wondering, into a superb restaurant, all red plush, white table-cloths, and silver cruets, as unlike as could be the old tavern or coffee house with its sanded floor, its wooden benches, its bowls of punch and chocolate, and its broadsheets and spittoons. He laid his gloves neatly on the table beside him. Still she could hardly believe that he was the same man. His nails were clean; where they used to be an inch long. His chin was shaved; where a black beard used to sprout. He wore gold sleeve-links; where his ragged linen used to dip in the broth. It was not, indeed, until he had ordered the wine, which he did with a care that reminded her of his taste in Malmsey long ago, that she was convinced he was the same man. 'Ah!' he said, heaving a little sigh, which was yet comfortable enough, 'ah! my dear lady, the great days of literature are over. Marlowe, Shakespeare, Ben Jonson – those were the giants. Dryden, Pope, Addison – those were the heroes. All, all are dead now. And whom have they left us? Tennyson, Browning, Carlyle!' – he threw an immense amount of scorn into his voice. 'The truth of it is,' he said, pouring himself a glass of wine, 'that all our young writers are in the pay of booksellers. They turn out any trash that serves to pay their tailor's bills. It is an age', he said, helping himself to hors-d'œuvres, 'marked by precious conceits and wild experiments – none of which the Elizabethans would have tolerated for an instant.'

'No, my dear lady,' he continued, passing with approval the turbot au gratin, which the waiter exhibited for his sanction, 'the great days are over. We live in degenerate times. We must cherish the past; honour those writers – there are still a few left of 'em – who take antiquity for their model and write, not for pay but—' Here Orlando almost shouted 'Glawr!' Indeed she could have sworn that she had heard him say the very same things three hundred years ago. The names were different, of course, but the spirit was the same. Nick Greene had not changed, for all his knighthood. And yet, some change there was. For while he ran on about taking Addison as one's model (it had been Cicero once, she thought) and lying in bed of a morning (which she was proud to think her pension paid quarterly enabled him to do) rolling the best works of the best authors round and round on one's tongue for an hour, at least, before setting pen to paper, so that the vulgarity of the present time and the deplorable condition of our native tongue (he had lived long in America, she believed) might be purified – while he ran on in much the same way that Greene had run on three hundred years ago, she had time to ask herself, how was it then that he had changed? He had grown plump; but he was a man verging on seventy. He had grown sleek: literature had been a prosperous pursuit evidently; but somehow the old restless, uneasy vivacity had gone. His stories, brilliant as they were, were no longer quite so free and easy. He mentioned, it is true, 'my dear friend Pope' or 'my illustrious friend Addison' every other second, but he had an air of respectability about him which was depressing, and he preferred, it seemed, to enlighten her about the doings and sayings of her own blood relations rather than tell her, as he used to do, scandal about the poets.

Orlando was unaccountably disappointed. She had thought of literature all these years (her seclusion, her rank, her sex must be her excuse) as something wild as the wind, hot as fire, swift as lightning; something errant, incalculable, abrupt, and behold, literature was an elderly gentleman in a grey suit talking about duchesses. The violence of her disillusionment was such that some hook or button fastening the upper part of her dress burst open, and out upon the table fell 'The Oak Tree', a poem.

'A manuscript!' said Sir Nicholas, putting on his gold pince-nez. 'How interesting, how excessively interesting! Permit me to look at it.' And once more, after an interval of some three hundred years, Nicholas Greene took Orlando's poem and, laying it down among the coffee cups and the liqueur glasses, began to read it. But now his verdict was very different from what it had been then. It reminded him, he said as he turned over the pages, of Addison's *Cato*. It compared favourably with Thomson's *Seasons*.[8] There was no trace in it, he was thankful to say, of the modern spirit. It was composed with a regard to truth, to nature, to the dictates of the human heart, which was rare indeed, in these days of unscrupulous eccentricity. It must, of course, be published instantly.

Really Orlando did not know what he meant. She had always carried her manuscripts about with her in the bosom of her dress. The idea tickled Sir Nicholas considerably.

'But what about royalties?' he asked.

Orlando's mind flew to Buckingham Palace and some dusky potentates who happened to be staying there.

Sir Nicholas was highly diverted. He explained that he was alluding to the fact that Messrs.—[9] (here he mentioned a well-known firm of publishers) would be delighted, if he wrote them a line, to put the book on their list. He could probably arrange for a royalty of ten per cent on all copies up to two thousand; after that it would be fifteen. As for the reviewers, he would himself write a line to Mr.—, who was the most influential; then a compliment – say a little puff of her own poems – addressed to the wife of the editor of the — never did any harm. He would call —. So he ran on. Orlando understood nothing of all this, and from old experience did not altogether trust his good nature, but there was nothing for it but to submit to what was evidently his wish and the fervent desire of the poem itself. So Sir Nicholas made the blood-stained packet into a neat parcel; flattened it into his breast pocket, lest it should disturb the set of his coat; and with many compliments on both sides, they parted.

Orlando walked up the street. Now that the poem was gone – and she felt a bare place in her breast where she had been used to carry it – she had nothing to do but reflect upon whatever she liked – the extraordinary chances it might be of the human lot. Here she was in St. James's Street; a married woman; with a ring on her finger; where there had been a coffee house once there was now a restaurant; it was about half past three in the afternoon; the sun was shining; there were three pigeons; a mongrel terrier dog; two hansom cabs and a barouche landau. What then, was Life? The thought popped into her head violently, irrelevantly (unless old Greene were somehow the cause of it). And it may be taken as a comment, adverse or favourable, as the reader chooses to consider it upon her relations with her husband (who was at the Horn), that whenever anything popped violently into her head, she went straight to the nearest telegraph office and wired to him. There was one, as it happened, close at hand. 'My God Shel', she wired; 'life literature Greene toady –' here she dropped into a cypher language[10] which they had invented between them so that a whole spiritual state of the utmost complexity might be conveyed in a word or two without the telegraph clerk being any the wiser, and added the words 'Rattigan Glumphoboo', which summed it up precisely. For not only had the events of the morning made a deep impression on her, but it cannot have escaped the reader's attention that Orlando was growing up – which is not necessarily growing better – and 'Rattigan Glumphoboo' described a very complicated spiritual state – which if the reader puts all his intelligence at our service he may discover for himself.

There could be no answer to her telegram for some hours; indeed, it was probable, she thought, glancing at the sky, where the upper clouds raced swiftly past, that there was a gale at Cape Horn, so that her husband would be at the mast-head, as likely as not, or cutting away some tattered spar, or even alone in a boat with a biscuit. And so, leaving the post office, she turned to beguile herself into the next shop, which was a shop so common in our day that it needs no description, yet, to her eyes, strange in the extreme; a shop where they sold books. All her life long Orlando had known manuscripts; she had held in her hands the rough brown sheets on which Spenser had written in his little crabbed hand; she had seen Shakespeare's script and Milton's. She owned, indeed, a fair number of quartos and folios, often with a sonnet in her praise in them and sometimes a lock of hair. But these innumerable little volumes, bright, identical, ephemeral, for they seemed bound in cardboard and printed on tissue paper, surprised her infinitely. The whole works of Shakespeare cost half a crown and could be put in your pocket. One could hardly read them, indeed, the print was so small, but it was a marvel, none the less. 'Works' – the works of every writer she had known or heard of and many more stretched from end to end of the long shelves. On tables and chairs, more 'works' were piled and tumbled, and these she saw, turning a page or two, were often works about other works by Sir Nicholas and a score of others whom, in her ignorance, she supposed, since they were bound and printed, to be very great writers too. So she gave an astounding order to the bookseller to send her everything of any importance in the shop and left.

She turned into Hyde Park, which she had known of old (beneath that cleft tree, she remembered, the Duke of Hamilton fell run through the body by Lord Mohun[11]), and her lips, which are often to blame in the matter, began framing the words of her telegram into a senseless singsong: life literature Greene toady Rattigan Glumphoboo; so that several park keepers looked at her with suspicion and were only brought to a favourable opinion of her sanity by noticing the pearl necklace which she wore. She had carried off a sheaf of papers and critical journals from the book shop, and at length, flinging herself on her elbow beneath a tree, she spread these pages round her and did her best to fathom the noble art of prose composition as these masters practised it. For still the old credulity was alive in her; even the blurred type of a weekly newspaper had some sanctity in her eyes. So she read, lying on her elbow, an article by Sir Nicholas on the collected works of a man she had once known – John Donne. But she had pitched herself, without knowing it, not far from the Serpentine.[12] The barking of a thousand dogs sounded in her ears. Carriage wheels rushed ceaselessly in a circle. Leaves sighed overhead. Now and again a braided skirt and a pair of tight scarlet trousers crossed the grass within a few steps of her. Once a gigantic rubber ball bounced on the newspaper. Violets, oranges, reds, and blues broke through the interstices of the leaves and sparkled in the emerald on her finger. She read a sentence and looked up at the sky; she looked up at the sky and looked down at the newspaper. Life? Literature? One to be made into the other? But how monstrously difficult! For – here came by a pair of tight scarlet trousers – how would Addison have put that? Here came two dogs dancing[13] on their hind legs. How would Lamb have described that? For reading Sir Nicholas and his friends (as she did in the intervals of looking about her), she somehow got the impression – here she rose and walked – they made one feel – it was an extremely uncomfortable feeling – one must never, never say what one thought. (She stood on the banks of the Serpentine. It was a bronze colour; spider-thin boats were skimming from side to side.) They made one feel, she continued, that one must always, always write like somebody else. (The tears formed themselves in her eyes.) For really, she thought, pushing a little boat off with her toe, I don't think I could (here the whole of Sir Nicholas' article came before her as articles do, ten minutes after they are read, with the look of his room, his head, his cat, his writing-table, and the time of the day thrown in), I don't think I could, she continued, considering the article from this point of view, sit in a study, no, it's not a study, it's a mouldy kind of drawing-room, all day long, and talk to pretty young men, and tell them little anecdotes, which they mustn't repeat, about what Tupper said about Smiles;[14] and then, she continued, weeping bitterly, they're all so manly; and then, I do detest Duchesses; and I don't like cake; and though I'm spiteful enough, I could never learn to be as spiteful as all that, so how can I be a critic and write the best English prose of my time? Damn it all! she exclaimed, launching a penny steamer so vigorously that the poor little boat almost sank in the bronze-coloured waves.

Now, the truth is that when one has been in a state of mind (as nurses call it) – and the tears still stood in Orlando's eyes – the thing one is looking at becomes, not itself, but another thing, which is bigger and much more important and yet remains the same thing. If one looks at the Serpentine in this state of mind, the waves soon become just as big as the waves on the Atlantic; the toy boats become indistinguishable from ocean liners. So Orlando mistook the toy boat for her husband's brig; and the wave she had made with her toe for a mountain of water off Cape Horn; and as she watched the toy boat climb the ripple, she thought she saw Bonthrop's ship climb up and up a glassy wall; up and up it went, and a white crest with a thousand deaths in it arched over it; and through the thousand deaths it went and disappeared – 'It's sunk!' she cried out in an agony – and then, behold, there it was again sailing along safe and sound among the ducks on the other side of the Atlantic.

'Ecstasy!' she cried. 'Ecstasy! Where's the post office?' she wondered. 'For I must wire at once to Shel and tell him . . .' And repeating 'A toy boat on the Serpentine', and 'Ecstasy', alternately, for the thoughts were interchangeable and meant exactly the same thing, she hurried towards Park Lane.

'A toy boat, a toy boat, a toy boat,' she repeated, thus enforcing upon herself the fact that it is not articles by Nick Greene on John Donne nor eight-hour bills nor covenants nor factory acts[15] that matter; it's something useless, sudden, violent; something that costs a life; red, blue, purple; a spirt; a splash; like those hyacinths (she was passing a fine bed of them); free from taint, dependence, soilure of humanity or care for one's kind; something rash, ridiculous, like my hyacinth, husband I mean, Bonthrop: that's what it is – a toy boat on the Serpentine, ecstasy – it's ecstasy that matters. Thus she spoke aloud, waiting for the carriages to pass at Stanhope Gate, for the consequence of not living with one's husband, except when the wind is sunk, is that one talks nonsense aloud in Park Lane. It would no doubt have been different had she lived all the year round with him as Queen Victoria recommended. As it was the thought of him would come upon her in a flash. She found it absolutely necessary to speak to him instantly. She did not care in the least what nonsense it might make, or what dislocation it might inflict on the narrative. Nick Greene's article had plunged her in the depths of despair; the toy boat had raised her to the heights of joy. So she repeated: 'Ecstasy, ecstasy', as she stood waiting to cross.

But the traffic was heavy that spring afternoon, and kept her standing there, repeating, ecstasy, ecstasy, or a toy boat on the Serpentine, while the wealth and power of England sat, as if sculptured, in hat and cloak, in four-in-hand, victoria and barouche landau.[16] It was as if a golden river had coagulated and massed itself in golden blocks across Park Lane. The ladies held cardcases between their fingers; the gentlemen balanced gold-mounted canes between their knees. She stood there gazing, admiring, awestruck. One thought only disturbed her, a thought familiar to all who behold great elephants, or whales of an incredible magnitude, and that is how do these leviathans to whom obviously stress, change, and activity are repugnant, propagate their kind? Perhaps, Orlando thought, looking at the stately, still faces, their time of propagation is over; this is the fruit; this is the consummation. What she now beheld was the triumph of an age. Portly and splendid there they sat. But now, the policeman let fall his hand; the stream became liquid; the massive conglomeration of splendid objects moved, dispersed, and disappeared into Piccadilly.

So she crossed Park Lane and went to her house in Curzon Street where, when the meadow-sweet blew there, she could remember curlew calling and one very old man with a gun.

She could remember, she thought, stepping across the threshold of her house, how Lord Chesterfield had said – but her memory was checked. Her discreet eighteenth-century hall, where she could see Lord Chesterfield putting his hat down here and his coat down there with an elegance of deportment which it was a pleasure to watch, was now completely littered with parcels. While she had been sitting in Hyde Park the bookseller had delivered her order, and the house was crammed – there were parcels slipping down the staircase – with the whole of Victorian literature done up in grey paper and neatly tied with string. She carried as many of these packets as she could to her room, ordered footmen to bring the others, and, rapidly cutting innumerable strings, was soon surrounded by innumerable volumes.

Accustomed to the little literatures of the sixteenth, seventeenth, and eighteenth centuries, Orlando was appalled by the consequences of her order. For, of course, to the Victorians themselves Victorian literature meant not merely four great names[17] separate and distinct but four great names sunk and embedded in a mass of Alexander Smiths, Dixons, Blacks, Milmans, Buckles, Taines, Paynes, Tuppers, Jamesons – all vocal, clamorous, prominent, and requiring as much attention as anybody else. Orlando's reverence for print had a tough job set before it, but drawing her chair to the window to get the benefit of what light might filter between the high houses of Mayfair, she tried to come to a conclusion.

And now it is clear that there are only two ways of coming to a conclusion upon Victorian literature – one is to write it out in sixty volumes octavo, the other is to squeeze it into six lines of the length of this one. Of the two courses, economy, since time runs short, leads us to choose the second; and so we proceed. Orlando then came to the conclusion (opening half-a-dozen books) that it was very odd that there was not a single dedication to a nobleman among them; next (turning over a vast pile of memoirs) that several of these writers had family trees half as high as her own; next, that it would be impolitic in the extreme to wrap a ten-pound note round the sugar tongs when Miss Christina Rossetti[18] came to tea; next (here were half-a-dozen invitations to celebrate centenaries by dining) that literature since it ate all these dinners must be growing very corpulent; next (she was invited to a score of lectures on the Influence of this upon that; the Classical revival; the Romantic survival, and other titles of the same engaging kind) that literature since it listened to all these lectures must be growing very dry; next (here she attended a reception given by a peeress) that literature since it wore all those fur tippets must be growing very respectable; next (here she visited Carlyle's sound-proof room at Chelsea) that genius since it needed all this coddling must be growing very delicate; and so at last she reached her final conclusion, which was of the highest importance but which, as we have already much overpassed our limit of six lines, we must omit.

Orlando, having come to this conclusion, stood looking out of the window for a considerable space of time. For, when anybody comes to a conclusion it is as if they had tossed the ball over the net and must wait for the unseen antagonist to return it to them. What would be sent her next from the colourless sky above Chesterfield House, she wondered? And with her hands clasped, she stood for a considerable space of time wondering. Suddenly she started – and here we could only wish that, as on a former occasion, Purity, Chastity, and Modesty would push the door ajar and provide, at least, a breathing space in which we could think how to wrap up what now has to be told delicately, as a biographer should. But no! Having thrown their white garment at the naked Orlando and seen it fall short by several inches, these ladies had given up all intercourse with her these many years; and were now otherwise engaged. Is nothing then, going to happen this pale March morning to mitigate, to veil, to cover, to conceal, to shroud this undeniable event whatever it may be? For after giving that sudden, violent start, Orlando – but Heaven be praised, at this very moment there struck up outside one of these frail, reedy, fluty, jerky, old-fashioned barrel-organs[19] which are still sometimes played by Italian organ-grinders in back streets. Let us accept the intervention, humble though it is, as if it were the music of the spheres, and allow it, with all its gasps and groans, to fill this page with sound until the moment comes which it is impossible to deny is coming; which the footman has seen coming and the maid-servant; and the reader will have to see too; for Orlando herself is clearly unable to ignore it any longer – let the barrel-organ sound and transport us on thought, which is no more than a little boat, when music sounds, tossing on the waves; on thought, which is, of all carriers, the most clumsy, the most erratic, over the roof tops and the back gardens where washing is hanging to – what is this place? Do you recognise the Green and in the middle the steeple, and the gates with a lion couchant on either side? Oh yes, it is Kew! Well, Kew will do. So here then we are at Kew, and I will show you to-day (the second of March) under the plum tree, a grape hyacinth, and a crocus, and a bud too, on the almond tree; so that to walk there is to be thinking of bulbs, hairy and red, thrust into the earth in October; flowering now; and to be dreaming of more than can rightly be said, and to be taking from its case a cigarette or cigar even, and to be flinging a cloak under (as the rhyme requires) an oak, and there to sit, waiting the kingfisher, which, it is said, was seen once to cross in the evening from bank to bank.

Wait! Wait! The kingfisher comes; the kingfisher comes not.

Behold, meanwhile, the factory chimneys, and their smoke; behold the city clerks flashing by in their outrigger.[20] Behold the old lady taking her dog for a walk and the servant girl wearing her new hat for the first time not at the right angle. Behold them all. Though Heaven has mercifully decreed that the secrets of all hearts are hidden so that we are lured on for ever to suspect something, perhaps, that does not exist; still through our cigarette smoke, we see blaze up and salute the splendid fulfilment of natural desires for a hat, for a boat, for a rat in a ditch; as once one saw blazing – such silly hops and skips the mind takes when it slops like this all over the saucer and the barrel-organ plays – saw blazing a fire in a field against minarets near Constantinople.

Hail! natural desire! Hail! happiness! divine happiness! and pleasure of all sorts, flowers and wine, though one fades and the other intoxicates; and half-crown tickets out of London on

Sundays, and singing in a dark chapel hymns about death, and anything, anything that interrupts and confounds the tapping of typewriters and filing of letters and forging of links and chains, binding the Empire together. Hail even the crude, red bows on shop girls' lips (as if Cupid, very clumsily, dipped his thumb in red ink and scrawled a token in passing). Hail, happiness! king-fisher flashing from bank to bank, and all fulfilment of natural desire, whether it is what the male novelist says it is; or prayer; or denial; hail! in whatever form it comes, and may there be more forms, and stranger. For dark flows the stream – would it were true, as the rhyme hints 'like a dream' – but duller and worser than that is our usual lot; without dreams, but alive, smug, fluent, habitual, under trees whose shade of an olive green drowns the blue of the wing of the vanishing bird when he darts of a sudden from bank to bank.

Hail, happiness, then, and after happiness, hail not those dreams which bloat the sharp image as spotted mirrors do the face in a country-inn parlour; dreams which splinter the whole and tear us asunder and wound us and split us apart in the night when we would sleep; but sleep, sleep, so deep that all shapes are ground to dust of infinite softness, water of dimness inscrutable, and there, folded, shrouded, like a mummy, like a moth, prone let us lie on the sand at the bottom of sleep.

But wait! but wait! we are not going, this time, visiting the blind land. Blue, like a match struck right in the ball of the innermost eye, he flies, burns, bursts the seal of sleep; the king-fisher; so that now floods back refluent like a tide, the red, thick stream of life again; bubbling, dripping; and we rise, and our eyes (for how handy a rhyme is to pass us safe over the awkward transition from death to life) fall on – (here the barrel-organ stops playing abruptly).

'It's a very fine boy, M'Lady,' said Mrs. Banting, the midwife, putting her first-born child into Orlando's arms. In other words Orlando was safely delivered of a son on Thursday, March the 20th,[21] at three o'clock in the morning.

*

Once more Orlando stood at the window, but let the reader take courage; nothing of the same sort is going to happen to-day, which is not, by any means, the same day. No – for if we look out of the window, as Orlando was doing at the moment, we shall see that Park Lane itself has considerably changed. Indeed one might stand there ten minutes or more, as Orlando stood now, without seeing a single barouche landau. 'Look at that!' she exclaimed, some days later when an absurd truncated carriage without any horses began to glide about of its own accord. A carriage without any horses indeed! She was called away just as she said that, but came back again after a time and had another look out of the window. It was odd sort of weather nowadays. The sky itself, she could not help thinking, had changed. It was no longer so thick, so watery, so prismatic now that King Edward – see, there he was, stepping out of his neat brougham to go and visit a certain lady opposite [22] – had succeeded Queen Victoria. The clouds had shrunk to a thin gauze; the sky seemed made of metal, which in hot weather tarnished verdigris, copper colour or orange as metal does in a fog. It was a little alarming – this shrinkage. Everything seemed to have shrunk. Driving past Buckingham Palace last night, there was not a trace of that vast erection which she had thought everlasting; top hats, widows' weeds, trumpets, telescopes, wreaths, all had vanished and left not a stain, not a puddle even, on the pavement. But it was now – after another interval she had come back again to her favourite station in the window – now, in the evening, that the change was most remarkable. Look at the lights in the houses! At a touch, a whole room was lit; hundreds of rooms were lit; and one was precisely the same as the other. One could see everything in the little square-shaped boxes; there was no privacy; none of those lingering shadows and odd corners that there used to be; none of those women in aprons carrying wobbly lamps which they put down carefully on this table and on that. At a touch, the whole room was bright. And the sky was bright all night long; and the pavements were bright; everything was bright. She came back again at mid-day. How narrow women had grown lately! They looked like stalks of corn, straight, shining, identical. And men's faces were as bare as the palm of one's hand. The dryness of the atmosphere brought out the colour in everything and seemed to stiffen the muscles of the cheeks. It was harder to cry now. Water was hot in two seconds. Ivy had perished or been scraped off houses. Vegetables were less fertile; families were much smaller. Curtains and covers had been frizzled up and the walls were bare so that new brilliantly coloured pictures of real things like streets, umbrellas, apples, were hung in frames, or painted upon the wood. There was something definite and distinct about the age, which reminded her of the eighteenth century, except that there was a distraction, a desperation – as she was thinking this, the immensely long tunnel in which she seemed to have been travelling for hundreds of years widened; the light poured in; her thoughts became mysteriously tightened and strung up as if a piano tuner had put his key in her back and stretched the nerves very taut; at the same time her hearing quickened; she could hear every whisper and crackle in the room so that the clock ticking on the mantelpiece beat like a hammer. And so for some seconds the light went on becoming brighter and brighter, and she saw everything more and more clearly and the clock ticked louder and louder until there was a terrific explosion right in her ear. Orlando leapt as if she had been violently struck on the head. Ten times she was struck. In fact it was ten o'clock in the morning. It was the eleventh of October. It was 1928.[23] It was the present moment.

No one need wonder that Orlando started, pressed her hand to her heart, and turned pale. For what more terrifying revelation can there be than that it is the present moment? That we survive the shock at all is only possible because the past shelters us on one side and the future on another. But we have no time now for reflections; Orlando was terribly late already. She ran downstairs, she jumped into her motor-car, she pressed the self-starter and was off. Vast blue blocks of building rose into the air; the red cowls of chimneys were spotted irregularly across the sky; the road shone like silver-headed nails; omnibuses bore down upon her with sculptured white-faced drivers; she noticed sponges, bird-cages, boxes of green American cloth. But she did not allow these sights to sink into her mind even the fraction of an inch as she crossed the narrow plank of the present, lest she should fall into the raging torrent beneath. 'Why don't you look where you're going to? . . . Put your hand out, can't you?' – that was all she said sharply, as if the words were jerked out of her. For the streets were immensely crowded; people crossed without looking where they were going. People buzzed and hummed round the plate-glass windows within which one could see a glow of red, a blaze of yellow, as if they were bees, Orlando thought – but her thought that they were bees was violently snipped off and she saw, regaining perspective with one flick of her eye, that they were bodies. 'Why don't you look where you're going?' she snapped out.

At last, however, she drew up at Marshall & Snelgrove's[24] and went into the shop. Shade and scent enveloped her. The present fell from her like drops of scalding water. Light swayed up and down like thin stuffs puffed out by a summer breeze. She took a list from her bag and began reading in a curious stiff voice at first as if she were holding the words – boys' boots, bath salts, sardines – under a tap of many-coloured water. She watched them change as the light fell on them. Bath and boots became blunt, obtuse; sardines serrated itself like a saw. So she stood in the ground-floor department of Messrs. Marshall & Snelgrove; looked this way and that; snuffed this smell and that and thus wasted some seconds. Then she got into the lift, for the good reason that the door stood open; and was shot smoothly upwards. The very fabric of life now, she thought as she rose, is magic. In the eighteenth century, we knew how everything was done; but here I rise through the air; I listen to voices in America; I see men flying – but how it's done, I can't even begin to wonder. So my belief in magic returns. Now the lift gave a little jerk as it stopped at the first floor; and she had a vision of innumerable coloured stuffs flaunting in a breeze from which came distinct, strange smells; and each time the lift stopped and flung its doors open, there was another slice of the world displayed with all the smells of that world clinging to it. She was reminded of the river off Wapping in the time of Elizabeth, where the treasure ships and the merchant ships used to anchor. How richly and curiously they had smelt! How well she remembered the feel of rough rubies running through her fingers when she dabbled them in a treasure sack! And then lying with Sukey – or whatever her name was – and having Cumberland's lantern flashed on them! The Cumberlands had a house in Portland Place now and she had lunched with them the other day and ventured a little joke with the old man about almshouses in the Sheen Road. He had winked. But here as the lift could go no higher, she must get out – Heaven knows into what 'department' as they called it. She stood still to consult her shopping list, but was blessed if she could see, as the list bade her, bath salts, or boy's boots anywhere about. And indeed, she was about to descend again, without buying anything, but was saved from that outrage by saying aloud automatically the last item on her list; which happened to be 'sheets for a double bed'.

'Sheets for a double bed,' she said to a man at a counter and, by a dispensation of Providence, it was sheets that the man at that particular counter happened to sell. For Grimsditch, no, Grimsditch was dead; Bartholomew, no, Bartholomew was dead; Louise then[25] – Louise had come to her in a great taking the other day, for she had found a hole in the bottom of the sheet in the royal bed. Many kings and queens had slept there – Elizabeth; James; Charles; George; Victoria; Edward; no wonder the sheet had a hole in it. But Louise was positive she knew who had done it. It was the Prince Consort.

'*Sale bosch!*' she said (for there had been another war; this time against the Germans).

'Sheets for a double bed,' Orlando repeated dreamily, for a double bed with a silver counterpane in a room fitted in a taste which she now thought perhaps a little vulgar – all in silver;[26] but she had furnished it when she had a passion for that metal. While the man went to get sheets for a double bed, she took out a little looking-glass and a powder puff. Women were not nearly as roundabout in their ways, she thought, powdering herself with the greatest unconcern, as they had been when she herself first turned woman and lay on the deck of the *Enamoured Lady*. She gave her nose the right tint deliberately. She never touched her cheeks. Honestly, though she was now thirty-six, she scarcely looked a day older. She looked just as pouting, as sulky, as handsome, as rosy (like a million-candled Christmas tree, Sasha had said) as she had done that day on the ice, when the Thames was frozen and they had gone skating—

'The best Irish linen, Ma'am,' said the shopman, spreading the sheets on the counter – and they had met an old woman picking up sticks. Here, as she was fingering the linen abstractedly, one of the swing-doors between the departments opened and let through, perhaps from the fancy-goods department, a whiff of scent, waxen, tinted as if from pink candles, and the scent curved like a shell round a figure – was it a boy's or was it a girl's? – young, slender, seductive – a girl, by God! furred, pearled, in Russian trousers; but faithless, faithless!

'Faithless!' cried Orlando (the man had gone) and all the shop seemed to pitch and toss with yellow water and far off she saw the masts of the Russian ship standing out to sea, and then, miraculously (perhaps the door opened again) the conch which the scent had made became a platform, a dais, off which stepped a fat, furred woman, marvellously well preserved, seductive, diademed, a Grand Duke's mistress; she who, leaning over the banks of the Volga, eating sandwiches, had watched men drown; and began walking down the shop towards her.

'Oh Sasha!' Orlando cried. Really, she was shocked that she should have come to this; she had grown so fat; so lethargic; and she bowed her head over the linen so that this apparition of a grey woman in fur, and a girl in Russian trousers, with all these smells of wax candles, white flowers, and old ships that it brought with it might pass behind her back unseen.

'Any napkins, towels, dusters to-day, Ma'am?' the shopman persisted. And it is enormously to the credit of the shopping list, which Orlando now consulted, that she was able to reply with every appearance of composure, that there was only one thing in the world she wanted and that was bath salts; which was in another department.

But descending in the lift again – so insidious is the repetition of any scene – she was again sunk far beneath the present moment; and thought when the lift bumped on the ground, that she heard a pot broken against a river bank. As for finding the right department, whatever it might be, she stood engrossed among the handbags, deaf to the suggestions of all the polite, black, combed, sprightly shop assistants, who descending as they did equally and some of them, perhaps, as proudly, even from such depths of the past as she did, chose to let down the impervious screen of the present so that to-day they appeared shop assistants in Marshall & Snelgrove's merely. Orlando stood there hesitating. Through the great glass doors she could see the traffic in Oxford Street. Omnibus seemed to pile itself upon omnibus and then to jerk itself apart. So the ice blocks had pitched and tossed that day on the Thames. An old nobleman in furred slippers had sat astride one of them. There he went – she could see him now – calling down maledictions upon the Irish rebels. He had sunk there, where her car stood.

'Time has passed over me,' she thought, trying to collect herself; 'this is the oncome of middle age. How strange it is! Nothing is any longer one thing. I take up a handbag and I think of an old bumboat woman frozen in the ice. Someone lights a pink candle and I see a girl in Russian trousers. When I step out of doors – as I do now,' here she stepped on to the pavement of Oxford Street, 'what is it that I taste? Little herbs. I hear goat bells. I see mountains. Turkey? India? Persia?' Her eyes filled with tears.

That Orlando had gone a little too far from the present moment will, perhaps, strike the reader who sees her now preparing to get into her motor-car with her eyes full of tears and visions of Persian mountains. And indeed, it cannot be denied that the most successful practitioners of the art of life, often unknown people by the way, somehow contrive to synchronise the sixty or seventy different times which beat simultaneously in every normal human system so that when eleven strikes, all the rest chime in unison, and the present is neither a violent disruption nor completely forgotten in the past. Of them we can justly say that they live precisely the sixty-eight or seventy-two years allotted them on the tombstone. Of the rest some we know to be dead though they walk among us; some are not yet born though they go through the forms of life; others are hundreds of years old though they call themselves thirty-six. The true length of a person's life, whatever the *Dictionary of National Biography*[27] may say, is always a matter of dispute. For it is a difficult business – this time-keeping; nothing more quickly disorders it than contact with any of the arts; and it may have been her love of poetry that was to blame for making Orlando lose her shopping list and start home without the sardines, the bath salts, or the boots. Now as she stood with her hand on the door of her motor-car, the present again struck her on the head. Eleven times she was violently assaulted.

'Confound it all!' she cried, for it is a great shock to the nervous system, hearing a clock strike – so much so that for some time now there is nothing to be said of her save that she frowned slightly, changed her gears admirably, and cried out, as before, 'Look where you're going!' 'Don't you know your own mind?' 'Why didn't you say so then?' while the motor-car shot, swung, squeezed, and slid, for she was an expert driver, down Regent Street, down Haymarket, down Northumberland Avenue, over Westminster Bridge, to the left, straight on, to the right, straight on again . . .

The old Kent Road was very crowded on Thursday, the eleventh of October 1928. People spilt off the pavement. There were women with shopping bags. Children ran out. There were sales at drapers' shops. Streets widened and narrowed. Long vistas steadily shrunk together. Here was a market. Here a funeral. Here a procession with banners upon which was written 'Ra—Un', but what else? Meat was very red. Butchers stood at

the door. Women almost had their heels sliced off. Amor Vin—
that was over a porch. A woman looked out of a bedroom
window, profoundly contemplative, and very still. Applejohn
and Applebed, Undert—.[28] Nothing could be seen whole or read
from start to finish. What was seen begun – like two friends
starting to meet each other across the street – was never seen
ended. After twenty minutes the body and mind were like scraps
of torn paper tumbling from a sack and, indeed, the process of
motoring fast out of London so much resembles the chopping
up small of identity which precedes unconsciousness and perhaps
death itself that it is an open question in what sense Orlando can
be said to have existed at the present moment. Indeed we should
have given her over for a person entirely disassembled were it
not that here, at last, one green screen was held out on the right,
against which the little bits of paper fell more slowly; and then
another was held out on the left so that one could see the
separate scraps now turning over by themselves in the air; and
then green screens were held continuously on either side, so that
her mind regained the illusion of holding things within itself and
she saw a cottage, a farmyard and four cows, all precisely life-
size.

When this happened, Orlando heaved a sigh of relief, lit a
cigarette, and puffed for a minute or two in silence. Then she
called hesitatingly, as if the person she wanted might not be
there, 'Orlando?' For if there are (at a venture) seventy-six different times all ticking in the mind at once, how many different
people are there not – Heaven help us – all having lodgment at
one time or another in the human spirit? Some say two thousand
and fifty-two. So that it is the most usual thing in the world for
a person to call, directly they are alone, Orlando? (if that is one's
name) meaning by that, Come, come! I'm sick to death of this
particular self. I want another. Hence, the astonishing changes
we see in our friends. But it is not altogether plain sailing, either,
for though one may say, as Orlando said (being out in the
country and needing another self presumably) Orlando? still the
Orlando she needs may not come; these selves of which we are

built up, one on top of another, as plates are piled on a waiter's hand, have attachments elsewhere, sympathies, little constitutions and rights of their own, call them what you will (and for many of these things there is no name) so that one will only come if it is raining, another in a room with green curtains, another when Mrs. Jones is not there, another if you can promise it a glass of wine – and so on; for everybody can multiply from his own experience the different terms which his different selves have made with him – and some are too wildly ridiculous to be mentioned in print at all.

So Orlando, at the turn by the barn, called 'Orlando?' with a note of interrogation in her voice and waited. Orlando did not come.[29]

'All right then,' Orlando said, with the good humour people practise on these occasions; and tried another. For she had a great variety of selves to call upon, far more than we have been able to find room for, since a biography is considered complete if it merely accounts for six or seven selves, whereas a person may well have as many thousand. Choosing then, only those selves we have found room for, Orlando may now have called on the boy who cut the nigger's head down; the boy who strung it up again; the boy who sat on the hill; the boy who saw the poet; the boy who handed the Queen the bowl of rose water; or she may have called upon the young man who fell in love with Sasha; or upon the Courtier; or upon the Ambassador; or upon the Soldier; or upon the Traveller; or she may have wanted the woman to come to her; the Gipsy; the Fine Lady; the Hermit; the girl in love with life; the Patroness of Letters; the woman who called Mar (meaning hot baths and evening fires) or Shelmerdine (meaning crocuses in autumn woods) or Bonthrop (meaning the death we die daily) or all three together – which meant more things than we have space to write out – all were different and she may have called upon any one of them.

Perhaps; but what appeared certain (for we are now in the region of 'perhaps' and 'appears') was that the one she needed most kept aloof, for she was, to hear her talk, changing her selves as quickly as she drove – there was a new one at every corner – as happens when, for some unaccountable reason, the conscious self, which is the uppermost, and has the power to desire, wishes to be nothing but one self. This is what some people call the true self, and it is, they say, compact of all the selves we have it in us to be; commanded and locked up by the Captain self, the Key self, which amalgamates and controls them all. Orlando was certainly seeking this self as the reader can judge from overhearing her talk as she drove (and if it is rambling talk, disconnected, trivial, dull, and sometimes unintelligible, it is the reader's fault for listening to a lady talking to herself; we only copy her words as she spoke them, adding in brackets which self in our opinion is speaking, but in this we may well be wrong).

'What then? Who then?'[30] she said. 'Thirty-six; in a motor-car; a woman. Yes, but a million other things as well. A snob am I? The garter in the hall? The leopards? My ancestors? Proud of them? Yes! Greedy, luxurious, vicious? Am I? (here a new self came in). Don't care a damn if I am. Truthful? I think so. Generous? Oh, but that don't count (here a new self came in). Lying in bed of a morning listening to the pigeons on fine linen; silver dishes; wine; maids; footmen. Spoilt? Perhaps. Too many things for nothing. Hence my books (here she mentioned fifty classical titles; which represented, so we think, the early romantic works that she tore up). Facile, glib, romantic. But (here another self came in) a duffer, a fumbler. More clumsy I couldn't be. And – and – (here she hesitated for a word and if we suggest 'Love' we may be wrong, but certainly she laughed and blushed and then cried out –) A toad set in emeralds! Harry the Archduke! Blue-bottles on the ceiling! (here another self came in). But Nell, Kit, Sasha? (she was sunk in gloom: tears actually shaped themselves and she had long given over crying). Trees, she said. (Here another self came in.) I love trees (she was passing a clump) growing there a thousand years. And barns (she passed a tumble-down barn at the edge of the road). And sheep dogs (here one came trotting across the road. She carefully avoided it). And the night. But people (here another self came in). People? (She repeated it as a question.) I don't know. Chattering, spiteful, always telling lies. (Here she turned into the High Street of her native town, which was crowded, for it was market day, with farmers, and shepherds, and old women with hens in baskets.) I like peasants. I understand crops. But (here another self came skipping over the top of her mind like the beam from a lighthouse). Fame! (She laughed.) Fame! Seven editions. A prize. Photographs in the evening papers (here she alluded to the 'Oak Tree' and 'The Burdett Coutts' Memorial Prize [31] which she had won; and we must snatch space to remark how discomposing it is for her biographer that this culmination to which the whole book moved, this peroration with which the book was to end, should be dashed from us on a laugh casually like this; but the truth is that when we write of a woman, everything is out of place – culminations and perorations; the accent never falls where it does with a man). Fame! she repeated. A poet – a charlatan; both every morning as regularly as the post comes in. To dine, to meet; to meet, to dine; fame – fame! (She had here to slow down to pass through the crowd of market people. But no one noticed her. A porpoise in a fishmonger's shop [32] attracted far more attention than a lady who had won a prize and might, had she chosen, have worn three coronets one on top of another on her brow.) Driving very slowly she now hummed as if it were part of an old song, 'With my guineas I'll buy flowering trees, flowering trees, flowering trees and walk among my flowering trees and tell my sons what fame is'. So she hummed, and now all her words began to sag here and there like a barbaric necklace of heavy beads. 'And walk among my flowering trees', she sang, accenting the words strongly, 'and see the moon rise slow, the waggons go . . .' Here she stopped short, and looked ahead of her intently at the bonnet of the car in profound meditation.

'He sat at Twitchett's table', she mused, 'with a dirty ruff on . . . Was it old Mr. Baker come to measure the timber? Or was it Sh—p—re?' (for when we speak names we deeply reverence to ourselves we never speak them whole). She gazed for ten minutes ahead of her, letting the car come almost to a standstill.

'Haunted!' she cried, suddenly pressing the accelerator. 'Haunted! ever since I was a child. There flies the wild goose.[33] It flies past the window out to sea. Up I jumped (she gripped the steering-wheel tighter) and stretched after it. But the goose flies too fast. I've seen it, here – there – there – England, Persia, Italy. Always it flies fast out to sea and always I fling after it words like nets (here she flung her hand out) which shrivel as I've seen nets shrivel drawn on deck with only sea-weed in them; and sometimes there's an inch of silver – six words – in the bottom of the net. But never the great fish who lives in the coral groves.' Here she bent her head, pondering deeply.

And it was at this moment, when she had ceased to call 'Orlando' and was deep in thoughts of something else, that the Orlando whom she had called came of its own accord; as was proved by the change that now came over her (she had passed through the lodge gates and was entering the park).

The whole of her darkened and settled, as when some foil whose addition makes the round and solidity of a surface is added to it, and the shallow becomes deep and the near distant; and all is contained as water is contained by the sides of a well. So she was now darkened, stilled, and become, with the addition of this Orlando, what is called, rightly or wrongly, a single self, a real self. And she fell silent. For it is probable that when people talk aloud, the selves (of which there may be more than two thousand) are conscious of disseverment, and are trying to communicate, but when communication is established they fall silent.

Masterfully, swiftly, she drove up the curving drive between the elms and oaks through the falling turf of the park whose fall was so gentle that had it been water it would have spread the beach with a smooth green tide. Planted here and in solemn groups were beech trees and oak trees. The deer stepped among them, one white as snow, another with its head on one side, for some wire netting had caught in its horns. All this, the trees, deer, and turf, she observed with the greatest satisfaction as if her mind had become a fluid that flowed round things and enclosed them completely. Next minute she drew up in the courtyard where, for so many hundred years she had come, on horseback or in coach and six, with men riding before or coming after; where plumes had tossed, torches flashed, and the same flowering trees that let their leaves drop now had shaken their blossoms. Now she was alone. The autumn leaves were falling. The porter opened the great gates. 'Morning, James,' she said, 'there're some things in the car. Will you bring 'em in?' words of no beauty, interest, or significance themselves, it will be conceded, but now so plumped out with meaning that they fell like ripe nuts from a tree, and proved that when the shrivelled skin of the ordinary is stuffed out with meaning it satisfies the senses amazingly. This was true indeed of every movement and action now, usual though they were; so that to see Orlando change her skirt for a pair of whipcord breeches and leather jacket, which she did in less than three minutes, was to be ravished with the beauty of movement as if Madame Lopokova[34] were using her highest art. Then she strode into the dining-room where her old friends Dryden, Pope, Swift, Addison regarded her demurely at first as who should say Here's the prize winner! but when they reflected that two hundred guineas was in question, they nodded their heads approvingly. Two hundred guineas, they seemed to say; two hundred guineas are not to be sniffed at. She cut herself a slice of bread and ham, clapped the two together and began to eat, striding up and down the room, thus shedding her company habits in a second, without thinking. After five or six such turns, she tossed off a glass of red Spanish wine,[35] and, filling another which she carried in her hand, strode down the long corridor and through a dozen drawing-rooms and so began a perambulation of the house, attended by such elk-hounds and spaniels as chose to follow her.

This, too, was all in the day's routine. As soon would she come home and leave her own grandmother without a kiss as come back and leave the house unvisited. She fancied that the rooms brightened as she came in; stirred, opened their eyes as if they had been dozing in her absence. She fancied, too, that, hundreds and thousands of times as she had seen them, they never looked the same twice, as if so long a life as theirs had stored in them a myriad moods which changed with winter and summer, bright weather and dark, and her own fortunes and the people's characters who visited them. Polite, they always were to strangers, but a little wary; with her, they were entirely open and at their ease. Why not indeed? They had known each other for close on four centuries now. They had nothing to conceal. She knew their sorrows and joys. She knew what age each part of them was and its little secrets – a hidden drawer, a concealed cupboard, or some deficiency perhaps, such as a part made up, or added later. They, too, knew her in all her moods and changes. She had hidden nothing from them; had come to them as boy and woman, crying and dancing, brooding and gay. In this window-seat,[36] she had written her first verses; in that chapel, she had been married. And she would be buried here, she re-flected, kneeling on the window-sill in the long gallery and sipping her Spanish wine. Though she could hardly fancy it, the body of the heraldic leopard would be making yellow pools on the floor the day they lowered her to lie among her ancestors. She, who believed in no immortality, could not help feeling that her soul would come and go forever with the reds on the panels and the greens on the sofa. For the room – she had strolled into the Ambassador's bedroom – shone like a shell that has lain at the bottom of the sea for centuries and has been crusted over and painted a million tints by the water; it was rose and yellow, green and sand-coloured. It was frail as a shell, as iridescent and as empty. No Ambassador would ever sleep there again. Ah, but she knew where the heart of the house still beat. Gently opening a door, she stood on the threshold so that (as she fancied) the room could not see her and watched the tapestry rising and falling on the eternal faint breeze which never failed to move it. Still the hunter rode; still Daphne flew. The heart still beat, she thought, however faintly, however far withdrawn; the frail in-domitable heart of the immense building.

Now, calling her troop of dogs to her she passed down the

gallery whose floor was laid with whole oak trees sawn across. Rows of chairs with all their velvets faded stood ranged against the wall holding their arms out for Elizabeth, for James, for Shakespeare it might be, for Cecil, who never came. The sight made her gloomy. She unhooked the rope that fenced them off. She sat on the Queen's chair; she opened a manuscript book lying on Lady Betty's table; she stirred her fingers in the aged rose leaves; she brushed her short hair with King James' silver brushes; she bounced up and down upon his bed (but no King would ever sleep there again, for all Louise's new sheets) and pressed her cheek against the worn silver counterpane that lay upon it. But everywhere were little lavender bags to keep the moth out and printed notices, 'Please do not touch', which, though she had put them there herself, seemed to rebuke her. The house was no longer hers entirely, she sighed. It belonged to time now; to history; was past the touch and control of the living. Never would beer be spilt here any more, she thought (she was in the bedroom that had been old Nick Greene's), or holes burnt in the carpet. Never two hundred servants come running and brawling down the corridors with warming pans and great branches for the great fireplaces. Never would ale be brewed and candles made and saddles fashioned and stone shaped in the workshops outside the house. Hammers and mallets were silent now. Chairs and beds were empty; tankards of silver and gold were locked in glass cases. The great wings of silence beat up and down the empty house.

So she sat at the end of the gallery with her dogs couched round her, in Queen Elizabeth's hard arm-chair. The gallery stretched far away to a point where the light almost failed. It was as a tunnel bored deep into the past. As her eyes peered down it, she could see people laughing and talking; the great men she had known; Dryden, Swift, and Pope; and statesmen in colloquy; and lovers dallying in the window-seats; and people eating and drinking at the long tables; and the wood smoke curling round their heads and making them sneeze and cough. Still further down, she saw sets of splendid dancers formed for the quadrille.

A fluty, frail, but nevertheless stately music began to play. An organ boomed. A coffin was borne into the chapel. A marriage procession came out of it. Armed men with helmets left for the wars. They brought banners back from Flodden and Poitiers and stuck them on the wall. The long gallery filled itself thus, and still peering further, she thought she could make out at the very end, beyond the Elizabethans and the Tudors, some one older, further, darker, a cowled figure, monastic, severe, a monk, who went with his hands clasped, and a book in them, murmuring—

Like thunder, the stable clock struck four. Never did any earthquake so demolish a whole town. The gallery and all its occupants fell to powder. Her own face, that had been dark and sombre as she gazed, was lit as by an explosion of gunpowder. In this same light everything near her showed with extreme distinctness. She saw two flies circling round and noticed the blue sheen on their bodies; she saw a knot in the wood where her foot was, and her dog's ear twitching. At the same time, she heard a bough creaking in the garden, a sheep coughing in the park, a swift screaming past the window. Her own body quivered and tingled as if suddenly stood naked in a hard frost. Yet, she kept, as she had not done when the clock struck ten in London, complete composure (for she was now one and entire, and presented, it may be, a larger surface to the shock of time). She rose, but without precipitation, called her dogs, and went firmly but with great alertness of movement down the staircase and out into the garden. Here the shadows of the plants were miraculously distinct. She noticed the separate grains of earth in the flower beds as if she had a microscope stuck to her eye. She saw the intricacy of the twigs of every tree. Each blade of grass was distinct and the marking of veins and petals. She saw Stubbs, the gardener, coming along the path, and every button on his gaiters was visible; she saw Betty and Prince, the cart horses, and never had she marked so clearly the white star on Betty's forehead, and the three long hairs that fell down below the rest on Prince's tail. Out in the quadrangle the old grey walls of the house looked like a scraped new photograph; she heard the loud speaker

ORLANDO AT THE PRESENT TIME

condensing on the terrace a dance tune that people were listening to in the red-velvet opera house at Vienna.[37] Braced and strung up by the present moment she was also strangely afraid, as if whenever the gulf of time gaped and let a second through some unknown danger might come with it. The tension was too relentless and too rigorous to be endured long without discomfort. She walked more briskly than she liked, as if her legs were moved for her, through the garden and out into the park. Here she forced herself, by a great effort, to stop by the carpenter's shop, and to stand stock-still watching Joe Stubbs fashion a cart wheel. She was standing with her eye fixed on his hand when the quarter struck. It hurtled through her like a meteor, so hot that no fingers can hold it. She saw with disgusting vividness that the thumb on Joe's right hand was without a finger nail and there was a raised saucer of pink flesh where the nail should have been. The sight was so repulsive that she felt faint for a moment, but in that moment's darkness, when her eyelids flickered, she was relieved of the pressure of the present. There was something strange in the shadow that the flicker of her eyes cast, something which (as anyone can test for himself by looking now at the sky) is always absent from the present – whence its terror, its nondescript character – something one trembles to pin through the body with a name and call beauty, for it has no body, is as a shadow without substance or quality of its own, yet has the power to change whatever it adds itself to. This shadow now, while she flickered her eye in her faintness in the carpenter's shop, stole out, and attaching itself to the innumerable sights she had been receiving, composed them into something tolerable, comprehensible. Her mind began to toss like the sea. Yes, she thought, heaving a deep sigh of relief, as she turned from the carpenter's shop to climb the hill, I can begin to live again. I am by the Serpentine, she thought, the little boat is climbing through the white arch of a thousand deaths. I am about to understand . . .

Those were her words, spoken quite distinctly, but we cannot conceal the fact that she was now a very indifferent witness to

the truth of what was before her and might easily have mistaken
a sheep for a cow, or an old man called Smith for one who was
called Jones and was no relation of his whatever. For the shadow
of faintness which the thumb without a nail had cast had deepened
now, at the back of her brain (which is the part furthest from
sight), into a pool where things dwell in darkness so deep that
what they are we scarcely know. She now looked down into
this pool or sea in which everything is reflected – and, indeed,
some say that all our most violent passions, and art and religion,
are the reflections which we see in the dark hollow at the back of
the head when the visible world is obscured for the time. She
looked there now, long, deeply, profoundly, and immediately
the ferny path up the hill along which she was walking became
not entirely a path, but partly the Serpentine; the hawthorn
bushes were partly ladies and gentlemen sitting with card-cases
and gold-mounted canes; the sheep were partly tall Mayfair
houses; everything was partly something else, as if her mind had
become a forest with glades branching here and there; things
came nearer, and further, and mingled and separated and made
the strangest alliances and combinations in an incessant chequer
of light and shade. Except when Canute, the elk-hound, chased a
rabbit and so reminded her that it must be about half-past four –
it was indeed twenty-three minutes to six – she forgot the time.

The ferny path led, with many turns and windings, higher and
higher to the oak tree, which stood on the top. The tree had
grown bigger, sturdier, and more knotted since she had known
it, somewhere about the year 1588, but it was still in the prime
of life. The little sharply frilled leaves were still fluttering thickly
on its branches. Flinging herself on the ground, she felt the
bones of the tree running out like ribs from a spine this way and
that beneath her. She liked to think that she was riding the back
of the world. She liked to attach herself to something hard. As
she flung herself down a little square book bound in red cloth
fell from the breast of her leather jacket – her poem 'The Oak
Tree'. 'I should have brought a trowel,' she reflected. The earth
was so shallow over the roots that it seemed doubtful if she

could do as she meant and bury the book here. Besides, the dogs would dig it up. No luck ever attends these symbolical celebrations, she thought. Perhaps it would be as well then to do without them. She had a little speech on the tip of her tongue which she meant to speak over the book as she buried it. (It was a copy of the first edition, signed by author and artist.) 'I bury this as a tribute,' she was going to have said, 'a return to the land of what the land has given me,' but Lord! once one began mouthing words aloud, how silly they sounded! She was reminded of old Greene getting upon a platform the other day comparing her with Milton[38] (save for his blindness) and handing her a cheque for two hundred guineas. She had thought then, of the oak tree here on its hill, and what has that got to do with this, she had wondered? What has praise and fame to do with poetry? What has seven editions (the book had already gone into no less) got to do with the value of it? Was not writing poetry a secret transaction, a voice answering a voice? So that all this chatter and praise and blame and meeting people who admired one and meeting people who did not admire one was as ill suited as could be to the thing itself – a voice answering a voice. What could have been more secret, she thought, more slow, and like the intercourse of lovers, than the stammering answer she had made all these years to the old crooning song of the woods, and the farms and the brown horses standing at the gate, neck to neck, and the smithy and the kitchen and the fields, so laboriously bearing wheat, turnips, grass, and the garden blowing irises and fritillaries?

So she let her book lie unburied and dishevelled on the ground, and watched the vast view, varied like an ocean floor this evening with the sun lightening it and the shadows darkening it. There was a village with a church tower among elm trees; a grey domed manor house in a park; a spark of light burning on some glass-house; a farmyard with yellow corn stacks. The fields were marked with black tree clumps, and beyond the fields stretched long woodlands, and there was the gleam of a river, and then hills again. In the far distance Snowdon's crags broke white

among the clouds; she saw the far Scottish hills and the wild
tides that swirl about the Hebrides. She listened for the sound of
gun-firing out at sea. No – only the wind blew. There was no
war to-day. Drake had gone; Nelson had gone. 'And there', she
thought, letting her eyes, which had been looking at these far
distances, drop once more to the land beneath her, 'was my land
once: that Castle between the downs was mine; and all that moor
running almost to the sea was mine.' Here the landscape (it must
have been some trick of the fading light) shook itself, heaped
itself, let all this encumbrance of houses, castles, and woods slide
off its tent-shaped sides. The bare mountains of Turkey were
before her. It was blazing noon. She looked straight at the baked
hill-side. Goats cropped the sandy tufts at her feet. An eagle
soared above her. The raucous voice of old Rustum, the gipsy,
croaked in her ears, 'What is your antiquity and your race, and
your possessions compared with this? What do you need with
four hundred bedrooms and silver lids on all your dishes, and
house-maids dusting?'

At this moment some church clock chimed in the valley. The
tent-like landscape collapsed and fell. The present showered
down upon her head once more, but now that the light was
fading, gentler than before, calling into view nothing detailed,
nothing small, but only misty fields, cottages with lamps in
them, the slumbering bulk of a wood, and a fan-shaped light
pushing the darkness before it along some lane. Whether it had
struck nine, ten, or eleven, she could not say. Night had come –
night that she loved of all times, night in which the reflections in
the dark pool of the mind shine more clearly than by day. It was
not necessary to faint now in order to look deep into the darkness
where things shape themselves and to see in the pool of the
mind now Shakespeare, now a girl in Russian trousers, now a
toy boat on the Serpentine, and then the Atlantic itself, where it
storms in great waves past Cape Horn. She looked into the
darkness. There was her husband's brig, rising to the top of the
wave! Up, it went, and up and up. The white arch of a thousand
deaths rose before it. Oh rash, oh ridiculous man, always sailing,

so uselessly, round Cape Horn in the teeth of a gale! But the brig was through the arch and out on the other side; it was safe at last!

'Ecstasy!' she cried, 'ecstasy!' And then the wind sank, the waters grew calm; and she saw the waves rippling peacefully in the moonlight.

'Marmaduke Bonthrop Shelmerdine!' she cried, standing by the oak tree.

The beautiful, glittering name fell out of the sky like a steel-blue feather. She watched it fall, turning and twisting like a slow-falling arrow that cleaves the deep air beautifully. He was coming, as he always came, in moments of dead calm; when the wave rippled and the spotted leaves fell slowly over her foot in the autumn woods; when the leopard was still; the moon was on the waters, and nothing moved between sky and sea. Then he came.

All was still now. It was near midnight. The moon rose slowly over the weald. Its light raised a phantom castle upon earth. There stood the great house with all its windows robed in silver. Of wall or substance there was none. All was phantom. All was still. All was lit as for the coming of a dead Queen. Gazing below her, Orlando saw dark plumes tossing in the courtyard, and torches flickering and shadows kneeling. A Queen once more stepped from her chariot.

'The house is at your service, Ma'am,' she cried, curtseying deeply. 'Nothing has been changed. The dead Lord, my father, shall lead you in.'

As she spoke, the first stroke of midnight sounded. The cold breeze of the present brushed her face with its little breath of fear. She looked anxiously into the sky. It was dark with clouds now. The wind roared in her ears. But in the roar of the wind she heard the roar of an aeroplane[39] coming nearer and nearer.

'Here! Shel, here!' she cried, baring her breast to the moon (which now showed bright) so that her pearls glowed like the eggs of some vast moon-spider. The aeroplane rushed out of the clouds and stood over her head. It hovered above her. Her pearls burnt like a phosphorescent flare in the darkness.

And as Shelmerdine, now grown a fine sea-captain, hale, fresh-coloured, and alert, leapt to the ground, there sprang up over his head a single wild bird.

'It is the goose!' Orlando cried. 'The wild goose . . .'

And the twelfth stroke of midnight sounded; the twelfth stroke of midnight, Thursday, the eleventh of October, Nineteen hundred and Twenty Eight.

Index

A., Lord, 135
Abbey, Westminster, 39
Addison, Joseph, 119, 138, 145
Alexandra, Queen, 55
Anne, Queen, 136
Archduchess Harriet of Finster-
Aarhorn (*see* Archduke Harry),
77, 126–8
Archduke, Harry, the, 169
Arlington House, 137

Bartholomew, Widow, 161, 162,
165
Bartolus, Captain Nicholas
Benedict, 109, 115, 138
Basket, Butler, 163
Boswell, James, 154
Brigge, John Fenner, 90, 94
Browne, Sir Thomas, 51, 54, 57
Browning, Robert, 193

C., Marquis of, 135, 169
Canute, the elk-hound, 169
Carlyle, Thomas, 193
Carpenter, Nurse, 50
Charles the Second, King, 83
Chesterfield, Lady, 134
Chesterfield, Lord, 148, 201
Chubb, Eusebius, 158
Cicero, 71
Clorinda, 23
Consort, the Prince, 208
Cumberland, Earl of, 21, 208

Deffand, Madame du, 139
Donne, John, 62, 198
Drake, 226
Dryden, John, 119, 138, 219
Dupper, Mr., 49, 53, 58, 120,
121, 181

Elizabeth, Queen, 15, 16, 17, 18,
19, 69
Euphrosyne, 23

Favilla, 23
Field, Mrs., 50
Frost, the Great, 24

Gladstone, Mrs., 177
Greene, Nicholas (afterwards
Sir), 58–65, 71, 192, 225
Greenwich, 60
Grimsditch, Mrs., 49, 51, 53, 74,
120, 121, 208
Gulliver's Travels, 146
Gwynn, Nell, 83

Hall, the falconer, 53
Hartopp, Miss Penelope, 91
Hercules, Death of, tragedy by
Orlando, 65

Isham, Mr., 58

James the First, King, 24, 47, 69
Johnson, Samuel, 154

229

THE END

Notes

GENERAL NOTE

Orlando is a *roman à clef*, written to entertain and also perhaps to comfort Vita Sackville-West. It is full of knowing detail about Knole, the Sackvilles' ancestral home near Sevenoaks where Vita had grown up and from which she was finally exiled when her father died in January 1928, during the writing of *Orlando*. Part of Woolf's intention was the re-creation, within the novel, of the home that Vita had lost, and much of the information she used was drawn from Vita's account of it in *Knole*. But Woolf had also visited Knole, and had listened attentively to Vita talking about her love for it. For that reason, these notes also draw on Vita's expanded fourth edition of *Knole* (1958) as well as on Charles J. Phillips's two-volume *History of the Sackville Family* (1930) (hereafter, *Phillips*) which also provides a *catalogue raisonné* of the paintings and drawings in the house at that time. In writing *Orlando*, Virginia accepted Vita's view of the Sackvilles that 'their interest lay in their being so representative. From generation to generation they might stand, fully equipped, as portraits from English history' (*Knole*, p. 28).

In what follows, further material has been taken from Woolf's own *Letters* and *Diary*, from Victoria Glendinning's biography, *Vita* (1983), and from the *Letters of Vita*. On the MS, see 'Orlando: An Edition of the Manuscript' (ed. Madeline Moore, *Twentieth Century Literature*, 25, 1979, pp. 303–55). Much the most important single source of information has been Nigel Nicolson, who annotated a volume of *Orlando* for our text editor, Brenda Lyons, especially for this edition; we would like to thank him particularly warmly for all his help. In addition, Sandra Gilbert would like to express her deep gratitude to Susan Fox for invaluable research assistance.

PREFACE

The list of contributors in the preface, which includes many of Woolf's favourite authors, as well as her friends, is part of the joke begun when she subtitled *Orlando*, 'A Biography' (see *Letters*, III, pp. 493, 547, 554, where she asks her nephew Quentin Bell, Hugh Walpole and Charles Sanger for permission to use their names here).

CHAPTER I

1. *a Moor*: a North African. It is difficult to know in what context Orlando's actual ancestors would have fought against Moors in North Africa, though his literary ancestor, Charlemagne's knight, Roland or Orlando, the hero of Ariosto's epic poem *Orlando Furioso* (1532), had fought against them and been driven mad by love (see the introduction, p. xxv). According to the MS, the novel's action begins in 1553 when Thomas Sackville, like Orlando, would have been sixteen; the time sequence quickly moves on to the end of Elizabeth's reign (which began in 1558).

2. *fields of asphodel*: where the immortals or the happy dead live. The asphodel is a lily-like flower – Vita had found it growing wild in Persia on her visit in 1926 (*Vita*, p. 157).

3. *northern mists . . . coronets on their heads*: 'The Sackvilles are supposed to have gone into Normandy in the ninth century with Rollo the Dane' (*Knole*, p. 29).

4. *an heraldic leopard*: mentioned as decorating the Tudor gables (*Knole*, pp. 2, 3).

5. *the shapely legs, the handsome body*: what follows, according to Nicolson, is a recognizable description of Vita Sackville-West, even down to the detail that she 'was a trifle clumsy' (p. 13). Woolf, like the book's narrator, wrote admiringly of Vita's legs (e.g. to Jacques Raverat, 26 December 1924, as 'her real claim to consideration', *Letters*, III, p. 150; or in her diary a year later, *Diary*, III, 21 December 1925, p. 52).

6. *Aethelbert: A Tragedy in Five Acts*: like Orlando, Thomas Sackville, first Earl of Dorset, wrote a five-act tragedy inspired by early English history, *Gorboduc*, performed in 1561 (*Knole*, pp. 33, 41).

7. *Stubbs, the gardener*: Stubbs was the name of the head gardener at Knole when Woolf was writing (Nicolson).

NOTES

8. *the house was a town*: Woolf exaggerates Vita's descriptions of Knole
   as 'a medieval village', 'a jumbled village', just as below (p. 16)
   where Knole's four acres become five (*Knole*, pp. 1, 18).

9. *a place crowned by a single oak tree*: Vita often wrote under an oak in
   Knole park, on a high mound known as the Mast Head (Nicolson).
   The oak tree, traditionally associated with English kings, later
   provides the title for Orlando's major poem, his equivalent of
   Vita's prize-winning poem *The Land*. Its title suggests the value of
   roots, family and Englishness.

10. *Sometimes one could see the English Channel ... London ... Snowdon*:
    none of these places can actually be seen from Knole, but this
    panoramic sweep (echoed in the novel's time scheme) seems to
    have been part of her plan for the book from its first conception:
    'Suddenly between twelve & one I conceived a whole fantasy to be
    called "The Jessamy Brides" ... Two women, poor, solitary at the
    top of a house – one can see anything (for this is all fantasy) the
    Tower Bridge, clouds, aeroplanes ... The Ladies are to have Con-
    stantinople in view. Dreams of golden domes ...' (*Diary*, III, 14
    March 1927, p. 131).

11. *Mrs. Stewkley's sitting-room ... hodden brown*: a 'Mrs Stewkly' is
    named as 'At the parlour table' in a list of Knole household servants
    from 1613 (*Knole*, p. 78); hodden is a coarse woollen cloth; the
    unidentified writer is William Shakespeare, whose portrait was in
    the Poets' Parlour at Knole. Vita later wrote, 'I often entertained
    wild dreams that some light might be thrown on the Shakespeare
    problem by a discovery of letters or documents at Knole' (*Knole*,
    4th edn, 1958, p. 57).

    Woolf had associated Shakespeare at work with the mystery of
    creativity in her short story 'The Mark on the Wall': 'A man who
    sat himself solidly in an arm-chair, and looked into the fire, so – A
    shower of ideas fell perpetually from some very high Heaven down
    through his mind. He leant his forehead on his hand, and people,
    looking in through the open door ...' (*Shorter Fiction*, p. 85.)

12. *the great Queen herself*: Queen Elizabeth gave Knole to Thomas
    Sackville in 1566, and visited the house on a royal progress in 1573.
    There was a portrait of her in the Brown Gallery (*Phillips*, I, p. 190;
    II, p. 423). Woolf's portrayal of Queen Elizabeth was partly in-
    spired by her waxwork effigy, then at Westminster Abbey, of
    which she wrote a description soon after completing *Orlando*: 'Her

eyes are wide and vigilant; her nose thin as the beak of a hawk; her lips shut tight; her eyebrows arched; only the jowl gives the fine-drawn face its massiveness' (*New Republic*, 11 April 1928; reprinted in 'The Fleeting Portrait', *CE*, IV, p. 205). Woolf's friend Lytton Strachey drew a comparable portrait of the ageing queen in his *Elizabeth and Essex* (published December 1928), but Woolf did not apparently read it until after the publication of *Orlando* in October (see *Diary*, III, 25 November 1928, p. 208).

13. *she heard the guns in the Channel*: Vita had told Virginia of hearing the guns in France from Knole during the First World War (Nicolson). Woolf had herself heard them on the downs at Asheham in 1916 (see 'Heard on the Downs', *Essays*, II, pp. 40–42).

14. *the great monastic house*: Knole had passed from Archbishop Bourchier and Cardinal Morton to Henry VIII, and thence to Queen Elizabeth who gave it to Thomas Sackville. Although the unnamed house in *Orlando* is said to have been given to Orlando's father, Orlando himself is also identified with Thomas Sackville, both as a poet and playwright (Sackville had written *Gorboduc* and the moralistic poem *A Mirror for Magistrates*), as the Queen's 'young cousin', and in receiving various honours from her. Like Sackville, Orlando becomes Lord Treasurer and Lord High Steward, is dubbed Knight of the Garter (see p. 18), and is sent to Scotland 'on a sad embassy to the unhappy Queen' (p. 18), i.e. to warn Mary Queen of Scots of her impending execution (*Knole*, pp. 34–5).

15. *booming at the Tower*: i.e. at the Tower of London, to celebrate the defeat of the Spanish Armada in 1588.

16. *Richmond*: Queen Elizabeth lived at Richmond Palace, to the south-west of London, dying there in 1603. She was succeeded by James I.

17. *Doris, Chloris, Delia, or Diana*: these might be typical names of mistresses in love poems: the Elizabethan poet Samuel Daniel wrote a sonnet sequence to Delia; while the Restoration poet Charles Sackville, sixth Earl (1638–1706), 'left us gay and artificial stanzas to Chloris and Dorinda' (*Knole*, p. 115).

18. *Wapping Old Stairs*: in east London, near the Tower and running down to the docks. Woolf's fascination with Elizabethan voyages is evident in what follows: the Spanish main was the north-east coast of South America, from Panama to the Orinoco River; the Azores are islands off the coast of Portugal, where in 1591, the

explorer Sir Richard Grenville's ship *Revenge* was sunk as he fought against the Spanish. (Her essay on Hakluyt's Voyages, 'Trafficks and Discoveries', is reprinted in *Essays*, II, pp. 329–36.)

19. *Earl of Cumberland*: 'a picturesque figure. He was Elizabeth's official champion at all jousts and tilting, a nobleman of great splendour ... [he had] the love of adventure which carried him eleven times to sea, to the Indies and elsewhere' (*Knole*, pp. 48–9). He was the father-in-law of Richard Sackville, third Earl of Dorset, and there was a portrait of him in the Brown Gallery (*Phillips*, p. 423). The reference to Cumberland building almshouses in the Sheen Road later in this paragraph looks like a private joke. On 27 August 1932, Woolf dictated the following response to an inquiry on this topic:

> [Mrs Woolf] cannot recollect that she had any authority for saying that Lord Cumberland founded almshouses; she thinks it probable that having some recollection of old almshouses in that neighbourhood, she fathered them upon Lord Cumberland on the spur of the moment.

These early nineteenth century almshouses stood just around the corner from Hogarth House, Richmond, where the Woolfs lived from 1915–24. There is a further reference to them near the end of the novel (p. 208).

20. *Clorinda, Favilla, Euphrosyne*: Nigel Nicolson identifies Clorinda with Rosamund Grosvenor, Vita's first, and at one time best-loved, friend (*Vita*, pp. 23–4, 48). Euphrosyne ('joy') was one of the three classical Graces (Woolf had used the name for the boat in her first novel, *The Voyage Out*, 1915). As 'one of the Irish Desmonds', she may recall the portrait in the Leicester Gallery of Catherine Fitzgerald, Countess of Desmond (*Knole*, p. 14).

21. *The Great Frost*: occurred in January 1608. Woolf knew of it from Thomas Dekker's pamphlet 'The Great Frost/Cold Doings in London, except it be at the Lottery', reprinted anonymously in Edward Arber's *An English Garner* (I, 1877, pp. 77–99). Some details are taken from his pamphlet, e.g. 'the high mortality among sheep and cattle', but Woolf's account is more fantastic, so that the rocks of the Peak District ('some parts of Derbyshire') are attributed to 'a kind of petrification'. Dekker described how the Thames became 'a very pavement of glass', and the citizens played games and sold

food and drink on the frozen river; he also described the plight of a man trapped on an ice floe as the result of the sudden thaw with which the frost ended. Woolf had a letter from Vita of 31 January 1927 describing Moscow and 'all the traffic passing to and fro across the frozen river as though it were a road; and sleighs everywhere . . .' (*Letters of Vita*, p. 183.)

22. *the north-west passage . . . Armada*: Elizabethan explorers had hoped to find a sea route to the Far East by sailing around the north coast of America. The Spanish Armada was the fleet sent by Philip II against Elizabeth in 1588 (see Note 15, above).

23. *London Bridge*: built at the narrowest point of the river, the old bridge carried shops and houses on it, and the ice would have been deepest here. The Surrey side is the south side of the river.

24. *corantoe and lavolta*: Renaissance dances, the first characterized by quick running steps ('courante'), the second a dance for a couple, involving high leaps.

25. *Princess Marousha Romanovitch*: later referred to as Sasha, this character may partly have been suggested by 'La Muscovite', whose pastel portrait hangs in the sitting-room at Knole and who is addressed in Charles Sackville's poem 'Arno's Vale' (*Knole*, p. 173); but Woolf's main inspiration was Vita's great love, Violet Trefusis. On 13 October 1927 Virginia wrote to Vita: 'Tomorrow I begin the chapter which describes Violet and you meeting on the ice . . . Do give me some inkling what sort of quarrels you had. Also, for what particular quality did she first choose you?' The same letter links Vita (rather than Violet) with emeralds, however: 'I want to see you in the lamplight, in your emeralds' (*Letters*, III, p. 430).

26. *Je crois avoir fait . . . la sienne*: Sasha's French here was supplied by Vita who, like Orlando, was bilingual in French and English. She was apparently translating Woolf's phrases, 'I think I met a gentleman of your family in Poland last summer', and 'The ladies of the English Court ravish me with their beauty. Never have I seen so graceful a lady as your Queen or so fine a head dress as she wears.' Vita also supplied the translation of 'rigged up like a Maypole' (see p. 28), as well as a number of other phrases that Woolf did not finally use (*Letters of Vita*, 26 April 1928, p. 284).

27. *George Villiers*: (1592–1628) was King James's favourite, later made Duke of Buckingham.

28. *the Tower . . . Royal Exchange*: the Yeomen of the Guard, known as

'Beefeaters', guard the Tower and wear a distinctive red Tudor uniform. The Temple Bar, the gate between Westminster and the old City of London, was topped with iron spikes, on which the heads of executed rebels were displayed. The Royal Exchange was built as a money market in 1564, on the corner of Threadneedle Street in the City.

29. *a white Russian fox*: Nigel Nicolson suggests that this refers to the Russian bear-cub given to Vita by Ivan Hay when she was nineteen; it had to be put down (*Vita*, p. 41). Orlando had earlier compared Sasha to 'a fox in the snow' (p. 26). Virginia later described Violet Trefusis (whom she did not meet until 1932) as 'like a fox cub, all scent and seduction' (19 January 1941, *Letters*, VI, p. 462).

30. *the arras . . . at home*: Vita wrote of the Leicester Gallery that 'the tapestry sways, and the figures on it undulate and seem to come alive (*Knole*, pp. 14–16); but Nicolson identifies this with the tapestry in the Venetian Ambassador's room.

31. *the philosopher is right*: Robert Burton takes this view in his *Anatomy of Melancholy* (1621), but as an Anglican he would have disapproved of the Anabaptists, a radical sect who aroused great fear since they did not believe in the sacraments (including baptism) and were permitted to conform outwardly.

32. *palanquin*: a canopy.

33. *sennight*: in seven days' time (archaic).

34. *the cross of St. Paul's*: a deliberate anachronism – old St Paul's had a square tower that was burnt down in the fire of London of 1666. It was rebuilt with a dome and cross by Christopher Wren (see also pp. 38, 117 and 157).

35. *stags . . . bucket*: this happened at Knole once according to Nicolson. Vita described a stag wandering into the banqueting-hall on one occasion during the summer when the doors were left open (*Knole*, p. 4).

36. *cony catchers*: Elizabethan slang for 'confidence tricksters' (literally, rabbit catchers).

37. *Punch and Judy show*: a traditional children's show performed with glove-puppets in a small booth, in which Punch first beats, then kills, his wife Judy. Orlando is watching a street performance of Shakespeare's *Othello* (as the index reference shows).

38. *Methinks . . . should yawn*: *Othello*, V. ii. 99–101; perhaps with an allusion to the total eclipse of the sun on 29 June 1927 which the

Woolfs and Vita and Harold Nicolson travelled up to Richmond in
North Yorkshire to see (30 June 1927, *Diary*, III, pp. 142–4), and
which she also wrote of in 'The Sun and the Fish' (*CE*, IV,
pp. 178–83).

39. *Jour de ma vie!*: 'Day of my life', the Sackville family motto, derived
from the Battle of Crécy (1346) where one of the family had fought
(Nicolson).

40. *Drake, Hawkins, and Grenville*: heroes of Elizabeth's naval wars
against the Spanish.

41. *the Irish rebels*: the English government under Elizabeth and James
made a series of attempts to colonize Ireland. Lands in Donegal
and Tyrone had been declared forfeit in December 1607, and later
in 1608 a further rebellion broke out. In the MS, the old nobleman
is exceptional among those dying in the flood; for the rest, 'Nobody
of very high birth seemed to be included . . . as if the thaw had
been the work of these rebels . . . which seemed to show that the
upper sort had received warning & made for safety.'

42. *standing out to sea*: sailing out to sea.

CHAPTER II

1. *The biographer . . . truth*: at much the same time as Woolf began
writing *Orlando* she completed an essay on 'The New Biography'
(*CE*, IV, pp. 229–35), in part a review of Harold Nicolson's *Some
People*. It opens with a quotation from Sir Sidney Lee: 'The aim of
biography is the truthful transmission of personality.' Woolf goes
on to argue that truth and personality are opposed, and that though
truth is required in a biography it does not combine easily or
comfortably with fiction or with the depiction of inner life. Themes
from this essay are taken up again on p. 55.

2. *of what nature life?*: Orlando's seven-day sleep, a figure for oblivion
or death, prepares us for his Jacobean preoccupation with 'the
skull beneath the skin', on display in this chapter, as well as for
other unexpected developments.

3. *Mrs. Grimsditch*: all the names listed here are taken from the third
Lord Dorset's catalogue of his household between 1613 and 1624
(*Knole*, pp. 78–81). At the parlour table are listed (among others),
Mrs Field, Mrs Grimsditch, Mrs Stewkly, Mr Dupper, Chaplain; in
the Nursery, Nurse Carpenter; at the Laundry Maids' Table, Mrs

Judith Simpton, Faith Husband and Grace Robinson, a Blacka-moor.

4. *the crypt where his ancestors lay*: the crypt of Orlando's ancestors lies beneath the house, symbolizing an awareness of death below or behind all human existence and prompting Orlando to a Hamlet-like soliloquy over the old bones. The Sackville family vault is not actually at Knole but at Withyham parish church. The Jacobean diarist Anne Clifford recorded visiting 'my Lord Treasurer's tomb' there and returning in tears. Vita added, 'I have been down into that vault myself, and it is not a cheerful expedition. In a small, dark cave underground, beneath the church, among grey veils of cobwebs, the coffins of the Sackvilles are stacked on shelves ...' (*Knole*, p. 71.)

5. *Thomas Browne*: (1605–82), a Norwich doctor famous for his elo-quent Latinate prose (cf. 'the delicate articulation of one of the doctor's longest and most marvellously contorted cogitations', p. 52). *Hydriotaphia, or Urn Burial* (1658) is a meditation on death, time and eternity. According to *Knole* (p. 105), Richard Sackville, third Earl of Dorset, recommended Browne's *Religio Medici* to Sir Kenelm Digby when the latter was imprisoned during the Civil War. Digby was so impressed with the book that he sent back a long letter of his *Observations* on it to Lord Dorset. Woolf had always admired Browne's prose (see *Essays*, III, pp. 153–9, 368–71).

6. *asphodel*: see Chapter I, Note 2.

7. *every gift . . . beaten gold*: the four acres have now become nine; this catalogue of Orlando's possessions suggests the 1624 household inventory (see *Knole*, pp. 95–6; and Note 35, below).

8. *a great inlaid cabinet . . . cedar wood*: this cabinet belonged to Vita, and was where she kept all her most intimate letters. It may be what Virginia had in mind when she asked Vita, 'Will this letter go into the cupboard?' (30 October 1927, *Letters*, III, p. 434). Orlando's prolific writings parallel those of Vita, both as a child and a young woman (*Vita*, pp. 25–6, 33). The play printed by John Ball suggests Vita's *Chatterton*, privately printed at Sevenoaks in 1909 (Nicolson). Orlando's poem 'The Oak Tree', whose writing extends throughout the book, corresponds to Vita's long poem *The Land* (see Chapter I, Note 9).

9. *of rainbow and granite*: this passage closely echoes Woolf's essay 'The

New Biography' (see above, Chapter II, Note 1) in its distinction between 'truth as something of granite-like solidity and personality as something of rainbow-like intangibility'. The essay ends with a reference to Harold Nicolson's 'mixture of biography and autobiography, of fact and fiction, of Lord Curzon's trousers and Miss Plimsoll's nose . . .' The 'even now (the first of November, 1927)' is likely to have been the actual date of composition since, according to the MS, she began Chapter II on 29 October. *Orlando* was begun on 8 October 1927 and completed on 17 March 1928 (see *Diary*, III, pp. 161, 176; *Letters*, III, pp. 428, 474).

10. *This is the face . . . Twitchett's room*: the face is Shakespeare's (see Chapter I, Note 11). Twitchett is Orlando's mother's waiting maid (see p. 12).

11. *how difficult it is for a nobleman to be a writer*: in *Knole* (p. 32) Vita quoted Edmund Gosse to the effect that Thomas Sackville was 'a born poet . . . diverted from poetry by the pursuits of statesmanship', and thus 'a very good instance of the disadvantage of fine birth to a poet'. Woolf told Vita's cousin Edward Sackville-West, 'How no aristocrat can write a book' (Letter to Vita, 17 February 1926, *Letters*, III, p. 241), and in a slightly later essay, 'The Niece of an Earl', made the related point that 'It is from the middle class that writers spring' (*CE*, I, p. 222).

12. *shawms . . . had burst in*: Woolf may be thinking of the classical myth, according to which the head of the poet Orpheus was torn from his shoulders by a 'horrid rout' of frenzied women, perhaps with a distant echo of Milton's *Lycidas*, where love is also a threat to poetic achievement. Shawms are antique wind instruments.

13. *Sir Boris . . . the Spaniard*: Woolf here echoes the 'long monotonous list of Sir Jordans, Sir Andrews, Sir Edwards, Sir Richards' (*Knole*, p. 30).

14. *the vales of Tempe*: in Greece, close to Mount Olympus, and praised for their beauty in classical poetry.

15. *Giles Isham of Norfolk*: Sir Gyles Isham (1903–76) was Woolf's second cousin, son of her cousin Millicent (née Halford Vaughan). On going down from Oxford in 1926, he became a Shakespearean actor.

16. *the glories of blood and state*: the opening lines of James Shirley's best-known poem, from his play *The Contention of Ajax and Ulysses* (1659):

The glories of our blood and state
Are shadows, not substantial things.

17. *Lady Winchilsea's fan*: Ann Finch, Countess of Winchilsea (1661–1720), wrote poems, some of which Woolf discusses in Chapter IV of *A Room of One's Own* (1928; Penguin Books, 1945). This phrase echoes the title of Wilde's play, *Lady Windermere's Fan* (1892).

18. *Nicholas Greene of Clifford's Inn*: an imaginary writer, supposed to live in a small court off Fleet Street (where Virginia and Leonard had lived in the year following their marriage). Greene is partly based on the Elizabethan hack writer, pamphleteer, poet and playwright, Robert Greene (1558–92), notorious for his envy of Shakespeare, whom he denounced as 'an upstart crow, beautified with our feathers'. He later reappeared in Chapter III of *A Room of One's Own* as the seducer of Shakespeare's (imaginary) sister Judith: 'at last Nick Greene the actor-manager took pity on her; she found herself with child by that gentleman and so . . . killed herself one winter's night . . .'

19. *Flodden . . . Agincourt*: the English defeated the Scots at the Battle of Flodden (1513), and had defeated the French at Agincourt a century earlier (1415).

20. *Malmsey*: a sweet Madeira wine.

21. *Shakespeare . . . Donne*: Orlando's heroes are the major dramatists and poets of his day. John Donne, the love poet and Dean of St Paul's, according to Izaac Walton, sometimes preached in the Chapel at Knole, and left Lord Dorset several pictures in his will (*Knole*, 4th edn, 1958, pp. 32, 69). The dramatist Ben Jonson had his portrait in the Poets' Parlour and is said to have enjoyed the patronage of Richard Sackville, third Earl of Dorset (1589–1624) (*Knole*, p. 59). For Browne, see above, Note 5.

22. *La Gloire*: glory.

23. *Cock Tavern in Fleet Street*: setting for a scandalous scene in which Charles Sackville, sixth Earl of Dorset, was involved (*Knole*, p. 117). Leonard and Virginia used to dine there when they lived round the corner at Clifford's Inn.

24. *Cicero*: Roman statesman (106–43 BC) whose prose style was much admired and imitated during the Renaissance.

25. *three hundred years ago*: in the MS, a passage follows insisting that Greene's 'impure' sayings have had to be suppressed in the interests

of Modesty (who appears again in the masque in Chapter III), even though Greene had a letter from Shakespeare relating the true story of Mr W.H. and the dark lady, which he 'gave to Orlando as a pleasant curiosity and a keepsake', but which had to be burnt. The MS adds, 'No one of British blood will censure us for the course we took.'

26. *a teg from a ewe*: a two-year-old (male) sheep from a female.

27. *the finest elk-hounds*: Vita kept elk-hounds (she inherited Canute from her father – see p. 169); one hound did have puppies under the dinner table at Long Barn, where Vita was then living (Nicolson). Like Vita, Orlando turned to dogs and gardening for consolation.

28. *Time passed*: Woolf here mocks the middle section, 'Time Passes', of her previous novel, *To the Lighthouse* (1927). The meditation on time that follows gives light-hearted expression to a serious artistic problem for the novelist.

29. *deserts of vast eternity*: from Andrew Marvell's 'To his Coy Mistress', itself a meditation on the nature of time:

> But at my back I always hear
> Time's winged chariot hurrying near.
> And Yonder all before us lie
> Deserts of vast eternity.

30. *fleets*: glides away, vanishes.

31. *budget*: the contents of a bag or bundle.

32. *scrolloping*: a word invented by Woolf to denote a rambling, looped and decorated movement (see also p. 159).

33. *There it lay . . . spring*: Vita loved this paragraph and quoted the final sentence from it in an appendix to the fourth edition of *Knole* (1958, p. 215). Writing immediately to Virginia to thank her for the novel, she added a postscript: 'You made me cry with your passages about Knole, you wretch' (11 October 1928, *Letters of Vita*, p. 306).

34. *King Jamie, my Lord*: the King's Bedroom at Knole was said to have been furnished for the reception of James I. During the Restoration, Charles Sackville, sixth Earl of Dorset, had it provided with 'a set of furniture made entirely in silver: table, hanging mirror, and tripods'. Like Orlando, he 'cannot have known when he had had enough of a good thing' (*Knole*, p. 15). James I's son, Charles I, had

been executed in 1649, and Oliver Cromwell, on behalf of Parliament, ruled England during the interregnum. Charles II came to the throne in 1660. The Sackville family had been committed royalists (see *Knole*, pp. 97, 106, 107, 110).

35. *Three hundred and sixty-five bedrooms*: according to *Knole* (p. 4) there were 7 courts, 52 staircases and 365 rooms (not bedrooms) in the house, to correspond to the divisions of days and weeks in the year. The inventory that follows, though much exaggerated, is inspired by one of 1624 (*Knole*, pp. 95–6).

36. *great trees . . . flooring*: the floor of the Cartoon Gallery at Knole is formed of 'solid tree trunks, split in half, with the rounded half downwards' (*Knole*, p. 10).

37. *galleries . . . mermaids on their backs*: in classical legend Daphne fled from Apollo and was transformed into a laurel. There was a blue and green tapestry that constantly stirred in the breeze in the Venetian Ambassador's bedroom, a room lovingly described by Vita in *Knole*; the carved chairs in the Brown Gallery were 'for ever holding out their arms, for ever disappointed', and in the ballroom there was a frieze of mermaids and dolphins that Vita had loved as a child (*Knole*, pp. 15–16, 13, 11). Early editions of *Knole* and Charles Phillips's history describe the tapestries in the Venetian Ambassador's bedroom variously as medieval or classical in theme – Apollo and Diana or Ulysses and Circe perhaps – but a guidebook to Knole written by Vita for the National Trust in 1948 says that they depict scenes from *Orlando Furioso* (see Chapter I, Note 1).

38. *round schoolboy hand*: like Vita's (Nicolson); for 'The Oak Tree', see Chapter I, Note 9.

39. *the Archduchess Harriet*: based on Lord Henry (Harry) Lascelles, who pursued and proposed to Vita in 1912 (*Vita*, pp. 48–51); later, in 1922, he married the Princess Royal. Virginia asked Vita, 'What used you and Lord Lascelles to talk about' (23 October 1927). Vita replied, 'He was always very tongue-tied, so we didn't get very far. He had nice hands' (25 October 1927, *Letters of Vita*, pp. 255–6). Scand-op-Boom may have been suggested by Bergen-op-Zoom, where Edward Sackville, fourth Earl of Dorset, had fought a duel (*Knole*, p. 184).

40. *Jacobi or of Topp*: 'This suit [of tilting armour], which is one of the gems of the Wallace Collection, had been made in 1575 by Jacob Topp or Jacobi for Sir Thomas Sackville' (*Knole*, p. 99).

41. *King Charles . . . Nell Gwyn was on his arm*: Nell Gwyn (1650–87) was an actress, the mistress of Charles II and also of Charles Sackville, sixth Earl of Dorset; a portrait in the Spangle dressing-room was supposed to be of Nell (*Knole*, pp. 122, 124–6; *Phillips*, II, p. 428). Sackvilles traditionally served as ambassadors, though mainly in France or the Netherlands. Vita's husband Harold Nicolson served in the British Embassy at Constantinople from 1911–14, and she began married life there in November 1913 (Nicolson; and *Vita*, p. 69).

CHAPTER III

1. *his Bath . . . Dukedom*: Orlando is now made a Knight of the Order of the Bath, and promoted from Earl to Duke, apparently as a reward for his services as ambassador in Constantinople. His honours parallel those of Lionel Sackville, seventh Earl, who was made Knight of the Garter in 1714 (Orlando already held this honour – see p. 18) and Duke of Dorset in 1720.

2. *the revolution . . . the fire*: these occur in Constantinople during Orlando's service there, although they also recapitulate the revolution of 1652 and the Great Fire of 1666, perhaps half a century earlier, in England.

3. *cheroot*: a cigar cut at both ends. Nicolson observes that Virginia smoked them, and often tried unsuccessfully to persuade Vita to do so too.

4. *the domes of Santa Sofia*: Constantinople had been an element in the novel from its first conception (see above, Chapter I, Note 10). In addition to its significance for Vita, Woolf had visited it in October 1906 with her brother Adrian, her sister and Violet Dickinson, recording, 'the morning veil of mist, & the stately domes that shine through' and the great cathedral of Santa Sofia 'like a treble globe of bubbles frozen solid' (*A Passionate Apprentice*, pp. 357, 347). The hills of Pera lie on the further (Turkish) side of the Golden Horn, and the Galata Tower stands on its heights.

5. *journeys there alone on foot*: Nicolson points out that this passage suggests Vita's journey over the Persian mountains. Early in 1927 Vita went out to Tehran to join Harold, and they made a walking expedition into the Bakhtiari mountains, described in letters to

Virginia, and later in her travel book *Twelve Days* (1927). The gypsies (whom Orlando joins later in this chapter) in some respects resemble the Bakhtiari tribe that Vita met there.

6. *Circassian*: from the region of the Caucasus mountains between the Black Sea and the Caspian Sea.

7. *Janissaries*: the soldiers belonging to the Sultan's Guard.

8. *hookah*: a water pipe. Orlando's boredom with diplomatic cere-monial reflects Vita's as described in letters to Virginia from Tehran early in 1927: 'Correctness is the order of the day, so we never get any further' (19 February); 'We've had a series of dinner parties, thank you, one of them indistinguishable from the other' (4 March, *Letters of Vita*, pp. 192, 202).

9. *Ramadan*: ninth month of the Islamic year, observed by fasting during daylight hours.

10. *the diary of John Fenner Brigge*: Woolf uses this occasion to parody eighteenth-century diaries and letters. In the MS, some of the gaps in Brigge's letter are filled in slightly differently so that the 'tableau vivant' (p. 91) 'represented the masque of Comus by our ... English poet Milton'. Among those performing are 'the bearers of some of our greatest names in England, such as Howard, Stanley, Herbert, Sackville, Talbot ...' (at which point the branch breaks). The masque anticipates that attendant on Orlando's sex change, while the names of great English families occur to Orlando later in the chapter (see below, Note 22).

11. *blue-jackets*: sailors of the Royal Navy.

12. *Rosina Pepita*: Vita's maternal grandmother was Josefa de Oliva, a famous Spanish dancer better known as 'Pepita'. She lived with Lionel Sackville-West, second Lord Sackville, and bore him five children of whom the youngest, Victoria, was Vita's mother. In 1910, Victoria's older brother Henry brought a lawsuit against Vita's father (who was also his cousin, and the legitimate son of Lionel's younger brother) on the grounds that Lionel and Pepita had in fact been married, and he was thus heir to Knole (see Chapter V, Note 27; and *Vita*, pp. 2, 30).

13. *bastinado*: punishment by caning, especially on the soles of the feet.

14. *red boxes*: used for official documents.

15. *three figures enter*: Orlando's second seven-day sleep recalls the earlier one, at the outset of Chapter II; a masque of three sisters now intervenes, attempting to prevent her 'indecent' discovery of the

change in her body. They are dismissed by Truth to the 'still unravished heights of [suburban] Surrey', protected by concealing ivy and curtains.

16. *let other pens . . . sexuality*: Chapter XLVIII of Jane Austen's *Mansfield Park* begins, 'Let other pens dwell on guilt and misery. I quit such odious subjects as soon as I can, impatient to restore everybody . . . to tolerable comfort.'

17. *her Seleuchi hound*: when Vita was staying with Gertrude Bell in Baghdad in February 1926 she bought a Seleuchi puppy, to take to Tehran, as a present for Harold (*Vita*, p. 156).

18. *Broussa*: modern Bursa, old capital of the Ottoman empire, is on the hills above the sea of Marmara in north-west Turkey. Virginia had travelled out there in 1911 when her sister Vanessa, on holiday there with her husband Clive Bell and Roger Fry, was suddenly taken ill. Orlando's gypsy guide from Constantinople, Rustum, is named after one of the heroes in Firdawsî's great Persian epic, the *Shâh-nâma* (or Book of the Kings).

19. *Thessalian*: hills in northern Greece, west of Bursa and across the sea.

20. *Marmara . . . Parthenon*: from the mountains behind Bursa it may be possible to glimpse Greece across the sea of Marmara, but it would not be possible to see Athens, crowned with the Acropolis on which stands the Parthenon, the temple of the maidens. Woolf had visited Athens in 1906, on her travels to Constantinople. On the sense of the panoramic, see Chapter I, Note 10.

21. *withys*: thin branches, usually of willow, used in basket-making.

22. *Howards and Plantagenets*: old English families, the Plantagenets were royal, the Howards merely aristocratic, as were the Talbots (see above, Note 10, and p. 105).

23. *Mount Athos*: a monastery in north-east Greece, from the vicinity of which women and female animals are strictly forbidden.

24. *burnous*: hooded cloak worn by Arabs.

25. *heavy carts . . . tree trunks*: Orlando's vision of her home under snow recalls Virginia's first visit to Knole in January 1927:

> . . . cart bringing wood in to be sawn by the great circular saw. How do you see that? I asked Vita. She said she saw it as something that had gone on for hundreds of years. They had brought wood in from the Park to replenish the great fires like

this for centuries: & her ancestresses had walked so on the snow with their great dogs bounding by them. All the centuries seemed lit up, the past expressive, articulate; not dumb & forgotten . . .

(23 January 1927, *Diary*, III, p. 125.)

CHAPTER IV

1. *paduasoy*: strong corded silk, much worn in the eighteenth century.
2. *shiver*: a tiny piece, a shaving (echoing Orlando's 'delicious tremor').
3. *pleasaunce*: a pleasure ground.
4. *like a Guy Fawkes*: the effigy of Guy Fawkes (who conspired against James I) is burnt on 5 November, i.e. 'grotesquely or absurdly dressed'.
5. *samphire gatherers*: samphire is a kind of edible seaweed. This sentence echoes Edgar's account of Dover cliffs in *King Lear* (IV. vi. 14–15):

   > Half way down
   > Hangs one that gathers samphire, dreadful trade!

   The phrase 'mopping and mowing' (i.e. making faces) is also used by Edgar who, disguised as mad Tom, refers to the demon 'Flibbertigibbit, of mopping and mowing' (IV. i. 61–2). Lionel, first Duke of Dorset, appears in a view of Dover Castle by John Wootton (1727), which was hanging on the great staircase at Knole (*Phillips*, II, p. 417).
6. *So good-bye . . . half Yorkshire*: 'Ladies of Spain' is a sea shanty. Half Yorkshire is an indirect allusion to the extensive estates of Henry Lascelles, figured in the story as the Archduchess Harriet (Nicolson; see below, Note 20).
7. *a dome . . . poet's forehead*: the dome of St Paul's (rebuilt by Christopher Wren after the Great Fire of 1666) reminds Orlando of the forehead of Shakespeare (glimpsed on p. 16). For Woolf, 'Shakespeare was androgynous' (*A Room of One's Own*, 1928; Penguin Books, 1945, p. 97), and this seems to calm Orlando's anxieties about her femaleness. Thoughts of Shakespeare's 'great lines' lead on to those of the seventeenth-century poet John Milton, whose style suggests a cathedral bell, ringing inside Orlando's mind – and perhaps outside too.

8. *orgulous, undulant, superb*: these Latinate words suggest the neo-classical style, just then coming into fashion. Both 'orgulous' and 'superb' mean proud or exalted; 'undulant' means rising and falling like (or on) waves.

9 *the Cocoa Tree ... Papists*: the Cocoa Tree was strictly a chocolate (rather than a coffee) house, at 64 St James's Street; around 1745 it became a centre for Jacobites (who would largely have been Papists, i.e. Catholic sympathizers). At this time political activists and men of letters met at (particular) coffee houses. John Dryden (1631–1700) was the leading Restoration poet and later in life a Catholic convert (i.e. a Papist). Joseph Addison (1672–1719) was an essayist and an Anglican. He was lampooned by Alexander Pope (1688–1744), also a Catholic. There were portraits of Dryden and Pope in the Poets' Parlour at Knole, and one of Addison in the Leicester Gallery (*Phillips*, II, pp. 439, 433). Dryden was a frequent visitor and a close friend and beneficiary of Charles Sackville, the sixth Earl, to whom he dedicated his *Essay of Dramatic Poesy*; Pope wrote an epitaph for the Earl's monument at Withyham (*Knole*, pp. 144–5, 151).

10. *home in Blackfriars ... suits*: the Sackvilles owned Dorset House at Blackfriars (now demolished), and Vita's mother had lived there at one time (Nicolson). Bow Street Runners were policemen, named after the Bow Street law courts, near Covent Garden. The case against Orlando parallels the 'Pepita' case, brought against Lionel Sackville-West by his illegitimate cousin Henry in 1910 (see above, Chapter III, Note 12).

11. *in Chancery*: under the jurisdiction of the Lord Chancellor for the duration of the case. Chancery lawsuits were those that could not be resolved in the regular courts; the Chancellor's court was notoriously slow.

12. *Mrs. Grimsditch, Mr. Dupper ... Canute*: see Chapter II, Notes 3, 35.

13. *the arras ... pot-pourri*: see Chapter I, Notes 4, 30; Chapter II, Notes 34, 35, 36. One particular silver hair brush in the King's Bedroom was supposed to have belonged to King James (though later editions of *Knole* dismiss this); Knole had a special recipe for pot-pourri, derived from Lady Betty Germain, a friend of the first Duchess of Dorset, whose portrait hung in the bedroom named after her (*Knole*, p. 172).

14. *the Prayer Book ... Royal blood*: the prayer book of the executed

Mary Queen of Scots is in the Chapel at Knole (Nicolson; and see above, Chapter I, Note :4).

15. *that doctor . . . Browne*: see above, Chapter II, Note 5.

16. *High battlements of thought*: in her letter thanking Virginia for *Orlando*, Vita wrote, 'There are a dozen details I should like to go into . . . phrases scattered about (particularly one on p. 160 [p. 124] beginning "High battlements of thought, etc." which is just what you did for me) . . .' (11 October 1928, *Letters of Vita*, p. 305.)

17. *Hair, pastry . . . dissemblables*: dissemblables, the antithesis of 'semblables', are things unlike one another. For an earlier 'humane jumble', see Chapter II, p. 55.

18. *that obscene vulture*: is lust (see p. 82), though whether felt by Orlando for the Archduchess or by the Archduchess herself remains obscure.

19. *twenty million . . . gape*: Lord Lascelles inherited Harewood House and large estates (and income from them) in Yorkshire (Nicolson; and *Vita*, pp. 49, 50). The Archduke seems particularly concerned with the opportunities for hunting on his estates; the gape is a disease of poultry; 'the does slipped their young', means they miscarried or gave premature birth to them.

20. *the Archduke . . . up again*: on his lack of conversation see above, Chapter II, Note 39.

21. *Fly Loo*: loo is a card game in which penalties are paid into a pool. Fly Loo, played at Knole, seems to involve betting on which sugar lump the flies will settle. Apparently Vita did once win by gluing a dead fly to a lump of sugar (Nicolson).

22. *dipping sheep . . . scab*: the summer section of Vita's poem *The Land* (Orlando's 'The Oak Tree') describes the process of sheep washing or dipping. The scab is a skin disease.

23. *so dark . . . so soft*: cf. Ben Jonson's 'Celebration of Charis, IV, Her triumph': 'O so white! O so soft! O so sweet is she!'

24. *a drop falling or a fountain rising*: important images for Woolf: a fountain of joy rises, at different times, for Mrs Ramsay, Lily Briscoe and Cam in *To the Lighthouse* (1927), while the gathering and falling drop haunts Bernard in *The Waves* (1931).

25. *off she drove*: in the MS this passage is followed by a description of Orlando's house at Blackfriars (see above, Note 10), which is rather underfurnished, though the library is well-stocked, and includes Ariosto, as well as *The Faerie Queene*, Montaigne and many Elizabethan plays.

26. *if the reader . . . her face*: the picture on p. 111 of Vita holding a scarf over her shoulders was probably taken by Lenare in the summer of 1927 (see letter to Vita, 30 Oct. 1927, *Letters*, III, p. 434). There are two 'photographs' of Orlando dressed as a man: 'as a Boy' (the frontispiece) and 'as Ambassador' (p. 87), but as his hands are invisible in the second portrait, this passage probably refers to the frontispiece. The much quoted notion that 'it is clothes that wear us and not we them' exposes the artifice of gender roles.

27. *if Orlando was a woman*: Nicolson points out that the details of Orlando's behaviour in this paragraph are all applicable to Vita, who dressed fast, drove fast and maintained that, since the south was downhill, the Nile must flow uphill.

28. *the heroine of the celebrated lawsuit*: according to Nicolson, this is connected not to the 'Pepita' case of 1910 (see above, Chapter III, Note 12) but to another much publicized lawsuit of 1913 brought against Vita's mother concerning a legacy left her by John Murray Scott, in which Vita was called to give evidence (*Vita*, pp. 57–8).

29. *billets*: short informal letters, or notes.

30. *routs*: large evening parties, receptions.

31. *the reign of Queen Anne*: 1702–14.

32. *her spaniel Pippin*: the actual name of Vita's spaniel (Nicolson).

33. *great writer . . . invisible*: this idea also occurs in Henry James's short story 'The Private Life' (1892), which Woolf read in 1921, and took some notes on in preparation for writing a review of James's ghost stories, though she did not in the end mention it (*CE*, I, pp. 286–96).

34. *Madame du Deffand*: (1697–1780), a French aristocrat and wit, she corresponded with Voltaire and Horace Walpole, and was hostess to a salon of well-known writers and philosophers. Her celebrated witticism, the 'mot de Saint Denis' (see the next paragraph), concerns the legend that St Denis had walked two leagues carrying his head in his hands: *'la distance n'y fait rien; il n'y a que le premier pas qui coûte.'* (The distance is nothing; it is only the first step which is difficult.)

35. *our modern Sibyl*: a sly reference to the London hostess Lady Sibyl Colefax who lionized Woolf and whom she associates in her diary with the 'party consciousness' (27 April 1925, *Diary*, III, p. 13).

36. *Link-boys*: carried torches (links). South Audley Street is in Mayfair,

behind Park Lane, and on its corner stands Chesterfield House, built for Lord Chesterfield (see Note 44, below) in 1750. In 1927 it was occupied by Lord Lascelles and Princess Mary.

37. *Piccadilly Circus . . . her own sex*: Woolf regularly associated Piccadilly with prostitutes and therefore with the evils of patriarchy, though later in this chapter there is a lighter portrayal of their way of life.

38. *the Rape of the Lock . . . at a ball*: these lines are from Pope's *The Rape of the Lock* (1714), canto II, 105–9.

39. *congee*: bow made when leaving.

40. *Addison . . . Spectator*: Addison wrote essays both for the *Spectator* and the *Tatler*. This passage is in fact from the *Tatler* (116, Thursday 5 Jan., 1710) and is the final paragraph of a case brought against the hooped petticoat. A tippet is a cape or scarf, a muff is a cylindrical covering for keeping the hands warm, and both were often made of fur or feathers. This passage, like the quotation from Pope, continues the emphasis on the limitations imposed on women, which is one of the central themes of this chapter.

41. *Swift . . . Gulliver's Travels*: (1726); the quotation is from the fourth book, 'A Voyage to the Houyhnhnms' (a society of rational horses), Chapter X. Swift's *Journal to Stella*, partly written in a private code, is referred to in the phrase, 'talks baby language to a girl'. Swift was a friend of Lady Betty Germain (see above, Note 13) and his portrait hung in her room (*Phillips*, II, p. 426).

42. *the Round Parlour*: at Knole, the Poets' Parlour (also known as the Round Parlour or the Dining Room) is hung with portraits of the sixth Earl's (Charles Sackville's) literary friends, including Dryden and Pope (*Knole*, pp. 148–9; and see above, Note 9).

43. *plates at dinner*: 'It is also related that Dryden, when dining with Dorset, found a hundred-pound note hidden under his plate' (*Knole*, p. 149).

44. *Lord Chesterfield*: (1694–1773) Chesterfield was a friend of Pope, but disliked by Dr Johnson. This slightly misquoted piece of misogyny (he actually wrote, 'Women, then, are only children . . .') is from his posthumous *Letters to his Son* (5 September 1748; published 1774). A pastel portrait of Lord Chesterfield hung in the sitting-room at Knole (*Phillips*, II, p. 437). In the MS this passage is both more oblique and more openly critical of Chesterfield, who is classed with Mr Arnold Bennett, Mr Desmond McCarthy and Mr Orlo Williams as among 'the most illustrious of the tribe of

masculinists' (on these, see *A Woman's Essays*, Penguin Books, 1992, pp. 30–38). She adds that Chesterfield 'forgot that children sometimes see things which their elders try to keep hidden. He forgot too that children grow up.'

45. *Mr. Pope ... of Women*: Pope's second Epistle, 'To a Lady: of the Characters of Women' (1735), includes several satirical portraits of contemporaries, though Woolf probably had in mind the opening lines:

> Nothing so true as what you once let fall,
> Most women have no Characters at all.

Pope's treatment of Orlando is reminiscent of Nick Greene's in Chapter II.

46. *the plain Dunstable of the matter*: a phrase meaning 'in plain language', deriving from the very straight road from London to Dunstable. Woolf would have found it spoken by a maidservant in Samuel Richardson's *Clarissa* (1748).

47. *women ... each other's society*: the sense of women speaking to one another behind closed doors is also strong in Woolf's next book, *A Room of One's Own* (1928; Penguin Books, 1945, especially Chapter V). Vita's cousin Edward Sackville-West complained to Virginia that 'Mr S.W.', quoted in this passage, referred to him, especially as a reference to Orlando's cousin appears on the following page, where her poems are mistakenly attributed to him (Edward Sackville-West also wrote poetry). Woolf wrote back to him mendaciously, according to Nicolson, 'Mr. S.W. was (if anybody) Sydney Waterlow. How could it have been you?' (21 November 1928, *Letters*, III, p. 559).

48. *and clip the nut trees*: Harold Nicolson had planted nut trees at Long Barn. Orlando's night wanderings dressed as a man parallel Vita's (*Vita*, pp. 83, 95, 99).

49. *a duel ... followed them*: in 1920 Vita had run away with Violet Trefusis to Amiens, pursued by both their husbands (Nicolson; and *Vita*, p. 108).

50. *shadows' names*: Samuel Johnson (1709–84), poet, lexicographer and man of letters, was the major literary figure of the second half of the eighteenth century; James Boswell (1740–95) was his friend and biographer; the blind Mrs Williams was a member of Johnson's household. Joshua Reynolds's portrait of Samuel Johnson (1769) hung in the Reynolds Room (*Phillips*, II, p. 419).

51. *light, order and serenity*: Woolf characterizes the age of Enlightenment, contrasting it on the one hand with the violence of Elizabethan England and on the other with the approaching clouds of the nineteenth century.

CHAPTER V

1. *the constitution of England was altered*: both in the narrow sense – that is, the principles according to which a state is governed were changed – and, more loosely, in the sense that the character or nature of England changed.

2. *the brothers Adam*: eighteenth-century architects and interior designers whose style was characterized by neo-classical elegance.

3. *muffin . . . and the crumpet*: two different kinds of cake, usually eaten at tea-time, toasted and with butter.

4. *obfusc green*: to obfuscate is to darken or obscure. In the MS this sentence is followed by a description of the Squire's chill and his desire to cover everything in sight: 'to muffle, to conceal, now became the chief pursuit of the educated classes'.

5. *British Empire . . . existence*: i.e. in order to accommodate the superfluous population.

6. *scrolloping*: see Chapter II, Note 32; the threatening vegetation recalls that of Andrew Marvell's 'The Garden'.

7. *pyramid, hecatomb, or trophy*: the statue of Queen Victoria outside Buckingham Palace was put up in 1911. In its place Woolf imagines a kind of funeral pyre (a hecatomb is a huge public sacrifice) of Victoriana, including: the Queen's own widow's weeds, worn since Prince Albert's death in 1861; crystal palaces, alluding to the one built for the Great Exhibition in 1851; bassinettes, i.e. wicker baby-prams; military helmets, suggestive of the Empire; Christmas trees, introduced to England by Prince Albert; and 'extinct monsters, globes, maps', suggesting the discovery of dinosaurs as well as of far-off countries. The female figure may be Chastity, or an ideal of womanhood such as 'The Angel in the House' (see 'Professions for Women', *CE*, II, pp. 285–6); the gentleman is the Victorian patriarch, dressed in the fashion of his day. The royal family were famous both for their domesticity and their bad taste.

8. *a crinoline*: a wide-hooped petticoat.

9. *Elizabeth . . . to princes?*: these words are usually supposed to have

been spoken by the dying Elizabeth to Lord Burghley's son, Robert Cecil: 'Little man, little man! thy father, if he had been alive, durst not have used that word.'

10. *bombazine*: a heavy dress material made from wool and silk; black bombazine was regularly used for mourning – 'widow's weeds'.

11. *1586 ... three hundred years now*: 1586 is probably the year *Orlando* opens (the chronology in *Knole* gives this as the year Sackville received the house from Elizabeth, though 1566 is the date given in the text). Vita took six years to write her poem 'The Land' ('The Oak Tree'), and Virginia mocked her for it, according to Nicolson. At this point, the MS includes a long account of Orlando's search for her writing self: she returns to the sixteenth and seventeenth centuries, citing lines from Thomas Sackville's 'Induction' to the *Mirror for Magistrates* and Charles Sackville's lyric, 'Tell me, Dorinda, why so gay', in an effort to overcome her writer's block and negotiate the unsympathetic spirit of the age.

12. *caracole ... her life*: curves and caracoles are graceful manoeuvres made on horseback. The verses that follow parody the drearier verse of the period.

13. *pinchbeck*: an alloy resembling gold.

14. *indissolubly linked together*: this image of marriage may derive from Shelley's 'Epipsychidion' (1821), where it is figured as

> [. . .] the beaten road
> Which those poor slaves with weary footsteps tread
> [. . .] and so
> The dreariest and the longest journey go.

These lines provided the title of E. M. Forster's second novel, *The Longest Journey* (1907).

15. *Lord Melbourne*: Queen Victoria's first prime minister, often pictured announcing her accession to the eighteen-year-old Queen.

16. *lachrymose ... mellifluous fluencies*: lachrymose means tearful; mellifluous fluencies are honey-sweet flowings or effusions.

17. *the Archduke ... Botany Bay*: Lord Lascelles had married Princess Mary, the Princess Royal, in 1922; Botany Bay is the place in Australia where British convicts were sent for punishment.

18. *Canute and Pippin*: Orlando's (and Vita's) elk-hound and spaniel.

19. *the moor ... Six feathers*: this scene is inspired by Emily Brontë's

novel *Wuthering Heights* (1847), in which the heroine, Catherine, loves the moor and its wild birds (in delirium she pulls the feathers out of her pillow, naming the birds they come from). Woolf included an essay on '*Jane Eyre* and *Wuthering Heights*' in *The Common Reader* (1925) (reprinted in *CE*, I, pp. 185–90).

20. *Sir Bedivere . . . Arthur*: this episode forms the climax of Tennyson's poem 'Morte d'Arthur' (1842), later incorporated into his *Idylls of the King* (1869).

21. *Armada . . . Nelson*: the Spanish Armada was defeated in 1588; Lord Nelson fought the French and Spanish at sea, being killed at Trafalgar in 1805. This wide historical sweep parallels the book's geographical panoramas.

22. *a man on horseback*: this scene recalls, while reversing, the first encounter between Jane Eyre and Mr Rochester in Charlotte Brontë's novel, *Jane Eyre* (1847). Out walking, Jane is overtaken by a rider whose horse slips on some ice so that he sprains his ankle in the fall. Her first words to him are: 'Are you injured, sir?' (I, Chapter XII.)

23. *Marmaduke Bonthrop Shelmerdine, Esquire*: a romantic version of Harold Nicolson. Vita's pet (family) name was 'Mar', and she sometimes referred to herself and Harold as 'the mars', thus Marmaduke. A woman called Shelmerdene appears in Michael Arlen's novel *These Charming People* (1923), having, like Harold, 'returned to England after a long absence abroad in Persia'. Harold, like 'Shel', had ancestors from Skye, was comparatively poor, had actually sailed round the Horn and frequently had to live abroad, since he was in the diplomatic service (Nicolson).

24. *brig*: a two-masted, square-rigged sailing vessel.

25. *Peelers*: policemen, named after Sir Robert Peel who established the London police force in 1829. Several of his letters relating to the Battle of Waterloo are quoted in *Knole* (pp. 208–14).

26. *the estates . . . Palmerston's*: desequestrated, i.e. released from being held in chancery, where Orlando's estates had been for the duration of the trial; tailed and entailed, i.e. settled as the inalienable possession of her and her heirs; Lord Palmerston was prime minister from 1855–65.

27. *the whole town . . . rejoicings*: after the Sackvilles won the 1910 'Pepita' case, all Sevenoaks turned out to celebrate (Nicolson; and *Vita*, p. 35). Barouches and landaus are different kinds of four-wheeled

carriages and The Bull and The Stag are pubs in Sevenoaks. Vita remembered leaving the car for a carriage at the top of the hill; when they reached Sevenoaks itself, the horse was taken out of the traces and the carriage pulled through the main street all the way to Knole itself, amidst a cheering crowd (Vita Sackville-West, *Pepita*, 1937, pp. 227–9).

28. *the castle . . . Gladstone*: the castle is Windsor Castle; W. E. Gladstone was yet another of Victoria's prime ministers, this time in the later part of her reign.

29. *parenthesis . . . Orlando's life*: Woolf is again parodying her own previous novel *To the Lighthouse*, in which the deaths of several of the main characters are enclosed in square brackets to mark them off from the rest of the text.

30. *top-boom mizzen . . . larboard*: nautical terms – Marmaduke explains to Orlando how various sails and spars are adjusted in the process of sailing. Starboard is the right-hand side of the ship when facing forwards, larboard (now usually referred to as 'port') is the left.

31. *Pascal*: Blaise Pascal (1623–62), French religious philosopher.

32. *Bishop Berkeley*: (1685–1753) Irish philosopher who believed that matter only existed in so far as it was perceived.

33. *Lady Derby*: Lady Mary Sackville-West, Vita's great aunt, married Lord Derby, an eminent Victorian statesman (*Knole*, p. 180).

34. *a ship in full sail . . . sails quivering*: this passage, with its sudden transpositions, is strongly reminiscent of De Quincey, and, in particular, the three-decker in summer seas, bearing down on a little pinnace, in 'Dream Fugue' in 'The English Mail Coach' (1849).

35. *they reached the Chapel*: Vita married Harold Nicolson on 1 October 1913 in the chapel at Knole (Nicolson; and *Vita*, p. 61). Orlando's marriage takes place during a thunderstorm (see *Knole*, p. 17: 'The chapel looks strange and lovely during a midnight thunderstorm: the lightning flashes through the stone ogives of the east window . . .'). The thunder conveniently drowns out the moment in the wedding ceremony when the bride promises to obey the bridegroom. Woolf associated the image of the bird dashed against the glass with passion – see, for example, *Night and Day* (1919; Penguin Books, 1992, p. 334).

CHAPTER VI

1. *And then . . . girls*: these four lines are from the 'Spring' section of Vita's poem *The Land* (1926, p. 49). The fritillaries are 'snaky' because of their spotted heads – this variety is also known as 'snake's head fritillary'. The presence of the Egyptian girls, implying the desire of women for women, disturbs the narrative and is smuggled in as an item of contraband past the literary censors of the age.

2. *the Hogarth Press*: begun by Leonard and Virginia in 1917, the Hogarth Press published a variety of modern writing, including Virginia's own.

3. *the poet*: Lord Byron wrote in *Don Juan* (Canto I, stanza 194):

> Man's love is of his life a thing apart,
> 'Tis woman's whole existence.

   George Sackville, fourth Duke of Dorset (1794–1815), had known Byron at school (*Knole*, pp. 203–5).

4. *think of a gamekeeper*: as Lady Chatterley does in D. H. Lawrence's novel *Lady Chatterley's Lover*, published in Florence in 1928 and read by Vita in July (*Vita*, p. 199). Woolf must have known of it by reputation earlier that year, since the gamekeeper also appears in the MS. The male novelist who defines love as 'slipping off one's petticoat and –' also suggests Lawrence.

5. *Let us go, then . . .*: the writer's visible inertia is contrasted with the activity of nature, which is celebrated in rhyme. Vita was later to include this passage in her anthology of poetry *Another World Than This* (1945, p. 131), in which she also published for the first time Charles Elton's 'Luriana, Lurilee', recited at the dinner party in *To the Lighthouse* (1927; Penguin Books, 1992, pp. 120–21).

6. *another in Mayfair*: in 1907 Vita's mother bought a house in Hill Street, off Berkeley Square (Nicolson; and *Vita*, p. 23), where Vita often used to stay.

7. *Sir Nicholas!*: Nick Greene has changed with the times, becoming 'the most influential critic of the Victorian age', a pillar of the establishment who takes tea with duchesses (see p. 195). Vita wrote to Harold on 11 October 1928: 'Nicholas Greene you will recognize as [Edmund] Gosse' (*Vita*, p. 202). A year earlier, Virginia had gone to hear Vita read a lecture chaired by Gosse:

She was fawned upon by the little dapper grocer Gosse who kept
spinning round on his heel to address her compliments . . . &
to be drawing round the lot of them thicker and thicker, the
red plush curtains of respectability. There was Vita, who was
too innocent to see it . . . I dont regret my wildest, foolishest,
utterance, if it gave the least crack to this respectability.

(30 October 1926, *Diary*, III, p. 115.)

Gosse wrote a regular column for the *Sunday Times* and it is here
that Orlando reads his article on John Donne (see p. 198). Woolf
wrote an essay on 'Edmund Gosse' in 1931 (*CE*, IV, pp. 81–7).

8. *Addison's* Cato . . . *Thomson's* Seasons: Addison's *Cato* (1713) is a
neo-classical tragedy. Thomson's *Seasons* (1726–30) is a long four-
part nature poem, anticipating *The Land* in structure.

9. *royalties . . . Messrs.* —: Sir Nicholas is referring to the proportion of
the cost of a book paid to the author for every copy sold. Vita's
The Land was actually her fourth book to be published by William
Heinemann (who had previously published *Knole and the Sackvilles*).

10. *a cypher language*: while Harold was in Tehran (from November 1925
to May 1927), he and Vita sent each other telegrams in a cypher
called 'unicode' (Nicolson). The code itself (e.g. 'Rattigan Glumphoboo') is indecipherable, but might be a parody of James Joyce's
Finnegans Wake, sections of which were published from 1922 onwards as *Work in Progress*.

11. *the Duke of Hamilton . . . Lord Mohun*: Hyde Park had often been the
setting for duels. Knole has portraits of the second Marquis of
Hamilton in the Great Hall and one of a Major Michael Mohun, a
noted duellist, in the Poets' Parlour (*Phillips*, II, pp. 416, 441).

12. *the Serpentine*: an artificial lake that runs through the centre of Hyde
Park and Kensington Gardens. As a child, Woolf walked twice a
day in Kensington Gardens and often sailed boats on the Serpentine
or the Round Pond. In 'A Sketch of the Past' she recalls her boat
sailing to the middle of the pond and suddenly sinking (*Moments of
Being*, p. 86).

13. *tight scarlet trousers . . . two dogs dancing*: the red trousers belong to a
guardsman; the dogs on their hind legs recall Dr Johnson's notorious comparison: 'A woman's preaching is like a dog's walking on
his hinder legs. It is not done well: but you are surprised to find it
done at all.' These overtones of militarism and misogyny may

explain Orlando's sense that as a woman she could not write about them in the same way as the essayists Addison or Charles Lamb would have done: 'one must never, never say what one thought'.

14. *Tupper said about Smiles*: two minor Victorian writers – Martin Tupper wrote facile verses ('pretentious twaddle'), while Samuel Smiles preached the smug doctrine of self-help.

15. *eight-hour bills . . . factory acts*: Victorian legislation to limit the hours in a working day.

16. *four-in-hand . . . barouche landau*: different types of carriages.

17. *four great names*: Tennyson and Browning, Charles Dickens and George Eliot. The names that follow all belong to genuine and identifiable, but mainly minor, poets, writers and historians of the Victorian age. At this point, the MS includes a much longer account of the differences between Victorian literature and its antecedents, and, in particular, of the way in which writing has been gentrified and professionalized – far more books are now published and many of them are 'not books pure and simple but books about books'. Orlando goes to hear Sir Nicholas lecturing on the Romantic poets and is almost suffocated (see above, Note 7). As writers grow more respectable, patrons are no longer sought after: Christina Rossetti turns down an invitation to tea. Lady A. takes Orlando to see Carlyle but is chased away by his wife: 'Be off with you, fool! . . . I'd have you know my Thomas is asleep.' They visit Tennyson at Freshwater, only to be intercepted by Emily in her wheelchair, who prevents them reaching the house: 'My husband is writing a poem.' Writers are now 'enclosed in a sound-proof room and protected by a wife'. Volumnia Fox (Virginia Woolf) is now only remembered because Arnold Bennett once devoted half an hour to demolishing this poor scribbler: 'She would have been forgotten anyhow, and the half hour spent on her might have given us another of his masterpieces.'

18. *Miss Christina Rossetti*: (1830–94) an intense and highly individual poet, the subject of Woolf's 1930 essay 'I am Christina Rossetti' (*CE*, IV, pp. 54–60). Poetic patronage has changed since Dryden's day (see p. 147).

19. *Suddenly she started . . . barrel organ*: here, as earlier in the novel, changes in the life of the body become occasions of anxiety and disturbance within the text: the next event befalling Orlando, while apparent to the footman and the maid-servant, cannot easily be

announced. The narration is interrupted first by the sound of the barrel-organ, then thoughts of Kew Gardens (where the lives of the plants were associated, for Woolf, with the rhythms of the body – see Chapter XXV of *Night and Day*, 1919), and then by a series of exclamations which recall, without exactly quoting, Milton's lines:

> Hail wedded Love, mysterious Law, true source
> Of human offspring . . .
> (*Paradise Lost*, Book 4, lines 750–51.)

20. *their outrigger*: a light rowing boat (they seem to be on the river at Kew).

21. *a son . . . 20th*: Vita had two sons, Ben and Nigel; when they asked which of them this was supposed to be, Woolf replied, 'Both of you' (Nicolson). Neither was born on 20 March, though this date is suggestively close to 17 March (1928), when Woolf completed *Orlando* (see letter to Vita, 20 March 1928, *Letters*, III, p. 474; and Note 39, below); it had been begun the previous October (like the bulbs, 'thrust into the earth in October', at Kew, p. 203).

22. *King Edward . . . lady opposite*: Edward had been a great visitor of ladies, among them, Mrs Keppel, mother of Violet Trefusis (*Vita*, p. 23). With the Edwardian age come modern conveniences – motor-cars, electric light and running water.

23. *eleventh of October . . . 1928*: the novel's date of publication and presentation to Vita, who, like Orlando, was then thirty-six (p. 209).

24. *Marshall & Snelgrove's*: a large department store in Regent's Street.

25. *Louise then*: Louise Genoux was Vita's French maid (Nicolson; and *Vita*, p. 191). She has no time for the Prince Consort because he was German – '*Sale bosch!*' (i.e. dirty German). The date is now post-1918; the First World War, in which Germany invaded France, has taken place; George V succeeded Edward in 1911.

26. *a little vulgar – all in silver*: 'The King's bedroom is the only vulgar room in the house . . . ' (*Knole*, p. 15; and see above, Chapter II, Note 34.)

27. *a person's life . . . Biography*: Virginia Woolf's father, Leslie Stephen, was the first and most important editor of the *Dictionary of National Biography*, and received a knighthood for his work on it.

28. *Ra—Un . . . Undert—*: Orlando is driving south out of London, in the direction of Sevenoaks and Knole. As she goes, Woolf describes

the constantly interrupted view from the car window, perhaps seeing it as symbolic of the fragmentary nature of modern city life. The words on the banner probably stand for 'Rally of the Unemployed' or 'Rally against Unemployment' (popular demonstrations against unemployment had begun again in the spring of 1928, when Woolf was writing this section); 'Amor Vin—' is the opening of the Latin tag, 'amor vincit omnia' ('love conquers all', perhaps an indication that this is the porch of a brothel), and Applejohn and Applebed are undertakers, thus completing the cycle of love and death.

29. *Orlando did not come*: Orlando's search for another self invokes the theme of the inadequacy of writing to represent lived time or lives, while allowing a recapitulation of the selves as they have appeared in the novel.

30. *What, then? Who, then?*: Orlando's stream of consciousness as expressed here parodies the staccato, exclamatory style used by James Joyce.

31. *Oak Tree . . . Prize*: Vita's poem *The Land* had won the Hawthornden Prize in 1927 (Nicolson; and *Vita*, p. 172). Vita used the prize money to plant a grove of nut trees at Long Barn. Woolf renamed the prize after Angela Burdett-Coutts, the great Victorian philanthropist, perhaps to make the point that such prizes are seldom established in women's names, and in any case cannot have the same significance for a woman as for a man.

32. *porpoise in a fishmonger's shop*: this description of Vita, which Virginia often teased her with, derived from a shopping trip to Sevenoaks they made together late in 1925 (see 21 December 1925, *Diary*, III, p. 52; and Nicolson). Woolf wrote to Vita, 'Aint it odd how the vision at the Sevenoaks fishmongers has worked itself into my idea of you?' (5 February 1927, *Letters*, III, p. 326).

33. *There flies the wild goose*: the unattainable wild goose may symbolize supernatural intervention (see the introduction, p. xxxviii); or else the search for self or for an elusive reality (perhaps identical with that described at the end of *A Room of One's Own*: 'whatever it touches, it fixes and makes permanent' (1928; Penguin Books, 1945, p. 108); or, as in the MS, 'the secret of life'. As Shelmerdine lands at the end of the poem, it appears again.

34. *whipcord breeches . . . Lopokova*: Orlando changes into Vita's favourite country dress. Lydia Lopokova was a ballerina, married to the economist (and Bloomsburian) Maynard Keynes.

35. *red Spanish wine*: Vita always drank a Spanish wine called Allella (Nicolson).

36. *In this window-seat* . . .: the different rooms of Knole are evoked for the last time (see above, Chapter IV, Note 13; and earlier notes).

37. *the loud speaker* . . . *Vienna*: the radio's transference of sound through space parallels the movement of Orlando's memory, traversing the history of the house.

38. *old Greene* . . . *Milton*: the Hawthornden Prize had been presented to Vita by John Drinkwater on 16 June 1927 – Virginia went to the presentation (*Diary*, III, p. 139; and Nicolson). Orlando contrasts the reception of the poem with the private experience of writing it.

39. *the roar of an aeroplane*: Harold Nicolson had once flown from Paris, landing on the cricket field at Knole, while Vita had called, 'Here Hadji, here!' (Nicolson.) In the darkness, her pearls are like the phosphorescent flares used to light up runways. The MS ends as follows:

And as Shelmerdine leapt from the aeroplane & ran to meet her a wild goose with its neck outstretched flew above them.

> Shel! cried Orlando
> The [wild] goose is –
> '[The secret of life] is . . .'

The End.   March 17th
                                                                1928

Appendix

A list of the substantive readings from the first British (Hogarth Press) and first American trade (Harcourt Brace) editions, excluding variants in punctuation, capitalization and spelling. Further minor differences between the texts are that the British first edition numbers chapters in Roman numerals, the American in Arabic; the British 'Contents' page lists the preface but not the index, while the American lists the index but not the preface; no reference to the jacket illustration occurs in the American edition (since it had a different jacket) but a few extra entries appear in the American index. Page and line numbers given below refer to this edition, the first entry being from the British first edition, the second from the American first edition.

5.28   Keynes; Mr. Hugh Walpole; Miss Violet Dickinson;] Keynes; Miss Violet Dickinson;

6.5   Raymond Mortimer; Lady Gerald Wellesley;] Raymond Mortimer; Miss Emphie Case; Lady Gerald Wellesley;

6.8   Nicolson; and my sister, Vanessa Bell] Nicolson; my sister, Vanessa Bell

11.26   winter and summer] winter or summer

12.14   reach whatever seat] reach what ever seat

14.17   thirty or perhaps forty,] thirty, or forty perhaps,

17.1   a commanding hand, too; a hand] a commanding hand; a hand

19.31   blame Orlando?] blame him?

20.22   bade him do.] bade him.

21.7   Old Stairs and the beer gardens] Old Stairs and such places

21.33   their loves had been active;] their love was active;

23.2   Euphrosyne – so he called them] Euphrosyne – to give them the names he called them

26.32   raved, so he stared.] raved, so he called her.

27.2   had eyes] had those eyes

27.12   bite; shut] bite and shut

28.36   Maypole (comme une grande perche   ]   Maypole (une grande perche

31.1   pailful   ]   pail full

37.3   they would fly. They would take ship to Russia.   ]   they would fly north; thence to Russia.

39.26   vanished it was   ]   vanished and was

39.29   lit up and the strangest   ]   lit up the strangest

39.34   transformation. As they approached   ]   transformation. The sounds too seemed closed and concentrated. As they approached

40.35   orange peel on to the ice which a dog   ]   orange peel at the actors which a dog

42.3   in these purlieus   ]   in this purlieus

44.8   gay city had been stood   ]   gay city had stood

44.13   huge and massy fragments   ]   huge and many fragments

45.4   were dashed against a tree and sunk   ]   were dashed to death and sunk

52.10   he looked like; know   ]   he looked like, and know

52.11   what he thought – and it is for readers such as these that we write –   ]   what he thought and felt and it is for readers such as these alone that we write –

56.34   man with big, bright eyes.   ]   man with bright eyes.

58.6   solitude of years   ]   solitude of many years

59.34   but the lips hung loose and slobbered.   ]   but the lips slobbered.

60.2   servility of a well-trained domestic's face; it   ]   servility of the face of a well-trained domestic; it

62.8   the Elizabethan age was inferior   ]   the Elizabethan was inferior

65.15   would seem very dull   ]   would seem dull

67.1   'For', he said, 'I have done with men.'   ]   'For,' he said, patting the little brutes on the head, 'I have done with men.'

67.13   Dogs and a bush were the whole of it.   ]   A dog and a bush were the whole of it.

68.29   coloured it a thousand tints, and filled it with   ]   coloured it all the tints of the rainbow and filled it with

73.27   and their windows were lit though they lay dying.   ]   and the windows were lit though they were dying.

75.16   ninety-nine pages more   ]   twenty-nine pages more

82.8 Thus he rushed] Then he rushed

83.5 Howbeit, the Fates were hard] [No new paragraph in American edition]

84.18 and even to use the imagination.] and even to make use of the imagination.

85.14 The houses were white as egg-shells and as bald.] The houses were bare and bald as egg-shells.

89.33 they conjured up] they conjured him up

91.7 lest the native population should be seized ... fraught with] lest the native population ... fraught with

91.14 valuable, if only because it impressed upon them ... the superiority] valuable ... because it impressed upon them ... superiority

92.15 the cynosure of all eyes] the sinecure of all eyes

94.15 applied remedies] applied the remedies

97.11 where there are ivy and curtains in plenty.'] where there are curtains in plenty.

97.35 he was a woman.

       The sound of the trumpets]
       he was a woman.
       The sound of the trumpets

101.7 the older men and women] the elder men and women

101.17 ramparts, to the breasts of doves, and the flanks of kine.] ramparts, and the plains to the flanks of kine.

102.34 blank version poem,] blank verse poem,

110.7 if I can't swim,] if I can swim,

113.30 wonder, as she pitted] wonder if, as she pitted

114.26 war-horse, nor even] war-horse, not even

118.9 on top, a covey of swans floated, orgulous] on top, floated a covey of swans, orgulous

119.16 aware by a succession] aware of a succession

123.4 The poet's, then, is the highest] The poet's, then, in the highest

123.11 Thoughts are divine, etc. Thus] Thoughts are divine. Thus

125.8 their meaning, she threw] their meaning upon the mind, she threw

131.26 seems to hint] seem to hint

132.15 in Orlando, which is to be found if the reader will look at page

144, even in her face. If] in Orlando, which is to be found even in her face. If

132.25 been the same.] been the same too.

133.10 would argue, for example, if Orlando was a woman, how did she] would argue how, for example, if Orlando was a woman, did she

133.29 rattling on the cobbles.] rattling over the cobbles.

135.21 into such an excitement?] into such excitement?

137.4 none to answer, 'is this', she finished her sentence all the same, 'what people call life?' The spaniel] none to answer, 'is this what people call life?' The spaniel

138.9 suffering from the effect of three honeyed words] suffering from the poison of three honeyed words

138.25 glimpse she had of these great men from the deck] glimpse she had of the poets from the deck

139.17 that the world has seen.] that the world has known.

143.8 What are "we"?'] What are we?'

145.2 men of genius. Nor were they so different from the rest of us as one might have supposed.] men of genius, yet after all they were not much different from other people.

149.19 beneath a fine willow tree.] beneath a willow tree.

150.19 the young woman looked up at him] the girl looked up at him

153.3 lose it. The task is made still more difficult by the fact that she found it] lose it. What makes the task of identification still more difficult is that she found it

153.14 of breeches she exchanged the seductiveness] of breeches she turned to the seductiveness

154.25 the great Roman shadow,] the great rolling shadow,

154.27 that ever left human lips;] that have ever left human lips;

156.16 All was darkness;] All was dark;

157.1 The great cloud which hung,] This great cloud which hung,

157.29 grown; trousers were fastened] grown and trousers fastened

157.30 legs the country gentleman soon transferred] legs he soon transferred

157.31 tables were covered; nothing was left bare.] tables were covered too.

158.8   dogs, mats, and china ornaments, the home –]   dogs, mats, and antimacassars, the home –

162.5   on one day at least of every year,]   on one day at least every year,

162.13 but no, she detested]   but not, she detested

163.12 end. Meanwhile she began]   end. And so she began

163.18 tried drama.]   tried the drama.

163.26 pool, which, I dare say, has the same carp in it.]   pool, with, I dare say, the same carp in it.

164.2   she began to decorate]   she tried to decorate

165.19 as though it were asking]   as though they were asking

165.27 the third finger]   the second finger

167.23 to be the left hand]   to be the left finger

168.21 She became nervous lest]   She had become nervous lest

173.10 irises and gentian.]   irises and gentians.

173.16 and then thought 'No,]   and then she thought, 'No,

174.11 things which will be described]   things besides, which will be described

174.27 hastily from the breakfast-room]   hastily out of the breakfast room

174.29 Mercifully its tail]   Mercifully his tail

175.20 to heave that overboard,]   to stow that overboard,

175.29 could say anything, which is tantamount]   could say anything they liked, which is tantamount

175.32 London, things which]   London, which

180.11 in our eyes, some of it rubs off on our thoughts)]   in our thoughts, some of it rubs off on our words)

180.32 their brooms and their saucepans]   their brooms, their saucepans

182.12 taking care lest it should slip past the joint of her finger.]   taking care that it should not slip past the finger joint.

182.14 on the third finger]   on the second finger

183.11 lest the pen might have been]   lest it might have been

183.17 As she wrote she felt some power (remember we are dealing with the most obscure manifestations of the human spirit) reading over her shoulder, and when she had written 'Egyptian girls', the power told her to stop.]   At this point she felt that power (remember we are dealing with the most obscure manifestations of the human spirit) which had been reading over her shoulder, tell her to stop.

184.23   whatever sum the Hogarth Press may   ]   whatever sum the publisher may

184.25   predicament into which   ]   predicament in which

187.5   wasp. Where there is blood there is life. And if killing   ]   wasp. And if killing

187.29   and begin at least to think of a gamekeeper   ]   and begin to think, at least of a gamekeeper

190.12   Human beings alone are thus gifted.   ]   Human beings alone have this power.

190.36   lordships' legs, they haven't taken to reading there.   ]   lordships' legs, 'they haven't taken to reading there.'

192.23   some time or other. But where?   ]   some time or other before. But when? But where?

192.31   'Sir Nicholas!' she exclaimed.   ]   'Sir Nicholas!' she replied.

198.7   ceaselessly in a circle.   ]   ceaselessly in a circle round her.

198.12   on her finger. She read a sentence and looked up at the sky; she looked up at the sky and looked down at the newspaper. Life?   ]   on her finger. She was distracted between the two. She looked at the paper and looked up; she looked at the sky and looked down. Life?

199.35   ridiculous, like my hyacinth, husband I mean, Bonthrop: that's what it is – a toy boat on the Serpentine, ecstasy – it's ecstasy that matters. Thus she spoke aloud,   ]   ridiculous, 'like my hyacinth, husband I mean, Bonthrop: that's what it is – a toy boat on the Serpentine, it's ecstasy – ecstasy.' Thus she spoke aloud,

202.2   lectures on the Influence   ]   lectures upon the Influence

202.6   all those fur tippets   ]   all these fur tippets

204.32   the midwife, putting her first-born child into Orlando's arms. In other words   ]   the midwife. In other words

206.5   cry now. Water was hot   ]   cry now. People were much gayer. Water was hot

206.31   one side and the future   ]   one side, the future

206.32   ran downstairs, she jumped into her motor car, she pressed the self-starter.   ]   ran downstairs, jumped into her motor car, pressed the self-starter.

209.17   a girl's? – young, slender, seductive – a girl, by God! furred,

pearled, in Russian trousers; but faithless, faithless!] a girl's
– furred, pearled, in Russian trousers – young, slender, seductive – a girl, by God! but faithless, faithless!

209.28 shop towards her.] shop toward her.

209.33 white flowers, and old ships that it brought] white flowers
and Russian sailors that it brought

211.12 dispute. For it is a difficult business –] dispute. Indeed it is
a difficult business –

211.35 was written 'Ra—Un',] written in great letters 'Ra—Un,'

212.9 the chopping up small of identity which] the chopping up
small of body and mind, which

212.30 person to call, directly] person to say, directly

213.32 all were different] all these selves were different

214.21 morning listening to the pigeons on fine linen;] morning
on fine linen; listening to the pigeons;

214.22 Spoilt? Perhaps. Too many things for nothing. Hence my
books (here she mentioned] Spoilt? Perhaps (here another
self came in). My books (here she mentioned

214.32 Trees, she said. (Here another self came in.) I love trees (she
was passing a clump) growing there a thousand
years.] Trees, she said. (She was passing a clump. Here
another self came in.) I love trees, trees growing there a
thousand years.

215.2 question.) I don't know. Chattering, spiteful,] question.)
Chattering, spiteful,

215.6 I like peasants.] Peasants I like.

215.10 and we must snatch space to remark] and we must here
snatch time to remark

215.12 this culmination to which the whole book moved, this peroration with which the book was to end, should be dashed from
us] this culmination and peroration should be dashed
from us

215.27 here and there like a barbaric necklace] here and there
(another self came in) like a barbaric necklace

215.28 she sang, accenting the words strongly, 'and see the
moon] she sang, 'and see the moon

216.15 came over her (she had passed through the lodge gates and
was entering the park).] came over her as she passed
through the lodge gates into the park.

216.26   established they fall silent.] established there is nothing more to be said.

217.9   significance themselves,] significance in themselves,

218.2   as theirs had stored in them a myriad moods] as theirs had been had stored in them a myriad moods

218.7   each other for close on four centuries now.] each other close on four centuries now.

218.13   come to them as boy and woman, crying and dancing,] come to them as child, as man, crying and dancing,

218.34   however faintly,] however faint,

219.1   laid with whole oak trees] laid with oak trees

220.30   the marking of veins and petals.] the markings of veins and petals.

220.31   on his gaiters was visible; she] on his gaiters; she

223.3   as if whenever the gulf of time gaped] as if every time the gulf of time gaped

223.24   a shadow without substance] a shadow and without substance

223.29   comprehensible. Her mind began to toss like the sea. Yes, she thought,] comprehensible. Yes, she thought,

224.17   partly something else, as if her mind had become a forest with glades branching here and there; things came nearer, and further, and mingled and separated and made the strangest alliances and combinations in an incessant chequer of light and shade. Except when Canute,] partly something else, and each gained an odd moving power from this union of itself and something not itself so that with this mixture of truth and falsehood her mind became like a forest in which things moved; lights and shadows changed, and one thing became another. Except when Canute,

225.26   and the garden blowing irises] and the gardens blowing irises

226.4   Nelson had gone. 'And there', she thought,] Nelson had gone. 'And that,' she thought,

226.17   on all your dishes,] on all the dishes,

226.23   fields, cottages with lamps in them,] fields, lamps in cottage windows,

226.33   Cape Horn. She looked into the darkness. There was] Cape Horn. There was

227.15   sky and sea. Then he came.   ]   sky and sea. It was then that
         he came.

227.27   As she spoke, the first stroke of midnight sounded.   ]   Im-
         mediately, the first stroke of midnight sounded.

READ MORE IN PENGUIN

In every corner of the world, on every subject under the sun, Penguin represents quality and variety – the very best in publishing today.

For complete information about books available from Penguin – including Puffins, Penguin Classics and Arkana – and how to order them, write to us at the appropriate address below. Please note that for copyright reasons the selection of books varies from country to country.

In the United Kingdom: Please write to *Dept. EP, Penguin Books Ltd, Bath Road, Harmondsworth, West Drayton, Middlesex UB7 ODA*

In the United States: Please write to *Consumer Sales, Penguin Putnam Inc., P.O. Box 12289 Dept. B, Newark, New Jersey 07101-5289.* VISA and MasterCard holders call 1-800-788-6262 to order Penguin titles

In Canada: Please write to *Penguin Books Canada Ltd, 10 Alcorn Avenue, Suite 300, Toronto, Ontario M4V 3B2*

In Australia: Please write to *Penguin Books Australia Ltd, P.O. Box 257, Ringwood, Victoria 3134*

In New Zealand: Please write to *Penguin Books (NZ) Ltd, Private Bag 102902, North Shore Mail Centre, Auckland 10*

In India: Please write to *Penguin Books India Pvt Ltd, 11 Community Centre, Panchsheel Park, New Delhi 110017*

In the Netherlands: Please write to *Penguin Books Netherlands bv, Postbus 3507, NL-1001 AH Amsterdam*

In Germany: Please write to *Penguin Books Deutschland GmbH, Metzlerstrasse 26, 60594 Frankfurt am Main*

In Spain: Please write to *Penguin Books S. A., Bravo Murillo 19, 1° B, 28015 Madrid*

In Italy: Please write to *Penguin Italia s.r.l., Via Benedetto Croce 2, 20094 Corsico, Milano*

In France: Please write to *Penguin France, Le Carré Wilson, 62 rue Benjamin Baillaud, 31500 Toulouse*

In Japan: Please write to *Penguin Books Japan Ltd, Kaneko Building, 2-3-25 Koraku, Bunkyo-Ku, Tokyo 112*

In South Africa: Please write to *Penguin Books South Africa (Pty) Ltd, Private Bag X14, Parkview, 2122 Johannesburg*

READ MORE IN PENGUIN

Published or forthcoming:

Ulysses James Joyce

Written over a seven-year period, from 1914 to 1921, *Ulysses* has survived bowdlerization, legal action and bitter controversy. An undisputed modernist classic, its ceaseless verbal inventiveness and astonishingly wide-ranging allusions confirm its standing as an imperishable monument to the human condition. 'Everybody knows now that *Ulysses* is the greatest novel of the century' Anthony Burgess, *Observer*

Nineteen Eighty-Four George Orwell

Hidden away in the Record Department of the Ministry of Truth, Winston Smith skilfully rewrites the past to suit the needs of the Party. Yet he inwardly rebels against the totalitarian world he lives in, which controls him through the all-seeing eye of Big Brother. 'His final masterpiece . . . *Nineteen Eighty-Four* is enthralling' Timothy Garton Ash, *New York Review of Books*

The Day of the Locust *and* The Dream Life of Balso Snell
Nathanael West

These two novellas demonstrate the fragility of the American dream. In *The Day of the Locust*, talented young artist Todd Hackett has been brought to Hollywood to work in a major studio. He discovers a surreal world of tarnished dreams, where violence and hysteria lurk behind the glittering façade. 'The best of the Hollywood novels, a nightmare vision of humanity destroyed by its obsession with film' J. G. Ballard, *Sunday Times*

The Myth of Sisyphus Albert Camus

The Myth of Sisyphus is one of the most profound philosophical statements written this century. It is a discussion of the central idea of absurdity that Camus was to develop in his novel *The Outsider*. Here Camus poses the fundamental question – Is life worth living? – and movingly argues for an acceptance of reality that encompasses revolt, passion and, above all, liberty.

READ MORE IN PENGUIN

Published or forthcoming:

The Diary of a Young Girl Anne Frank

This definitive edition of Anne Frank's diary restores substantial material omitted from the original edition, giving us a deeper insight into her world. 'One of the greatest books of the twentieth century . . . If you have never read Anne Frank's diary, or haven't read it for years, this is the edition to buy' *Guardian*

Brideshead Revisited Evelyn Waugh

The most nostalgic of Evelyn Waugh's novels, *Brideshead Revisited* looks back to the golden age before the Second World War. It tells the story of Charles Ryder's infatuation with the Marchmains and the rapidly disappearing world of privilege they inhabit. 'Lush and evocative . . . expresses at once the profundity of change and the indomitable endurance of the human spirit' *The Times*

Oranges John McPhee

From Thailand, where the sweetest oranges are as green as emeralds, to Florida oranges so juicy it is said they should be peeled in the bath, the orange exists in bounteous varieties. John McPhee has woven together history, anecdote and science to create a definitive guide to the world of oranges. 'A classic of American reportage. McPhee is quirky, original and intensely curious' Julian Barnes

Wide Sargasso Sea Jean Rhys

Inspired by Charlotte Brontë's *Jane Eyre*, *Wide Sargasso Sea* is set in the lush landscape of Jamaica in the 1830s. Born into an oppressive colonialist society, Creole heiress Antoinette Cosway meets and marries a young Englishman. But as Antoinette becomes caught between his demands and her own precarious sense of belonging, she is eventually driven towards madness.

READ MORE IN PENGUIN

Published or forthcoming:

Love in a Cold Climate and Other Novels Nancy Mitford

Nancy Mitford's brilliantly witty, irreverent stories of the upper classes in pre-war London and Paris conjure up a world of glamour and decadence, in which her heroines deal with hilariously eccentric relatives, the excitement of love and passion, and the thrills of the Season. But beneath their glittering surfaces, Nancy Mitford's novels are also hymns to a lost era and to the brevity of life and love.

The Prime of Miss Jean Brodie Muriel Spark

Romantic, heroic, comic and tragic, schoolmistress Jean Brodie has become an iconic figure in post-war fiction. Her glamour, freethinking ideas and manipulative charm hold dangerous sway over her girls at the Marcia Blaine Academy, who are introduced to a privileged world of adult games that they will never forget. 'A sublimely funny book ... unforgettable and universal' Candia McWilliam

Sons and Lovers D. H. Lawrence

Gertrude Morel, a delicate yet determined woman, no longer loves her boorish husband and devotes herself to her sons, William and Paul. Inevitably there is conflict when Paul falls in love and seeks to escape his mother's grasp. Lawrence's modern masterpiece reflects the transition between the past and the future, between one generation and the next, and between childhood and adolescence.

Cold Comfort Farm Stella Gibbons

When the sukebind is in the bud, orphaned, expensively educated Flora Poste descends on her relatives at Cold Comfort Farm. There are plenty of them – Amos, called by God; Seth, smouldering with sex; and, of course, Great Aunt Ada Doom, who saw 'something nasty in the woodshed' ... 'Very probably the funniest book ever written' Julie Burchill, *Sunday Times*

READ MORE IN PENGUIN

Published or forthcoming:

A Confederacy of Dunces John Kennedy Toole

A monument to sloth, rant and contempt, a behemoth of fat, flatulence and furious suspicion of anything modern – this is Ignatius J. Reilly of New Orleans. In magnificent revolt against the twentieth century, he propels his monstrous bulk among the flesh-pots of a fallen city, a noble crusader against a world of dunces. 'A masterwork of comedy' *The New York Times*

Giovanni's Room James Baldwin

Set in the bohemian world of 1950s Paris, *Giovanni's Room* is a landmark in gay writing. David is casually introduced to a barman named Giovanni and stays overnight with him. One night lengthens to more than three months of covert passion in his room. As he waits for his fiancée to arrive from Spain, David idealizes his planned marriage while tragically failing to see Giovanni's real love.

Breakfast at Tiffany's Truman Capote

It's New York in the 1940s, where the Martinis flow from cocktail-hour to breakfast at Tiffany's. And nice girls don't, except, of course, Holly Golightly. Pursued by Mafia gangsters and playboy millionaires, Holly is a fragile eyeful of tawny hair and turned-up nose. She is irrepressibly 'top banana in the shock department', and one of the shining flowers of American fiction.

Delta of Venus Anaïs Nin

In *Delta of Venus* Anaïs Nin conjures up a glittering cascade of sexual encounters. Creating her own 'language of the senses', she explores an area that was previously the domain of male writers and brings to it her own unique perceptions. Her vibrant and impassioned prose evokes the essence of female sexuality in a world where only love has meaning.

READ MORE IN PENGUIN

Published or forthcoming:

A Clockwork Orange   Anthony Burgess

Fifteen-year-old Alex enjoys rape, drugs and Beethoven's Ninth. He and his gang rampage through a dystopian future, hunting for terrible thrills, until he finds himself at the mercy of the state and the ministrations of Dr Brodsky, the government psychologist. *A Clockwork Orange* is both a virtuoso performance from an electrifying prose stylist and a serious exploration of the morality of free will.

On the Road   Jack Kerouac

On the Road swings to the rhythms of 1950s underground America, with Sal Paradise and his hero Dean Moriarty, traveller and mystic, the living epitome of Beat. Now recognized as a modern classic, its American Dream is nearer that of Walt Whitman than F. Scott Fitzgerald, and it goes racing towards the sunset with unforgettable exuberance, poignancy and autobiographical passion.

Zazie in the Metro   Raymond Queneau

Impish, foul-mouthed Zazie arrives in Paris from the country to stay with her female-impersonator Uncle Gabriel. All she really wants to do is ride the metro, but finding it shut because of a strike, Zazie looks for other means of amusement and is soon caught up in a comic adventure that becomes wilder and more manic by the minute. Queneau's cult classic is stylish, witty and packed full of wordplay and phonetic games.

Lolita   Vladimir Nabokov

Poet and pervert Humbert Humbert becomes obsessed by twelve-year-old Lolita and seeks to possess her, first carnally and then artistically. This seduction is one of many dimensions in Nabokov's dizzying masterpiece, which is suffused with a savage humour and rich verbal textures. 'You read Lolita sprawling limply in your chair, ravished, overcome, nodding scandalized assent' Martin Amis

READ MORE IN PENGUIN

Published or forthcoming:

Seven Pillars of Wisdom T. E. Lawrence

Although 'continually and bitterly ashamed' that the Arabs had risen in revolt against the Turks as a result of fraudulent British promises, Lawrence led them in a triumphant campaign. *Seven Pillars of Wisdom* recreates epic events with extraordinary vividness. However flawed, Lawrence is one of the twentieth century's most fascinating figures. This is the greatest monument to his character.

A Month in the Country J. L. Carr

A damaged survivor of the First World War, Tom Birkin finds refuge in the village church of Oxgodby where he is to spend the summer uncovering a huge medieval wall-painting. Immersed in the peace of the countryside and the unchanging rhythms of village life, Birkin experiences a sense of renewal. Now an old man, he looks back on that idyllic summer of 1920.

Lucky Jim Kingsley Amis

Jim Dixon has accidentally fallen into a job at one of Britain's new redbrick universities. A moderately successful future beckons, as long as he can survive a madrigal-singing weekend at Professor Welch's, deliver a lecture on 'Merrie England' and resist Christine, the hopelessly desirable girlfriend of Welch's awful son Bertrand. 'A flawless comic novel . . . It has always made me laugh out loud' Helen Dunmore, *The Times*

Under Milk Wood Dylan Thomas

As the inhabitants of Llareggub lie sleeping, their dreams and fantasies deliciously unfold. Waking up, their dreams turn to bustling activity as a new day begins. In this classic modern pastoral, the 'dismays and rainbows' of the imagined seaside town become, within the cycle of one day, 'a greenleaved sermon on the innocence of men'.

READ MORE IN PENGUIN

Published or forthcoming:

Swann's Way   Marcel Proust

This first book of Proust's supreme masterpiece, *A la recherche du temps perdu*, recalls the early youth of Charles Swann in the small, provincial backwater of Combray through the eyes of the adult narrator. The story then moves forward to Swann's life as a man of fashion in the glittering world of *belle-époque* Paris. A scathing, often comic dissection of French society, *Swann's Way* is also a story of past moments tantalizingly lost and, finally, triumphantly rediscovered.

Metamorphosis and Other Stories   Franz Kafka

A companion volume to *The Great Wall of China and Other Short Works*, these translations bring together the small proportion of Kafka's works that he thought worthy of publication. This volume contains his most famous story, 'Metamorphosis'. All the stories reveal the breadth of Kafka's literary vision and the extraordinary imaginative depth of his thought.

Cancer Ward   Aleksandr Solzhenitsyn

One of the great allegorical masterpieces of world literature, *Cancer Ward* is both a deeply compassionate study of people facing terminal illness and a brilliant dissection of the 'cancerous' Soviet police state. Withdrawn from publication in Russia in 1964, it became a work that awoke the conscience of the world. 'Without doubt the greatest Russian novelist of this century' *Sunday Times*

Peter Camenzind   Hermann Hesse

In a moment of 'emotion recollected in tranquility' Peter Camenzind recounts the days of his youth: his childhood in a remote mountain village, his abiding love of nature, and the discovery of literature which inspires him to leave the village and become a writer. 'One of the most penetrating accounts of a young man trying to discover the nature of his creative talent' *The Times Literary Supplement*

BY THE SAME AUTHOR

'Woolf is modern ... With Joyce and Eliot she has shaped a literary century' Jeanette Winterson, *The Times*

Mrs Dalloway

Clarissa Dalloway, elegant and vivacious, is preparing for a party and remembering those she once loved. In another part of London, Septimus Warren Smith is shell-shocked and on the brink of madness. Smith's day interweaves with that of Clarissa and her friends, their lives converging as the party reaches its glittering climax. Past, present and future are brought together one momentous June day in 1923.

The Waves

Tracing the lives of a group of friends, *The Waves* follows their development from childhood to youth and middle age. The novel is remarkable for the rich poetic language that conveys the inner life of its characters: their aspirations, their triumphs and regrets, their awareness of unity and isolation. Separately and together, they query the relationship of past to present, and the meaning of life itself.

Between the Acts

Outwardly a novel about life in a country-house in whose grounds there is to be a pageant, *Between the Acts* is also a striking evocation of English experience in the months leading up to the Second World War. Through dialogue, humour and the passionate musings of the characters, Virginia Woolf explores how a community is formed (and scattered) over time.

Selected Short Stories

Virginia Woolf tested the boundaries of fiction in these short stories, developing a new language of sensation, feeling and thought, and recreating in words the 'swarm and confusion of life'. Defying categorization, the stories range from the more traditional narrative style of 'Solid Objects' through the fragile impressionism of 'Kew Gardens' to the abstract exploration of consciousness in 'The Mark on the Wall'.

BY THE SAME AUTHOR

A Room of One's Own *and* Three Guineas

A Room of One's Own is one of the great feminist polemics, ranging in its themes from Jane Austen and Charlotte Bronte to the silent fate of Shakespeare's gifted (imaginary) sister and the effects of poverty and sexual constraint on female creativity. *Three Guineas* was published almost a decade later and breaks new ground in its discussion of men, militarism and women's attitudes towards war.

To the Lighthouse

To the Lighthouse is, on the surface, the story of a family holiday, but it is also a portrait of a marriage, of parenthood and childhood, of grief, tyranny and bitterness. Written with an astonishing and beautiful lyricism, it is told almost entirely through the reflections of its characters.

Also published:

The Crowded Dance of Modern Life
The Diary of Virginia Woolf Volumes 1–5
Jacob's Room
Night and Day
The Voyage Out
A Woman's Essays
The Years

Mrs Dalloway, *read by Eileen Atkins, and* Orlando, *read by Tilda Swinton, are also published as Penguin Audiobooks.*